18 Acres of England

Chris Oswald

NEWMORE PUBLISHING

First edition published in 2018 by Newmore Publishing.

ISBN 978-1-9997868-6-1

Cover design by Book Beaver.

Book design and layout by Heddon Publishing.

Chris Oswald has lived in America, Scotland and England and is now living in Dorset with his wife, Suzanne, and six children. For many years he was in international business but now has a little more time to follow his love of writing. His books have been described as dystopian but they are more about individual choice, human frailty and how our history influences the decisions we make, also about how quickly things can go so wrong.

To my parents, the very best.

End of Shift   1

Prison Visit   7

Change and No Change   18

Letter One   25

Day Trip to Charlottesville   32

Letter Two   41

Contents of the Trunk   47

A Day in the Life   60

Letter Three   72

Corporate Rungs   78

Call in the Night   86

Constitutional Matters   95

Certain Frank Conversations   103

Letter Four   113

Mothers and Children   122

Legal Aspects   132

Politics and Problems   140

Letter Five   152

Two Months to Serve   159

Daniel Roberts Esquire   167

Revelation   174

Of Nationhood and All that Follows   184

Standstill or Showdown?   194

Letter Six   201

Panic Stations   206

Diplomatic Niceties   216

Fight Back   228

That Failing Feeling   239

Caribbean Conference   246

Excursion   261

Letter Seven   272

The Seat of Government   281

Under Attack   289

Letter Eight   300

The Date   307

False Imprisonment   315

Be Prepared   331

Letter Nine   346

The State Versus Jameson   354

Back in Charlottesville   367

Letter Ten   377

Trade Off   394

Prison Reform   404

Full Week   412

Epilogue   426

18 Acres of England

End of Shift

The joke had worn thin by fourth grade. The instigator, his father, had long since disappeared but the joke had not gone with him.

Ben flicked the disc through to his favourite, *A Boy called Sue*, and pulled out of the car park. It had been a long shift. He worked out the pay as he always did, fourteen hours at $8.50 an hour made $85 plus $17 and $17, the total coming to $119, plus the overtime premium the union was fighting to get enhanced. Not bad. He would stop for gas and get a four-pack. In a good week he had two four-packs. This would be his second this week. He would send a little more home to his mother as well. Better than that, he would drive out to Still City on Sunday and take her the cash. He pressed the back button to listen to his favourite all over again. He would only have one beer tonight because he had to be back on duty at 6am, just ten hours' time, and it was an hour each way through the traffic to and from his studio apartment.

Ben had done the calculations a thousand times. In an average month he took home $1842 after union fees, life assurance, retirement and taxes. His rent was $500. He was lucky because Mrs Jameson had not put up the rent since her husband died, over three years ago now. Instead, Ben listened when Mrs Jameson wanted to talk. That happened often. She had a lot to talk about, having lost first her son to leukaemia, then her daughter to maximum security, and her husband to an early grave.

Ben needed $75 for the electric meter and $125 for the car payment on his 2016 Chevy. Then there was $400 to his mother for rent of his childhood home. Most months, he sent a little more. That left gas, food and entertainment to pay for; there was not much left over to save of course, but he did have $1800 in a deposit account at the bank.

At the lights he watched a hamburger wrapper dance in the wind, maybe searching out a companion? His car was eight back from the lights so he would start moving thirty-two seconds after they turned green. He always allowed four seconds a car and was usually dead-on. He ran through the rest of the week in his mind. Today was Thursday, the first Thursday in March. Tomorrow might be ten hours or it might be fourteen. It depended on the level of security at the White House. It changed from one day to the next. The only certain thing was that when he had a short shift of eight hours, he was always finished by two-thirty in the afternoon. That was how he planned his social life. Every second Friday his and Patrick's schedules coincided and they had a short shift together, hence they went bowling. They had both become pretty good over the six years since Ben had moved to DC. Patrick and he were fourth in the league, with good prospects of moving up to third place this year.

Ben's mind wandered through a dozen different convoluted thoughts as he worked his way across town, dealing with the late evening commuter traffic. There was constant noise, oscillating between horns, cries, the relentless thump of heavy bass music, laughter and sirens; always sirens somewhere on his route back. His mother usually featured in his thoughts, also his ambition to go to university, fading steadily with each passing year, dreams receding inexorably, like hairlines. The shrinking ship that was his future sometimes changing course to tease him before heading back to the horizon. He swung his old car right and right again, into Thomas B. Eldridge Avenue, the border between smooth and rough, genteel and risky. It started as a grand, tree-lined avenue and reduced steadily as his car lights picked out the houses, like rows of wine in a supermarket going from premium to bargain offers. By half-way down the mile-long road there were no elegant trees anymore. Had there never been any trees in the lower half or had they been uprooted by residents objecting to the leafy greenness as presenting too wholesome an image?

At the end of Thomas B. Eldridge he turned right again into Booker Street, noticing the dead end sign had been spray painted with silver-gold luminous paint, like a child's depiction of the night-time sky. He pulled his car up off the road into the front-yard-turned-parking-lot of Mrs Jameson's house, the last house on the left by the railroad track. He took the same parking spot each day, not by reference to the lease, but by convention. Mrs Jameson did not have a car but the three renters all did and they squeezed their vehicles in to the space available.

"Hello," he said to himself. "Why is the front door open?" It was not a good neighbourhood. He grabbed his lunch box and his four-pack and locked the car. Mrs Jameson was on the top step, looking out over the street from her slight vantage point, hands wringing in excitement, eyes dancing for once.

"Ben!" she cried. "You will never guess what." Her tiny fifty-year-old frame reminded him of a worn but still functioning motorcycle: tatty, faded, pitted in places, but as strong as the day it rolled out of the factory. Her clothes let her down, carried over from another generation. Ben supposed they were only available in thrift shops or Goodwill. She wore pink slacks and a white blouse, covered in a flowered wrap-around apron. Her almost white hair completed the picture, with the curlers still in. Every time he saw her he expected to see a cigarette hanging out of the side of her mouth. Only Mrs Jameson had given up smoking when her daughter went inside. Ben knew that all available money went on the daughter's comforts rather than hers. Yet still she did not put the rent up, even when Ben had suggested it.

"Ben, she's coming home!" Only she was not, as Ben learned on going into her ground-floor sitting room, directly below his tiny apartment. She was just moving closer. "She's moving from California to Ohio. We can go see her at weekends!" Mrs Jameson was suddenly a little girl being told she could have a birthday party and a new dress for it as well.

"When is she moving?" Ben asked. Mrs Jameson showed him the letter. "March the fourth? That means she has moved already."

"Oh gosh," replied Mrs Jameson. "Does it say about visiting hours?"

Ben turned over to the back of the letter before replying.

"Yes, it says every Saturday and Sunday from 2pm to 5pm, call first to check visiting privileges have not been revoked." Ben knew the next question coming his way so he answered it in advance. "Yes, I'll take you there for sure."

"This Sunday?"

"This Sunday." His mother would have to wait. She would understand; besides, he had not yet called her and would go there instead on his next short shift day.

"When did you last see her?" Ben asked, then wished he had not, for Mrs Jameson was now in floods of tears. The tautness of her face seemed collapsed like a child's broken toy: wires, rubber bands and clips all over the place.

"Eight years last September. I just could not get the money together to go to California. We took out two mortgages and a bank loan to fund her lawyer, not that it did any good." The strain was pouring out of her now. "My baby, my little girl." She cried and cried while Ben held her hand and tried to soothe her.

"You'll see much more of her now. I'll take you whenever I can." He would need to factor the gas into his tight budget. Later, he looked up Zanesville on his phone and shocked himself with the 740-mile round trip he had committed to.

***

It was half past midnight before Ben opened his studio door and surveyed again his little kingdom. A realtor might describe it as 270 square feet of true ethnicity, highlighting the remaining period features as if they added real value to the quality of occupancy. He or she would have concentrated on the fine plasterwork; evidence the house had been built for a railroad manager, long since gone. Or perhaps they would have pointed out the chandelier that still hung from what had been the upstairs sitting room when it had been a family home. Ben had often lain in bed on mornings off and counted how many of the fourteen light fittings still functioned. It had been eleven when he moved in six years ago, now down to seven.

He had one window looking over the back yard and rail tracks beyond. Then there was a comfortable chair, a table, a bed in one corner, his kitchen in the opposite corner. He had invested in a microwave, a trashcan, a toaster, and a large and overflowing bookcase; everything else came with the room. He had not eaten that evening and no longer wanted a beer. He drew the blinds, switched on the bedside light, and brushed his teeth in the sink. He would have a shower in the morning. He had four hours to sleep before the routine started again.

Despite the late hour, Ben read for ten minutes. He read every night. It was his sanctuary, his escape. It represented who he wanted to be. He read history, philosophy, science; anything that told him of the wider world. It was his education, his university.

Thankfully, Friday was another fourteen-hour shift. He needed the money. He would work as many hours as they gave him.

***

"Will you be coming to lunch on Sunday now?" Patrick's easy-flowing Irish accent was always a joy to hear. It reminded him, like his reading, that there were other places, other lives, other worlds to visit. They were in the basement canteen, sitting at a table on the far side by the window. Ben was pretending to be eating something bought in the canteen, but really drinking coffee from his flask.

"I can't. I'm taking Mrs Jameson out for the day. But thanks for the invite."

"Where're you going to?"

"Oh, wherever she wants to head. I promised her a while back and she keeps my rent real low so it doesn't hurt to spend some time with her." He had never told anyone about Mrs Jameson's daughter. Even with his best friend, it did not seem right. He feared any link with a convicted criminal would lose him his job.

"You should buy a house like Siobhan and I have done. Money on rent is wasted."

"Yeah, but I'm alone and Siobhan must earn a lot more than you and I as a nurse. Besides, you've got tenure and seniority."

"And the part-time income as union official." Patrick reminded him.

"Yeah, you've done alright, especially as you came across without even a green card."

"Siobhan would've liked to see you. I think she's sweet on you!"

"Get away!"

"OK, guys. Time to get back to work." Brad Meadows, their genial supervisor, called over to them from three tables away. Brad was just sitting down with a bacon sandwich and a large cup of coffee.

"It's alright for some," Patrick replied in a way Ben never would. "Extended breaks must be the latest perk for management."

"I wish," Brad said. "I've just been in to see Mr Reading about the new security briefing. All supervisors were called. There are going to be some changes."

"What changes?" Ben could not afford a cut in hours.

"Don't worry, Ben, it's not a step back." Brad knew that Ben would work any hours he could. "If anything, it's going to be the opposite. We're taking responsibility for a wider area. There'll be a department meeting on Monday. You'll get the full picture then."

Prison Visit

Ben was the sort to make plans. It was just how he was; a lonely job and an active, intelligent mind. He measured his shift not in hours but in plans made. Hence by Friday evening, after fourteen long hours on patrol, he had the trip to Zanesville planned to perfection. Mrs Jameson laughed when she heard the timings to the minute, then remembered it was for her and her daughter, and bit back the laughter, converting it to warm smiles of appreciation.

"We'll leave at 6.45am as it is five hours forty-three minutes driving time. That gives us one hour twenty-two minutes for stops, traffic and emergencies. You need to call on Saturday evening to check the visit can go ahead. I emailed your ID and my driving licence to them this morning before work and they emailed back to say we can both visit. You were on the register and I've been added. Look at the rules on the attachment to the letter, Mrs Jameson. It says no physical contact other than at the beginning and end of each session, no direct gifts; all intended gifts have to be handed in to the officials, who will inspect them and decide whether they can be passed on. There are a few more here. No alcohol and so on. I'll fill the tank after work on Saturday. If we stay to 5pm on Sunday we'll get back at 11.10, allowing thirty minutes for a stop and refuel. That's generous on the stop so I'm hoping to be back a little before eleven."

They left three minutes early on Sunday morning. They drove in silence for the first twenty minutes, as if weighing each other up on first acquaintance. Outside, it was not a promising start to the day, with wind whipping rain to an acute diagonal and the middle-aged Chevy bumping through deep rain-filled ruts in the road, almost like a carefully selected stone skimming along the surface of a lake. There were few other cars on the roads out of the city and as the sun rose behind them it seemed to spotlight them as if a solo act on a vast stage. Even the sound effects were muted: a dog barking but losing interest quickly; a door banging dully on its hinges repeatedly but fading with each swing; a distant siren sounding lost, unable to locate the accident or crime scene it sought.

Into this strange, silent start to a city normally full of activity, Mrs Jameson eventually spoke.

"Thank you for taking me, Ben. It's real good of you."

"Hey, that's OK," he replied, taking his eyes off the road to look briefly at his landlady. "To tell you the truth I'm looking forward to meeting Dakota, I mean like after all you've said about her."

"She's a good sort, Dakota." That ended that particular conversation.

Several more sprouted over the next few hours as they steamed west, hitting Hancock and I68 in good time. Each failed to blossom because Mrs Jameson was too nervous to sustain small-talk. Ben's GPS showed the time to go ticking down. He got the impression that a part of Mrs Jameson did not want to arrive, but the sun was lighting their way from behind and the wind was bowling them along. There was no stopping them. They drove past the prison twenty minutes ahead of schedule, at 12.15. Ben drove on to find a coffee shop.

"There's one," Mrs Jameson said. "The Rest Stop." They pulled in and Ben wished they had not, but there was nowhere else to go, straight roads through farmland with no settlements in sight.

"You must be visiting," the waitress wore a 1950s uniform in pink and white. Her hair was peroxide and yearned to be its natural grey. Some of the coffee spilt over onto the table both times she poured. "Let me guess, mother and brother?"

"We're just passing through," Mrs Jameson replied, sitting up as if at war.

"That's what they all say, honey. No shame in one going off the rails. Now my kids kept away from drugs but then I raised them proper. What's that saying? Spare the child or something like that. Well I sure as anything did not spare no child!" She cackled as she spoke and kept it up while they ordered. Ben spotted a shot of spit landing on the table-top and shuddered. A dozen locals seemed to enjoy the show, sniggering into their coffee and pancakes. Several were in prison guard uniform, extended stomachs bulging over belts slung low yet still managing to get a few more pancakes down.

Ten minutes later she was back with two plates of eggs, ham and waffles with syrup. It was not what Ben had ordered but he did not care.

"So, what's she in for? Has to be drugs of course, that's what most of them are in for. Was she a courier then?"

"I want to see the manager."

"Ben, don't make a fuss."

"You're looking at her," the smug waitress replied, shifting her weight and dropping her order pad into Ben's eggs, so the yolk crept up the paper like the rising tide. "There's only me and my boyfriend who cooks and if you want to meet him be my guest."

"Let's go," said Ben, standing up and throwing a ten and two fives on the table. "This place ain't fit for pigs."

"Well, we're certainly a notch or two above jail scum," she called to their backs. "But then pigs generally are in my experience." This always got the maximum laugh from the audience.

"See you at visiting time," one of the guards yelled. "Pat-down is real fun. You're going to love it!"

It took twenty minutes of gentle driving along near-deserted roads to calm Mrs Jameson down. They eventually drove to a strip mall on the edge of Zanesville and got hot dogs and cokes from a Boy Scout's barbecue in the parking lot. They sat on the wall and watched golfers going into a shop called The Golf Cart, which had a banner splashed across its window saying 'Up to 70% off clubs. Final Day of Super Sale Sunday'. Nobody came out with clubs under their arms.

"It's time to go," Ben said, checking the time on his phone again. "The letter said to get there fifteen minutes early."

Mrs Jameson was shaking before she entered the prison.

After an aggressive pat-down from a humourless female officer, she was close to tears. Ben, affronted himself, knew that he had to be there for her and carefully guided her to table eighteen. It was like an enlarged classroom, except instead of desks there were regimented tables bolted to the white concrete floor. Each table was set up with the exact number of chairs to visitors, with wide gangways in between.

"My God, it's grim," Mrs Jameson whispered, clinging to Ben's arm. Several parties were already together; other visitors were waiting for their prisoner to appear. "Where is she?"

"They said they don't call her until we are sitting down. Here, you take this chair and I'll sit to one side." They sat, Ben caught a guard's eye and he called out that number eighteen was ready.

Twenty seconds later, the door at the back of the room swung open and an orange figure shuffled out. Ben's first reaction was that it was not Dakota, but the guard leading her made directly for table eighteen.

"Jameson D. 174632F," was all the guard said and they were alone; as alone as you can be in a busy prison visiting room. Mrs Jameson and her daughter stared at each other for a long moment then embraced, tears flowing.

"Mother," was all Dakota said.

"My baby, my little girl."

Ben had time to look at Mrs Jameson's daughter carefully. She looked fifteen years older than twenty-eight. The left ear lobe facing him was missing, a nasty scar rising up her neck, as if a knife had been whipped out of hiding and driven upwards in a rapid movement to cause as much damage as possible, thankfully missing her face. But then he looked at that face. Her eyes were deeply lined with dark rings, panda effect, against her dead pale skin. This, then, was what prison pallor looked like. Her skin could not hold less tone; even her lips appeared dull and pained, as if some sadistic nurse had carefully drawn the blood out of them with a syringe. Then he saw the large spots dominating her cheeks, forehead, and behind the ears; evidence of poor diet and limited washing. Her hair was quite short, just long enough not to be thought of as butch, but it was not the least attractive. It was badly cut, lank and greasy, with a few strands of grey offsetting her natural mid-brown. Pinned to her orange suit was a name badge with name, number and photo, and "Zanesville Penitentiary" in large black letters, matching the back and front of her clothes. Underneath her orange suit was a skeleton but not much more.

"Who is this, Mother?" After their embrace, Dakota turned to Ben. It was then he saw the other scars. Evidently Mrs Jameson knew about the scars because she did not comment on them.

"This is my lodger, Ben Franklin. He kindly drove me here." The name appeared to mean nothing immediately to Dakota. She whispered her thanks and turned back to her mother.

Ben had two and a half hours to observe while mother and daughter caught up on eight hard years; hard for both of them. He looked Dakota over closely, noticing the hesitancy of every movement, as if seeking permission before shifting in her seat. She spoke in a low voice, hands often by her face, feeling her scars, tampering with her spots, playing with her lanky hair, looking around for danger like a wild animal, eyes constantly moving. He imagined her senses were alert at all times. He noticed how thin her wrists were. Once he bent down to tie his shoelaces, really to look at the lower half of her under the table. Her manacled ankles were the same fragile state. On her feet were brown plastic sandals over short white socks.

After a while, he tried to look at others in the room, aware that he was watching Dakota intently. He forced himself for three minutes to watch the next table where a black American woman in her sixties was laughing with three younger visitors. She was not thin, rather bulging with rings of fat from her face downwards. They wobbled as she laughed, so the whole had a fluid effect, like there was no real boundary to her body.

Another time he did a survey. It was approximate because he could look left, right and straight ahead but could not look behind him without risking causing offence. He could see twenty-two tables. He counted them again by ethnic background. There were four Hispanics and Dakota as the only white person. That made seventeen tables occupied by black inmates. He remembered seeing another white person on his way in. He estimated there were another twelve tables behind him with one more white person to count. That meant about 6% were white. The vast majority were black. He tried to remember the ratio of the overall population. He knew that in the 2021 census it had been 51% white across the whole country but could not remember the black population, only that the Hispanics were just ahead of the blacks at that point.

A third time he looked at the guards spaced out amongst the room, black-and-white uniforms in an orange sea. What were they really like? Were they all tough, mean people like those in the Rest Stop? Or did they have an average amount of humanity? Perhaps the job only attracted the extremes. Most applicants lacked all compassion, while a handful had bags of it. But where was the proof for that wild theory? Could you tell the level of compassion by someone's features? Or by their eyes, or the set of their mouth? Moreover, what was it like to be an inmate, entirely dependent on the compassion of others? Everybody depended on compassion to some extent but here was a situation where every inmate's existence was either bearable or not, depending on whether there was a dose of true human feeling in those that controlled every aspect of their life.

But each time he looked away, each distraction he sought to give Mrs Jameson and her daughter a little privacy in that crowded room, he felt a compulsion to look back at Dakota. Despite her unhealthy, worn appearance, she was the focal point of the room for him. He had not listened to the conversation between mother and daughter but decided now that he would.

"Mom, this is a great place, nothing like the last place. I'm in a dorm instead of a cell. I can use the library as much as I want, well… within reason. The screws in the library aren't so bad. I can get on with my studies."

"Are you studying?" Ben asked, feeling like he was butting in on their conversation. But she turned to him, smiled, and her whole face changed, warmth and friendliness bursting out as if they had been imprisoned alongside the body.

"Yep, got a BA last year and right in the middle of a Masters now."

"What subject?" A part of him thought how come she has done it with all these restrictions and I have failed with all the opportunity in the world?

"History. In fact, I know quite a lot about your namesake, the original Benjamin Franklin." So she had taken aboard his name after all. "My Masters thesis is on a friend of his called Richard Sutherland. He was instrumental in bringing about peace at the end of the War of Independence."

"That's great, I read a lot of history. And thanks for not making a joke about my name, linking it to electricity or bifocals!" It was the old joke worn thin, but she had avoided it.

"That's OK, I figured you had not chosen the name for yourself and would not welcome a stupid joke about something you had no control over."

"Time please, ladies, gents and inmates. Ten minutes for goodbyes."

"I'll come next week," Mrs Jameson promised. "That is OK, isn't it, Ben?"

"Yes, it's OK, sure." He would have to change his shift. Others did that but he had never made a request before. He looked at Dakota and saw that she understood his thoughts, understood what he would have to do. They looked at each other, deep into each other's eyes for a few seconds, until Dakota said, "Mother, only if Mr Franklin can do it. You can't go promising his time in advance."

"No, for sure, I can do it, no problem," Ben lied. "We'll

put ourselves down for next week on the way out. Dakota, it's a real pleasure meeting you. I'll step back now and let you say goodbye to your mother." He stood up and addressed a guard. "Ma'am, can I leave now?" Dakota also stood up, awkwardly, due to her leg shackles, held out her hand and Ben held out his, noticing another viscous scar running across the palm of her right hand which was cold, delicate, small, bony and scarred. Somehow he felt her touch for a long time afterwards.

"See you next week, then."

"Right, next week." Then he turned to Mrs Jameson. "I'll be in the waiting area."

He was first in the waiting area, all the others still saying goodbye. There was only one guard; a short, petite woman he might have considered asking out in other circumstances. Her blonde hair was tied back in a rigid bun and she had hazel eyes that did not seem unkind.

"Hi, I'm just waiting for the other visitor in my party." It seemed a pointless thing to say, so he added, "We were visiting Dakota Jameson. She's just moved from California." The way he said it sounded like she had woken up one morning and decided on a whim to move across country.

"I know her," the guard replied. "She just came in the other day. She will be pleased to be here."

"Why's that?"

"She was in Centerville Maximum Security. We are only Medium Security. She will have a lot more freedom here. There is a lot more she can do with her time."

"That's good. That's great news. She said it was much better here. How long has she got to serve?"

"You mean before she's eligible for parole? I'll need to look it up." She flicked a few keys on the computer. "September 1st, 2045."

"My God, that's seventeen more years in here!"

"That's if she gets parole first time through. Most people it takes three or four times. She got just over forty-two years back in '18 so without parole but with good behaviour she will get out on, let me see, November 1st 2059. But my guess would be somewhere between '45 and '59, maybe around '48 or '49." Ben was going to ask what the conviction was for but Mrs Jameson arrived at that moment. He just had time to notice the guard's name badge read "V. Bennet".

"Thanks Miss Bennet."

"That's OK." Then she raised her voice, "Come along everybody now, visiting time is over. Please make your way to the exit where you'll need to sign out. Anybody not signing out will not get in next time. Line up please, you can't all get out at once."

The drive back was dead on schedule. They left at 5.10pm and were back home by 10.55. They had one fuel stop at which they also bought sandwiches and coffee and went to the bathroom. It was a classic 'as planned' expedition, cruising most of the way at 65mph, with no hold ups and only a minor thickening of traffic as they approached their destination. However, for once, Ben's mind was not on the schedule, planned stops or average fuel consumption.

"Mrs Jameson, can you tell me about Dakota's case?" They were easing out of the prison visitors' car park, turning left to head away from the sun. The rain had ceased and the early evening springtime light picked out flowers, birds, mailboxes, and the grilles of approaching cars; anything it could make dance and then play with the colours.

"She had just turned eighteen. She was never super pretty but had a lot going for her, like clever and open. She was infatuated with a boy in the group she hanged out with. He was a bad one." It was painful for Mrs Jameson and Ben felt for her, but he had to know. He had to know more about Dakota. Slowly, the story came out, as Ben's car moved at a steady pace on cruise control away from the prison, eastwards towards the capital and their home.

Dakota had undoubtedly been used and nobody else had gone to jail over this bust. Mrs Jameson spoke of the dreadful night in 2019. She and her husband had been woken at 3am by the police pounding on their door, breaking it in, not waiting for a sleepy Mr Jameson to answer it. They had pulled the house to pieces with their search, but found nothing, no drugs. Yet Dakota had been stopped carrying a plastic bag with a $150,000 street value of crack cocaine at the bottom in a large envelope ready for posting and written in her own hand. It had been addressed to a PO Box in Maryland.

At first, Dakota had said she knew nothing of it and, fatefully, lied to cover up her would-be boyfriend. Then she changed her story, at the insistence of the lawyer her parents hired, to say she had written the envelope at Dan Roberts' request. He had handed it to her with the bulky package sealed already and asked her to put the address on and send it. But if this was true, where was the note in Dan's handwriting giving the address for her to copy out? It was in the bag; only it was not. There was nothing in there except a lunch box and a cardigan. There was no note, nothing to link Dan to the drugs.

"It did not help that she lied to the police. Our lawyer argued that she had done so through infatuation with Dan Roberts but there was absolutely no link to Dan any way you look at it. We called him as a witness and he denied everything. He actually said Dakota had tried to give him the drugs because she was so infatuated and he thought she was joking or crazy and sent her away."

"So she was found guilty?" Ben asked, shortly after their fuel stop.

"Not at first. It was a hung jury the first time around and they went for retrial. The second time it was guilty. Our attorney seemed much less interested second time around, like he did not believe in her any more. The judge gave her just enough time to ensure she spent her sixtieth birthday in jail. She said criminals like Dakota needed to be kept off the streets. Oh Ben, what a terrible time it's been. The poor girl, my poor baby." Long, deep sobs followed and Ben took his arm off the steering wheel and placed it around Mrs Jameson's small, shrunken shoulders. They remained like that for almost 100 miles until they reached the suburbs of DC and Ben needed both hands to drive.

There was no more talk that night. Mrs Jameson was spent and Ben had a lot to absorb. Besides, it was late and he had early shift in the morning. He saw Mrs Jameson into her apartment on the ground floor and climbed the stairs to his room. He would, as usual, read for ten minutes and have a shower in the morning. When in bed he opened a book on his namesake and looked through the index for Richard Sutherland. There were several entries concerning his time in Paris, but Ben drifted off to sleep half way through the first one, the bedside light still on and the book slowly slipping from his fingers.

Change and No Change

Days of work followed in their timeless routine: short shifts, long shifts and shifts that began before dawn and finished after dark. Monday's meeting meant a lot of extra work. They were taking on security for a wider area, including the Smithsonian and the Washington Monument.

"It was a management failure their end, leading to some serious security breaches. Our firm has taken over the whole lot. We've got some increase in staff, taking on the best of their group, but it is going to mean a lot more hours on the job. I don't want us to let Corporate down." Mr Reading, the pompous manager who lived and breathed his job, explained the situation. They were crammed into the main security office, Ben and others staying on after their shifts to hear the news. "So, I need 110% over this period while we bed down the new responsibilities and train the new hires. Any questions? Good, take over Meadows." Mr Reading made an exit.

"Brad, can I have a word?" Ben grabbed his supervisor as soon as the meeting was over. "I'm all for extra hours but I want to ask you a favour."

"What is it, Ben?" Brad was a good soul and he knew Ben was a solid worker, topping the league last year at 3,562 hours on the job. He would always do what he could for Ben, especially as in six years he had hardly asked for anything. "Come with me to the car park while we talk." They quickly agreed that Ben, despite being single, could have every second Sunday off, starting with this coming Sunday, in return for four fourteen-hour shifts and two eight-hour shifts a week. The bowling would have to wait.

So the work went on with the new rhythm of many long days on the job. Patrick was less happy. He liked the pay but had two young children.

"Pat, take it for now. Save up a little nest egg. It probably won't last long, everything is always changing." Ben's advice was ever practical.

Sunday came and Ben found himself looking forward to the Zanesville trip. He had found a couple of hours during his busy days to read up a little on Richard Sutherland. He could not find much in the library situated at the better end of Thomas B. Eldridge and there was not much on the internet, either. He did find out that Richard was a Scot and a wealthy merchant. He had moved from Cromarty in the north of Scotland to Glasgow to work for his uncles, who traded in tobacco. His uncles sent him to North Carolina where he ran their business operations, importing slaves and taking payment in tobacco, cotton and sugar from the West Indies. He next spent twelve years in Virginia before moving to London. By then he was a wealthy man. He set up on his own and bought and sold arms, slaves and tobacco, but also started to get involved on the fringes of public life. There was apparently a long chapter on him in a book on the War of Independence called *The Peacemakers*. It was not in the library that day because it was out on loan, but Ben reserved it for when it came back.

He had not had time to visit his mother but had called her twice during the week and sent a cheque for $200.

"Same routine, Mrs Jameson." Ben had stopped by on Saturday evening. "I've filled the car with gas, so we can stop half way again for a refill, just like last time, then stop again on the way back."

"I need to pay you back for the fuel, Ben."

"No way, this is my treat."

"I can't let…"

"Mrs Jameson, I'll let you pay for the gas if you put up the rent to a market rate and backdate it three years. Otherwise it's no way."

Instead of trying to stop this Sunday for something to eat, Mrs Jameson brought sandwiches and a large bottle of water. They pulled off the interstate fifty miles short of Zanesville and ate the sandwiches with the car doors open to catch a beautiful, fresh breeze.

"Just think, Ben, Dakota won't feel this breeze, stuck inside those hateful walls."

"What about the appeal?" Ben asked.

"We ran out of money. We had to cut back the research. Our lawyer wouldn't work for nothing. The first two trials cost us everything we had and could borrow. Remember we were still getting over the medical bills from Walker's leukaemia. I remember the day the lawyer, Albert Essington II, called us into his office to say, 'no pay no work'. He was hard as nails. We'd given him $75,000 for the appeal work and he said it was not enough. We scraped together another $20,000 to cover his court time but all the research just stopped right then. They say justice is available to all but if you don't have any money you just can't buy any damn justice." It was not often Mrs Jameson swore.

"What was the research he was doing?"

"It was all about Dan Roberts, lots of surveillance on him. We thought if we could show he was a common criminal it would reflect well on Dakota. So we were looking for others who had maybe suffered the same way as her."

"Did you find any?"

"Some, but nothing definite. And then Essington would not release some of the research without a further payment. There was a lot of dirt around Dan Roberts but we were struggling to get any to stick. Essington said another $50,000 would cover it but we were completely out of funds and could not borrow any more. We had to just take our chances with the appeal case in court."

Ben knew the rest. It had not worked out and Dakota's sentence was confirmed, along with the guilty verdict. He had not known the family then but he reckoned that was what had killed Mr Jameson. Officially it was heart failure but he had been healthy all his life until the blow of Dakota's arrest and conviction.

It was a bright day, a day for driving long distances. They passed pretty farmsteads with unusual barns, land that looked unchanged since the first settlers. It was still early in the year but there was a feeling that winter was over. Slow, lumbering trucks came up to them, driven by farmers or carpenters or plumbers, ; a constant stream of small business making up what was America. The little wind that had accompanied their lunch stop had drifted away, creating a stillness that spoke of permanence. This was how it would always be: jobs to do, markets to sell to, homes to go to, prisons to populate, prisoners to visit. The temperature rose steadily as they drove, from 39 degrees when they started to 61 as they approached Zanesville and the object of their journey.

Mrs Jameson answered all Ben's questions, until the last half-hour, when she fell silent. Ben left her to herself and drove on with his own thoughts.

"Hi, Mother," Dakota said, embracing Mrs Jameson as she spoke. "Hi, Mr Franklin. It was good of you to come and to bring Mother." The way she smiled, it was like opening a special book and reading again the treasured words within. She seemed unchanged from the previous Sunday: same manacled shuffle; same tone to her skin; same muted voice; same lank, badly-cut and greasy hair. This would be how it would always be, then; steady aging but otherwise unchanged week in, week out. How do you measure time when nothing ever changes?

Yet time was the one thing a prisoner had to measure.

Ben's survey results were sustained for the second visit. There was 70%-plus black population in the visiting room. He wanted to ask Dakota whether that was the proportion in the general prison population but was embarrassed to do so. He looked for V. Bennet and nodded when he saw her against the wall in front of him. She smiled weakly then looked away. "No touching there," she called, her voice ten times the volume and confidence of Dakota's, yet still very much quieter than most of the guards'. Ben followed her eyes to see a young black child who would not let go of his mother, the inmate. She tried to ease him away gently but he would not let go. Bennet made to walk over there but a large male guard with a swagger that made Ben think he was an actor in a Western got there first.

"The lady said no touching. What part of that don't you understand?" It was unclear whether he was talking to the inmate mother or the frightened child, his dark glasses hiding the direction of sight.

"I'm sorry, Mr Wartsand, it's just my Billy is frightened." The boy still would not let his mother go and buried his head in her orange overalls, her large prison badge resting neatly on his short, fuzzy hair.

"Visiting rights suspended." The guard turned to the father and said, "You and the kid leave now. Bennet, take Frampton away." Then, as if suddenly aware that he had an audience of almost 100 people, he turned to the room at large and said, "We won't take no breaking the rules. Break the rules and visits over. Period."

"Nice guy," whispered Ben.

"One of the best," agreed Dakota. For the hundredth time in their seven-day acquaintance, Ben wondered how Dakota coped with this, day in and day out for nine years now, possibly thirty-three to go. And still to study and get a degree? He wanted to ask her so much but did not want to break into Mrs Jameson's time with her only remaining child.

Towards the end, when ten minutes was called and Ben felt he should leave early and give some time to them alone, he did lean forward and tell Dakota about his tiny bit of research on Richard Sutherland, the subject of her Masters degree.

"Wow, you actually took the time to look him up. He was a real interesting person. He was an entrepreneur of his day. He had fingers in all sorts." She was clearly fascinated by her research; her face shone in a way it never should in prison, not with artificial lighting and rules on every conceivable thing. "He was into all sorts of trades which we would say were questionable, but they were OK at the time and he was a humane person."

"Last five minutes," Bennet called as she made her way to the door to set up the departure sign-off in the waiting room. That was presumably her task each week.

"I've got to go," said Ben. "I'd love to talk more about it next time."

"Sure, and thanks for everything."

Downstairs in the waiting room, Ben sought out Bennet.

"Miss Bennet, can I ask you something?"

"Of course, but I can't promise to reply," she said with a smile.

"Well, that little kid and his mother, was that really necessary?"

"They broke the rules. That's the consequence. Surely you don't expect me to criticise a fellow officer?" But her eyes and her body language gave a contrary message. They said clearly that she was shocked by the big guard's actions. It was not necessary at all. She looked directly at Ben and her eyes were too honest to confuse the answer.

"Another question for you, please."

"Be quick, the mob will be down in a second," she joked to hide her emotion.

"Do you get many successful exonerations of convictions?"

"Your girlfriend is innocent?" she asked, her voice sounding tired, like she had heard it all before.

"She's not my girlfriend. She's my landlady's daughter. And yes, I think she probably is innocent."

"Rule of thumb, one in a hundred gets exonerated. Another two in a hundred get their sentences reduced on appeal and one in two hundred get a full pardon. That leaves ninety-six and a half hoping to impress the parole board, except that ten of those have no chance as they are on life without parole." She gave the facts, just as she had learned in basic training.

"Thanks, it just seems such a waste, especially when at worst it was a stupid mistake by an eighteen-year-old girl."

"Those are the facts. My job is not to argue about them but to enforce the rules." Then came her usual calling-out as everyone started to come down the stairs. "Move along, ladies and gents, sign out on the way out. Anybody not signing out won't be coming back."

"Thanks, Miss Bennet." Ben turned to leave as Mrs Jameson walked up to him.

"One more thing," she said, her voice much lower now. "If you believe Jameson is innocent, keep fighting, keep hoping and trying, only don't build her hopes up too much."

"Thanks." He wanted to touch her hand to show his appreciation but it seemed a wholly inappropriate thing to do.

Letter One

The letter arrived on Thursday, clearly marked, back and front, 'Federal Penitentiary'.

"It's from Dakota!" Mrs Jameson was waiting on the steps when Ben got back at five past nine. "I got one too. She hoped you would not mind her writing you."

"Not one bit." He was pleased. He pulled open the envelope and saw the 'Censored' stamp on each page. It was a long letter. She had lots of time.

"I've made a pot roast," Mrs Jameson said. "I'll warm it up while you sit right down in this easy chair and read your letter. You can tell me about it while we eat if you like."

Ben was delighted to be offered pot roast, along with a beer poured inexpertly by Mrs Jameson so that the froth spilled over the edge of the glass and onto the sleeve of his jacket. Mrs Jameson giggled and said she had not poured a beer since her husband died. Ben settled down, took a long draught of the beer, and opened up the letter, reading half aloud to himself, as if he were a grand old storyteller from a different age.

Dear Mr Franklin,

I hope you don't mind me writing you without an invitation but I was so touched that you looked up Richard Sutherland and I wanted to share my research with someone who showed real interest. I don't think you were just being polite. I saw your genuineness. But if you were just being polite please disregard this letter as the rants of an inmate with nothing better to do with her time.

The funny thing is I got interested in Richard Sutherland through my BA studies on Benjamin Franklin. Mom told me it was your father gave you that name, claiming he was related to the first BF, then that he had left when you were only a month old and disappeared, leaving your mom to bring you up. She also told me how hard you work to support your mother now that she can't work anymore and I think that is a truly wonderful thing. But enough of my ramblings, I am writing to tell you about Richard Sutherland, not to go on about my thoughts.

Sutherland was born the son of a preacher of the Church of Scotland in Cromarty. That is apparently a beautiful portion of northeast Scotland, somewhere below Sutherland, the county that must have given him his name. Sutherland means 'South Land', which it was for the Vikings. The Church of Scotland was very strict Presbyterianism and I imagine Richard having a studious, simple upbringing close to God.

As Ben read he got more and more drawn into the story. It was coming alive to him, living history; a stage set in his mind while Dakota supplied plot, characters and scenery.

In 1723 he was sent to Glasgow to learn the tobacco trade with his uncles, his father's brothers. In 1732, when he was 26, he moved to Charleston, South Carolina. Here he set up a trading house and made a new fortune for his uncles. He was importing slaves from Africa and exchanging them for tobacco and cotton. Then he added stops for his ships in the Indies and started loading up with sugar as well. He moved to Virginia in 1737 and did the same thing there, buying lots of land in the northern part of the state, prime real estate now. Then finally he moved to London and set up on his own. He made another fortune supplying arms and equipment to the army in the Indian Wars, or the Seven Years War as they call it in Britain. After peace in 1763, he was one of the richest people in Britain, helped by the fact he married a rich sugar heiress; not that it was a happy marriage, more that it was loveless and cold.

He loved his time in America and wanted to help as relations deteriorated during the run-up to Independence. He was devastated when war broke out between his country of birth and his adopted country. Then in 1782 he was sent by the British Government to Paris to negotiate with none other than Benjamin Franklin! They became firm friends. They worked hard on a peace treaty that was fair to both sides. Then something happened and Sutherland was relieved of his office and went back to Scotland where he died a little over a year later. My thesis is trying to establish what happened.

"Good letter?" Mrs Jameson asked.

"It's all about her thesis. It's real interesting."

"She must have recognised a kindred spirit."

"What do you mean?"

"You're always reading. She was real touched that you researched her subject on top of a seventy-hour workweek. But finish the letter, I won't interrupt you anymore." She put down a plate of pot roast, beans and potatoes plus another beer, this time in its bottle.

"She is researching this guy called Richard Sutherland, who died almost 250 years ago, just after the end of the War of Independence. He owned lots of land all around here, huge plantations. I need to check what land that is, exactly. I need to go find out where the records are kept and go through them on my next day off."

But Ben had a far better idea that evening and next day went to see his manager, Mr Reading, in his small but well-furnished White House office. He imagined his manager being the type who would drop into conversations at parties: "I was in my office at the White House…"

"Sir, do you think I might be assigned to the Smithsonian? I'm real interested in getting an education and would love to think I was helping to guard these national treasures."

"What? No, I can't handle any more schedule changes. Out of the question."

But later, just as Ben's shift was entering its last hour, he was called back to Mr Reading's office. "Wright's resigned. He only worked Tuesdays and Thursdays. You can have his shifts if you like."

"But every second Thursday is my day off."

"Take it or leave it, Franklin."

"I'll take it, sir. Do I report there tomorrow?" It was Thursday tomorrow and he had the day off, had arranged to go and see his mother.

"Yes, 6am." All his days started at 6am.

"I'll be there." That was one more problem off Mr Reading's desk. Meadows would have to find a substitute for Franklin for three days every two weeks, but that was his problem. He couldn't mother them all.

His new supervisor was from the old firm. He was nine months from retirement and did not care for responsibility. By 6.30am, Ben had assigned himself to the National Museum of American History, part of the Smithsonian empire. He had been there several times before as a visitor. Now that he was a security employee he had access to the document archives.

"Is there a way to search for specific things, like a specific person?" He asked innocently when the assistant curator volunteered to show him around on the first morning.

"Yep, most things are catalogued in the system. It's easy to use. You just type a name, or anything, into this box and it lists all the known references. Look." She typed in 'Thomas Jefferson' and the screen filled with hundreds of references. Then she looked at Ben's name badge and with a half-smile typed in 'Benjamin Franklin'. The screen filled up just as quickly.

"Can I try?"

"Sure, anytime. Let me show you the layout of the building first. It's very quiet here until 10am, opening time. You'll have lots of time to play with the system." Then she added with the other half of that smile: "I wrote the system. It's my baby."

"Wow," said Ben, and followed her to the stairs.

He had been told to take his morning break before 10am so at 9.25 he was at the computer in the main lobby, behind the reception desk. He typed in 'Richard Sutherland'. There were no known references. He tried each name alone. There was none for Sutherland and hundreds for Richard. Then he tried 'Richard Paris Franklin' but seemed to get mainly references to Franklin's stay in Paris generally. It would take hours to go into each one and check them out.

"Are you open, my man?" The clear British upper-class accent cut across the silence of the museum lobby. Ben looked up with a start to see a tall, wavy haired man in his early forties. He was impeccably dressed in a blazer and what looked like a college tie.

"Not quite yet, sir. 10am opening." The clock on the wall said a quarter to.

"I'm Professor Sir John Fitzroy, King's College, Cambridge. I only have today in this fine city and have a lot to crack on with."

"Can I see ID?" The professor handed over his passport. Ben looked at him and decided to let him in early.

"What were you doing on the computer terminal?" Sir John asked as Ben completed the pass paperwork he had just learned.

"I was having my coffee break."

"And?"

"I was trying to find any reference to someone my friend is doing a thesis on. He was around during the War of Independence."

"Come, come, man, let's have a name. My specialism is 18th Century British American relations."

"Richard Sutherland."

"1706 to 1784. Lived for twenty years in America, pal of Franklin and Lord North, the PM at the time of the war. Earned a packet. Famous for being extraordinarily ugly."

"I didn't know that."

"Young man, what we do know and what we don't know are two very different scales. Spent my life in education but could put everything I know on a pinhead." His staccato way of speaking made it hard for Ben to understand. "Won't find anything in there." He pointed dismissively towards the computer terminal. "Was all hushed up."

"So where?" But the Professor was gone, summoned by the Museum Director, who was ashamed at having not noticed Sir John entering the building. At least Security had been there and had seemed to engage him properly in conversation. She would thank that new guy later on.

Ben's shift was complete by 2.30 that afternoon. He asked if he could stay on in the lobby to do some research. The assistant curator checked with the Director and came back with the answer that anything that fine young man wanted to do in his own time was OK with her. So, with half an eye watching for Professor Fitzroy, Ben tapped every conceivable combination of relevant words into the catalogue search engine. There was nothing on Sutherland.

"It's like he was wiped off the face of history," he murmured to himself, gulping his fourth coffee of the day.

"Professor Sir? Can I see you a moment?"

"Running late for Dulles, my flight, have to get a cab."

"I'll drive you, Professor." It was an inspiration. He would be able to get to Dulles before the traffic built up too much, drop the professor about 3.45 and make it to his mother's house by 5pm.

"One condition?"

"Sir?"

"You address me correctly for the remainder of our probably short acquaintance." He grinned as he spoke, displaying that it was a joke from 3000 miles away.

"How do I do that?"

"Just 'Sir John'."

"Let's go, Sir John, we have a flight to catch!"

"Correction, I have a flight to catch. You have an airport to find and pronto."

Later in the car, winding through the traffic lanes as vehicles built up like ants in a new colony, Sir John asked why Ben or his friend was interested in Richard Sutherland.

"She's in jail, Sir John; got a long long sentence at age eighteen for planted coke. She's twenty-eight and got a history degree last year from a maximum-security prison in California. Now she's studying for a Masters and concentrating on Sutherland and what happened to him. I just wanted to try and help."

"You admire her, don't you? It's obvious from the way you talk about her."

"I suppose I do, yes. She has achieved much more than me under real bad circumstances."

"How long has she got to go of her sentence?"

"Thirty-two years come June 18th."

"My God!"

"She can apply for parole in seventeen years."

"All her youth?" Sir John could not take it in. "Surely it must be a terrible crime."

"Possession of coke, but she was framed."

"Isn't that what they all say?"

Ben slammed on the brakes, turned to his passenger and said, "Maybe, but this time it is true. She is innocent." There was an awkward moment before Sir John broke the ice.

"You were contracted to get me to the airport, not the side of some unknown freeway. But I retract my earlier comment and hope you forgive my thoughtless remark."

"Sure, of course."

After a few minutes, they pulled into the big sweep at the front of Dulles Airport. Ben drew his car up to the passenger drop-off point.

"Thanks," said Sir John. "Listen, rather than risk offending you with an offer of payment for the fuel or your time, I would like to help if I could. You won't find any documents in the museum. But there are some in a private collection in Charlottesville, Virginia. Here's my card. Call me in a few days' time, say on Monday." He wrote a second number on the back of the card. "That is my personal mobile. I'll make contact with the document owner and plead your case. Call and I will give you his contact details if he is willing to let you see what he has." He got out of the car with his briefcase and small, brown leather travel bag and leant back in to shake hands. "I've enjoyed meeting you, Ben. Thanks for the ride." He closed the door and made as if to walk away, then returned suddenly. "What's the girl's name?"

"Jameson, Dakota Jameson."

"Dakota? Why can't you crazy Americans stick to established names? Cheerio now!"

Day Trip to Charlottesville

Shifts changed and changed again. The only thing certain in Ben's work life was change. But Brad was true to his word and Ben had every second Sunday off. Brad was the sort who tried always to cater for the minor needs of those who were solid workers. He joked with Pat but relied on the quiet dedication of Ben, who would nearly always stay late or come in early.

But now Ben was not at work, but driving on his own to Charlottesville. It was April 8th and spring was being serious about making progress before summer swept in to take its place. The snow of late March had melted, only a few patches in cold, shady corners of parking lots to remind people of the five inches that had descended one night and the four inches two days later. As Ben swung onto US29 South off the interstate, he saw emerging daffodils rising from the roadside grass, poking their yellow heads up as if to say, 'Is it time now? Have we slept long enough?' They were met with the sun's affirmative; it was time for new growth. Ben checked his GPS. He was in good time. He would make the Hunt Ridge Estate with twenty minutes to spare. He slowed down a little to conserve fuel. He only needed ten minutes spare for emergencies. What would he find at Hunt Ridge? Well, he would know soon enough. He settled back at the slower speed, put *A Boy called Sue* on again and wondered what Dakota was doing this Saturday morning. She had to work in the laundry: dirty, heavy, steamy work. She was trying to get assigned to the library but most inmates wanted to potter around amongst the books rather than doing more arduous work. Last Sunday, Ben had screwed up his courage and asked Bennet, the female guard, if she could make the change to the work schedules to accommodate Dakota's wishes.

"She is, after all, an academic. She is well into her MA."

"No promises, but I will see what I can do." They had made it a sort of unofficial date to meet for the last ten minutes of the visiting period. Gradually, respectfully, he was learning a little about her. She was twenty-two years old, married to her high school sweetheart because of a sudden pregnancy, unhappy at home and at work. She was, without doubt, too soft, too understanding, to work in a jail. In Ben's opinion, she needed to toughen up or look for other work. He had asked her last Sunday about other opportunities.

"There's not much else that will let me look after Kyle during the day and come here weekends and evenings when my husband is home." Ben noticed that her husband did not have a name. He was just 'my husband', linked to her forever by one silly mistake of an eighteen-year-old, or rather one silly mistake by two eighteen-year-olds.

"Hello. This is Ben Franklin. I've come by appointment to see Mr Williams." Ben spoke into the entry speaker system at the wrought iron gates that marked the start of the Hunt Ridge Estate.

"What are you visiting for?" The voice came back immediately.

"Eh, the documents. Mr Williams said I was to come at 11am on April 8th."

"OK, take a left at the fork in the drive and follow round to the stables on your right hand side, about half a mile."

"Thanks." The gates swung open silently and closed again as soon as Ben's car was through. He forked left, seeing a glimpse of a colonial mansion up the right fork, went down into a wooded dip and up onto a rise in the land that seemed to cross the whole property like a straightened-out Iron Age fort. "That must be Hunt Ridge," he murmured to himself.

The stable complex was more like three quarters of a mile; Ben recorded it on his milometer. From the ridge, he looked directly down at a huge complex, a medieval village. It had a central cobbled yard with half a dozen horses standing around, flanked by long, low stables with lofts, he presumed for hay or something. To one side was a ranch house with a picture-perfect white picket fence and a huge GMC pickup truck in the drive. To the other side was a mish-mash of barns of all styles, housing horseboxes, tractors and other equipment. The entrance into the stable complex had an arch with a window above it and a slanted flagpole; there was no flag but a pair of muddy jodhpurs tied to the base moved heavily in the wind. The road ran down in an S shape, the other side of the ridge, crossing a brook with a barrel-effect bridge made of thick planks and girders. There were large trees everywhere: forked oaks, maples, beeches, and massive cedars. It was like a movie set.

"Hi, you're Ben, right? Got the documents?"

"No, I came for documents. Mr Williams said I should come see some old documents he has."

The stable manager looked oddly at him. "Mr Williams?" He called and hurried over to him, Ben following. "This gent says you told him to come about some documents. We let him in thinking he was bringing the documents for the new horses."

"Ben Franklin, sir." Ben held out a hand. Frank Williams grabbed it and shook energetically. But something was wrong. This Frank was not much older than Ben. The Frank Williams he was meeting was in his late eighties.

"That's Grandpa," Frank explained, guessing the cause of Ben's confusion. "He's not too well. You'll need to tell me what this is about and see if I can help." But before Ben could answer, Frank went on. "Do you ride? We need one more."

"No sir, I've never even been near a horse."

"Well, now's the time to try. We need one more rider for the photo. Everything else is ready."

"Well, I'll try but I don't know what I am doing."

"You'll be OK. Do this for me and then we'll go find these documents. I'll have a word with Grandpa for you."

Ben agreed and was led off by the stable manager to get changed in one of the stables. Five minutes later, feeling rather uncomfortable in jodhpurs, green jacket, silk tie and riding hat, he was being briefed on the essentials of horse riding.

"Straight back. Both hands on the reins; no, like this, see? Remember you are in control. We'll go once round the yard, then do the photos. Ready?"

Ben mounted the seventeen-hand horse from a mounting block and looked down from a great height to the others standing around. He liked the easy movement of the horse as he was led around the yard on a rope. He tried the reins. At first, he pulled too hard and caused the beautiful stallion to shake its head and whine, stepping sideways at the same time. But the next time he had it right. The horse moved around the corner of the yard and into the next straight.

"We've got a natural here!" someone called, meaning to be light-hearted, but the silence from others ruined the joke. Clearly Ben was a natural.

After the photos, Frank Williams came over to Ben and suggested they ride together to the big house to see about the documents. "Somebody will bring your car up and take the horse back."

They rode up the side of the ridge to its crest and then along the top until they could see the mansion below them.

"It must have dozens of rooms." Ben stopped to take in the view.

"About sixty, excluding the kitchens and bathrooms. It's been in our family forever but Grandpa made a fortune and did a lot of upgrades about twenty years ago. It will be mine one day and I have plans for it."

"Your father is…"

"No, Frank Williams II is very alive." Frank laughed. "He just wants nothing to do with this. He works for a charity and makes about $30,000 a year. I grew up in a two-bedroom house on the wrong side of town."

"So did I!" Ben replied. "My father left early on and it was just Mom and me."

"Well, my mother left and it was just Dad and me! How do you like the horse?"

"I love it; it is such a great feeling. I would love to do it again."

"Come any time. I can see that you are made to sit on a horse. You just know how to handle him. What do you do for a living?"

"I am a security guard at the White House. Long hours and low pay."

"But a vital task and a patriotic one." Ben felt a glow of value, of appreciation. Frank continued. "Hey, let's race to the house. You haven't let him rip yet so you raise yourself up and bend forwards and kick gently but firmly, like this." Frank shot away. Ben copied him and soon caught up.

"He's like the wind!" he cried as he overtook Frank and streaked down the gentle slope towards the house, only to realise that there was no brake pedal. Pulling back hard on the reins as a natural instinct, Ben flew forwards over the horse's head and landed awkwardly on the lawn leading up to the house, just short of the gravel drive.

"Are you OK?" Frank had caught Ben's stallion and led it over to where Ben was picking himself up.

He was fine, just a little bruised and shocked.

"Get back on. It's the best thing to do."

"I don't know if I should." He felt rather foolish, having flown past Frank and then come off so easily. But he very much wanted to get back on, to extend the ride a little further.

"Come on, don't let it get to you. We'll just walk up to the house and dismount at the door. It's always the best thing to do. Everybody falls from a horse, it's part of the learning experience and you have done so much better than others for a first time." Frank jumped down and cupped his hands for Ben's right foot.

"Alright." The two horses walked sedately across the expansive drive and up to the wide steps leading up to the wrap-around porch and front door beyond. At that moment Ben's car came up the drive. A stable-hand jumped out and took both horses.

"Take them back to the stables, Joe. I'll come down later."

Five minutes later, Ben was waiting in a large, triple aspect sitting room, one side having borrowed light from an octagonal orangery full of plants Ben had never seen before. He sat in a comfortable armchair, rubbing his knee where it had twisted slightly from the fall. Above the fireplace was a large portrait of who he assumed was the grandfather with his young son by his side. It looked like they were out on Hunt Ridge. They had rifles cupped in their arms, Davy Crockett style. Frank had left him to go and talk to his grandfather. He was back within a few minutes.

"I've asked Terrence to get the box," he said. "It is pretty large but should fit into your car easily."

"You mean I am to take it home with me? I was expecting to look at the papers here."

"Grandpa said to give you the box."

"But it is your heirloom. There could be valuable papers in there."

"Ben, he said to give it to you and that is what I am doing. I will inherit everything here and I just don't care for old papers. I barely read a book from one year to the next. I'm a magazine man myself." Then, on seeing Ben's disbelief, he added, "There are only four things I care about in the world. They are horses, women, friends, and making money, probably in that order. History just does not feature. Grandpa told me about your friend in jail and how you are trying to help her. If I can get rid of an old trunk and help you help her at the same time, then I am all for it. Ah, here is Terrence. Put it in Mr Franklin's car please, it is the blue Chevy out front. Then tell Mr Urquart that the trunk has been picked up. Now, Ben, how about we rustle up some grub, I'm starving and you did me a good turn today with the photos."

The rustling up of grub was not quite how Ben would have managed it. They moved to the orangery and were served rare steak 'from our own herd' with mushrooms and fried potatoes and salad. They both had a beer and then cheese and biscuits. Terrence brought the food in on fine tableware, helped by a shy girl of eighteen or so in a black skirt and white shirt. She was pretty, with masses of freckles on a fine face, but almost entirely bald. Ben could not help staring at her as she served the food. She had a kind of deep-down confidence that did not get flustered as Ben stared; she just got on gracefully with her work.

"She is a cancer survivor," Frank explained when they were alone again. "She has had masses of chemo and we hope is in remission now. We hire several of them to work around the house as it gives them a way of earning money and also getting health insurance. Otherwise they find it impossible to get anything other than casual work."

"That's good of you."

"No, it is self-interest, actually. As they can't get work anywhere else they are real loyal and do a great job here." But Ben knew it was far more than that. However the Williams family had made their money, they were good people at heart.

"How did you make your money?" Ben asked.

"It goes back a long way. There were Williams living here in Revolutionary times. More recently, Grandpa started an arms business and then sold out thirty years ago. Now we buy companies that are in trouble and break them up, sell off the pieces to the highest bidders, close down unprofitable sections and generally make a killing." Suddenly the penny dropped.

"You bought United Hardware, didn't you?"

"That was the first deal I worked on, back in 2017. I was fresh out of UVA. Do you know about it?"

"My mother was laid off from the Still City plant. They used to make all the hinges and locks there but production was moved to Mexico. There was a huge fight with the unions."

"I remember it. Ben, are you mad about it?"

"Yes." The single word conveyed everything.

"Has your mother worked since?" That question showed that Frank knew something of the employment conditions in Still City.

"She was hurt badly in the riots. She broke her back, hit by something. We never found out who or what hit her but she was hospitalised for six months and has great difficulty walking now."

"Is she bitter?"

"No, not her style," Ben replied, paused a second, and then decided to come out with it. "But I am."

"I can see that." Frank ate in silence.

Ben did not feel hungry anymore. After a few moments, he stood up. "Mr Williams, it has been a pleasure meeting you and thank you for the old papers. I need to be getting back now."

"Ben, think on something a moment. I can't be responsible for all the bad events following a takeover. Some I accept are our fault but a lot of it is down to the previous management, who did not bite the bullet and do the things they needed to do. I know in this case I was too eager to make as much money as I could and we could have handled it better, but we are not the cause of the problem, just someone who is responding to the situation they find."

"I understand." But Ben was in wooden mode. He did not want to be there any longer.

"Think if we had not stepped in. Each factory in United Hardware would have gone bankrupt and every single person would have lost his or her job. We closed down the six worst performing locations and sold the rest to an organisation that has invested in them. I dare say they now employ more people than ever before."

"But not my mother, and nobody cared that she ended up a half cripple."

"Let me do something, then. I could…"

"No. We manage fine without any help."

On the drive back, Ben could not get this conversation out of his mind. Here was a man who made a rich living by breaking up businesses, upsetting lives without as much as a thought, yet he gave opportunity to cancer survivors and had shown generous hospitality to Ben, a stranger to him. Ben could not understand why things were becoming so complicated. Suddenly he was dealing with changing shifts at work, visits every two weeks to a girl in prison for a crime she did not commit, the inadequacies in his mind that he had no education while an inmate his own age was working on a

Masters, and now the realisation that his host for the day and kind donor of the papers he sought on Richard Sutherland was implicated in his mother's misfortunes. Inside five weeks his life had become a muddle of confliction and he yearned for the simple days again.

Rather than give it any more thought, he turned instead to his gas mileage, calculating that the weight of the trunk took off almost a mile a gallon from average consumption, compared to the trip down. He had not lifted the trunk but Terrence, the butler, had. It would probably be around sixty to eighty pounds. So how does that compare to the weight of the car?

But then maybe he was just driving a little faster. In a few more miles of driving time he would work out the extra cost in fuel of the trunk of old papers he carried, and his ETA, to see whether he was averaging a faster speed back. They were simple calculations he could do in his head.

Letter Two

Dear Ben,

I agree that it is far nicer to be less formal and for us to use first names. I am delighted that you consider me your friend. And that you wrote me back so promptly, especially when you are working such long hours and dedicate so much of your precious time off to visiting me. When you and Mom visit I spend most of my time talking with her so I feel like my writing to you is making up for this by dedicating time outside visiting hours to you. I look forward to your visits enormously. Zanesville is much better than my last place and I am still hoping to get a better job, but the highlights of my time here are when I walk through that door and see Mom and you sitting waiting for me. It makes my life worth living, it really does. But no more about me, I am dying to tell you about some of my discoveries of Richard Sutherland.

Ben paused a moment, aware that the rest of the letter would be all about the past. Now was the time to make any adjustments, as he would soon be lost in the world Dakota was discovering. He got up from his one comfortable chair and fetched a beer from the refrigerator, made a corned beef sandwich and turned off the main light, leaving just a reading light above the chair. It gave a theatrical mood to his studio apartment.

Richard was deeply frustrated. He had been almost two weeks in Paris and was yet to meet Franklin. It was high summer, hot and sultry, no breeze to freshen the air and cool tempers. Franklin's departure for Berlin, just before Richard had arrived, was an irritant that his tired bones did not feel like coping with. Would the famous American negotiator make any difference? He hoped so. He loved both his own country and his adopted country, remembering clearly where he had lived as a young man. He had loved that time. The sense of building something new, fresh-sawn planks, clearings in trees, new piers jutting out into the rivers as if they wanted to reach out and be a part of the world. There had been a sense of adventure, of sharing, now often reduced to dogma and belligerence on both sides. Such was the nature of war. And this was really a civil war, the worst of all kinds. The colonies had been awash with opportunity, but that was before the pamphleteers had moved in. He would give it the best he could and then beg to be relieved. He was too old for these games and his house in Dumfriesshire was still to be completed. Would he ever see the work done?

Richard was staying with a friend; a wealthy French merchant, Charles Dubois, a rival from his days in Virginia. The house was two stone-throws from the Palace of Versailles and Richard had a suite of rooms on the second floor. Charles had welcomed him warmly, despite their two countries being at war, saying in his near-perfect English, "My friend, you are always welcome."

Charles Dubois' hospitality was legendary for its lavishness. The home was made of three spacious houses knocked together to include ballroom, library, smoking room and several drawing and dining rooms, spread over two floors with the bedrooms above. Madame Dubois was a generous host with several people at one time as houseguests. Parties followed parties; musicians seemed to be in a permanent state of either setting up or gathering up their equipment. Richard was used to entertaining but found this to be on a scale beyond his experience or desire to participate in. Charles noticed this and took Richard aside early in his stay, explaining that he should only attend the events that he wanted to and could always dine in his rooms if he so chose. "I want you to be comfortable and at ease." So Richard took him at his word and dipped into the functions like a child tasting an array of sweets, choosing only those that really appealed to him. He enjoyed these tasters quite considerably, but often wondered how on earth his old friend could afford such enormous extravagance. Charles once let him know the annual rent on his Versailles house. It was more than Richard's entire estate had cost in Dumfriesshire.

But there was one side of the hospitality that Richard found disturbing and the irony of his disquiet was not lost on him. The man who made his first fortune from slavery disliked intensely that the whole of the Dubois household staff were slaves, selected from the best of the best and trained to the manners and routine of a wealthy French household. Charles had explained that this was the fashion in Paris. Richard had been allocated a manservant with the unlikely name of Rupert. He was blacker than black, with a vivacious grin and young, dancing eyes, but a seriousness of purpose that contrasted with his jovial features. He made Richard think of a man grown old and wise before his time, his physical characteristics lagging behind. Rupert remembered little of his African heritage. Richard quizzed him and learned something of the sea fishing in long canoes, his family and the endless dry grasslands with crooked trees and rivers that disappeared for long months at a time. He sometimes heard Rupert humming beautiful tunes with enchanting rhythms but the man had clearly long-since forgotten the words.

"Do you resent being taken away?"

"Yes, Master. I remember being taken by the bad men."

"But are you angry?"

"No, Master. I am not angry." To Richard's question of how that could be, he just answered, "The sun shines here also and life is too short to carry burdens. I go light-footed in the world. That is the best way." Another time he said, "I carry my wealth with me, I have it here." And he beat his chest to indicate his heart. It was conversations such as these that made Richard uneasy; the contrast with his Presbyterian upbringing was stark. And Rupert seemed to see right into Richard, understanding what and who he was but being content to remain what and who he himself was.

Rupert came in early one morning full of smiles. "Sir, Master Sir! Mr Franklin is back again from his travels. I heard it in the kitchen this very morning. I heard he is coming here to meet you at 10 o'clock."

"Quick, help me get ready, Rupert." Rupert, Richard had noticed, loved a challenge and always rose to it. Richard was fed, washed, and dressed in best coat, cravat and new silk stockings by half past nine. He used the spare half an hour to go through his brief from Lord Shelburne again and to remind himself of the objectives he hoped to achieve. After almost eighty years on this earth, in which he had travelled across continents and made multiple fortunes, Richard suddenly felt inexplicably nervous, just like when, as a young trainee clerk, he had first turned up at his uncles' offices in Glasgow sixty years earlier. He had heard so much about this famous American, this delver into so many things. In contrast, Richard's life seemed inadequately narrow, concentrating on trade, balance sheets and networks. There were no discoveries, no inventions, no ideas to Richard's name, just a lot of money and property.

But Richard Sutherland had nothing to be concerned about. Benjamin Franklin and he became firm friends from the first meeting. Franklin had praised Richard's prowess in trade and then said, "By God, Richard, we need to get agreement to end this blasted war. Our two countries should be firm friends, not enemies."

"I agree, Benjamin. Let's start with where we have agreement and common ground and then deal with the problems. You have clearly won the war on the ground. We hold the cards at sea with our navy being supreme."

They got straight down to business that first meeting and found they agreed on so much.

Within weeks they had a set of principles to work with. All the frustration of July 1782 was blown away by the time August sent its strong rays down on the two bowed heads as they walked together in deep concentration, either in the extensive garden of Charles Dubois or the side streets deep in Paris, touring the sites and visiting the best coffee shops. Benjamin was an expert guide, seeming to know something about everything. Richard found himself sending optimistic reports back to London and Benjamin Franklin confirmed he was doing the same to Philadelphia.

"Rupert?" Richard called one evening in mid-September.

"Yes sir, right here, sir." Rupert came right up to him.

"Rupert, I might be going back to London soon and then on to Scotland to supervise the completion of my house."

"Of course, sir. I think you will be pleased to go."

"Yes, I am getting very old, but I want to do something for you before I go."

"A present, sir?"

"The ultimate present, Rupert. I want to buy your freedom."

"No thank you, sir."

"What?"

"Sir, I am very grateful that you have thought of this but here I *have a wife and three children and I am happy. I am very happy. I don't have a desire to change things."*

"Are you really sure, Rupert? I can set your whole family free if you like." But Rupert would not have his mind changed. Charles Dubois was a good master and he intended to stay with what he knew.

"There is nothing I want for and if I were free I would face the struggles you face with making money, decisions on everything. Right now, I have a different type of freedom."

"Rupert, you have slavery."

"Yes sir, I have a type of freedom called slavery and it is not so bad a thing."

All Richard could get out of Rupert was a promise that if ever he changed his mind he would get in touch with Richard for whatever help he needed. Richard held out his glass for more cognac and sighed as the brown liquid eased into the crystal. What he would do now for a dram of whisky instead of the brandy, but none was available anywhere in Paris that he knew of, the two countries still being at war.

As autumn brought in great gales and floods of rain, they made steady progress. America would have its independence: that had been clear for some time now. But why was the response from the old colonies becoming so patchy and changeable?

Suddenly it was Dakota's voice coming through instead of Richard's. Ben sat up straight in his chair.

Ben, I don't understand why they had this agreement and then months went by in which they seemed to do nothing. Richard was recalled and shortly afterwards retired up to Scotland. He was accused of being too lenient with the colonists. But what happened? The same deal was signed nine months after Franklin and Sutherland agreed it. It is a mystery. I don't know whether I will be able to determine what has gone on from prison because it is deeply frustrating having to make application for documents and books and then three weeks later you might get them or it might be denied. I guess there are not that many libraries and museums that want to extend lending rights to Zanesville Medium Security

Federal Penitentiary! I have to go to work now in the laundry so I
will send this letter and start another one tonight.
All the best from Dakota.

Ben stared at the letter for several minutes, not wanting to be
dragged back to the present, contemplating what Dakota
would be doing at 9.15pm on a Thursday evening. She was
probably getting ready for bed, like he needed to do as it was
an early start in the morning. She shared an overcrowded
dorm with numerous other inmates in bunks. No privacy
other than a sheet pulled across the entrance and secured
under the bunk above, lights on all night, snoring,
nightmares, angry shouting carrying across the dorm like
shells across a battlefield. All the disturbance he had was an
electric guitar whining across the street in fits and starts of
enthusiasm and the occasional horn in the next street over.
Even the freight trains at the back rumbled quietly on their
single-track journeys. And he had the privacy of his own
room: no need for self-rigged sheet-curtains across his bed.
Why was his life so thoroughly ordinary, decent and
wholesome, while Dakota's was full of anger and risk? Could
one mistake as an eighteen-year-old make all that difference?
That made him think of Frank Williams, living in luxury,
going from deal to deal making more and more money,
while his father worked for the homeless and lived in four
rooms with the interstate pounding at his door. But Frank
Williams was a good man in large part. It was too much to
think about so Ben tossed his empty beer bottle, brushed his
teeth, and got into bed, reading some of his copy of *The
Peacemakers* the library had located for him before drifting off
to sleep.

Contents of the Trunk

It was actually not that heavy. Ben could lift it easily from the back seat of his car where it had sat for over a week due to his hectic work schedule. Mrs Jameson suggested he take it to her front room, the one her husband had sat in and which was never used now. It was set up as a combined sitting and dining room so it had a large mahogany polished table, with a fine layer of dust that she brushed off, darting just ahead of him and flicking the duster left and right as he lowered the trunk onto the table.

"This can be your work room. So you can lay out all the papers carefully and organise them," she said. "I'll bring you coffee and cookies to keep you going," she added with a laugh, making light of her deep appreciation for what he was doing for her daughter. Dakota's letters were so much brighter now. Part of that was her moving to a medium security facility and the visits from Ben and her but a large part, Mrs Jameson knew, was that someone else was taking an interest in Dakota's studies. Mrs Jameson did not mention to Ben the frequent questions about him in Dakota's letters to her. *Did he like his last letter? Is he really interested in my subject? Does he ever talk about me? Really, do you think he likes me? Do you mean he actually went to Charlottesville to get the papers? And he fell off his horse?* Mrs Jameson could picture her girl laughing quietly as she imagined Ben riding for the first time. It was little things like this, she knew, that made Dakota's life bearable.

The contents of the trunk were largely copies of letters from Benjamin Franklin to statesmen back home, reporting on what was going on in Paris or London. Ben could tell they were copies because most of them started with 'This is a fair copy of the report from B. Franklin on affairs in Paris', or similar wording. He went through each letter, sorting them by date and then by recipient, making a pile of any that were from July 1782 until the end of 1783.

With growing dismay, Ben saw the pile of letters from London increase while the Paris pile was scarcely added to. He willed the next bundle, and then the one after that, to be from Paris, but this seemed to be largely a collection of London letters. He read a few of them, although the language and handwriting were difficult to the untrained. They seemed witty and observant and included insight into that roaring metropolis, that melting pot of world sailors, traders, business people, aristocrats, scientists and cranks. Everyone in London had something to say and they seemed to shout it from every corner, every window, every doorway. He imagined a city that was alive in so many ways. Warehouses brim-full of exotic merchandise, pickpockets forever on the lookout for the next opportunity, preachers, soldiers and tramps everywhere. And then he could imagine the sound also. There would be noise from every direction, conflicting, contrasting, merging together, a great big cry of human activity at maximum volume.

In contrast, the few letters from Paris were much more subdued, giving Ben the impression of a quiet, ordered, structured, but almost depressed, city where initiative and ambition were displayed only behind closed doors. Benjamin Franklin still had observations, but they were muter than the noise of London.

There were also only six letters from Paris and three of those dated from before Richard's arrival in late July 1782. One was a warm appreciation for 'my new dear friend, Richard Sutherland' and another was in similar vein, striking a positive note on discussions for a hopeful outcome in the very near future. That was dated 10th September 1782.

The last letter from Paris was the most interesting. It was also by far the shortest. It seemed to refer to a communication to Franklin but the paper was torn and Ben could not make out to whom the letter was addressed. It was only four lines and spoke of his 'disgust at the outturn of events and the turn tailing of the body of opinion after he had negotiated such respectable and hopeful an outcome as could be reasonably expected'. What could it mean? On impulse, Ben called Sir John in England and read the letter to his voicemail. He looked at his phone as he closed off the call and suddenly realised the time. "I'm late for work," he cried, running upstairs to get changed.

He was twelve minutes late but nobody noticed. His almost retired supervisor at the Smithsonian seemed more interested in calculating his pension than in arranging the schedules and checking on each member of staff. It was a late night shift as they were open to 10pm and Ben knew he had a long shift the next day and an early shift the day after. So it would be Saturday afternoon before he could get back to the trunk. But then the trunk was bare and it had not shed any light on anything.

On Saturday afternoon, he rolled his car into his normal spot outside Mrs Jameson's house and flicked off the engine. It had been a hard few days. As soon as he had got home on Friday night he had been called out again and spent several hours searching the grounds because someone had seen something in the shadows and the President was in residence, just back from a trip to China. Now he had what was left of Saturday afternoon free and all day Sunday as well so they could visit Dakota.

"Mrs Jameson, normal time tomorrow, the tank is… Oh, hi Sir John, what are you doing here?"

"Studying the bloody architecture of 1940s backstreet DC," he replied, before adding, "What the blue blazes do you think I am doing? You left a crazy phone message and then are surprised to see me?"

"But all this way?"

"I was in New York, 'matey', so not that far to come." He had an aggressive way of talking but his eyes twinkled, belying the abrasive impression Ben suspected him of cultivating.

"So you want to see the letter?"

"No, I want to go and watch a movie. What do you think? Lead on then, and let's see what you have."

"Is there nothing else?" Sir John asked twenty minutes later after studying the copy letter very carefully. "Are you sure?"

"Look," said Mrs Jameson, "an empty trunk." She lifted up the bowed lid and both Ben and Sir John peered in. It was completely empty. Ben took the lid from Mrs Jameson and laid it back down.

"I'm surprised Mr Williams gave you these documents," Sir John said. Ben told him the story of his visit, after getting two beers from his apartment upstairs. Mrs Jameson thought it was nice to have someone use her front room again so left it to them, going to the kitchen to cook them some supper. It was the least she could do for Ben and his strange friend.

"I know Frank Junior a little, but his grandfather I know much better. He is a benefactor to our college. So, you fell off the horse? First time riding?"

"Yeah, but I really liked it."

"So do I."

"You ride?"

"All my life. My kids are crazy about it, too. We have six horses back at home, one for each of us, plus a pony the children used to ride. My wife does carriage driving also."

"Do you live on a farm in England?"

"It's called a farm but most of the land was sold off before we bought it. It has eighteen acres now, a few small fields and a big one. Got another beer? I've got quite a thirst."

A second beer was followed by Mrs Jameson's fried chicken with beans and corn bread. It was growing dark when Sir John stood up suddenly. "I need to find an hotel. Are there any half-decent ones nearby?"

"You should stay here," Mrs Jameson replied. "You can have the spare bed in my room and move it in here. There is the bathroom right next door."

"Well, if you're sure?"

"I'm sure. But we have to be off early in the morning. We're visiting Dakota and it's a long drive."

"We leave at 6.45," put in Ben.

"That's fine. I get up at 5.30 every day anyway and it is easier in the mornings over here with jetlag. But the other end of the day is something else, so unless you people have some serious objections I need to lay my head down. Can we move the bed now?"

After the bed was settled and Ben had gone upstairs, Sir John asked Mrs Jameson to sit down a moment. "I want to know all about the case that led to Dakota being sentenced."

So Mrs Jameson took a deep breath and told the story again, starting with Walker's death in 2015, because that is when it seemed the world had stopped and turned inside out for the Jameson family. Sir John was a good listener and asked a few questions; at first general ones, but increasingly focused on Dakota's representation throughout the trial and appeal. "So how much did you pay the lawyer?"

"In total?" she asked. "Well, it was $215,000 for the trial and then $75,000 for the appeal. Plus, he wanted another $20,000 to attend the appeal. Then there were the expenses. We paid those monthly and I just made the last payment in February this year. He said he would accept $2,000 a month and that was for, let me see now, it must have been nine years and three months."

"So 111 months at $2,000 is another $222,000. So that brings the grand total to $532,000?"

"I suppose so, but then there was that other bill for the private detective. That was just under $60,000."

"So our grand total is around $590,000?"

"That sounds about right."

"Scandalous," Sir John muttered. "Well, thank you for that, now that bed looks very attractive to my weary body so I will say goodnight and thank you for the hospitality."

Mrs Jameson fussed a few minutes longer over her strange English guest, settling him down as well as she could. Then she sat in her kitchen long into the night, thinking about her decimated family and wondering what Dakota was doing right now. It had been her husband's idea to name their first child Dakota in memory of where they had lived when he was in the Air Force and they were first married. She thought back to those days fondly. Dakota had not been an easy baby. It had been a long and painful birth.

Then she had slept peacefully for the forty-eight hours she stayed in the Air Force hospital, luring Mrs Jameson into thinking it was going to be a breeze. But as soon as she got back home, her bellowing started and it seemed like it did not finish until her first birthday. By then Mrs Jameson was pregnant with Walker. He was so different: as easy-going as Dakota had been stressed. They were both adorable to look at, hair the whiter side of blond, and sky-blue eyes, taking after their father. They were firm friends from the start. Nothing could separate them. Once Dakota had said, "Mom, I wish Walker was not my brother because then I could marry him." She could have eaten both her two little children, she loved them so much. Those were the happy Dakota days. Then they had moved to DC, bought this house, and there was every reason to think the happy days would go on forever.

Every time Mrs Jameson went down this road it ended in tears, great big shaking sobs. It had started with Walker's illness a dozen years ago and was not over yet. Would she live to see Dakota free again? The question haunted her. But at least she was going to see her tomorrow. She picked up her favourite photograph, a picture she had taken twenty-five years ago. It was of her husband, with Dakota on his back and the toddler Walker clinging to his front as their father struggled along, almost on all fours. She sat a long time looking at the photograph before she finally hauled herself off to bed.

In the morning, she overslept. Sir John had already left, announced with a brisk note thanking her for his stay at the Hotel Jameson. Give his best to Ben and say he would be in touch. There was a postscript on the reverse that just said. 'Thanks for filling me in on Dakota. I told Ben I would like to help and, while there's not much I can do, I would like to try in any way you might ask so please do. I'm often in the States and will be at Georgetown University over the next couple of days'. She had planned to get up early and make

Sir John some breakfast. Instead, she had Ben knocking on her door asking if she was ready.

"Just coming." She put on the first clothes she could find, brushed her hair and teeth and left within ten minutes of waking. She was going to see her daughter.

***

For Albert Essington II, life was good. His third wife was a scorcher, more than ten years his junior, with full wavy black hair and long legs, and a delicious sense of fun and adventure. She was taller than him, but he did not care. His first wife looked after the kids; now early-teens when they know everything but nothing, a boy first and a girl a year younger. He saw them at Thanksgiving and Christmas and for one hellish week each summer. But he phoned on their birthdays and was generous with gifts. His second wife had left him after four months and he had no idea where she was, but was just grateful that it left him free when Maggie came along a year later.

His house was a beauty, too, with swimming pool and tennis court; compulsory for their neighbourhood, of course, as were the Porsche and Range Rover. Other accruements included the golf club membership, the Italian-style villa on the Far Shore, and, the latest addition, the cinema room in the basement. This had all the latest gadgets and, while most others had cinema rooms, his was set apart by being cutting edge.

He swung the Range Rover through the electric gates and drove at too fast a speed up the twenty-degree incline of the drive, screeching to a stop by the front door.

"You're back early." Maggie spoke through her champagne glass. "Want some champers?"

"Wimp's drink." He made that comment most days, before going to the huge glass drinks cabinet and pouring himself a Scotch and ice. "Decided to work from home."

"Your files are in the bedroom."

"Can you show me where?"

"Sure thing," she giggled, grabbing the bottle of champagne as she went for the stairs. "Follow me, you insatiable little workaholic!"

That was when the home office phone went. "Ignore it," Maggie said, but Albert did not get where he was today by ignoring potential clients.

"Essington."

"Good afternoon, Mr Essington. My name is Sir John Fitzroy. I wonder if you might spare a few moments of your valuable time."

"When?"

"Now."

"But…"

"Never mind, I'll call my back-up lawyer instead. Goodbye, Mr Essington."

"Wait a minute." He looked back at Maggie waiting impatiently on the first stair. "It's aristocracy," he mouthed. "I'd be glad to meet you, Sir John. Can you come to my house?"

"I'll be there in ten minutes." It did not occur to Essington that Sir John had not asked for an address.

Exactly ten minutes later the doorbell rang, as if Sir John had been around the corner checking off the time on a stopwatch.

"I'm a baronet," he explained when Maggie asked him straight out if he was a real aristocrat.

"As in Magna Carta and all that?"

"As in Magna Carta, I suppose you could say. It is the lowest rank of the aristocracy, but ours is an ancient family dating back to the Norman Conquest. That is before Magna Carta of course."

"I knew that!" Maggie lied. "So it's more like Arthur and his round table."

"Maggie, don't go on so. Leave the baronet and me to talk business. Fetch us some drinks. What's your tipple, Baron?"

"Actually, it is 'Sir John'."

"Is that the name of a cocktail?" Maggie asked, enormously impressed by her humour, the champagne getting to her. She was rewarded by Albert guiding her out of the door.

"Bimbo," Albert said by way of explanation. "But the sex is good."

Sir John did not reply, recognising the brashness as another form of sycophancy. Albert spoke again into the silence. "What can I do for you Sir John?"

"It's more what I can do for you." As soon as Sir John uttered these lines he cringed with their corniness, straight out of a black-and-white movie in which tough guys talk tough and men do what men have to do. But he kept his nerve and waited for Essington to speak.

"Tell me more, I'm listening."

"Dakota Jameson."

"Who?" Albert genuinely did not remember.

"You were her lawyer in a federal drugs case back in 2018."

"So if I was?" He now remembered and a shard of intuition told him Sir John's visit was not going to bring a fat fee for minimal work. "I'm very busy right now and don't have time to concern myself with ancient history."

"You will have a lot more time pretty soon. I would say twenty years, judging by the way the courts of this fine land are handing down sentences these days."

"Get out now."

"I'm going. But I want you to know that we are on to you and I won't rest until you pay for the cruelty of letting down an innocent teenager."

"Hey, she was found guilty despite my representation."

"I would say 'because of your representation'," Sir John replied, standing up and leaving without another word. He would find a way to get to the bottom of this. Historians were in many ways detectives.

"You do-gooders make me want to vomit," Essington called after him. "The case was cut and dried, guilty as hell. The silly girl got what she had coming to her. That's called justice, Mr Fitzroy." Albert got himself another whisky, shrugged away the threat, and went to find Maggie.

***

Towards the end of a long day, Ben and Mrs Jameson were driving across Pennsylvania at a steady pace, the only irritant being the constant stream of heavy trucks that behaved as if the interstate was a private racetrack, packed in long, close convoy and changing lanes at will.

"She seemed so much more perky today," Mrs Jameson commented.

"That's the third time you've made the same comment on the way back," Ben reminded her.

"Well, it's true. Don't you think?"

"Without a doubt." Ben was not going to mention the bruising on Dakota's left arm, as if great iron pincers had grabbed her and dragged her along the prison corridor. "You know she has the most beautiful smile."

Dakota's news was that she had been allocated to the library, a top job usually only for those with long tenure at Zanesville. Ben had tried to thank Bennet afterwards, during their end of visit session, but Bennet had stonewalled him.

"It's just done on suitability," she had said in as official a manner as she could, but blushing slightly and addressing the floor rather than making eye contact.

"Well, it's a great move so whoever is responsible has my thanks." His thoughts returned to Dakota. She would be lying in her narrow bed, probably not yet asleep, thinking about her first day in the library. Once she had the knack of the requisition system it would be much easier for her to get the books she needed.

Much later, Mrs Jameson broke her quiet, happy silence again to ask Ben if he had early shift the next day.

"Yes, early and late. Long day tomorrow."

"Would you mind helping me move the bed back tonight, then?"

"Sure, we'll be back in ten minutes and we'll do it straight away and then I'm going to hit the sack."

It was Mrs Jameson who discovered the false lid of the trunk they had left as empty. She did it by stumbling while moving the bed and falling against the trunk, making the lid cave in.

"A hidden cavity," she said. Ben clambered over the bed to feel his way around the cavity.

"Damn, it's empty," he declared. "I thought maybe we had found something." He sat back on the bed, slanted now across the floor so that the top end was against the trunk. "Wait a minute. What's this?" He pulled out a yellowed document that had been taped against the back portion of the lid. "It looks like a deed of some sorts."

"You mean a property deed?" Mrs Jameson thought of the folded paper in the bank safe that proved her house had two mortgages on it.

"Yes, but I cannot understand it."

"Call Sir John."

"He will be long gone."

"No," Mrs Jameson replied. "He said he was going to spend a couple of days at Georgetown University. Call him."

Sir John was asleep, grumpy at first and then increasingly excited as Ben described what they had found.

"I'll be right over."

"This is a property deed," he confirmed, using his magnifying glass to decipher the words. "It is made out to Richard Sutherland. It is for land in Northern Virginia of all places!"

"Dakota said he had lots of land around DC," Ben confirmed.

"Had is the operative word. This is actually a deed of sale as well. It is a right strange old document! It seems he was selling 2,400 acres in Albemarle County; no, not selling but exchanging that large property for just a few acres close to the Potomac. It is hard to tell with these old references. Can we get more light on this document?" They moved to the kitchen where the strip light made the kitchen table seem like an operating room. Sir John studied the document for over twenty minutes without a sound. Ben yawned.

"Young man, if this is too tedious, you have my

permission to trot off to bed."

"No way." Ben was getting used to Sir John's humour. "I just thought you might like to tell us what it says."

"All in good time," he muttered, completely absorbed in the very clever document spread out on the kitchen table in front of him.

"It is a deed of exchange, but with a difference," he explained long after midnight. "I've never seen anything like it before." He tried his cup of coffee. "It's gone cold. Any chance of a refresh, Mrs Jameson?" He looked around at his mini audience, rather enjoying the tension he had created. "Well, it is a deed of exchange but it is for a huge 2,400 acre estate in Albemarle County for a tiny eighteen-acre parcel somewhere in what must now be the northwest of DC. It's an exchange of unequal value but there is a twist."

"What is it?" Ben asked into the silence. Then a premonition hit him and he gasped. "It's the White House, isn't it? Eighteen acres in Northwest DC: that is the grounds at the White House. Eighteen acres."

"My DC geography is not that good so I have no idea," Sir John replied. "But the twist is that these eighteen acres remain sovereign territory of the United Kingdom of Great Britain for perpetuity. There are a few conditions in tiny writing but, to all intents and purposes, that means, if you are right, Ben, that the White House is located on British soil. It has always been on British sovereign territory. Now, it refers to a second document as the revised treaty. If we could just find that." Like treasure hunters in a race, all three of them stared at each other for half a moment and then ran for the front room and the broken trunk by the bed. Ben was first in and he found the slightly torn document taped to the inside roof of the lid. It was a single page dated 3rd September 1783.

"The same date as the Treaty of Paris that ended the War of Independence," Sir John said. Then on quickly reading the document he added, "It rescinds the Treaty of Paris and reinstates all the colonies as British possessions in perpetuity. My God, it says independence for USA never actually happened. Look, here it says the bearer of this document is automatically a British citizen and is appointed Governor General of the thirteen states."

"Who signed it?" Mrs Jameson asked.

"Everyone who signed the Treaty of Paris."

"It has to be a hoax." Ben could not take it in.

"I'll get it checked out but I can't do that in America. We have to keep it very quiet. I'll take it to London. I know someone who will be very discreet. My God, if it is true it is going to turn the world upside down. We must keep this absolutely to ourselves while I check it out. Is that agreed?"

Mrs Jameson and Ben nodded and then said, "Yes, I agree," when Sir John said he wanted their spoken commitment to absolute silence.

"That crucially means no one. Not even Dakota." He made them both say that they agreed, not even Dakota.

Sir John slept that night in the front room again, after booking as early a flight the next day as he could find.

"I'll be in touch in a few days. Remember, not a word to anyone." Sir John glared his parting warning and was gone in the cab Ben organised for him, taking both documents with him.

A Day in the Life

Dakota always woke early. There was a time an hour before wake-up call when the constant noise of the dorm died down, as if the guards growing weary towards the end of their night shift decided to turn the volume knob down. Most inmates caught up on sleep but Dakota enjoyed the relative silence and seclusion and preferred to be awake. The other bugbear, the constant strip lights, seemed less obtrusive at this time. She mused that as day started they lost their power to break the darkness and seemed weak and pointless as a result.

She started each day with a routine she had invented. As she slowly came around, her back aching from the wafer-thin mattress, she needed something to fight the natural wave of despair. In the first months of incarceration she had given way to this despair. It had overwhelmed her as her nineteenth birthday came and went, marked just by a card and two chocolate bars from her parents, both of which were stolen from her within minutes. She had thought she could not go on; nobody could live like this. Then she had met a tiny old woman who had befriended her in an offhand manner, hiding emotion behind a hardened exterior. Elsie had been inside since she was eighteen, herself following the murder of her entire family. Even now, Dakota shuddered to think of the house burning to ash after a row with her parents about her boyfriend. Elsie had gone three-quarters crazy inside, as many did.

"Count your blessings." It was the one thing she had said that made sense and hit home. Ever since then, Dakota had started the day with a silent reflection on her blessings. Elsie had not been around long. She was moved to another facility after four months of acquaintance with Dakota, who learned years later from another transferee that Elsie had died of breast cancer shortly afterwards. It had been a painful slide towards death, with minimal medical care. Nobody in authority had thought it worthwhile to keep a crazy old inmate alive if it involved extra expenditure. Thus, they cut her sentence and released her soul.

Dakota's blessings had multiplied several times over during the last couple of months. Sometimes, mimicking an old song her father had sung, she called it her 'Reasons to be Cheerful' time. She had been moved to an infinitely more bearable prison. It was only medium security. That meant they thought she had hope for the future. The next logical step would be a low security facility; maybe even with work release. She was twenty-eight now and her counsellor had told her in their first monthly meeting that provided she behaved herself, she could expect the move to low security before her fortieth birthday. Then there was the impending move to the library, away from the dreadful laundry. She had heard only yesterday that this was happening and that she was starting there on Monday. That was a true blessing, allowing her to work with her beloved books.

There were many other reasons to be cheerful. They seemed to be stacking up right now. Yes, it was frustrating working on her Masters because of access to research material but, as her counsellor had pointed out, it was not as if she was in a rush. "You have all the time in the world." She had smirked and Dakota had nodded and said, "Yes, ma'am, I do." But she had a degree and she had obtained it in just eight years of study from a maximum-security facility. She proudly told herself each morning that she was one of only eleven inmates who had achieved this in the last decade.

But chief of her blessings were her visits. They had never been before and now suddenly they were like clockwork. Actually, not quite clockwork because they had sneaked in an extra one, so in March they had come three Sundays in a row. But she could count on them coming. And it was wonderful to see her mother becoming alive again. During each visit, she gauged her mother's health on an index. Zero was dead and 100 was perfect health. She felt like a doctor monitoring her patient at regular intervals, charting the recovery and feeling a sense of accomplishment as it happened. She had been shocked by how much her mother had aged during the eight-and-a-half years she had not seen her. After the first visit, Dakota had given her an eighteen score. Now, after seven visits, she was at forty-nine and rising. Dakota calculated it scientifically. She gave scores for subsectors of health – her mother's smile, her facial lines, her walk from the table afterwards, her general manner, her conversation, and double for the light in her eyes. She carefully weighed up each one and then calculated the total score. It was an objective test and it gave the results she wanted to see.

But Dakota had an honesty that came from her animal status. She had no belongings other than the few they allowed her. She had no freedom of dress, occupation or entertainment, save the books they allowed her. She ate what she was given, as a dog would. She obeyed instructions absolutely and immediately, not to curry favour but to have a chance of liberation as soon as possible. Sometimes she reflected that it was like a strict religious order with vows of poverty and obedience and humility. The only other option was to fight and that meant a longer sentence so was self-defeating. She was fighting by obeying.

And the honesty that was Dakota told her that the principle blessing of the many in her life was Ben Franklin, the oddly named security guard with a heart bigger than the prison walls that surrounded her. She lived for sight of him.

And when she closed her eyes she saw him each time, looking at her.

***

The bell rang, harsh against the peace before. Dakota threw off the thin blanket and swung her feet over the edge towards the concrete floor. There was another blessing. Her mother had brought new shower shoes on her last visit. She loved the newness of them and the tight way they fitted her feet with the thick rubber soles. But today was not shower day. Those were Tuesdays and Saturdays. Instead, she took off her orange nightie and put on her orange overalls with white t-shirt below, white socks and orange sandals. She brushed her short, straggly hair, remembering briefly how it had once been. But no time for what had once been. That way led depression and unpredictable behaviour. She checked her badge and grabbed her towel and toothbrush.

It was Friday today. While there were no guarantees in prison life, she knew that routine hardly ever changed. She was looking forward to porridge for breakfast. It was the best day for breakfast, other than Sunday when they had scrambled eggs. She shuffled in line, nodding to one or two other inmates. There was no talking allowed in line, just at the tables where they ate. She hoped to sit next to Janice who usually was in first and kept a space for her provided one of the gangs did not make her move to free up the table. Janice was her mother's age and was in for drugs, just like Dakota. But she was very different. She had been in and out of jail for a long time before getting a thirty-year sentence two years ago. Because they knew her they had moved her quickly to medium security. She was cheeky with the guards and they seemed to like her. She was a good person to be friends with.

"Morning," Dakota said. Following the ritual they had developed, she added, "Mind if I sit next to you?"

"Be by guest, honey, I don't think Clint Eastwood is going to take it today."

"So it's a Clint day today?" Some days it was George Clooney, others Kevin Costner. Once, bizarrely, it had been Ronald Reagan, but Janice had never explained why.

"Sure is. Porridge for brekkie and Smith's not on duty until Tuesday so it adds up to a great outlook for the weekend." Smith was nobody's favourite; a bloated figure with very poor health and small eyes and thin lips, an archetypal cruel-looking person for a casting director. She reminded Dakota of a portrait she had once seen of Henry VIII of England. She was an Assistant Warden with considerable authority. She was also a guard on the make because she resented her meagre salary, supplementing it with petty theft and extortion from the inmates. Rumour was she had gone to high school with the prison warden and then they had gone their separate ways. Smith had risen as far as she would go while Kinderly, with a Degree in Criminology, was her direct boss and was moving up rapidly. Smith would spend her entire career beating and cheating the prisoners at Zanesville, while the warden was passing through to Corporate.

"Second-last day in the laundry today," Dakota said, gulping down the lukewarm porridge before they were told to move on and get out of the dining hall.

"I forgot you're a bookworm type. Never saw the point of it myself." Janice had once confided to Dakota that she had skipped most of her education and, while she could rattle with the best verbally, she had limited reading and writing skills. She had refused Dakota's offer of help, saying she was too old to start on book-learning. Janice was assistant supervisor in the laundry and was happy with her lot. "I'll miss you," she added suddenly, another moment of honesty.

There was a sudden rush for the food counter. Dakota and Janice sprang up. There must be some leftover porridge. But the guards waved them down. There had been a little left but it had gone now.

"We need to sit closer to the counter," Janice said, but both of them knew that those spaces were prime real estate and they had no chance.

"Morning. Mind if I sit with you?" It was Hannah, the only other white person in Dakota's dorm.

"Be my guest, honey. I don't think Donald Sutherland is going to take it today."

"So it's a Donald day today?" Hannah spoke between mouths of porridge. She was behind and did not want to miss out. They would be calling time any moment now.

"Jan, why don't you sit with the other blacks?" Dakota had always wanted to ask her.

"No reason." But the usually verbose response was missing and spoke for itself by its curtness.

"Time, move out now."

"Damn!" mumbled Hannah, stuffing spoonfuls of

porridge into her mouth at speed.

"I said move!"

***

Val Bennet was frightened. Her husband frightened her. He had been such fun to be around in high school but five years of drink, no exercise and junk food had seen to his temper as well as his looks. She was frightened of everything about him: the anger that was more evident every day, his violence, his sneering condescension, his bullying 'know all' nature. It worked very well that he worked weekdays at the prison and she did weekends. She liked to see how long she could go without seeing him other than the cursory and mundane, passing over responsibility for their boy.

It did not help that he was a senior guard, above her in experience and pay grade. He might soon even become a supervisor. Then he would be unbearable.

Val pondered her life gloomily as she dropped her son with her mother. She had been called in to work today because they were short-staffed. Hopefully she would be on a different wing to her husband. She had no desire to see his brash bulk any more than she had to. Why had things turned out so poorly for her? Everything had been bright and hopeful before.

"He's a little unwell, Mom, so call me if you need me."

"Believe it or not, I have dealt with sick kids before." Why was her mother so cold with her? One day she would get up the courage to talk to her about it, but not today. She needed to rush or she would miss the thirty-minute slot at work for payment and would have a half hour docked from her wages.

"Please God, let me be on D wing," she prayed, knowing her husband was on A wing today. D wing had a separate staff room for breaks so there would be little chance of seeing him until tonight when they got home.

"You're on D wing today, Bennet."

"Thank you, Lord."

"What did you say?"

"Nothing, sir."

"Laundry room." That was hot and humid but at least it was D wing.

***

"Jameson, you are daydreaming. You have been staring at that basket for five minutes."

"I'm sorry, Miss Bennet." Val saw the fear in Dakota's eyes and hated her job even more. "I'll get right on to it."

"Wait a moment." Val fished a couple of dollar bills out of her skirt pocket. She just could not be that hard, however much she tried. "Go get two coffees from the machine in the hallway outside the staff room. I take mine white, no sugar."

"And the other one?"

"Whatever you have. Here's a chit to go there." She scribbled out a permission slip.

Dakota had not had a real machine cup of coffee since her trial. She just could not believe her luck. She was back in four minutes with the two cups of coffee, rushing so as not to be told off.

"Thank you, Miss Bennet."

"Come outside with me." There was a loading dock outside the anteroom to the laundry.

"I'm not allowed."

"You are with me. I'll say you were helping me with something." There was an air of collusion in the way she spoke. Dakota reluctantly followed the guard outside. The landing dock was a long raised concrete platform, overlooking a yard with D wing to the right, C wing to the left. Val leant against the railings with her back to the yard. Dakota stood in front of her, not knowing what to expect. She sipped at her coffee; it seemed all so wrong in front of a guard.

"Dakota?" At first, she did not respond, she was not used to a guard using her first name. "Dakota?" Val said again, more hesitantly.

"Yes, Miss Bennet."

"I just wanted to talk to someone."

"What about?" Was this some trick to get her in trouble? The coffee tasted great but was it worth the risk? Dakota wished she were safely back with the others, working the washers and presses. What could this guard want with her?

Suddenly, Val could not stop herself. The last five years of her life poured out: the hopes, the pregnancy shock, the aftermath, her parents, his parents, the rushed marriage, the birth, their home, her disappointment, her fear, the job, everything about how unhappy she was.

"Do you love your husband, Miss Bennet?" Dakota dared to ask, her right hand clasped against the paper coffee cup, her left fingers drumming against the side of her overalls.

"No."

"Then you should leave him. Better a five-year mistake than a lifetime sentence." Would that incite the barrage of abuse she expected at any moment? Guards and inmates just did not mix. Everyone knew that.

"But I don't know if I can. I have nowhere to go."

"Miss Bennet, I know your husband. He is as mean as they get." She did not add that every inmate knew that he was unfaithful to her. He was looking for it, too. "You can look after yourself. Get your son into day care and get the tax credit and you can work full-time here."

"But I hate this job too and I'll never be any good at it."

Dakota realised this to be true. Bennet would never be any good at the job because she was a gentle, considerate person. Yet she was in as harsh an environment as she could imagine. It was like a war zone in there. Now Dakota's fear was gone, replaced by compassion for what she saw – a lost person in the wrong place, trying to make it work but fighting against the tide.

"Then look for something else."

"But what? There is nothing else in Zanesville." At that moment Val looked like a little sister asking for advice. Dakota saw this and also that there was no point in stating the obvious; that she must move somewhere else. She was lost, depressed, miserable. Now was not the time to face reality.

"I'll ask Ben on Sunday. He might have some good ideas."

"Ben Franklin? Yes, he might." She seemed to cheer up, then added. "He is a good man. He has talked to me a bit."

"Take heart, Miss Bennet, things will improve." On impulse, Dakota stepped forward and took the guard's hand, squeezing it gently. They made eye contact and Val gave a weak smile. Dakota only hoped that no one had seen her, as it was an invitation to trouble.

"Thank you."

"That's OK. Anytime, Miss Bennet." To Dakota, this was surreal, but more was to come.

"Dakota, will you call me Val when we are on our own?"

***

Lunch was a Spam sandwich, as it was on most weekdays. The cooked meal was at 5pm. At weekends, it went the other way because they wanted to close the kitchens early, hence cooked meal at midday and Spam sandwich in the afternoon. Dakota was lucky because Hannah was serving lunch and slipped an extra piece of Spam onto her tray. A piece of Spam was worth three cigarettes, not that Dakota smoked anymore. The packet she received from her mother each week was traded for other essentials. Ten cigarettes would get you a packet of plain biscuits, but anything with chocolate cost at least fifteen.

She sat with three friends so split the Spam in four. It was how she approached life. Janice called it stupid, but her opinion did not stretch to declining the quarter of Spam. They often talked about food. Today Dakota said what she would give for a juicy hamburger. They laughed and then raised it to a pizza with various toppings, then Tammy saw them with a steak and fries, washed down with a long cold and never-ending beer.

"I had a real coffee today."

"Yeah sure, and it had caramel flavouring and came with free refills."

"No, I did." But they would not believe her; deep as they were in their own game of make-believe.

The afternoon was spent in the laundry, but it was her last afternoon there. On Saturdays, they only worked half a day. She worked the machines as if she was a machine herself, everything in slow-motion automation. It was hot but the guards let them open the door onto the loading bay and the breeze was like freedom on their cheeks. They sang with Janice leading them in 'Captain Jack, meet me down by the railroad tracks', the echoes sounding like a ragged blues band at play.

"Keep it down, ladies," Bennet called but her voice was not heard above the vocals, then someone started drumming on the empty washing machine. Dakota saw Bennet look at her pleadingly.

"Guys, enough!" She shouted to be heard above the accelerating din. "If we get caught it will be no visiting privileges this week. I really don't want that to happen." They responded to Dakota's request and, giggling, started to whisper the same song. Soon, all work had been abandoned and they were rolling on the floor laughing, or gripping the sides of the machines, trying to control themselves.

It was none too soon for Val when the bell went at 4pm. She led the slightly more sober inmates back to the rec room and handed them over to the staff there.

"Sixteen inmates from laundry detail," she reported.

"Good, take a break and get back here in thirty minutes. You'll be finished after lockdown."

"But I was told it was only to the end of the work day. I've got my son to pick up."

"Bennet, do you want a job or not? Just because hubby is going up in the world doesn't mean you can pick and choose your hours to suit yourself."

"Sorry, sir."

Evenings were the most exposed time of all. It was obviously so because of two key factors. There was more free time and less supervision. The evening meal was complete by 5.20. They filed out of the dining hall and most days they could go to the rec room, the dorm or the bathroom. Dakota and her friends always chose the rec room as the safest. It was better populated and more scrutinised by the guards. She saw Bennet there and looked away, pretending to watch a game of cards. There was a DVD player at one end but it was the cause of unending fights for viewing privileges and Dakota knew to keep away. Mainly they sat on the floor in a huddle, ready to move on the moment a gang came their way, happy to do so.

"We're the 'non-gang'," Hannah had joked once. "Our aim is to keep away from everyone else." They achieved this through a mixture of appeasement, bribery and agility. The idea was to use your wits to survive and they were all survivors; that is what they had in common.

So, evenings were a mixture of cautious enjoyment of the company of the same old friends, tainted with being forever on guard against threats, looking out for each other, building those bonds that last forever.

Dakota had quickly become a central figure in this evolving group, despite being a recent arrival. Occasionally, a new inmate would join, sometimes only briefly, before drifting away to a gang or moved on suddenly to another prison. But Dakota liked her friends and would have it no other way. She had lived in maximum security for over eight years without any friends, watching her own back day after day, night after night. Hence a half-dozen friends was another blessing she counted every morning when the prison population finally slept and gave a little peace to their violent world.

It was a strange fact that they had so much time on their hands yet Dakota found getting time to study so difficult. Twice a week, on Wednesday and Saturday afternoons, she could go to the library, likewise on Sunday mornings. But it was not enough. But that was changing with her new job on Monday.

Lockdown was 7pm. That was the end of the day. That was when she said a brief prayer and then ran through the day again in her mind, trying to talk to God about good and bad, hopes and fears, until she drifted off despite the harsh light and harsher voices. Tonight, her thoughts were all about Bennet. It was unheard of for a guard to confide in an inmate, even stranger to seek advice and to collapse in a heap of sorrow and confusion. Dakota would talk to Ben on Sunday. She felt sure he would have an idea to help her.

Letter Three

My dear Ben,

I really enjoyed your letter, thank you so much for writing me. I read it six times the day I got it and read it every day at least twice more. You have a funny way of writing things. I would call it quaint, well Mother would, that's for sure.

Things are looking up here. I really enjoy my new job and have already sent away for some documents to London! The warden got an email asking who I was and what I wanted the documents for and she knew nothing about me so I suddenly got summoned to the warden's office, only they did not tell me where I was going, just put the chains on so I knew it was not a normal place to go. The warden is Mrs Kinderly. She asked me lots of questions about what I was doing and what I was studying and why and all sorts. Then she said if they were prepared to send the documents they would allow them to enter the prison and provided they got through the inspections I could have them for two weeks. I thanked her and was just about to leave when she said that she was impressed by my work ethic and it could only go well for me. She asked me a lot of questions about my studies and why I wanted to do it and stuff. So, I am waiting for the documents and the guard thought they would come the day after tomorrow!

Ben was used to the format of her letters now. There would be an introductory section, thanking him for writing and giving him an update on her life and activities behind bars, but always skimming over the bruises and sheer horror of 1,200 women living in close confinement, many with furious tempers and huge grudges against the world. He would always read that bit quickly to find out if she was OK, then he would take a break and a beer and settle down for the next section where somehow Dakota seemed to switch tenses and write as if she were Richard Sutherland almost 250 years ago. It was an amazing knack. "She should be a writer," he told himself often enough as he became absorbed in her scripts. She could make Franklin's diaries come alive to the reader. Richard wrote much less, but his diaries were factual, observant and full of detail. She obviously used both and built up what happened from these two sources and others where she could find them.

So now, beer in hand, shoes off, sitting back in the chair with just the reading light above him, he felt the years roll back to late 1782.

On November 15th Richard made his way into the coffee house. It was a noisy place with movement everywhere, whether waiters, customers or hawkers of books, paper, oranges, girls; anything that educated gentlemen might need on the spur of the moment. He had been here many times before, both alone and with Benjamin. Normally he thrived on the bustle and the sudden appearances of people he knew in coffee houses, loving the scent of business deals made on chance encounters over coffee. But that was in London. Over here he was held by most at arms-length because of the war. He could not do deals here despite knowing many of the merchants in the city. He would be in breach of his ministerial appointment and they were, of course, at war with Great Britain so it was pointless anyway. But he heard the chatter and it made him yearn to get back to the home environment as quickly as possible.

He made his way to a table at the back that was unoccupied and ordered hot chocolate for himself and for Franklin, who had said he might be a few minutes late.

"Bring it out when Monsieur Franklin arrives," he said in his imperfect French, knowing full well that the waiter understood him but would bring the drinks out when it suited him and not the customer. "Also, some dates." He knew those to be a passion of Benjamin's. He settled back, turned the chair slightly so he could view the room, and spent the waiting time observing the crowd. Although it was busy there was a subdued nature to everyone's conduct, as if they all were trading but wished they could be gentlemen of leisure. There was such a demarcation over here: trade was dirty, something you did on the way up and abandoned as soon as you could buy an estate. At home, there was some of the same, but most of the aristocracy was involved in enriching themselves even if they disguised their participation through agents or factors.

He did business regularly with several earls, even with members of the royal family from time to time. They joined the fluid consortiums that Richard was so good at putting together. They would kit out a ship and finance its cargo; another group he organised would insure it while it bore the immense risks of the triangle of trade between Britain, Africa and the Americas. But he also got involved with factories, financing the new steam locomotive and always buying land.

By the time Benjamin Franklin arrived, thirty minutes later, Richard was onto his second hot chocolate, deciding to drink Benjamin's rather than have it go cold. Other customers were eyeing Richard's table, as there was standing room only in the morning rush.

"Sorry I was late," Benjamin cried as he reached the table. "My God, the chatter that goes on, none of it much help and most of it being pip squeaks wanting to sound important. Still, one has to endure!"

"Yes, one must," agreed Richard. He had been a bit sour about waiting, conscious that he had taken a large table. But Benjamin's smile and enthusiasm were infectious. Richard found him liking the large American more and more.

"Bring more chocolate and I will have a roast duck if you please. And for you, Richard...? Are you sure? Just the duck for me, then. Ah, I see you already have some dates. How thoughtful of you, my dear friend." Then he added more quietly once the waiter had gone, "Well, Richard, what are we going to do about this little issue we have?"

They talked on for some time, exploring what to do and why all their efforts at getting a treaty agreed seemed to be floundering.

"I can't give you any more leeway," Richard said. "I am getting heavy criticism for being too generous as it is. If they recall me then you will get some hardnosed fellow who will want to undo everything we have agreed on."

"I know. It is a good deal and you have been very fair. The holdup is entirely in Philadelphia and I cannot understand it. All I get are requests for more detail, more background, and then endless letters about tiny little aspects. Frankly, it is as if there is a collective paralysis back home."

"We need to break that paralysis. The question is, how?"

"Let's walk a while," replied Benjamin. "Maybe the cold air will clear our minds." Once outside, their table taken instantly by a group that had been standing nearby, Benjamin spoke again. "Have you heard the rumours about your host?"

"More than rumours." They crossed the little square by silent agreement and headed down an alley to the Seine.

"What do you mean?"

"Charles has spoken to me about the problems he is facing. He invested heavily in the tobacco trade and that has been damaged beyond belief by the war yet, by his own admission, he did not cut back on his expenditure. He borrowed heavily to supplement his capital and then a ship he was a major owner in went down with an underinsured tobacco cargo in it. It is one thing after another, starting with the fact that he over-extended."

"It's a dreadful shame. Is there anything can be done about it?"

"Not much. He is giving up the house at the end of the year. He has found a much more modest one. He is selling the estate he purchased just two years ago, but he needs more capital to start again. If he sells everything he will cover his debts, but he needs something to set up again."

They reached a part where the road split into upper and lower ways along the banks of the river. The upper way was broad with restaurants, cafés and shops looking onto the Seine, the snake that slithered through the city. But the lower way was reached by steep steps and was narrow and slippery along its two-hundred-yard reach. The river lapped at the edge of the walkway, rising and falling as if it thought itself a sea.

They always took the lower path. It was a difficult route for two older men, but the very first time they had walked together along the river they had gone this way and now they always did. The path had a wall on the side opposite the river, rising to the upper way. Into the wall at regular intervals were alcoves with worn, weathered statues standing guard like angels watching not the virgin birth but the passing humanity, constructed in the image of God. The statues were all old except for one replacement. They were stone and some of the features had worn too smooth for the angles of human bodies but figures they were, looking over the constant *flow of dark water with eyes that did not seem to see. Richard found them frightening, yet was always drawn to them.*

The wind sent the rain sideways, causing it to beat against their bodies. That same wind kept changing its direction of attack, pushing them along one minute then thrusting them backwards or sideways the next. Half way along, Benjamin shouted that maybe it was not such a good idea to have come along the lower way today. At that moment, the wind seemed to make an extra effort and Richard was suddenly over the edge and into the river, grasping at a stone on the lower wall that stuck out from the others.

"Don't let go," Benjamin cried and thrust out his stick, shouting for help but shouting in English and no help came. Gradually Richard managed to climb up the four-foot wall, holding Benjamin's walking stick in his left hand and searching for any grip on the wall with his right. A minute after he fell in, he lay on the lower walkway, soaking and exhausted, his heart pounding, lungs heaving, trying to get his breath back. Finally, he stood up, but instantly was on his knees as a pain in his chest stabbed him repeatedly with a jagged knife. Or so it seemed to Richard. And to Benjamin who watched, tried to help, prayed for survival.

His prayers were answered. After a long time, Richard slowly got to his feet, dragging himself up with his hands clutched to Benjamin's arms for support.

"My friend, I thought we had lost you for a moment." But Richard did not answer immediately. After another few minutes of regulating his breathing he told his friend that it would take more than a swim in the river to get him down. But his exhausted, shattered voice said much more than the defiant words he spoke. With Benjamin's help this time he stayed on his feet and they made their careful way along the walkway to the far steps, climbed them slowly and hailed a hansom cab.

"You need to rest, my friend." Benjamin climbed into the hansom alongside Richard; he meant to stay with his friend until he was safely in his bed.

Rupert was summoned on entry to the Dubois household and took charge of the situation immediately. Within ten minutes, Richard was resting in bed, propped up on two pillows, the rain trying to break in at the huge windows to his bedroom but making no progress. It was getting dark now so Benjamin drew the curtains while Rupert scuttled off to fetch a pot of tea at Richard's request, taking the soaking clothes with him.

"We never finished our conversation," Richard said.

"It will wait. Everything can wait until you are better."

"But…"

"No buts, my dear friend. Now is the time for rest. Tomorrow, or the day after, we will work it all out. I will leave you now so you can sleep. I'll call by in the morning."

"Good night and thank you doubly. You saved my life…"

"Poppycock."

"And for being a good friend." Richard closed his eyes and settled into a deep, dreamless sleep. A few minutes later, Rupert sat at his side drinking the tea he had prepared for Richard, an expression of innocent Christian concern on the man born as a savage and saved by slavery.

Corporate Rungs

The rumour concerning Smith and Mrs Kinderly was correct in part. They had attended high school together, although they had not known each other. Smith was a senior during Mrs Kinderly's freshman year. Thus, three years separated them in age, but a lifetime in terms of outlook and opportunity.

Smith and her friends had only ever expected to work at the penitentiary just as their parents did. Federal jobs were more secure, less prone to lay-offs. Plus, they were unionised and took high school graduates whereas many commercial positions sought at least a two-year degree.

But there were other reasons why Smith left high school on 4th June 2005 and turned up for her first day of work at the prison on the seventh day of the same month. One was that, through favours and counter favours, she was guaranteed a job. It worked on seniority of parents' employment and loyalty to the union.

But the most significant reason was that it was the only job where she could exercise considerable power over others from the first day.

It was the only job she had ever wanted.

So a decade and more rolled by. She worked her way up and she worked her way in, ingenious small schemes making medium bucks. That was her modus operandi.

***

Smith, along with her parents and many others, had not seen the changes coming. Nor, to be fair, had the young Mrs Kinderly, then known by her maiden name of Iris O'Connor The changes came from different directions but brought the two high schoolers back together.

O'Connor had gone on to a good liberal arts college and graduated with a BA in English with a minor in American History. The rumour was wrong in this regard: she had not studied criminology, nor ever had any intention of working within corrections. She had moved to Chicago and joined Pillars of the Community Inc. as a graduate trainee on the fast-track. The business was recently listed on the stock exchange and growing fast as an outsourcer of all sorts of services. She had revolved around departments such as marketing, bid solicitation and accounting, before being posted to contracts execution as a junior manager.

Her parents, recently retired, had moved from Zanesville to Chicago to be near their only child. She had an apartment in a beautiful warehouse conversion while they had a neat, semi-suburban house thirty minutes away.

There was no reason ever to go back to Zanesville. That was what they all thought.

Then Pillars of the Community Inc. bid on their first Federal Penitentiary Contract, a small low-security facility in Georgia. It was explained to a gathering of managers that this was an experimental area for Pillars of the Community. It would be expanded rapidly if all went well. And O'Connor, with excellent annual reviews, was placed on the team to implement the trial. The team was based in Chicago, so both she and her parents breathed a sigh of relief that they did not have to move.

The next seven years saw a lot of change, however. First was the marriage to Michael J. Kinderly, a charming but ruthless middle-aged politician. They expected children, but none came. She tried to ignore the affairs but the birth of his first illegitimate son, also called Michael J., she took as the ultimate insult. The divorce was bitter, not because there had been any love but because of who he was as a person and because she saw her youth wasted with him.

She knew she could not have children, so she turned, at the age of 32, to her work, her career. Her parents suggested adoption but something in her ex-husband's dismissal of her made her want to reach the top. A child would be in the way.

So when her boss, the Director of Contracts, asked the rising executive to dinner in January 2024, she accepted willingly, not knowing whether it was personal or business.

She was thirty-four years old and had carefully cultivated her still radiant looks. She was willowy-tall with natural blonde hair and wore her smart business and casual clothes with a grace that belied the inner doubts and turmoil. She felt good about her career, but not about herself.

It was personal.

They had a passionate affair and Mrs Kinderly knew love for the first time.

She loved being loved.

And it was reciprocated. Declan Dacey was as passionate about her as she was about him.

Until she asked him to divorce his wife.

"I just can't leave her and Sonny Boy," he had said. Sonny Boy was the Daceys' only child; a beautiful sandy-haired and freckled boy of nineteen with traumatic brain damage and total paralysis following an automobile accident ten years earlier.

Iris was distraught; angry, sobbing and pleading so he came up with what, was the perfect solution, to him.

But not to her.

He confessed to his wife, became reconciled, found new love with her.

"I'm sorry, Iris, it has to end. I realise now that I love her above all else. I was looking for something else with you but all the time what I needed was under my nose." After the shock, Iris wondered which had been the greater insult to her fragile identity. Michael J.'s callous naming of his illegitimate son after himself or Declan's almost blasé explanation that she had helped him find his real love.

"How can we still work together?" she asked, trying to hold back the tears, trying for some little dignity.

"I'll sort it out." He tried to kiss her as you would kiss a friend but she shied away.

He did sort it out. He promoted her. It was the only gift he could still give.

It was a still intensely sorrowful and fragile Mrs Kinderly that turned up in July 2026 for her first day as Warden of the Zanesville Federal Medium Security Penitentiary.

She was greeted at the main gate by a delegation led by Smith, newly promoted to Deputy Warden.

Two people, both hungry, but for very different reasons.

***

It was then that Mrs Kinderly made her big mistake. Only six weeks into her new job, no one to share her problems with, lonely at home and work, aching for someone to care for her, she fell for a young inmate.

Stacy was nineteen; shy, spotty, big eyes grown wider for danger. On the outside, she would be described as petite and cute. On the inside, she was vulnerable. She had not learned to look down, to avoid eye contact. Instead, her big grey eyes pleaded for comfort and protection. But found anguish and turmoil.

She was a novice.

Mrs Kinderly was vulnerable in a different way. They came together when Stacy was detailed to clean Mrs Kinderly's office. Mrs Kinderly made the first move; Stacy looked so alone, so sensual in her orange overalls with her hesitant movements and wide eyes. They made love on the floor of the sumptuous office. Afterwards, Stacy wept. Mrs Kinderly held her on the floor, stroking her ragged hair.

"What do I call you?" Stacy whispered at last, looking into the warden's eyes with wonder streaked with a tiny pinch of happiness.

"Mrs Kinderly, of course. But I will call you Stacy. This will be our secret, Stacy. Do you understand?" Stacy nodded and dared to smile.

Then someone knocked on the door.

"Quick, behind the desk," Mrs Kinderly whispered, then spoke. "Enter… What can I do for you, Smith?"

"I wanted to check Warner was cleaning your office properly, Mrs Kinderly. Where is she?"

"I… I… sent her on an errand. She's a good little cleaner. I want to keep her. I can trust her to be discreet if she learns anything she should not."

"Of course, Mrs Kinderly, I'll just stay around until she gets back and then take her back to A wing."

"That won't be necessary. I'll bring her down later."

"But, Mrs Kinderly…"

"Smith, were you not listening to me? I said I would bring her down later when she has completed her work. I want her to give the bookshelves a complete clear out." Seeing Smith still as a rock, she raised her voice. "Smith, out now, unless you want to be on report." Stacy Warner could not help but give a smothered giggle at the most frightening guard in the whole prison being told off like a naughty child. Mrs Kinderly gave a belated coughing performance while also shuffling her chair across the floor: distractive noise. The door closed, but only after a quizzical look from Smith.

"Stacy, you should not have made a sound, silly girl." Mrs Kinderly, only minutes into the relationship, was developing a strong maternal instinct. Stacy naturally played her part.

"Sorry, Mrs Kinderly."

They made love a second time but first Mrs Kinderly locked the inner and outer doors. This time they made love slowly, relishing each other. Afterwards, they lay on the floor facing each other, Mrs Kinderly propped on her right arm, Stacy on her left. Could this be what she had been missing all those years in Chicago? She placed her index finger on Stacy's mouth, tracing around her lips, then running the finger up the centre of her face, over her pretty nose, between her sweet eyebrows, across her pallid forehead and into her lank hair. Stacy stayed rock-still.

"What are you thinking about?" Mrs Kinderly asked her inmate lover.

"My puppy. I got him for my birthday." Stacy's eyes filled with tears. Mrs Kinderly noticed the strangeness of her crying. There were no trickles down the cheeks, just great big teardrops sitting on her lower eyelids, glistening and reflecting the light around like tiny globes but refusing to drop, defying gravity.

"I'll look after you, Stacy. You'll be OK, you'll see." Mrs

Kinderly sat up and wrapped her arms around her lover, wondering at the inertness of her body. Yet she knew how to give the warden pleasure.

"Thank you, Mrs Kinderly." Stacy smiled amongst her tears, creating a rainbow effect. Mrs Kinderly, overcome with desire, leant over and kissed her full on the mouth.

For the rest of the morning they were consumed with each other. Eventually, Mrs Kinderly straightened her stockings, smoothed her skirt and did her hair in the mirror, noting that Stacy copied her every move, although dressed in prison overalls and with hair secured in simple fashion with a matching orange tie, it was hard to make herself remotely elegant. Mrs Kinderly took Stacy down to A wing and delivered her to Smith.

"Warner did good work today, please ensure she gets extra lunch. She deserves it."

"Yes, Mrs Kinderly." But Smith had other plans and they involved finding out the truth.

***

There was a power cut that night, discipline broken down temporarily while backup generators and flashlights were dug out. They traced the cause to an unused toilet block, waiting repairs. There they found Warner S. 135649G hanging from a torn light cable attached to the roof joists. She had locked herself in, torn the ceiling panels with her bare hands, ripped off the cord, blown the fuses and hung herself in the resulting darkness.

Nobody blamed Mrs Kinderly.

"She's only six weeks into the job," Declan said at the next board meeting. "But it is a blow to the image of Pillars, for sure."

Mrs Kinderly, no official blame attaching, felt enormous remorse until she confided in her pastor.

"The Lord gives and the Lord takes away."

"But I made love to a vulnerable girl. She must have felt awful afterwards to do this, to take her own life."

"Tell me, Iris, have you ever felt any inclination to lie with another woman?"

"No, I don't know what came over me. She seemed so vulnerable."

"I know exactly what happened."

"Then tell me, Pastor, for I'm in agony."

"Warner was a temptress. She was the devil come to take you down to Hell. She was an inmate, a criminal. The Lord has dealt with her and sent her to never-ending anguish. You, my dear, must be strong for the Lord and for the other inmates who need you to lead them into salvation. It is a sign. Do your job to the very best of your ability and save as many souls as you can."

So Mrs Kinderly reignited her ambition and set out to be the best warden of the most efficient prison in the Pillars of the Community fold. She swore that, while she might have fun with another man or even a woman, she would never love again.

And nothing would ever stand in the way of her ambition, her career.

And it was recognised at the highest level of the firm.

"She's our best hope for the future," Declan declared during the next Senior Personnel Review Meeting, held on the 14th floor of the Chicago skyscraper that had been renamed Pillars House. He loved entering at street level, door opened by Jennings, an elderly black man in a red uniform, then walking across the marble floor towards the elevators.

"Good morning, Mr Dacey."

"Good morning, Caroline," he would reply to the receptionist, his ego another notch above the place it had reached the day before.

"I think we should defer judgment until she has been in the job a little longer than six months." That was the head of HR; bald, glossy skin, expensive suit. Nobody but Declan knew that he had got the position with a fictitious résumé. Declan had him in his pocket.

So Declan disagreed and the head of HR acquiesced and

Mrs Kinderly became a VP and Associate Director. Her salary was now twenty times what it had been ten years earlier and the stock options made it imperative that the share price continued to rise. To achieve this, they needed to slightly beat expectations every quarter.

"So," Declan explained to Mrs Kinderly, sitting in the Westminster Hotel Dining Room with the President, the CEO and the COO, as well as the VP of Finance, "Iris, we need to screw every penny out of the system to boost our profits. We are relying on you to do that for us at Zanesville and the world will be your oyster if you achieve it."

"I understand, sir," replied Mrs Kinderly, all passion for him gone, replaced with a determination to achieve and rise to the pinnacle of the Pillars of the Community.

Call in the Night

The call came to Mrs Jameson as next of kin. She did not know what to do, except to go up the stairs and knock on Ben's door.

"Ben, are you awake?" It was close to 3am. Mrs Jameson had to call several times before he opened the door.

"What's the matter?"

"The prison," she wailed, unable to contain herself any more. Ben sat her down in his chair and held her gently until the sobbing was under control.

"Is Dakota OK?"

"No." Mrs Jameson started crying again.

"What is wrong with her?" He suddenly saw a life without Dakota. It was bleak, an existence. "Please, Mrs Jameson, what has happened to her?"

"Hospital, she's in hospital." Gradually the story emerged of Dakota's rape and assault.

"Which hospital? We must go there now."

"I don't know."

Ben called the prison. The hospital was Zanesville Memorial. They left minutes later, scooting through the backstreets of DC to get onto the interstate. They got fuel and two large coffees and drove on through the black night, as if following the star to Bethlehem.

"Did they say what condition she was in?" Ben asked but Mrs Jameson was unable to remember. She just kept seeing in her mind her little girl: perfect, untroubled, protected.

Ben called the prison to find out. He had to get Mrs Jameson to give permission for them to talk about Dakota with Ben.

"I see. How did this happen? Was there no supervision?" He remained on the phone a long time, wondering as he listened to the deputy warden how to pass the news on to Mrs Jameson.

They pulled into the car park at Zanesville Memorial at a little before nine that morning. When Ben stopped the car, pulling into a spacious bay at the back of the hospital, he felt like they were still somehow moving.

Mrs Jameson would not get out of the car, fearing the worst and not wanting to face it. It took several minutes to persuade her to enter the hospital. The warden had called Ben to say she was waiting for them at the hospital. That meant it was serious.

Mrs Kinderly was waiting outside the operating theatre with several of her colleagues. She rose when Ben and Mrs Jameson entered the room, showing her willowy, gangly frame; the body of a young teenager on a thirty-eight-year-old woman.

"Mrs Jameson, I am sorry to meet you under these circumstances."

Ben introduced himself as a family friend and asked how Dakota was.

"She does not appear to be that good," the warden replied. "They are coming out each half-hour to give an update. They will be out in a moment."

As if she had summoned the surgeon, he chose that minute to come out to report. "Mrs Jameson? And Mr Franklin? I am Dr Burrows, assistant to Professor Medici. She is doing the surgery. I'm very sorry but Dakota is not doing well. We fear that there has been massive internal bleeding from her injuries."

"Injuries?" exploded Ben then, looking at Mrs Kinderly, "What injuries?"

"Sir, can I suggest that we let Dr Burrows finish his report and get back to the surgery, then I can give all the explanations."

Dr Burrows' report was short. There was no definite news. Dakota was unconscious while they worked to stop the internal bleeding. Her brain seemed to be untouched but there were problems in several lower organs, including her kidneys. Several bones were broken and were being reset. Dr Burrows then made a hasty exit back to the operating theatre where he was needed. As the door swung closed behind him, all eyes turned to Mrs Kinderly.

"We are still investigating, obviously," she began, trying to retain composure, "but it would seem like Dakota Jameson was a victim of a vicious assault." To the inevitable questions of 'why?', 'who?' and 'how could it happen?' she waved her arms and raised her voice. "Please let me finish. I never condone violence in my prison and abhor the perpetrators. We are using every avenue to track down the aggressor."

"Mrs Kinderly, just tell us what you do know without any more mention of investigations or intentions." Mrs Jameson cut through the bluster with a steel blade of a voice, surprising both herself and Ben.

"Of course. Well, early indications are that the other party was a member of staff. That leads us to two possible outcomes. Either your daughter was the aggressor or the member of staff was. That is what we have to investigate."

"Who was the member of staff?"

"I am not at liberty to say at the moment."

"My daughter might be dying in there and you are hiding behind clever words. Tell me, how well do you know Dakota?"

"I've met her, of course."

"How many times?" Ben asked, sensing where Mrs Jameson was leading.

"Well, actually just once, the week before last. But that is not the point. The point is I cannot meet every inmate so we have a system. The counsellors report up to me."

"How often does she meet with her counsellor?"

"I believe the standard time is once a month. I'll need to check that."

"Do so," Ben said. "Now." Mrs Kinderly looked startled for a moment and then picked up her phone. A few minutes later she confirmed that Dakota had only had one meeting with her counsellor in the almost three months she had been there.

"We are a bit backed up," she said, as if they were dealing with traffic flows.

"So nobody really knows Dakota on your staff," Mrs Jameson spoke again. "Nobody would know that she is the last person on earth to start a fight or to provoke others. She was attacked and we need to know who did it. Do you have CCTV?"

"Of course."

"Then we will find out in the next few hours anyway, so you might as well tell me."

"It was a guard called Bennet."

"No way!" Shouted Ben, pushing back his chair and jumping up so that Mrs Kinderly shrunk back in alarm as the chair crashed to the floor. "I know her. She is as gentle as anything. She's the one decent human being you have working in that place."

"It's not her," Mrs Kinderly replied. "It is her husband, Hunter Bennet. He was just made supervisor last week. I am so surprised." Her voice had shrunk to the level of an inmate.

Then Professor Medici came out of the operating room, a beam on her round face.

"Mrs Jameson? Mr Franklin? I am pleased to be able to tell you that Dakota came through the surgery. We have managed to stop all the internal bleeding. There is some damage, particularly to her womb. But her kidneys were not as badly damaged as we first feared. I think there is every chance of a complete recovery, other than her womb. It is too early to say with regard to the possible damage done there."

"My God, my baby. When can I see her?"

"In about twenty minutes, Mrs Jameson. She is in post-op now and they will take her back to the recovery ward any minute. She should be starting to wake up around now."

"That is truly good news," Mrs Kinderly said. "If it is OK with you I will leave you here and go back to the prison to see how the investigations are going."

"Yes, of course. Just mind it is a proper investigation, not some cover-up."

"I give you my word."

***

Hunter Bennet was arrested later that morning. The CCTV

camera displayed it so clearly that the federal authorities could not try and protect their own but turned on him instead. He was handcuffed and drummed off to the local jail. The charge was assault and rape. This was added to when they searched the Bennet home and found Val Bennet unconscious, her pretty face bruised almost beyond recognition. An enterprising reporter snapped photos on her phone and they were all over the papers the next morning. Val was rushed to Zanesville Memorial but did not need surgery.

"Plenty of bed rest," the doctor ordered. "She has suffered from a serious shock. Where is her family?" Nobody around her bedside knew. The police were called and it turned out Val's mother had the child and would look after him for however long she was needed but would not come to the hospital.

"She's made her bed," was all that her mother said.

Val slept on and off during the afternoon and evening but then could not sleep at night. The clock in the ward ticked loudly and she watched the hands winding up the night to let daylight out, just as they would then wind up the day to let night back in. But she was not philosophical or poetic at all. She just saw the hands slowly making progress. She was in shock. She tried to block out the terrible happenings. Her husband had come home from work more drunk than ever. She had been feeling good about the day. He was on night shift and she was called in for the day shift so their time together would be minimal. She had called her mother, who had agreed to pick up Kyle after preschool and have him for the rest of the day.

She had not planned perfectly, however. She had left her work ID at home and after the trip to preschool had to come back to fetch it. It was then Hunter caught her in all his drunken glory.

"I saw you, you little bitch." He had slurred. "You slut. I saw you with that damn Jameson woman."

"I was just talking to her, Hunter. I was trying to help

her." It was a lie and Hunter knew it straight away, assumed the worst.

"You liar, I saw you holding hands like a couple of lovebirds. I expect you curled up in a laundry basket and had your way with her."

"No, Hunter, I swear I did no such thing." But the sweat of fear was all over her. And that fear smelt and Hunter knew instinctively he was on to something.

"What's the matter, girl, not getting enough at home?" He grabbed her, refused to let her go, downed her on the bed, jumped on top of her and thrust himself inside.

When he had satisfied himself, he calmly and coldly beat her. He concentrated on her face while she bleated helplessly, raising her arms to try and protect herself then gasping in pain as he kicked her in the unguarded stomach.

"I need a drink," he said calmly and left her on the bedroom floor, eyes open but turned inwards so they did not see but radiated out the terror she felt. That is where the police found her three hours later, shortly after they picked up her husband in an all-day bar five blocks from their house.

Rather than run the vivid images all over again, Val got up out of bed. At first she just walked up and down a few feet from her hospital bed, then grew bolder and walked past the next bed, then several more. Everyone in her ward was asleep. So eventually she walked on, into the corridor, past the drinks machines. That hurt, thinking of the coffees she had sent Dakota to get from similar machines to these. She walked on, hesitant steps but the walking soothed her. She was in a terrible marriage. Her thoughts seemed to overflow with sorrow, jumbling so she would start one thought and then jump to another and another like the operator on a fairground merry-go-round. Not one thought was carried through to a conclusion. Suddenly aware of this, she concluded quite neatly that the conclusions were all too depressing.

Then she stopped. She was lost in a vast network of corridors, swing doors and signposts. She did not know what ward she had come from. Should she just ask someone? But the corridors were deserted. It was the dead of night. Sometimes she heard noises in far-off places: human voices; the clash of metal on metal; the squeak of small wheels on hard floors. But they all sounded in another world. Somewhere she could not get to. She felt panic rising. She had to find someone. Then, approaching a right turn corner, she heard footsteps, then saw a shadow against the opposite wall. It was a big man. It was Hunter coming back for her. She screamed, then turned, felt a hand on her shoulder, struggled and screamed again. But then reason took over. The hand she felt was not threatening. Even if it were Hunter's he would never dare attack her outside the home. And this man did not smell like Hunter. She stopped, took a huge breath and turned around.

"Mr Franklin!" He did not respond. He did not recognise her.

"Mr Franklin, it's me, Bennet, from the prison."

"My God, Miss Bennet, what has happened to you?" Then he saw her eyes, saw the fear rolling through like the reel of an old movie. It was more than fear; it was terror. He understood then. "It was your husband did this to you?" Her face was multi-coloured, distorted, swollen, raw in places.

"Yes." That said with the same pitiful volume that the inmates used. She had always been on the edge of authority, approaching it with hesitancy. Now she was firmly on the other side, looking for instruction, for guidance, for someone to take charge. All this he saw in an instant, reading it in her eyes.

So Ben took charge. He had been on his way for coffee. But instead of the machines, he took her to the all-night restaurant and ordered her hot, sweet tea without asking her what she wanted. He led her to a table by the window. But the window, lacking light outside, just bounced back their images so it looked like there were four of them at the elongated table. At the far end of the restaurant, an old man slept in a wheel chair while his wife knitted, their coffee long ago finished. There was nobody else in the room.

"Why are you here, Mr Franklin?"

"Call me Ben if you want."

"I'm Val," she said with a self-conscious smile. Then it echoed back whom else she had given her first name to. "It's Dakota, isn't it?" Talking was painful and came out of the left side of her mouth; the right side had been more exposed to the beating.

"Yes, but she is probably going to be OK."

"Was it my husband?" Said so forlornly that Ben grabbed her hand and held it.

"Yes," was all he said.

They talked on for half an hour. Val re-lived again what Hunter had done to her, then Ben spoke of what he knew about Dakota's attack. There were many sobs from Val. He muted his anger in recognition of who he was talking to, also did not mention the rape.

"This is my fault," she wailed suddenly as the dark of night outside seemed to break through the window and attack her soul, her very inside person. "If I hadn't tried to befriend Jameson, I mean Dakota, this would never have happened."

Ben decided on instinct to half-agree with her, in order to help her.

"Your actions were a contributory factor, that's for sure. But you did not attack anyone. You cannot blame yourself for the actions of others. Your husband made a clear decision as an adult and that is not your responsibility." They fell silent then for a few moments, both cupping their drinks in their hands, both deep in very different thoughts. Val wallowed in her misery and perceived culpability. Ben was thinking of Dakota.

"You know it is not so different to Dakota's conviction," he said at last, disturbing Val's self-pity. He went on to explain. "Back in 2018 she was caught with a packet of drugs in her bag. She had agreed to take it to the post office and send it for her boyfriend, not knowing what was in it. In fact, he had said it was a necklace for his cousin, although he did not have a cousin. Perhaps she should have been more careful but she was in the grip of strong emotions and did not think clearly. Do you see the parallel? You were in a similar emotional state and, because Dakota is fundamentally a kind, considerate and empathetic person, you went against better judgment and confided in her. Just as she was not responsible for drug smuggling so you are not responsible for your husband's crimes. You were both contributory factors drawn in by emotion and failing to make a judgment but you are not responsible in any way for the underlying crime."

"Yes, I see. Thank you, Ben." She remained tentative but appeared a little more cheerful. "I think I better get back to bed now. I am suddenly exhausted."

Ben walked with her to the drink machines in a wide hallway. There were two silent wards going off from the corridor opposite that Val was sure she must have walked down. They tried the right-hand door and Val could see her empty bed across the room.

"It's this one," she said, releasing her grip on Ben's hand. "Will I see you tomorrow?"

"Yes. I'll come down and find you." He leant down and kissed her hand, her face being too raw to touch.

"Thanks, Ben. Thanks for being a friend. If I am allowed, I will go see Dakota tomorrow also."

She slipped through the door, looked back once and then crossed the room to reach her bed. Ben watched through the glass window of the door until she was in bed with the sheets and blankets pulled up tight against her neck. Around her the ward slept on, nurses and patients alike. Sleep as an essential part of recovery.

Constitutional Matters

Sir John could not sleep. He felt wired, exhausted, exhilarated. He paced the floor of his London flat, waiting for the taxi that was still four hours away, running through the journey in his mind. Taxi first to the airport, then through security and to the airline lounge; quick call to his wife, Anne, including messages for the children. Then the announcement for First Class passengers, followed by eight hours of pampered luxury on the way to DC. Touchdown meant he could turn on his phone again before Immigration and quickly catch up on events. Then it was taxi straight to the law offices of Hibbert, Fisher and Welling, or HFW as their logo promoted them to be. He knew nothing about them except what Frank Williams had told him. Both Franks would be there for the meeting. Nobody in the world knew the subject matter of this planned meeting, except for him. It gave him a thrill to think about it for a moment.

Having nothing else to do, he turned on his laptop and looked again at HFW's website. Their mission was to be the 'Go to firm for all constitutional matters with regard to the United States of America'. Well, he was going to them on a constitutional matter of enormous import so they should be pleased to see him.

He checked his bags, passport and credit cards for the fourth time that night. Then he checked the two documents again, plus the reports on their authenticity. He had gone first to the firm he had in mind to check their authenticity, then on to three other reputable firms. All had been in agreement. The documents dated back to the time of Independence and the signatures were genuine.

Three hours to go. His thoughts turned to Ben. He had liked Ben instantly. He imagined most people did, provided they were not too arrogant. He knew Frank Williams had warmed to him. He crossed the room and looked out of the window. There was the first hint of dawn away in the distance beyond his Docklands penthouse flat. Time was moving on, only too slowly. What else could he think about to pass the time? His thoughts of Ben led naturally to Mrs Jameson and then to Dakota. He wanted to help but his first attempt, his visit with that damn lawyer, had been pathetic. The man had laughed him down, secure in his knowledge that, whether it was incompetence or corruption, it was well hidden, deep down in some long-forgotten filing cabinet or email, or perhaps only in someone's memory. If Sir John was to help Dakota he would have to get a lot smarter.

At ninety minutes to go he had a shower, ate breakfast, called his wife, moved his suitcase and briefcase to the hall. That halved the remaining time. Then he read the documents again, sat in the hall on an upright chair, closed his eyes and tried to imagine he was Richard Sutherland. He was sure Richard Sutherland was key to this whole situation. There was something about him he could not define exactly. Was he a spy? If so, for which side? A double agent, maybe?

Then he suddenly remembered that, according to Ben, Dakota was doing a Masters about the man. Perhaps he could get to meet her; maybe she would have some ideas.

A car honked its horn way down on the street below, angering Sir John that his thoughts had been interrupted. But he was waiting for a car. He rushed to the window but could not see the street below, the angle being too sharp. Then his mobile rang.

"Your taxi, sir, for the airport."

"I'll be right down." The adventure was starting.

***

The offices of HFW were pleasing in their lack of pretentiousness. A friendly young lady rose instantly from the reception desk. She welcomed Sir John with an accent that spoke of southern hospitality.

"Sir, my name is Tammy and I will be happy to help in any way during your stay with us. Please just ask. If you will step this way, everyone is waiting to meet you."

Tammy led the way to the elevators and travelled with Sir

John up to the third floor. She chatted easily and was a good ambassador for the firm. Once in the main conference room she handed over to Marcus Hibbert to make the introductions, standing to one side to assist with coffee and biscuits as required.

Frank Williams Senior had done his work. As well as Marcus, the Senior Partner, both the other principals were there. Sir John shook hands with Kirsten Fisher, lead expert on governmental matters; a tall, thin lady like the mast of an ocean-going yacht, dressed like most lawyers in DC; conservatively but very strikingly - in a dark business suit and white silk blouse. Her features were attractive, with a well-set mouth and eyes that looked both intelligent and hard at the same time. Her aura was purposeful, ambitious but decent. He also met Mike Welling, who specialised in human rights. He had the classic look of a campaigner, slightly worn and scruffy at the edges, evidently less careful about his appearance than his colleagues. Everything about him, Sir John reflected, was slightly awry. His hair was a little too long for a law practice in the capital, his tie a bit loose, even his socks were that bit too colourful. He grinned and shook Sir John's hand warmly.

Then Sir John turned to his friend, Frank Williams Senior. With a start, he noticed the wheelchair. As he bent to give a brief hug, he could not help thinking how much he had aged in ten months since he had seen him last, although Frank was dressed impeccably as always. It was not hygiene or appearance that struck Sir John about his old friend, but something else. Life was slipping away.

Sir John had met Frank, the grandson, only once before at Frank's 21st birthday celebrations a decade or so before. Unlike his grandfather, however, Frank looked as if that decade had left him completely unchanged.

As well as the principals of the firm, Sir John was introduced to an elderly lady, Teresa Whitby, who was the company historian, and two younger lawyers whose names he did not remember.

"Ladies and gentlemen, shall we get down to business?"

Marcus suggested. "Unless, Sir John, you would prefer to rest and start properly in the morning."

"No, I slept on the aeroplane. I will be fine for now. I would like to get cracking, even if we have to break after a while." He looked around the room and saw interested and interesting faces. Trust Frank to know the best lawyers in every discipline. "But if I nod off while any of you are talking, please don't take it personally!"

The clock on the wall struck 5.30 as they took chairs and settled down, the younger lawyers opening up obligatory notebooks encased in tasteful matching leather holders embossed with 'HFW'. Sir John reached into his tatty, old but favourite briefcase for his notes and for the two documents. In a flash, he decided to do this correctly; despite his weariness he was going to sell this to them so that they kept coming back for more. So, rather than start talking, he took the two documents around the table to where Teresa Whitby sat at the far end, next to Marcus. As he progressed around the table he enjoyed being the centre of attention.

"Mrs Whitby, would you please be kind enough to peruse these two documents and tell everyone what you think?" It was a good tactical move. Teresa blushed with pride and bent her head over the documents for some minutes.

"In the meantime, and no rush please, Mrs Whitby, I thought I would recap on the discovery of these two documents." His clear British voice was compelling as he went through the short story, as they knew it, of the documents. Nobody interrupted until Sir John spoke of ownership.

"So, conclusively, it would appear that these documents belong to Frank, although how they got to be in his possession, I do not know. But..."

"They are not mine."

"Sorry?"

"They were mine but I gave them to that young fellow who Frank met."

"Ben Franklin." Frank assisted with the name.

"That's right, and no more suitable name could be

imagined."

This sparked a lawyerly debate on the principles of ownership and how goods passed from one to another. It would seem that Frank had a claim to ownership.

"But I gave them away and that is all there is to it. I live by my word. Without my word, I am nothing. I will not go back on it."

"Well it seems that is settled, then." Marcus' sonorous voice stopped the discussion and everyone fell instantly silent. All eyes now turned to Mrs Whitby, who blushed again from the attention and then spoke hesitantly. "Sir John, did you say that these documents have been authenticated?"

"Yes, and by four separate organisations. I have their reports here." He dipped into his briefcase and slid several copies of the four reports across the table to his audience. "Now, Mrs Whitby, would you mind giving a summary of the contents of these two documents?"

Theresa spoke in a quiet voice, a little shaky at first, but growing in confidence as she progressed. She quoted large portions of the two documents. Finally, she read out the name of each signatory, British and American. She finished to utter silence.

"My God," Marcus uttered eventually, speaking for them all. For a few moments longer, nobody could think of anything to say. There was no sound in the room; no coughs, no shifting of chairs, no sipping of coffee, long-gone cold, certainly no words. As the ornate wall clock ticked round to 6.22pm Marcus, as the senior lawyer present, felt an obligation to break the silence.

"So what we have is a situation where it would appear that our country does not exist. The United States of America does not exist."

This broke the floodgates. By 6.24 everyone was talking at once, not quite believing it, questioning it, seeking reasons how and why.

"Ladies and gentlemen, quiet please." Sir John raised his voice at 6.36. He had let the urgent questioning tumble out for over ten minutes. "The immediate question is not so much how this came about but what we are going to do about it."

"I'm sorry," Kirsten spoke. "But does this mean we are all British citizens? I just cannot take it in."

"Strictly speaking, you are all British subjects, not citizens, but because it is a constitutional monarchy it is effectively the same thing."

The next forty-five minutes saw an alternating between a babble of chatter, everyone talking at once, and a silence full of suspense as collectively they tried to consider what it all meant. During the talking times, they naturally broke into fluid groups, discussing such subsidiary subjects as the laws of USA being totally defunct, the nuclear deterrent, who would be in charge, what authority the police had. It was an unthinkable scenario that they just could not take in.

At 7.15 Sir John stood up. "Listen, this is momentous news indeed. I think everybody here needs to break off now, go home and perhaps we can meet again tomorrow morning. Would 8am suit?" He looked around the table at vacant stares and slow nods. "OK. until 8am. May I conclude by reminding you of the secrecy agreement you all signed when Frank set up the meeting."

As they filed out of the room, still shaking their heads as if to settle down the rampaging thoughts rushing around inside, Sir John drew both Franks to one side.

"Can I leave the documents with you until tomorrow for safe keeping? I have a bad feeling about leaving them in the hotel safe."

"Yes, come with us in our car to our apartment. We have a heavy-duty safe there. In fact, why don't you stay the night with us?"

"Are you sure? I don't want to be any trouble."

"You Brits are all the same, far too polite!"

But that joke was a little too close to the truth as Frank suddenly exclaimed, "Well it seems like we are all Brits now so, Grandpa, you and I are going to have to learn how to be polite."

Marcus drove slowly home, easing his graceful automobile from one lane to another without any recall of his track through the city. He took brief calls from each of his two partners.

"I don't know how this will work out but it is certainly exciting and will make the firm's reputation one way or another. Yes, I agree, we need to be loyal to our client first and foremost. We will always do that. Let's meet early tomorrow to discuss it more." They scheduled for 6am. Marcus then selected Tina Turner and turned up the volume to drown out the surrounding world. Many of his colleagues had been amazed when he had set up a new law firm at the age of seventy-four, especially with two partners thirty years his junior and without any pedigree in respectable law firms. But from first meeting them as his opponents on a complicated law case involving state rights against federal on extradition of a criminal to Mexico, he had wanted to back them. He had poured his retirement funds into the new firm and so far it had not paid back more than a moderate salary. He would be eighty on Christmas Eve. Maybe this would be the final making of the firm so that he could retire with honour.

Then he thought about his wife, as he did several times every day, more now that she was in her grave. On impulse he turned the heavy, sedate car left and left again and brought it to a stop in the ten-minute parking outside the cemetery. He visited her grave frequently, spoke little, no soliloquy like in corny movies, just silent communion until common sense settled like the first blanket of snow at the start of winter. The evening light through the leaves made a crazy patchwork as he walked the path he knew so well. As always, he read the tombstone:

'Rosie Hibbert, nee Folkes, in this world 1954 to 2019. Whether husband, mother, daughter or friend, her touch remains with us forever.'

He saw then in the rising gloom her cancer-wizened face,

pain wrought through it like mangled fenders in a wreck, her smile weakened but still present, her eyes dulled but still looking at him and the children with love and wonder. He took that face and turned back the years through sheer concentration, pushing out the pain of disease, winding back to their first date. It had been a blind date in 1974. She had been a second-year French major. He was studying law after four tours in Vietnam. They had laughed all the time, in fact really never stopped laughing, even when breast cancer hit them with a sledgehammer. They had married in Paris when she spent a semester at the Sorbonne. For their honeymoon, they had hitchhiked to the south and then stayed the summer in Marseille; she teaching English, he working as a sailing instructor to rich kids with little interest in boats, but their parents tipped well.

He spoke very little to Rosie these days, preferring silent companionship. He did give a brief update on their four children; not one was a linguist and none became lawyers either, but they were happy and balanced and loved. Then the silence settled and eventually her loving voice seemed to speak to him. After a long time he rose from his crouching position, realising it was now completely dark. He blew her a last kiss and made his way back to his car and then on to his empty house. The supper his housekeeper had left would be totally dried up in the low oven but at least he now knew what to do with the greatest legal question of his entire career.

Certain Frank Conversations

Ben traded on the goodwill he had built up over the years and begged more time off.

"It's just a kind of crazy time right now with my landlady's family. There is so much to sort out and I'm helping where I can."

Brad was OK with it but the unspoken question was, after years of being as reliable as clockwork, was Ben becoming shaky? He was still in credit with the work bank but the balance was being whittled down.

Ben needed the time off to meet Sir John and a bunch of lawyers. It was a fine Tuesday in mid-May; blossom was everywhere, as if God wanted to send down a different coloured shower every week to mark His glory. The sun magnified itself on everything it could: car windows; metal staircases; sidewalks of old mellow brick, bouncing its warmth back up to hit from every angle, heat dispelling everything that ever was winter. It was a good time of year. The heat was fresh and unburdened by humidity, like youth, untroubled by the cares that come with age.

Ben entered the offices of HFW, just as Sir John had done the previous week. The first thing he saw was a black welcome notice with his name amongst a half-dozen others, Sir John's included. Tammy came around the reception desk to meet him.

"Good morning, Mr Franklin. It is real nice to meet you."

"Thanks. How did you know who I was?"

"Sir John Fitzroy gave me your description."

"Which was?" He knew Sir John's humour and decided to have a bit of fun with this girl.

"Well, he just described you. You know: tall, thin, late twenties, light brown hair, that sort of thing."

"That does not sound like him at all. I would expect him to be a lot more frank."

"Well, if you must know, he said you were 'like a bloody bean pole with monkey-length arms and in need of a proper hair cut'."

"That sounds more like it!" Ben followed Tammy on the same route that Sir John had done several times now, across the hallway, up the elevator, out on the third floor, into the main conference room. As with Sir John's visits, everyone was waiting already, sitting around the beautiful Queen Anne mahogany table as if they normally worked at a $20,000 piece of antique furniture. Sir John did the introductions. Tammy poured coffee. Ben felt awkward in his Walmart suit, not worn since Mr Jameson's funeral three years earlier.

"Mr Franklin... may we call you Ben? Good, now I think you need to sit down because what we are going to talk about might shock you quite a lot."

***

Val was leaving hospital that day, as soon as the doctor did his afternoon rounds and signed the release paperwork. Her face was a mass of colour and distortion. When she looked in the hand mirror that the lady in the next bed had lent her she thought she was like a wounded soldier arriving at a convalescence home, all the blood cleaned away but leaving the damage clearer for everyone to see. She imagined the chief nurse saying: "Lieutenant Bennet will bear the scars for the rest of her life. But each time she looks at those scars perhaps she will remember how brave she was and how many people owe their lives to her."

But then she would look a little closer in the mirror and see not a hero but a victim, yet another victim of a disastrous-turned-violent marriage. She would become a statistic in a report. No, worse than that, she would be just one victim of many that made up the statistic, one ant in the colony.

Then her deflation brought about self-examination, quickly followed by self-hate. She was worthless and a failure. Her mother would not come to visit her. She had not seen Kyle in over a week. Ben had kept his word and visited her each day he was there at the hospital. He had cheered her up, warding off the darker thoughts, her sword and shield. Yet she had not once gone to see Dakota. She had said she would and had not. Each day she had a reason why it should be the next day. Only today was the last day.

"I am Valarie Bennet, a guard at Zanesville, and am known to the prisoner."

"Miss, I can't let you in. You are not on the visiting list. Are you a patient here?" The police officer on guard outside Dakota's room saw her bruised face and was suspicious. "I know, you are the guy's wife who he also beat up." That was said with a sneer, as if she was responsible for Hunter's actions after all. She suddenly felt like a criminal, so small, so in the wrong.

"Who makes up the visiting list?"

"The warden, of course. You know hubby is going to go away a long time and it won't exactly be a picnic inside for him as an ex-screw." But Val was not listening: she was already back through the swing door, rushing for her cell phone by her bed.

"This is Guard Valerie Bennet. I need to talk to Mrs Kinderly urgently. Yes, I will wait but please stress that it is urgent."

When she went back upstairs to Dakota's room the same police officer was on duty, his chair tipped back and his feet on the table opposite that held magazines for waiting visitors. She had to step over his legs to enter Dakota's room. Her determination was rewarded with more sniping.

"You're all the same, scum of the earth." He was tempted to spit at her as she passed but even he did not have the courage for that.

"Dakota?" Her determination evaporated at the threshold to Dakota's room. She had been just a little bit brave in getting in here, but the next few minutes called for a much higher level.

"Who is it?" Dakota tried to sit up but failed, as she could not put weight on her arms, arms that Val saw were encased in plaster.

"He broke your arms?"

"Miss Bennet?" Her facial bruises matched Val's. It was like a pale, worn reflection of her staring back up from the bed. But here was much more damage. There was an ugly metal brace on her teeth, her head was bandaged, the arms in plaster, and, looking down, one leg also.

"He handcuffed me to cell bars. I broke my arms and leg trying to get away."

"And then he beat you?"

"First he raped me, then he beat me. He put handcuffs in my mouth to stop me screaming. That's how I broke my teeth."

"My God, Dakota, I am so sorry."

"Don't apologise. You did not do anything to me."

"I'm still sorry. I don't mean like I am apologising for something I've done, but that I am so sorry that this has happened to you." She held Dakota's fingers with one hand and stroked her ragged, lifeless hair with her other. "He did the same to me." Dakota was only about five years older than her, but so worn out.

"I can see that. And I am sorry too."

"Only he did not handcuff me." That was enough talking for now. They sat on in silence a long time, the lights dimmed, Val stroking Dakota's hair. Had she done the right thing in telling Mrs Kinderly that she was going to try and persuade Jameson not to start legal action against the prison so that she would be allowed in? Frankly, she did not care.

***

"I'm am American," Ben shouted, slamming his fist on the table so that the coffee cups jolted in their saucers. "I can't do this."

"Ladies and gentlemen." Sir John selected particularly rich tones, designed to calm. "I am a great believer in staging news in order to make progress over time. We have, I think, heard quite enough for now. This is a momentous discovery with quite incredible consequences for all involved and for both nations. Let us pause and return this afternoon. Ben, would you care to join me for lunch? Frank and Frank, I would be delighted by your company as well. Good, can we go in your car, Frank? I took the liberty of booking a table at Chambreys."

"The best restaurant in town," Frank commented.

"Take the car by all means," the older Frank said in reply. "But I have some business to catch up with here. So the three of you go together and I am sure you will enjoy your lunch."

In the back of Frank Williams' limo, Sir John chose a different subject for discussion.

"Ben, Frank and I would like to try and help Dakota. I made a first recce but it did not go too well." He told Ben and Frank about the meeting at Essington's home.

"That is unfortunate," Frank said. "It has put Essington on alert without actually achieving anything. Look, we are here at Chambreys now. Why don't we put the constitutional matter to one side for an hour and strategize on how to help Dakota while we fill our bellies with a lot better food that she will be having."

Chambreys was pretentious, glitzy, over-the-top, and first-rate. They ordered beer while choosing from the hardboard menus backed in leather from a ranch in Texas, so said the note at the foot of the page. Sir John would have preferred something stronger but Ben had suggested beer and he went along with it. They sat at a table to one side of the main thoroughfare, hastily moved from outside the kitchen when the headwaiter saw that Frank Williams III was in the recently booked lunch party.

"Your usual table, Sir," he had said, congratulating himself for thinking so quickly.

"I come here quite often," Frank explained as they sat down and the waiter pulled out heavy linen napkins and laid them one at a time on their laps. He did it with a flourish that must have been part of their training because it looked so natural. Then Frank decided to lay it on thick, so raised his voice and said, "What is your recommended dish today? Sir John Fitzroy is over from his English estates and we want to impress him with the best our fair capital city has to offer."

Like all good headwaiters, this one heard the question from the other side of the room and was over in a second, gliding between the tables.

"Sir John, how nice it is to have you here. As to our humble offerings I would certainly suggest the…" Ben was not listening, nor looking at the menu, but rather soaking in the sumptuousness. He felt the tablecloth. It must weigh five pounds. He looked at the other diners. They screamed elegance and wit, everything demure and proper. His dark suit was cheap and shiny and he was sure everybody would have noticed it the moment he walked in. He was out of his comfort zone; displayed, no doubt, by the rising blush to his cheeks and neck.

"I'll have the same as Mr Williams," Ben said when it was his turn to order.

"OK," said Frank once the ordering was complete, Sir John insisting on a bottle of '16 Macon Villages ,to accompany the fish they had all ordered. "The question is what can we do with regard to Dakota Jameson. The objective has to be to cut her sentence or get her out early on parole."

"I disagree." Ben said. "I can't say I know Dakota that well, having just met her seven times in prison and then half a dozen days in the hospital. But…"

"Why the hospital?" Sir John wanted to know. So Ben told them the story of Dakota, Val, and the attacks by Hunter. The other two listened in silence, Sir John shaking his head and muttering "outrageous" from time to time.

"So," Ben concluded, "I don't think Dakota ultimately will be satisfied by anything other than a 'not guilty' verdict at re-trial. I don't think a sentence reduction or early parole, or even a pardon, will work with her because that will mean her admitting guilt."

"Then we have one hell of a problem on our hands," Sir John said.

"But let's think a minute about what we have going for ourselves," Frank replied, slicing the bones out of a fresh-water trout with the expertise of a fishmonger. "First…"

"First," interjected Ben, "we have her innocence."

"Too right," Frank replied. "But she was found guilty. And again on appeal. That is what we have to fight."

"Do you know how much Mr and Mrs Jameson paid her lawyer for the trial and the appeal? $590,000! And her lawyer said that was not enough to finish the job properly."

Sir John pulled a small notebook from his pocket. It had a tiny gold pencil set in its spine.

"Let's do this properly and take notes."

By the time they had drained their first coffees and the waiter was hovering with more, they had a list of eight items.

Sir John recapped. "One, her innocence. Two, the outrageous fees, suggesting poor representation. Three, her resilience. Four, the fact that she was set up by her then-boyfriend or the boy she wanted to be her boyfriend. Five, her educational achievements in prison. Six, the attack on her. Seven, the financial backing of Frank Williams. Eight, and perhaps most important, the support of each of us and, of course, of her mother."

"That's not a bad list," Frank said. "Now the question is what shall we do about it? We need to move on to the weaknesses of the other side."

"That's easy," replied Ben. "Two things. First, the lawyer and all that money he got; second, the old boyfriend. We need to track him down."

They talked about it more, making their coffee refills last that little bit longer. The restaurant was still packed, newcomers replacing those satisfied. Ben wondered how much money they made over one lunch period. He would work it out later, perhaps on his way home in the car.

They agreed as Sir John paid the bill that they would work together to tackle the problem from three angles. Sir John would investigate the old boyfriend, track him down, but not approach him until he reported back to Frank and Ben. Frank would find a way to approach the lawyer. Ben would quiz Dakota and her mother about events to try and find any weakness in the case against her.

Afterwards, back in the HFW offices, Ben and Sir John were alone in the bathroom.

"You're in love with Dakota aren't you?" The question made Ben stop dead, hands covered in soap, tap running.

"Yes, I suppose I am," he replied thoughtfully. "I suppose I do love her, yes." It had never occurred to him before, but she had become central in his life in a way nobody else ever had. He felt shriven now.

"We'll work it out, Ben. But please pay ball with me on this other question."

"Are you trying to make a deal?" Ben asked.

"No, Frank and I will do everything possible to get Dakota out of prison whether you go along with this constitutional issue or not."

"Why is this independence thing so important to you? You could just forget all about it. It is going to cause one hell of a mess."

"Forget about it? Forget about the greatest historical discovery since, well since God knows when? Ben, this is going to make me as an historian!" Sir John turned to leave the washroom, then came back as another thought came to him. "Ben, these documents are genuine."

"So? We can still burn them."

"But don't you see?"

"See what?"

"They were signed by the founding fathers." Sir John went through the logic that had just wound through his own mind. "That means your founding fathers did not want independence. Regardless of what they said at the time they signed their names to remain a part of Great Britain. That is a fact. We can't dispute that. Don't you think we should respect what they wanted?" He walked out of the washroom at that moment, thinking to leave on a high note before Ben could find reasons why it was not the case.

***

They voted late that afternoon. Everybody around the table

had one say, one hand they could raise in full view of their colleagues. Sir John wanted to lead the proceedings, relishing the limelight, but accepted reluctantly Frank's suggestion that Marcus Hibbert, as Senior Partner of the leading constitutional law firm in the United States, should be chairman of the meeting.

"I think we have three options to consider. But first of all I want everyone's agreement that whatever happens we all support wholeheartedly the majority vote." Marcus started his summing up as the sun slanted rays through the tall sash windows of their conference room, catching dust particles and seeming to send them swimming this way and that. They seemed directionless to Ben, sometimes suspended before darting off in random directions. He tried quietly to blow some of the nearer ones to influence their motion but he caught Sir John scowling at him so started to pay attention to Marcus Hibbert.

"First, we have the option to sit on it, perhaps indefinitely. Second, we can publicise this document and go with the full consequences, whatever they turn out to be. Third, well we just quietly destroy it. We have discussed this a considerable amount over the last week and a lot just today with Ben present. I think it is time to take a vote and see where we are. So, raise your hand if you agree with the first proposal, namely that we sit on it."

One of the managers from the law firm raised his hand.

"One vote. Now for the second proposal that we publicise it."

Sir John raised his hand, as did Teresa Whitby and both Franks.

"Four votes. Now on to the third proposal, that we destroy the documents."

Ben's hand shot up, along with the other two partners' and remaining manager's.

"An equal four votes." Marcus paused a moment as the impact of this came through to him. He was the chairman and his was the casting vote. He considered hard. His two partners had voted to destroy, as had Mannings, the manager he was thinking of offering a partnership to next year. But his clients had voted to go through with it. What should he do? And where was the principle of all this? Why had the founding fathers reneged on independence and decided to remain with Great Britain? And why had their wishes not been carried out? Was Sir John right that it was Sutherland and Franklin working together to stifle this before it became public? If so, how had they succeeded? That would be a fascinating story on its own. But the main thing was that the founding fathers had changed their minds and signed this new agreement. The fact that Sutherland and Franklin and maybe some others then hid it from the world was irrelevant. The bare truth was that the founding fathers wanted to go back on the claim for independence and remain with the mother country. This was what his wife's voice had said last night in the darkness of her resting place. So Marcus cleared his throat and said to the room.

"I vote to pursue this matter."

Thus they did.

And Marcus was right: the consequences were enormous.

Letter Four

My dearest Ben, it was so lovely to see you every day last week. It has quite spoilt me, such that the days when you are not here seem to go on forever and be utterly pointless.

You won't recognise this handwriting because it is not me writing with my broken arms! Instead, Val Bennet is writing it down for me. She calls herself my secretary and I can speak about her freely because she has promised to write down faithfully every word I say, so she can't alter the bits about her. She looks every bit the secretary. She is wearing a brown flared skirt with a yellow shirt and a brown and yellow scarf. Her hair is loose and looks real awesome. It is so nice to see her out of uniform. It makes me feel normal, almost like a person again, although there is a grumpy policeman just the other side of the door to my room. But at least we cannot see him. Val is looking real pretty despite her bruises that are starting to heal nicely but her face is quite a picture of colour! It reminds me of the leaves in fall. She gave me a look when I said she was pretty but she has promised to write down every word so I can say what I like about her. (Don't listen to a word Dakota says, I look a sight although it is good to be in civvies around her, more like normal life.)

So I will tell you something else about her. When you told me about Val being in the hospital and that she had also been attacked and that she would come to visit me the next day, well I thought that would be OK because she seemed to like me and none of the guards were ever the least bit personal other than her. And away from the prison it should be OK. But then she did not come the next day, nor the day after or for several days. But she did finally come and she has kept coming back ever since. I think I can safely say that we have become real firm friends despite me being an inmate and she being a guard. She comes every day now and we talk for hours. She is on sick leave. Sometimes she brings her son, Kyle, who is adorable. Then she takes him to the hospital crèche and she comes back and we talk and talk and talk like only women can do!

But this is enough of the present. Val went to the prison library and got the papers I had been working on. Like a true secretary she has been helping me organise them. We have made a fantastic discovery from the shipping documents for the port of London for December 1782. And then, you won't believe it but we actually found some of Richard Sutherland's diary entries. They were published in an old book called 'Diaries of the Great Traders of the Late Eighteenth Century.' It does not exactly sound like best-selling material but to me it was Heaven. There were fifteen diary entries from Richard over the course of a year and a half. I am itching to tell you about it all so please grab your beer, in fact get two because you can have one for me, settle back in your chair and let me tell you what we have found out.

Ben did as he was instructed. It was a treat to have two beers, as money was tight. His earnings were way down and the cost of the journeys to Zanesville and the motel for the week had eaten into his savings. He decided on one beer but, in a quirky response to her request, poured it into two glasses, one for himself and one for Dakota. He would drink his first and then Dakota's.

Christmas Eve 1782. Rupert quickly unpacked Richard's bags and his own small one also. The cabin was the best on the ship; Richard's money had ensured that. It ran along the stern and had towering windows of expensive glass with ornate framing. It was the captain's normally, but he frequently gave it up for a fare-paying passenger. He inspected the living space; a cot behind a screen for Richard, a table with leaves to extend it, a rim around the edge to prevent plates and glasses sliding off with the ship's motion, five chairs around it, a desk in the corner where the sixth chair was positioned and a cushioned bench running along underneath the windows.

With bags unpacked he went to inspect the private storeroom and pantry. This was his domain. He would sleep in the storeroom on a hammock. He had done that often before, having frequently travelled with his old master before he had a family and had begged to be allowed to settle down. Now he was travelling again and leaving his precious family behind in Paris. He felt a wave of homesickness wash over him, the bitter tang of salty loneliness soaking through his wool breeches and plain cotton shirt as if naked again in the pen on Bunce Island, awaiting that first dreadful journey to enslavement.

Then, not believing in self-pity, he shrugged it off, looking for something to do.

Richard found him forty minutes later scrubbing the pantry clean with a brush that looked like an old man, bristles being sparse and worn.

"Was it dirty?" Richard asked.

'No Master, not really, but I just wanted to be sure it was clean."

"Rupert?"

"Yes Master?"

"This journey will last maybe five weeks."

"Yes Master, I have done it before."

"It is the perfect time to teach you to read and write."

"Sir, I don't want…"

"You will do as you are told, young man. And you will do it well or you will have me to answer to." Richard then looked a little more kindly at him and said, "Think man, you could write to your family and Madame Dubois would read it to them."

"Kitty reads already, Master."

"Well then, it is settled. You must learn too. We will start after dinner."

The relationship had changed with the troubles of the Dubois household. It had been easy for Richard to make the arrangements. The loan had been quite considerable and the interest low, but secured on Dubois' remaining business interests. Richard knew he would get it back in instalments over ten years. But the final piece of the deal, the real sweetener, had been the acquisition of Rupert and his entire family for a sum on the generous side of their true valuation. Richard and Dubois had parted with genuine friendship, the wealthier assisting the poorer to get back on his feet. A reflection of that friendship was that they swore secrecy on their deal, Richard agreeing that the subsidy element might undermine confidence in Dubois' future business partners. Nobody knew of the transactions except Richard, Dubois and his wife. Rupert was thus in total ignorance of his change of owner, only knowing that he had been delegated to assist Mr Sutherland in his travels and when they were concluded he would be returned to his family.

"I understand we are getting way in two hours or so. Do you have enough stores for the journey?"

"Yes Master."

"Wine? Spices? Fresh meat and fruit? You picked up the cheeses?"

"Yes sir, all is in order. See in the storeroom here."

***

Richard was amazed by how quickly Rupert learned. The bench under the window became their study, with the books spread out on the cushion between them, the sea racing away outside as the wind blew them on their way.

Within two sessions Rupert had mastered the alphabet. Richard quizzed him relentlessly, enjoying stabbing at a letter on the sheet and hearing the name of the letter and its sound coming back each time. They worked on it almost non-stop on Christmas Day, only breaking when Richard sent bottles of good wine to the captain and officers with his best wishes and they invited him to the wardroom to celebrate. When he returned he found Rupert had written his name many times to practise the emerging neat handwriting he was developing. It was inevitably similar in style to Richard's, with great looping letter stems and exaggerated capitals at the start of each sentence, causing Richard to smile to himself.

Captain Boley was a lifetime sailor, hardened, softened and hardened again like the best timber, weathered in. He seemed to Richard to be 'of the ship', another short, stubby but vital mast or a reliable pump or capstan. He was always on deck, always where needed, and inspired his crew to work ever harder for their safety and prosperity. He led a service on Christmas Day and asked Richard and the First Lieutenant to read passages from the Bible. They were on the main deck, the crew of sixty-four gathered around the quarterdeck. Richard read from St Luke's gospel of the angel Gabriel and there being no room at the inn, his voice struggling over the rising wind which carried thickening rain and sleet. He wondered what type of man the innkeeper had been. Had he turned them away dismissively to the stable or had he sent them there and followed up with warm stew and wine, maybe blankets and some towels for the impending birth? Maybe he had even sent for Bethlehem's midwife and paid her bill. It was a comforting thought, though, that such kindnesses would have been repaid countless times over in Heaven. Then Richard felt the same internal anguish that visited him each time he stopped thinking of trade and everyday matters and turned to things more thoughtful. He had been born and raised a Presbyterian. By most accounts he still was one. But he could not make himself accept that faith alone brought you everlasting life. He could not deny an obligation within himself to do good works where he could and to look out for them.

The weather worsened during the following days. Richard and Rupert kept most of the time to the cabin, not wanting to distract Captain Boley or the crew. By New Year's Day, Rupert was reading Shakespeare. They read it together, Richard allocating the parts, as the sea and wind threw the ship here and there, playing with it as if cat and mouse.

"It is all three axes of motion," Richard said when the ship had been taken up by a wave the equivalent of several storeys, only then to be thrust back to the cellar, deep below the ground floor, but also skewed along, both forwards and to starboard at the same time. "God only knows what it is like to be working up aloft today."

"It is not an occupation I enjoy, sir."

"You have done it, then?"

"Yes, sir." When pressed by Richard, Rupert gave an account of his adventures as a very young man, barely more than a boy.

"I was a part of a crew sailing from Africa and bound for the West Indies. They were short-handed and my master offered me in their service. It must have been 1762, because war was waging everywhere and the crew was frightened of being taken by the British."

"Go on." So Rupert told of the desperate bid to save the ship when storm after storm hit them.

"It was hurricane season, sir, and we were leaking from every seam. Our foremast broke and then the main mast when we thought we had a lull and tried to put on sail. We wanted to get to port but the next storm came so fast it caught us all unawares. We were not too far from land but were not sure exactly where we were. We lost eight people at least overboard. They were just swept away by waves that towered over us. Several more sailors tumbled down from the spars, trying to get the sails in, but then the mast came down and we all went into the sea." Rupert paused at this point, but Richard put down his 'Complete Works of Shakespeare' and urged Rupert to continue.

"I was lucky. There was a mass of rigging spilled over the side of the ship. I climbed up it to get back on board, only to be told we were abandoning ship. There were only two lifeboats left undamaged and," Rupert paused again, clearly overwhelmed, "and they would not let me onto either one of them. They said 'no niggers in this boat' and pushed me back from each one. Then I heard the cries from below."

Richard intuitively knew what was coming next. The cargo was a human one, fresh from the shores of West Africa and bound for the sugar plantations of the Caribbean.

Rupert told the rest of the story in abbreviated form, almost like the pidgin English of the slaves. The crew, in their rush to save themselves, had left in the two boats with all the keys to the chains and padlocks holding the slaves. He opened the hatches and saw already that water was swirling around where they lay, the slaves desperate to raise themselves up and live another moment of terror, desperate for it not to end there and then in these pitiful, mad circumstances so far from their families and homes. Rupert had dived in, holding his breath until bursting point, trying to free any of the chains, but without success. He described their screams muffled to his ears by the water rushing in around him, also their kicking and shoving, frantic efforts to save themselves.

He had then got stuck with a chain wrapped around his left leg. One of the slaves, desperately trying to free himself, turning this way and that, ensnared Rupert in the chain. As his lungs gave way he felt the same frantic urgency. He was no more than them. He was the property of another, abandoned property when white lives were at stake. He tore at the chains and they gave way. He was free, rising up through the water, thrusting and pushing against dead and almost-dead bodies, until he broke the surface and could take in great big gasps of painful air, his head bumping repeatedly against the deck above. As he recovered, he looked around in the gloom. All had gone quiet, incredibly quiet. He had failed.

He swam back towards the hatch, only six inches of air between the water and the deck above and rapidly reducing. He felt the dead bodies. It was almost like they were free in death, swimming around, oblivious to their surroundings.

"I left the ship soon after. I found a small boat that had hit one of the cannons and was stove-in. I stretched a portion of sail over it on the outside and one more portion on the inside and tied them to the gunwales. It made a serviceable craft and I tipped it over the side and then climbed back down the broken rigging and got into my boat. I landed on the northern tip of Jamaica three days later. I was taken to the governor and sold in the next slave auction. That is when Monsieur Dubois acquired me. Everything has looked up since then."

Richard could not sleep that first full night of 1783. It was not the motion of the ship, somewhat more limited now as the gale blew itself out with long, low straggling sighs that whipped musically against the rigging. It was Rupert's story. He had not mentioned or known the name of the ship but for all Richard knew he could have been the owner, or at least an investor. He had done a lot of business on the slave triangle in the 1750s and 1760s, including multiple investments in foreign ships. He could be the man ultimately responsible for the death of a hold full of human cargo.

He was too hot with the blankets on, too cold with them off. The shrieking of the wind became the shrieking of the drowning slaves. The black ship beams were transformed into black limbs and torsos tossing and thriving for life. The half-moon outside the windows became the half-moon Rupert and the slaves could see when they looked out of the open hatch and saw life and freedom waiting there, tantalisingly beyond their reach while the water rose and rose and rose to flood their lungs with as painful a death as you could imagine. It is one thing to fall as a free man from a spar high above the ship and take your chances in the churning sea below, another to wait for the swirling waters to take the very life from you and *your companions without any hope of survival.*

Richard welcomed the dawn. The wind had died down, spent its anger on the sleepless man and now was a friend again with a constant, refreshing breeze to push the ship along at six knots. Richard and Rupert went on deck to watch the sea and the work on board to repair the ship. There were no masts down. It had not been that ferocious a gale. The crew sang shanties as they worked on broken rails and blocks and torn sails.

"Time to return to our studies," Richard said at last, after great lungfuls of salty air, tired bones refreshed, mind a little clearer.

The journey to Halifax, Nova Scotia, took thirty-four days. As they carefully worked their way up the coast of North America the cold intensified and Richard felt the brief respite after the storm slipping away. He was tired, very tried, but had one last mission to do.

From Halifax he had to get to Boston, then New York, and finally Philadelphia. He and Rupert did this in several hops over four weeks. They travelled as Americans, reputedly returning to Richard's estates in Northern Virginia. He had many friends in America, making it simple and comfortable to skip down the coast in small craft, stopping to stay with old contacts. To those with influence, he hinted that he was there as an Englishman on government business. To the rest he was another American returning home.

They reached Philadelphia on March 1st. Richard had been cold for weeks. No amount of rugs and blazing fires seemed to be able to warm him. He recognised that his body was starting to close down, just at the extremes so that his fingertips were constantly numb and his feet ached with no apparent cause.

The postscript this time was from Val, not Dakota who, as Val explained, had drifted off to sleep, exhausted by the effort of dictating the long letter.

Dear Ben,
I just wanted to say thank you for being there for me the other day. Afterwards, I was too scared to go see Dakota, but I had nothing to be worried about. She has been a great friend to me and we get

along great. I was feeling sorry for myself but Dakota has been through so much. She has three broken bones and her face is much worse than mine, plus she was hit with something sharp, cutting her head open. You know all this but I am only listing it because I want you to know that meeting Dakota properly has really opened my eyes to the world and what we can and should do for ourselves and for others.

I have sick leave now. The doctor thinks I will be off a month. I don't think I am going to go back to the prison. I will find something else for Kyle and myself, even if it means moving away from Zanesville.

Ben, Dakota tells me she is innocent. We were taught on the basic training course that every inmate considers herself innocent. But in her case I am convinced she is. You once asked me about the chances of getting an appeal or an early release. You are obviously interested in that. If there is anything I can ever do to help, please let me know. I would love to help.

Right, I better sign off. I will send this on the way home. There is no censorship because it is strictly a letter from me! I have to go pick up Kyle now, so all the best from your true friend Val and on behalf of your very great friend Dakota who is sleeping peacefully with a little smile on her face.

Ben read the letter again and then a third time, not heeding that it was late and he had to be up early. He sat in his chair long past midnight, thinking himself first in the ship with Richard and Rupert and then in the hospital room with Dakota and Val.

Finally, he brushed his teeth and went to bed, not reading this time, for he had read enough already that night.

Mothers and Children

Val wound up the window of her car as she swung into the drive of her mother's ranch house. It was not where she had grown up and the neat, shaped bushes and plastic, low-maintenance siding and lawns with the 'Tru-Care' signs showing who looked after them meant nothing to her. Her mother had moved to this two-bed property after her father left. That had been three years ago now. She had always thought it a happy marriage and a happy family with herself and her younger sister. But it seems it was not.

"You know Dad left the moment I finished high school and got a job," her sister, Verity, had once said to her. It had never occurred to Val that her father was itching to leave. Val had seemed to be his favourite, while Mother and Verity were always close. Looking back, she could see the division of the family as if it had always been there. Her father had worked thirty years at the prison, becoming assistant deputy warden, and got both Hunter and Val their jobs there. Then he had gone off with his pension and a younger woman to Florida and even Val, his favourite, only heard from him at Christmas and sometimes birthdays. She knew that the girl he had gone off with had left him and he had moved in with someone else but her signature on the Christmas cards was scribbled and illegible, so she did not know the new girlfriend's name.

She wondered, as she got Kyle out of the back of the car, how they could have gone on all those years of sharing just for the marriage to end like a car wreck ends lives. She wondered that every time she arrived at the neat ranch house with its fake blinds and low-maintenance aura. She was convinced that most of the time they had been happy.

"Mom, how are you?" She deliberately kissed her mother although her mother had stopped that pretence three years earlier. Val felt a new person and was going to build bridges.

"Passable." That is what her mother always said, then, "Hello Kyle dear. I've got something for you. It is a surprise for after lunch."

"Thank you for having him." Val took her mother's hands in hers, such was her determination. "It means a lot to me. Thank you."

"That's OK, Valerie." Her mother never shortened the name, whereas her father always had. But then her father had left them. Her mother was slightly embarrassed, sensing something different about her daughter. "I don't suppose you have time for a coffee." Said, old style, as a statement. Normally Val would have said no, she was in a rush, but thanks anyway.

"Of course I do, that would be great. I wanted to ask your advice about something anyway."

First real eye contact for three years, thought Val.

Over coffee on the sun deck, Kyle playing with dumper trucks and cranes in the sandpit, Val told her mother something of her emerging plans.

"I got a good high school diploma, 3.8 grade average. I want to make use of that. I don't want to go back to the prison to work. I want something better."

"Amen to that," her mother replied.

"Oh, I thought you approved."

"Far from it. I always thought you were too kind and sensitive for that place. You should get a job in an office or school or even a charity."

"That's what I am trying to do. That's why I need to buy some decent clothes today so I can go to interviews."

"Have you got the money?"

"I'll put it on a credit card. I better go now." Val drained her coffee and stood up. "I'll be back by 4pm if that is OK."

"Actually, I have an idea." Val's mother also stood up. "Bear with me a moment. Kyle, don't leave the sandpit. I will be back in a moment. I just want to show your mom something quickly." She led the way back to the hall and then to the spare bedroom, where Kyle sometimes stayed. But then on into a small walk-in closet. Down one side was a rail half full of good quality work clothes.

"Why don't you look through these first and see if anything grabs your fancy. We are the same size and it would save you a pretty penny if you like any of them."

"Wow, these are your old work clothes? I thought you had disposed of them when you retired."

Val's mother did not reply at first, but sat down on a round cushioned stool that once must have fitted under a dressing table.

"No," she said, then after another gap, "They were my link with something else. Now, I must get back to Kyle. Try on anything you like. I will never wear them again." She was up and gone, closing the bedroom door before Val could express her thanks.

Kyle called it the Bennet fashion show. Val never made it to the shops that day. Instead, she tentatively tried on a business suit, selecting a white shirt to go under the jacket, and then shyly went back to the sun deck.

"What do you think?" she asked.

"Super Mom, real smart." Kyle did a little dance as he sung "Smartie pants Mommy" over and over again.

"Quiet, Kyle, I want Granny to tell me what she thinks."

"Very elegant. You must be exactly the same size as me as they fit perfectly. Try some others on. I want to see each outfit. Gosh, that one takes me back!"

Hence Kyle's fashion show took place. Val spent the rest of the day parading one outfit after another. The two spectators devised a scoring system that caused shrieks of laughter when they differed so much in their opinions. Val's mother made lunch, then more coffee, then supper also and gave Kyle a bath, while Val smiled and indulged herself.

By 9pm Kyle was yawning repeatedly, although claiming he was not the least bit tired. It was time to go home.

"Don't go," her mother suddenly said. "It is so lonely here on my own. Stay the night." So they did, Kyle and Val squeezing into one bed. The next morning Val carefully laid out her new clothes in the back of her car and kissed her mother warmly. She was equipped for her new life, the life she had to sort out before the money ran out.

"Call me later," her mother said as they hugged. "It's so nice to be together again. Your bruises are easing also. The swelling is coming down. You are a very pretty girl, Valarie. You will find someone else once the divorce goes through. You are definitely doing the right thing leaving the prison."

"I know, I feel it in my bones," Val said, then, "Mom, come to lunch tomorrow. I'll cook something special."

"I'd like that. I'll bring the ice cream."

"Cool," said Kyle. "Can we have Jell-O too?"

***

Ben knew the route up through the hospital by heart. There were two ways to get to Dakota's room. It was slightly longer through the front entrance so he always parked at the back and used the door there and straight up the stairs one flight and then they were at the bank of elevators up to the sixth floor.

It was a Saturday afternoon in June and he and Mrs Jameson had had a long, slow journey out of DC and then heavy traffic all the way to Zanesville. To compensate, Ben suggested they did not stop for lunch but ate as they drove, Mrs Jameson passing sandwiches and an apple to Ben. She was in buoyant mood, looking forward to four days with her daughter. Ben would stay for a few hours and then drive back alone to DC as he had work on Sunday. He would return for her on Wednesday, his next day off.

"Prepare for a shock," the officer grinned maliciously as they passed through to Dakota's room.

It was a shock.

"Your hair!" Mrs Jameson exclaimed without thinking. "What have they done to your hair?" Dakota was sitting in the chair beside the bed with a hospital dressing gown and slippers over her hospital nightie. She was completely bald. The bruises were now nakedly displayed on her head, running up from her face like a multi-coloured three-dimensional tattoo. She had been crying. She had wiped the tears and still held a tissue in the left hand that, with the plaster restrictions, could just reach her face, but she could not disguise the glint of tears in her eyes.

"The warden came," she got out before the tears became a flood.

"But surely she did not cut your hair?"

"No, she brought someone to do it."

"But why?" Both Mrs Jameson and Ben went to her and stood either side of her, one against the window, the other half-perched on the bed. It was a while until Dakota unburied her head from her mother's squatted body and spoke again.

"They want me back in the prison and said I wouldn't be able to wash my hair in there. The nurses washed it here."

"But it is far too early to consider going back! What do the doctors say?"

"They all say it is too early but this room is costing a lot and then there is the guard at the door. They have to reimburse the Zanesville police."

"I'll go and find the doctor." Ben stood up and left the room, determined to sort this out.

"When do they want you back?" Mrs Jameson summoned up the courage to ask, already knowing that it was not going to be good news.

"This afternoon."

"No!"

Ben got nowhere. He spoke to the house doctor and even to Professor Medici on the phone. They were both against Dakota being moved. He then called the prison and asked to speak to Mrs Kinderly.

"It's not my decision," the warden explained. "It has come down from the top. It is costing the firm over $2,000 a day and impacting our budget. I'm sorry, Mr Franklin, but there is nothing I can do."

"What of her rights?" Ben demanded.

"Mr Franklin, she is a convicted felon serving a long sentence."

"So?"

"So, she does not have any rights. Now, I really have to go. I am late for a Health and Welfare Committee meeting. We will watch her carefully and call in any specialist help she needs. Please be assured she will have the best attention we can afford and will be looked after."

"Like last time." But Ben was talking to a dead phone.

Back in Dakota's room, Ben heard the news that Mrs Jameson would not be able to stay the four days and would need to come back that evening with Ben.

It was a grim afternoon. Clearly Dakota did not want to go back, had got used to the relative freedom of the hospital environment. They stayed until three guards came at 5.30. The one in charge was Smith, the brute who enjoyed imposing misery. It struck Ben as strange that such a senior guard should come on this detail.

"Ma'am we can't get her manacles on with the plaster on her leg."

"Regulations say manacles and handcuffs for all inmates when outside the prison perimeter," Smith replied, licking her lips. "You'll have to wrap the chain around the plaster and then fix the clasp back on the chain. Here, you oaf, like this." Smith grabbed the chain and wrapped it tightly around the plaster, looking into Dakota's eyes for signs of pain. Mrs Jameson left the room, returning five minutes later with Professor Medici. Smith was wrapping a second set of manacles around Dakota's arms, as the handcuffs also would not fit.

"Take those off."

"No." Smith seemed eager for a fight. Professor Medici remained absolutely calm, as if in the operating theatre. She spoke into her radio.

"Call Security to room 643. We need all available guards now." Then she stepped forward, seized the manacles Smith was holding and neatly clicked one side onto the bed, the other already being fastened to Dakota's right arm plaster.

"Call the press office and get a photographer up here right away." She called back into her radio as the first security guards rushed in.

"Stay by the door," she ordered. "Now, can we resolve this sensibly? This patient is not fit to be restrained in any way. She should not be leaving the hospital until next week at the earliest but your warden has made a plea and guaranteed her safety and security. Putting her in chains is not part of that guarantee."

"She's an inmate," Smith leered back. "Inmates are moved in chains. That's the fact you are forgetting."

"Nobody gets moved in chains in my hospital." Then as the press officer arrived she stepped it up a gear by informing the security guards that the prison officials were just leaving. As they stomped out, outnumbered and cameras clicking, Professor Medici winked at Dakota before rushing off to her next patient.

Ben left immediately and called Mrs Kinderly again, getting her agreement to Dakota not going back to prison until Wednesday and no chains or handcuffs of any description. In return he said they would not release the photographs to the newspapers and internet sites.

During the next four days Mrs Jameson virtually lived in Dakota's hospital room. She would get a taxi late at night to her motel, then one straight back again at breakfast time. It was, she reflected afterwards, the longest period of time she had spent with Dakota in a dozen years. They talked of old times, of fun times, of sad times. They talked of the family, outings to grandparents and treats to the movies. They talked of exam successes, girl scouts, church, boyfriends. They talked a lot about Walker, the son who had died of leukaemia three years before Dakota's arrest, and of their father. But sometimes they dared talk of the future. Mrs Jameson knew not to give too much hope but she also knew that hope gets you through so much.

Val turned up each morning, not staying too long because she realised it was an important time for mother and daughter together. She ran errands and wrote letters dictated by Dakota and did a little research on Richard Sutherland, cataloguing his diary entries and trying to use them to trace his movements, although at times he was being very secretive and there were large gaps. She enjoyed the work and loved reporting back to Dakota on her achievements. Mrs Jameson called the two of them her 'pair of black and blues' because of their vivid facial bruises, although Val's were healing much more quickly from the fresh air denied to Dakota.

On Wednesday morning Val arrived, clearly upset. She showed Dakota and Mrs Jameson a letter from Pillars of the Community Inc., the firm that ran forty prisons across America, including the Zanesville one.

"It's calling you back to work tomorrow morning. It's cutting your sick leave short because of a severe shortage of staff," Mrs Jameson said. "My goodness, that is the last thing you wanted."

"I have an interview tomorrow and one the next day. Look at this shift pattern; every weekday from 6am to 6pm. That is a sixty-hour week! And I have Kyle to look after, school is out too, for summer break."

"Did you not give notice?"

"No, I didn't think it was necessary with the sick leave."

"You must write a letter today and hand it in tomorrow. What is your notice period?"

"Two months," Val replied miserably.

"So your last day will be September 2nd. That is not too bad," Dakota said. Suddenly it all seemed clear to Val. She was upset about a two-month sentence, while Dakota was facing another thirty years.

"Of course I will," she replied, wiping her tears with the back of her hand. "It was just a shock. Now let me tell you what Kyle said today when we were having our breakfast..."

A little later, feeling chastised but with no chastiser evident, Val took her leave, knowing that the last few hours of relative freedom should be reserved for mother and daughter.

"I'll see you soon." She leaned over and kissed Dakota. She had not said she would see her inside, that was the cruel unspoken truth that hung around them like a great dump of snow about to happen, the air damp and heavy and cold with it.

"Same," Dakota said, trying to be brave. "Remember the resignation letter now. Write it tonight and hand it in first thing tomorrow."

"Yes boss," Val joked, but recognised there was an element of truth to it. She was a follower, not a leader like Dakota could be if she were not stuck inside for half a lifetime.

"I'll come out with you," Mrs Jameson said. As soon as they were in the lift, out of earshot of the police guard, Mrs Jameson asked Val about how it would be in prison.

"She has some good friends. They will stand by her. And then for the next two months I will look out for her. I will make it my mission to keep Smith at bay."

"But you can't show her favouritism," Mrs Jameson said. "Look out for her, protect her, but don't be obvious about it and risk charges of favouritism. That could backfire."

Val agreed, kissed Mrs Jameson goodbye and went out of the lift to the back entrance where Ben had advised her to park. Mrs Jameson hit the sixth floor button again and returned to her daughter, a great big smile on her strained face.

***

Later that evening, Dakota was pushed in her wheelchair back to her bunk, another inmate holding her bedding, as she was unable to do so. She was dressed in the orange dress that had been standard issue before the overalls and was still worn by some older inmates. They had been unable to fit the overalls over her plasters. The dress was a slightly faded version of the same orange, washed and pressed countless times by the heavy machines in the laundry. On her back and front she was clearly marked as who she was:

Jameson D. 174632F
Inmate Zanesville Federal Penitentiary

They had inspected her thoroughly and knew she was clean. Thankfully, Smith was not on duty that evening.

At her bunk, she had a reception committee of her friends. Together they made her bed for her, then Hannah brushed Dakota's teeth. They hugged her and said it was good to have her back.

"I know you don't want to be here, who in their right mind would? But we missed you."

"Thanks," said Dakota, climbing into her bunk, feeling again the thin mattress and board below, plus the board above that marked the top bunk, closing her in like she was sleeping in a coffin. She felt the concrete wall to the side with her left hand, the more able one.

Then Janice placed a pillow under Dakota's plastered leg.

"But that is your pillow."

"I don't need it," Janice lied convincingly.

"Thank you, thanks all." Tomorrow morning when she counted her blessings she would put her many friends, inside and outside, top of the list. She fell asleep, not crying as she expected, but thinking how very lucky she was.

Legal Aspects

Frank Williams III stood by the window of his expansive DC office, looking over the corner of H and 10th Street down below. It was ruinously expensive but worth every penny for the impression it gave. He doubted whether he would have completed the outrageous takeover of Horton Schnide Inc. without these lavish premises to woo the opposite numbers. He had made well over a billion dollars on that deal. His father had once said to him that for every dollar he gained some poor soul lost that much; more when you considered that someone had to pay for the legions of lawyers and accountants. But in the case of Horton Schnide Frank did not believe that. He had owned the bulk of it for ten months, sorted out the flight simulation business that was losing money and sold this segment on for more than he paid for the whole firm. The rest he had sold piecemeal, getting surprising amounts for the food businesses. He still owned the tractor division but his executive team was working on that.

Marcus Hibbert's sidekick, Mannings, would be here in a moment. It was best to have an anonymous lawyer rather than the instantly recognisable Hibbert who had spoken in public many times on constitutional and governmental matters. Mannings was a good lawyer, promising material for partnership.

The other party to the meeting was coming fifteen minutes later. He was Albert Essington, a small-time but wealthy criminal defence lawyer who, Frank and Mannings were now convinced, had colluded in the conviction of Dakota Jameson nine years earlier. But the problem was to prove it.

Essington arrived twelve minutes late deliberately, giving the appearance of someone with a lot of pressing business. As soon as he was announced, Frank made the decision to keep him waiting twice as long. So Chuck Mannings and he chatted about what they had done for 4th July, recognising the deep irony that strictly there was now no 4th July. Yet they had both enjoyed it; Frank with his horses, Chuck with the sailing boat he had just purchased.

"We had a glorious week on the Chesapeake," he said. "The weather was hot, some good winds for sailing, and the kids loved it."

When Albert was shown into the spacious office he saw a room bigger than his entire office suite. It had framed pictures of horses on the walls. He had no idea who the painter was but they were clearly of good quality. Even he, who had never been near a horse, could recognise the noble features as belonging to thoroughbred racehorses. The floor of the entire office was polished oak with thick Indian rugs. He noticed several distinct areas. To the right was a long boardroom-type table with a dozen high-back chairs around it with intricate spindles twisting and turning to form the backs. The desk area, alone bigger than his own office, was under the largest window looking onto H Street below. The desk was empty apart from some framed photographs of horses; the man was obviously a horse nut. On the other side of the room were three large sofas set to form a squared 'C' shape, with a shiny metal-and-glass coffee table in between. Then there was a fourth area with a small round oak table in the corner there were no chairs but papers were stacked neatly in several piles. The whole place spoke power; power that pinpointed its direction with laser-like purpose. Albert was impressed and intimidated in equal measure. It made his accomplishments over the years seem dingy and inadequate in comparison.

That was the intention.

"Mr Essington, my apologies for keeping you waiting." Frank offered a hand as if it was a polite duty he had to fulfil.

"That's alright," Albert found himself saying, but that was not what he had rehearsed while sitting in the corridor outside as Frank's secretary tapped away in her spacious office.

"Well my time is limited, so let's get down to business

straight away." Frank had risen to shake hands, as had Chuck when introduced. Both had sat back down again, Frank behind his desk, Chuck in a comfortable chair to the right and slightly behind the desk. There was nowhere obvious for Albert to sit. He looked around; should he go to the large table and drag a chair from there? Or remain standing? He hesitated, then Frank's secretary came in with coffee on a silver tray. She expertly moved one of the high-backed chairs with one hand to a position on its own in front of the desk but eight feet back, then handed him a cup and saucer. He was on his own, an island. There was nowhere to put down his coffee cup so he held it with both hands, one holding the saucer, the other steadying the cup. It rattled slightly in the saucer. He looked around for somewhere to put his briefcase, clasped under his arm, then rested it against the leg of the chair, except it kept slipping down flat on the polished floor. So he picked it up and placed it on his lap, under his coffee.

"The purpose of this meeting," Chuck took over with a clear and confident voice, "is to determine what can be done to reverse the decision on Dakota Jameson and what roles each of us might play in that. So, Mr Essington, think of it as an interview. Jameson has very powerful friends and we need to marshal the best resources to fight on her behalf." Albert thought fast, remembering the visit from that English aristocrat. He would have to be careful.

"What is your hourly rate?" Frank demanded, seemingly bored of the conversation already.

"Oh, um." Should he be reasonable or exaggerate it? He had not expected to be earning new fees. He went for exaggeration. "Usually it is $675 an hour, but I can look at reducing that to say, $600, if that goes down a bit better."

"$675 is not unreasonable," Frank replied. Then Chuck asked a series of questions over the next ninety minutes, many had no interest to Frank or him, but the pointless questions were peppered with a few of great interest, concerning files, procedures and tactics from the original trial and appeal.

"So Mr Essington, if we bring you on board you can make available all the old files and papers?"

"Yes, of course. They are all in our archives in my office." Albert knew they would never find the other ones.

"We will need them immediately."

"We will send over a contract for your services later today." Frank stood up and the meeting was over.

"Wow," said Albert as he walked into the lift and made his way down to the ground. There was a skip in his step all the way home as he thought of the thousand-plus hours he would be able to bill at $675 an hour. Should he have asked for more?

The contract was even more generous than he imagined. He would be paid $675 an hour with a 20% premium over forty billable hours a week. His assistants could bill at $300 with the same premium. He liked the difference in rate between himself and the hired help. They were valuable, but he was much more so. All expenses paid of course; that probably meant dinners, First Class flights, nice hotels. These people had more sense than money. The contract was already signed by Chuck Mannings and the note with it stressed the urgency of completion so he signed immediately and sent it back with the courier, promising himself he would read it properly that evening.

Then he settled back with a bourbon and ice at his poolside and dreamed of the future billings that had suddenly come his way. He wondered whether he could charge his 'interview' time. With mileage and travel time he was well over $2,000 already. Life was good when you were a hard-working attorney out for the kill.

***

It was Ben's turn to choose a restaurant for their catch-up meeting. He chose The Little Kitchen and was there first to get a corner booth. He ordered an ice-cold beer in response to the blistering heat outside. The Washington air sat heavily, the moisture close to condensing, turning everyone to a damp, hot, sweaty and bad-tempered state. The sounds of the city seemed muted, losing their energy as they fought their way through the water molecules that saturated the air. People were not out much anyway, other than the tourists, who seemed determinedly cheerful whatever the conditions they faced.

The Little Kitchen was his favourite diner. Run by May and Mavis, a couple of sixty-plus lesbians with interesting pasts and a scathing sense of humour, plus a determination to humiliate at every opportunity. It combined quite good food with an extreme casualness that saw customers helping out behind the counter and bartering as the norm. There were old framed, now tatty, newspaper clippings on the walls, describing it as 'quaint, authentic and of character'. Ben was entitled to several free meals because he had mended a tap that gushed water late at night when he had stopped in for a coffee to go. It had been a late night but considered a bargain when he now had to host Sir John and Frank with only $30 left in the bank for the balance of July.

His finances had taken a knock. He had spent hundreds of dollars on fuel while working the least hours he had ever worked with his other commitments seeming to crowd out work time. He would have to do something about it, but the draw of Dakota was too much. He had driven to Zanesville five times in the last three weeks. His car was overdue an oil change. He would do it in August when he was paid again.

He fiddled with his beer, getting depressed about money while waiting for the other two. He did not want to have to buy a refill. Then Sir John arrived. With his innate ability to hit the truth he declared that Ben was a bloody wimp to sip his beer on a scorcher of a day and ordered another, alongside one for himself as well. Now Ben would have to cover the bill. The free meal did not extend to beer also.

"I like this place," Sir John said, beer foam giving him a temporary white moustache. "Frank will be here in a moment."

They ordered steak and fries. These were preceded by a

decent salad, large enough almost to be a meal on its own.

"Better than a Spam sandwich," Ben said when the steaks were placed in front of them by May who joked, inevitably, about feeding them up and filling them out.

"Explain your statement," Sir John said. So Ben told them of the staple diet at Zanesville Penitentiary.

"You guys better keep out of trouble, then," May joked as she journeyed around the room with coffee pot in hand. The Little Kitchen was famous for its coffee. "That sounds worse than Mavis' cooking! Hear that, Mavis?" She called across the room. "Ben and his buddies are complaining that we don't have Spam sandwiches on the menu."

"I don't know," Mavis called back. "Give a man a decent steak and they want Spam. There's no satisfying men. That's why I'm sticking with you, my love!"

"Enough of this," cried Sir John. "Away with you, wicked woman. I have matters of great import to impart and they are not for your lewd ears."

"Mavis, we got ourselves a regular Shakespeare here, even has the accent." She went away, chuckling, spilling coffee into cups here and there, joking with everyone.

"Good," Sir John said. "I want to tell you about my discoveries concerning one Daniel Roberts Esq., erstwhile boyfriend to Dakota Jameson, currently incarcerated for heinous crimes she did not undertake." Sir John had a way of telling stories that invited listening, drawing his audience in.

"Well, our friend Mr Roberts is now a leading figure in the community. Which community? I hear you ask. And I answer, the political community. That's right, he is an aide to a senior member of Congress. He is a twenty-nine-year-old man with an apparently bright future so he probably will not want his seedy little past to catch up with him."

Sir John went on to recount that Dan Roberts had gone from druggy high school student with lank, long, greasy hair to mainstream respectability in a designer suit via a placement at a top university with a chunk of money changing hands to secure the spot.

"I had an interesting chat with the lady who runs

admissions at his university. She was quite enamoured with my title."

Daniel's university tutor and ambitious parents with connections led naturally to several summer internships, one of which had been with a genteel old congressman who had taken Roberts under his wing. He had gone back to work there on graduation and was now his right-hand man.

"Word is that he hopes to take over when the old congressman retires. He married the man's daughter in '25 and they now have twins, a son and daughter."

"Which district?"

"That is the incredible part of this story. You will never guess." Only Ben guessed straight away.

"Ohio," he said. "Whatever district covers Zanesville."

"Spot on, Sherlock. 12th District. Our Mr Roberts is hoping in 2030 to become Dakota's representative in Congress."

"Free meal includes a choice of apple or pecan pie with whipped cream, only we are out of whipped cream, unless you want that squeeze-tube stuff that tastes like cardboard."

"Apple, no cream," was followed by confirmations of the same from the other two, before Sir John ordered three more beers.

But Ben was not thinking about the cost of the beers. His mind was on the outrage of Roberts becoming a Congressman while Dakota rotted in prison for his crimes. True, it was the stupid excess of youth, and punished with a sledgehammer, but it had not been Dakota's excess but this protected young man's, now a pillar of the community. He missed the discussion about what they could do about it, such that Sir John's irritation was scathing when he had to repeat it afterwards in the car park.

"I haven't paid the bill." Ben suddenly remembered, interrupting Sir John.

"Forget that, my man. That has been covered."

"What do you mean?"

"I mean that I withdrew my wallet from my pocket and counted out the requisite notes, taking into account an obscene tip for the ladies who run that establishment.

Furthermore, I placed those notes upon the table by my own free will."

"But it was my shout."

"Ben, stop cackling. I am a millionaire, while Frank is a billionaire. You are clearly struggling to balance your work commitments with looking after the Jamesons. You have done that without complaint. Mrs Jameson has told us you refuse to take a dime in fuel costs. Frank and I applaud your attitude. If we choose to show our appreciation by funding the odd few beers then do not deny us the pleasure. Now I'm going to have to go over the plans all over again for you. Talk about in one ear and out the other."

Politics and Problems

"Buggeration!" Max Heaton did not often swear, believing strongly that more subtle use of English would gain his objectives. But he knew this made the occasional profane indulgence all the more effective.

Certainly his staff looked up from their 'glued to the table-top' posture that was normal for the pronouncement of truly bad news.

And this was truly bad news.

"West, I want a summary of our options on my desk first thing tomorrow morning."

"Yes, sir." Belinda West, Permanent Secretary to the Foreign Office, noted the use of her surname, underlining the tone of the order. Her second thought was how she would come up with options by start of day tomorrow. It seemed the coffin lid was closing on her career. She was already on a written warning from her boss. This was her last chance.

Then she remembered her son and her world closed in.

"West, are you hearing me? West?"

"Sir, sorry. I was just running through the ideas in my head." A lie, she had been thinking about Harry, her son, and that made her think of Andy, her estranged husband. Why couldn't he take some of the strain of Harry?

"Bel, can I suggest a meeting to delegate tasks today?" Her neat assistant addressed her as the meeting broke up. Georgie looked twenty but Bel knew she was closer to thirty.

"Yes, great idea, Georgie, please organise it."

Georgie called the Task Force for 10am. She included an agenda, although there was only one subject to discuss. It was padded out by dividing it up into (1) review of the situation, (2) consideration of possible options, (3) viability assessments, (4) recommendations/ further action and, finally, the obligatory Any Other Business.

Harry had been hell that morning, worse than usual. He had been hell last night for that matter, leaving Bel exhausted.

She was constantly exhausted. The tiredness ate into her bones like woodworm into a ship's timber, leaving her frail, distracted, anxious, snappy, quite unable to rise to the challenge.

And this was a challenge. Somehow she had to get a range of options to her political boss by first thing in the morning. Yet her fine mind was full of Harry. Instead of the subtleties of the United Nations she was wondering why he would not dress himself. In place of a strategy to counter the threat, her head was flowing with behaviour treatments for extreme autism.

And underneath all this she was angry, a hot–cold–hot anger that ate like flames in a bonfire yet burnt like ice. Why did Andy leave? Why was it acceptable for him to announce that he was unable to write his precious articles when under the stress imposed by Harry's autism and take off; a migrating bird who might come back next year but, equally, may shack up with another to breed again? Why was he allowed to term it a friendly separation when she was livid with his actions and unable to count him a friend, far less a husband? Why did society work in this way?

So the thoughts filled every day like a blur, delineated not by the coming of night, for darkness meant nothing to Harry, but by written warnings, confidential chats to buck her up, and quiet words from colleagues to reassure her.

Georgie saw all this and her thirty-year-old soul caved in every time she thought of Bel, her boss. She made it her quiet mission to aid and assist, plugging the gaps, finalising the documents that were left half-done, gathering help from all sources. Georgie tried to smooth things over, but the warnings and chats kept coming and Bel knew she was on her ninth life.

"We need ideas," Bel said. "So speak up." What about building more routine into Harry's life, she thought, then a look towards Georgie, who seemed to understand everything.

Georgie gave a faint smile and said, "As Mrs West has said, please put your ideas on the paper in front of you and then pass up to me. I will sort and collate and then we can go over them and choose the best ones to pursue. Note the plural, we need ideas rather than a single idea from each of you."

The first round produced little of worth but did at least provoke some discussion, various department members coming out of themselves bit by bit, reminding Georgie of small creatures terrified of becoming prey but needing to go out in the heat and hunt for themselves. It was a pinprick in the veil of defeatism that lay everywhere in Westminster, that some would say caused the problems in a depressing spiral of cause and effect.

"So we have several good ideas," Georgie exaggerated the truth to encourage. "The one that comes up most often is to bargain with something else that the UN wants to resolve. Some of you mentioned Gibraltar and two wrote down the Falkland Islands." Georgie looked pleadingly at Bel, she was at the limit of her own experience.

Bel saw her and responded. "It's called the Diplomatic Theory of Relativity," she started, some of her old vigour back in her voice. "Or Trading Places. If you are in danger of losing something important, try offering up something slightly less so."

"An exchange." Somebody else spoke up. "The Falklands for the permanent seat."

"It might work."

"But won't they take our offering and then come back next year with the same request?" Georgie surprised herself with her question. She was only there to direct proceedings and take notes, not to contribute.

"Exactly," said Bel in reply. "Good point. And there is another theory that comes into play here." She stopped and thought of Harry a moment. When he was younger you could persuade him to brush his teeth or get dressed with a tiny bribe, but after a while the bribes had to grow. "It's the theory of Blackmail Inflation. Each time a demand is placed, it grows."

"Danelaw," Georgie suddenly said. She had loved

studying Saxons and Danes at school. There was something romantic yet practical and solid about the creation of her adopted country.

"A perfect example." Bel beamed with pleasure at the contribution her assistant was making. "Now, what is the second idea?"

"A plea to their humanity, basically, to their better nature."

"That's unlikely to work." Bel thought of begging Harry to respond or behave. It never worked; rather, he enjoyed the attention it generated, provoking further bad behaviour. You could not reason with him. There was no other view than his. It was not selfishness; just that his were the only eyes on a world that only made sense when processed through his mind.

They met that morning until almost lunchtime, broke up with various tasks delegated and recorded by Georgie, then agreed, at Georgie's suggestion, to meet again at 4pm. It looked like they were making progress.

***

The phone call came at 3.25pm. The headmaster tried to sound calm but clearly was not, his attempt sounding false like a con artist working around in order to strike.

"Mrs West, Harry has been taken to St Thomas'. He was in a fight but is not badly hurt."

"My God, but he has never fought anyone before. Is he all right? I need to get there."

"I am on my way now, Mrs West, so I'll see you there. He lost consciousness for a short while but does not seem to be hurt. We thought it wise…"

"I'm on my way. Georgie? I have to go to hospital. It is Harry. I must go now."

"Which hospital?"

"St Thomas'."

"OK, let me know how he is and don't worry about anything here. We can cope." But Bel was gone.

Harry seemed in worse condition than the headmaster had indicated. When Bel arrived at the hospital he was unconscious again, breathing raggedly as if struggling with the pumps, twitching constantly from pain.

"We think his lung is pierced and his skull cracked. We have to operate immediately," the doctor said, then a nurse took Bel, white-faced like marble, to a nearby rest room and made her a cup of tea that was still there, stone-cold, several hours later when Georgie arrived.

"How is he?" Georgie asked, but was not heard. So she sat on the chair next to Bel and picked up her hand, held it then stroked it, then her arm and her left shoulder. After a long time, a different doctor and nurse came into the waiting room.

"Mrs West, I am afraid I do not have good news." The update was that Harry remained in a critical condition, breathing with the help of a machine, unconscious still.

After a while longer the headmaster returned, ashen-white, no pretence of jolly confidence now.

"What happened?" Georgie asked, in place of Bel, who still had not uttered a word.

"A fight." The young headteacher replied, not sure what to say.

"We know that, of course. But what happened to start the fight? Who else was involved?"

"There were two other boys and two girls. It seemed they were teasing Harry and it got out of hand. I'm afraid we've had a spate of bullying recently. We're trying to stamp it out." With Georgie persisting, the whole story came out. They constituted a gang, these four, in fact were the ringleaders of an emerging gang, recruiting daily. They had been pulled up for bullying Harry and two other vulnerable children but evidently the warnings had not been heeded for they had continued. It had been torment for Harry, never left alone during school hours. For weeks he had ignored their taunts, tried to block them out, humming loudly with hands over ears whenever they came near. Finally, he had started crying and that was the sign of weakness that triggered the brutal escalation. Harry formed a ball with arms and legs behind the big dustbins outside the school kitchens and they had battered him until he slid down the wall and lay like a spilled puddle on the ground. Then they had run, but a teacher had spotted them and gone to investigate, quickly calling ambulance and police when he saw the slumped teenager half-hidden in excess rubbish from the bins. He felt then for a pulse, not there, but remembered enough of his First Aid training and got the child breathing again just as the ambulance roared up into the playground and across to the growing crowd around the kitchens.

Throughout this Bel remained impassive, vacant, not communicative in any way. It was only when the doctor returned that she looked up. The clock had just ticked past one-thirty in the morning when the better news was announced.

"Mrs West, Harry regained consciousness a few minutes ago. He is asking for you. I think and pray we are through the worst."

"Thank God." Bel rose and made for the door, looking back at Georgie. "Thank you, Georgie. Thank you for everything."

"No problem," she replied. "I'll head off now, still got some more to do for Mr Heaton's report. No, don't worry about a thing. It is all done, just typing. I'll get to it now rather than leave it to the morning. I am so pleased that Harry is OK." She kissed Bel lightly on the cheek. "Please give that to him from me."

Georgie had lied about the state of the report. It was far from complete, in fact was just a handful of ideas. She sat in Bel's office with a sequence of plastic coffee cups from the machine on the landing and thought hard, sitting back in the chair, swivelled around with her legs resting on an open drawer so that the side of the drawer dug into her legs unless she shifted them every few minutes.

She decided to start from the beginning again. She stood up and went to the whiteboard tacked to the partition wall. The other side of the partition was her alcove and the main entrance to Bel's office but today she was the big boss, in the big swivel chair at the big desk, at least until 8.30am.

Georgie wrote on the board in big letters with her beautiful handwriting, learned in the Ukrainian school she had attended between the ages of five and eight, before the move to Britain with her parents.

Ways to change the United Nations' mind.

It took her two minutes to sketch out the valid but tame points from the sessions during the day. They amounted to (1) offer something else in its place, (2) plea to their reason/humanity and (3) undermine their position with some suggestion of scandal in order to buy time.

But this filled only one small portion of the whiteboard and Georgie felt as if something was missing. Something obvious. All of a sudden she knew. She closed the green pen she had been writing with and took the top off the red marker, writing a little more hurriedly now.

Hit back at them.

Then a line led away to:

Give them something more serious to think about.

Underneath this were several more lines, her writing getting sketchier as she wrote faster.

Be aggressive, hit them hard, don't take it lying down.

After a few minutes of speedwriting she stopped, took three steps backwards like an artist trying to get perspective, looked at the board again, realising that her work that night was only just starting. She went out to the landing for another coffee and then settled back at Bel's desk with her computer on.

The report was ready by 8am. Max Heaton's secretary did not want to let her in but Georgie persisted.

"Sir, Bel asked me to get this report to you. Unfortunately, there was an accident last night with her son and she had to leave suddenly."

"I didn't know she had a son. I thought she lived alone."

"She has one son, sir, who is heavily autistic and has been bullied a lot at school. He was beaten up yesterday and they had to operate."

"My God!" Even Max Heaton forgot about the pressing issue with the UN as he listened to Georgie's account of Harry's troubles. As she neared the end he picked up the phone and called for a car to go to St. Thomas'.

"But sir, the report, the problem with the United Nations?"

"I'll take a copy with me. Take a second copy round to Number 10 now. I'll go on there after the hospital. I'll call to make sure they are expecting you."

***

Picture the scene when a senior government minister makes any unplanned visit. Havoc reins, aides and bodyguards scrambling for order, to limit risks and to manage them as best they can. But it has its compensations. There was no need to find a car parking space, his chauffeur sliding across the ambulance parking bays so that Max could get out.

"I'll find somewhere nearby, sir, and be waiting for you." Already, prompted by the advance phone call, two orderlies were manhandling a special parking sign, one of them waving to the chauffeur, colleagues together, cogs in the machine of government.

They were met by a hastily-summoned manager, still fastening his tie as he strode out of the main entrance. He guided them directly to Harry's bedside in a sunny ward with other youngsters, some bouncing with energy, others lying quietly, holding on to life, just. Harry was neither, staring out of the window and humming a monotonous tune that varied only one note up and down from a central dominant. It was the never-ending rhythm that made it so distinctive.

"Foreign Secretary, I didn't mean for you to come here, you have so much to do. And the report I owe you, I will follow up immediately."

"Don't worry, Bel, you have other priorities. And the report is done. Georgie told me she collated all your thoughts and put it into final form. I read it on the way here. It's a fair effort." They exchanged a look that told Bel that Max knew Georgie was the mainstay of the overnight effort, but there was no condemnation in expression or voice. "But how is your son? And why did you not tell me about your problems? I put you under a lot of strain."

Max Heaton and Bel West retired to a waiting room that was empty. They spent fifteen minutes, probably the best investment of time Bel had made in her forty-eight years. Harry was recovering. Andy, her estranged husband, had not turned up yet. She thought he was in Turkey writing a novel.

"Bel, you should have let me know the pressures you were under. I made things worse when I could have helped you." He would help her now. "You will stay in charge, Bel, but with adequate support so you can devote some time to other issues as well as keeping control at work. We will find a couple of 'super deputies' to take some of the day-to-day strain."

But only one was needed. Georgie's promotion happened that same day. Georgie was given special responsibility for the urgent question of how on earth to retain the United Kingdom's permanent seat on the United Nations Security Council.

***

Harry seemed to shrug off his battering at the hands of his

school friends, although his inability to express himself meant nobody knew what he really thought and felt. Bel took him back to school a week later and went into a meeting of all involved: victim, perpetrators, parents, school, social workers, lawyers and police.

"I want to hear from the four children who did this to Harry." Bel cut across the headmaster and social worker, who seemed to be vying for the privilege of running the meeting, not thinking that Bel was a master of just such.

"I don't think that would be appropriate," someone in an expensive suit said. But one of the boys stood up anyway.

"My name is Edmund Jones and we have all discussed the things that we did." He looked briefly sideways at his parents for support; his mother squeezed his hand, father remaining impassive but looking into his son's eyes. "We did terrible things. We picked on a boy who could not answer us back. We taunted him and we would not let him go. We thought it made us strong and powerful, like we were in control, like we dominated him. But we were cowardly and hateful and vicious. We hate what we had become, like thugs and bullies, and we are very sorry that we picked on Harry and hurt him and that we threatened his life. We deserve to be punished and will do whatever you decide." At this point he looked directly at Bel, as if she was the judge about to sentence them. "Whatever we do in our lives we will remember this and we have all sworn oaths never to bully anyone again and to work hard to stop bullying and violence when we see it." Finally, he looked at Harry, then hung his head in shame as he sat down. But as Edmund lowered himself into his chair, Harry rose clumsily and walked around the table to Edmund. He lent over Edmund's chair and took his hand to shake it, his left hand on Edmund's shoulder.

"That's OK," he said in his slurred speech, pumping the other boy's hand vigorously and patting him on the shoulder. "Friends." The vigorous hand-pumping knocked against the large plastic water bottle, sending it rolling across the table, water spraying out, before landing in the lap of one of the lawyers, who jumped up and knocked her own coffee over, puddles of caffeine competing with the water.

But no one cared, not even the lawyer with the soaked skirt, for the outcome was positive and hope hung around like seedlings sprung into the air around them.

The chief social worker had a name for it: victim generosity. The lawyers packed up their briefcases, pads away, pens in jacket pockets, not disappointed at the curtailment of income but pleased for once not to be dealing with legalities and retribution. The soaked lawyer made a joke that at least she could go and change now.

The police constable, a round woman in her thirties, stayed on for the smaller meeting, shifting chairs to be closer to the others. Bullying in school was her passionate cause. Secretly delighted, she nevertheless had several tasks ahead of her. First, she quizzed each child and the parents, individually and collectively, wanting to be convinced of their contrition, but making sure beyond doubt. Then she had to consider charges.

"Mrs West, do you want to pursue charges?"

"No. I am convinced of the genuineness of their statements and attitude."

"And Mr Haylock," she turned to the headmaster, "does the school wish to pursue this matter through the courts?"

"No, Officer. I think that would be counter-productive. In fact, I am going to try and turn this into something positive. I am going to ask each of the four students to become anti-bullying ambassadors for the school and the wider community. If Mrs West agrees, I will inform the whole school of what happened, both last week and here today, and announce their appointment at the same time. I think we can make this a powerful force for good."

"Of course I agree, Mr Haylock. I would also urge speed because now is the time to act and build on the fine sentiments that Edmund and the others have shown today. I was full of anger, being so protective over Harry, but now I have no anger, just hope." She turned to the other parents in the room, the children having been dismissed, the five of them going off together, and said, "Your children did a terrible thing but say no more. Out of every evil, every bad deed can come hope and change and good. Your children have shown this to me today. It would be pointless to charge your sons and daughters and mete out a court judgment, perhaps taking them into borstal and maybe setting them on a path of embittered self-destruction. They have all shown remorse and Harry and I applaud the initiative to turn this into something good."

"Amen," said the police officer under her breath. No arrests today but a major step forward in what was becoming her lifelong mission.

***

"Sir, if I might say so, we don't have any really effective way of countering this aggressive stance on the permanent seat at the UN. Our best hope is to delay and hope something comes up that will give us some leverage."

Georgie loved her new role. Bel smiled to see the growth in her confidence. Max Heaton looked distracted, strangely lacking in energy; so unlike him. Georgie continued. "Bel believes we can hold off for six months by creating smoke screens about procedure, review, consultation, but we need to use that time to find something to really bargain with."

But what could they use?

"Georgie, I need you to find the leverage. Hold whatever meetings you like, use my authority to drag anybody into them, take weekends, do whatever you like, but within that six months we need to find something that will work. Bel, I think you should help me with the delaying tactics. I don't want to raise too many suspicions so we are going to have to cover it carefully."

"Yes, sir, I'd be glad to."

Letter Five

My dearest Ben,

I am sitting in the rec room, hanging out with my friends and thinking about you. I can write now, although only with my left hand. The plaster was replaced with a much smaller one when I was taken back to hospital for a check-up this morning. So please forgive my shaky left hand and I hope you can read this letter.

I miss you so much. It has only been four days since we saw each other, the day I was returned to prison. I am counting the minutes – no, the seconds, until I see you and Mother again next Sunday. I want, well it does not matter what I want.

I have kept busy these last four days. I have seen my 'secretary' around the place a few times. She is business-like, which it is best to be, I think. She did some great work on organising diary entries and the Museum of Trade and Enterprise in London has kindly sent me some more and some other information as well. So, Ben, my true, kind, good friend, my best friend, please settle back with your beer and let me tell you something of what I have discovered although having to write with my left hand it may take quite a while to tell you everything!

Ben had kept one can of the cheapest beer he could find for this occasion. Along with a pint of milk it had been the only thing in his refrigerator. He had no cash, after filling the car up that morning, and nothing in the bank until he was paid on Tuesday. He went to the fridge, opened the can, poured it into a glass and settled down with the reading lamp.

Richard arrived in Philadelphia in the early evening of March 1st 1783. The sun had not been seen all day, natural light dimmed by the heavy clouds hanging in the sky and threatening snow. He and Rupert saw odd flakes drifting down; sent like scouts to check out the destination, perhaps. Everybody was hustling to get prepared for the expected storm. Shutters were closing, wood being carried indoors, horses stabled, tarpaulins spread over carriages and carts outside houses that sent up cheeky trails of smoke, saying to the snow to come if you dare but we don't care.

"We need to find a comfortable inn," Richard muttered. "I say, you fellow, be so good as to direct us to the best inn in town."

"That will be the Patriot, sir, three blocks straight on and turn left on 4th Street. I'm going that way myself so will gladly guide you."

"Thank you my man. I am Richard Sutherland of Harrington, Virginia." Richard did not introduce Rupert; that would not be form.

"Pleased to meet you. I am Sidney Hollingsworth. I trade in pretty much anything so if you are here on business I am your man. Bear with me a moment while I fetch my horse." He was back in a minute on a beautiful black stallion that spoke of wealth.

"Right, this way, Mr Sutherland." They chatted easily along the half-deserted road as the snowflakes became regular, larger and settled on the muddy street and rough sidewalks. It was below freezing and the temperature was dropping every minute. Richard shuddered and then started a fit of coughing so that Rupert, following behind, reached forward and grabbed Richard's reins.

"Take care, sir," he said. "I have the reins."

"I'm sorry, Mr Hollingsworth, it has been a long, hard journey for an old man." The truth was every muscle ached and the chill went to the marrow. His fingers were numb constantly, not sure if that was the cold or life moving slowly out, such that his grip was weak and imperfect.

"I am in no hurry," he replied. "Catch your breath and we will move on when you are ready. We have covered half the distance to the Patriot already. You will soon be relaxing by the fire in your rooms with a stiff drink to warm your bones and some of their soup, for which they are famous."

They moved on after a few minutes but at a slower pace, the snow now like a thick white curtain, something to fight your way through. They reached the inn, dismounted, and went inside.

"I'll just see you safely settled," Sidney said.

'That's very kind."

"I'm sorry, sir, but we are completely full. Several patrons were due to leave today but have delayed their departure because of the storm."

"No space at all?" Richard asked. "We don't need much."
Rupert was reminded of 'no room at the inn'.

"No space for a gentleman, sir, I much regret. Only the common lodging."

"Then it will have to be that. We have horses outside."

But Sidney Hollingsworth would not let them proceed.

Mr Sutherland, I live not two blocks from here in a largish house, alone with my wife. We have no children at home, as my sons are away in the war. It would be our utmost pleasure to entertain and comfort you a little while you are in this city. No, please, I am deaf to all reasons why not and beg you to be sensible of my request for good companionship for my wife and I during the storm, otherwise we would be bored silly of our own company."

It was agreed. They moved on two more blocks to a row of solidly built houses set back from the road. It was too dark to see but Richard imagined the garden at the front to be full of roses and fruit trees, with a winding path around them.

Mr Hollingsworth opened the door, calling that they had guests and needed help. A stable boy ran up from the basement to lead the horses around to the stables in the back yard, while a round woman with a cheery face came out of the back rooms, wiping her hands on her apron.

"Good Lord, sir, they look all-in. Herbert, take their bags and coats. I suggest you go straight to the drawing room, sir, and warm yourselves while we sort out the rooms. Mrs Hollingsworth has retired for a little while prior to dressing for dinner. I shall send Betty to tell her we have guests and then to lay another place at the table." She looked briefly from Richard to Rupert, then said to Rupert without any awkwardness at all, "I expect you, sir, will want to come downstairs. The kitchen is very warm and cosy and we are all on friendly terms. You are most welcome to be with us."

It was arranged. Rupert went downstairs, Richard to the drawing room, then to a quickly prepared bedroom, with a fire starting to spread warmth. Rupert came up to lay out his clothes so he could wash and change before going down to the dining room.

"This is a fine house, sir," he commented. "It lacks the appearance of high society, but makes up for it in warmth."
Richard thought about Rupert's words a moment. He had been too

tired, too oblivious to all but his discomfort, to notice that the house was simple; no elaborate furniture or expensive paintings, drapes or chandeliers, yet had a simple, warm comfort that cheered from within.

"Yes, how right you are, Rupert. Do you have pleasant arrangements?"

"Oh yes, Master. Mrs Baker is very accommodating. She has placed me in a comfortable room of my own in the attic and has given me chocolate to drink and muffins ahead of our supper, which we will have after yours is served. She chats endlessly and Betty and Herbert seem kind souls. I am very pleased to be here instead of the inn, sir."

"Good, now please help me with this cravat, Rupert. My fingers are too tired to tie it properly."

Richard slept for twelve hours that night. The supper echoed Rupert's assessment of the house; simple, unpretentious, wholesome, while the company of Mr and Mrs Hollingsworth was carefully tempered by their observation that Richard was exhausted and in need of bed: light and pleasant conversation, not too taxing, certainly nothing political or too inquisitive.

Rupert slept for eight hours, an hour later to bed than Richard, after he had helped him retire, and three hours earlier to rise. There was an anteroom to Richard's bedroom so Rupert quietly turned it into a dressing room and laid out all Richard's clothes. He took advantage of his and Betty's skills to mend, wash and polish, feeling pleased with his efforts by the time he brought breakfast on a tray into Richard's room.

"Good morning, Master." He set the tray down and opened the curtains to a white world outside. "We had several feet of snow last night, sir, and it is still coming down." As if to demonstrate the truth of his words, he stepped to one side and used his arms to guide Richard's vision to the window.

"Did you sleep well, sir?"

"Yes, perfectly. And you?"

"Yes, sir." It always seemed strange to Rupert that this man, who had been responsible for the transportation of thousands of slaves across the Atlantic in terrible conditions, many dying on route, enriching himself in the process, could concern himself with one more piece of human property. Yet he did and always seemed concerned for Rupert, a slave. Perhaps it was the gradations of conscience depending on personal acquaintance. Rupert was intelligent and could see that Richard was fundamentally a good man, driven by considerations and a general respect for others, yet had brought so much terror and deprivation to thousands: retail care offset by wholesale cruelty, yet the brand seemed untarnished. What would his master have been like if he had actually been in daily contact with the slaves he transported for enormous profit? Which side, the humane or the mercantile, would have won out then?

"Dear sir, how nice to see you." The Hollingsworths rose as Richard walked into the morning room, as it was called, but doubled as a library and a smoking room in the evenings. Two walls were covered in bookshelves and there were a couple of card tables, two sofas, and a large fireplace. "I trust you slept well? Good, and breakfast was sufficient? Come and sit by the fire and let's get better acquainted. You were clearly very tired last night and we did not want to ply you with too many questions, but today we will let our curiosity off the rein!" Mrs Hollingsworth was all generosity and very talkative, a genteel version of Mrs Baker, the housekeeper downstairs in the kitchens.

They quickly established that first names were more appropriate. So Richard, Sidney and Sally Ann sat and talked until lunch was served. They were in a comfortable, warm cavern while around them the blizzard raged, finding new things to throw in its determination to cause damage but making little impression on the Hollingsworth household.

"We are shuttered down," Sally Ann joked.

As they talked over that day and the next two, Richard often wondered if he should state who exactly he was. He doubted he would be arrested, but he was an enemy alien and had therefore to be careful. It became increasingly obvious that the Hollingsworths were central to the independence movement in some form. They chatted amiably but Richard sensed clever questions dotted here and there.

Finally, on the evening of his third full day in their house, he decided to inform them of his intentions. But he would play it very carefully.

"I know Mr Benjamin Franklin," he said as they sat in the dining room, washing down roast venison with a claret that filled the mouth with flavour.

"So do we!" Sally Ann exclaimed. "We were almost neighbours until we purchased this house back in '58 and then, of course, he went to Europe."

"That's where I met him."

"You are not American, are you?" Sidney asked.

"I confess that I am not, although I have lived in Virginia and South Carolina and am excessively fond of this country."

"We could tell. There is a way about you. When did you leave America?"

"In '56."

"Much has changed since then. You have a refinement about you that speaks of an earlier age. Society has become a degree or two coarser since those days. So what brings you here while our countries are at war?"

It was then that Richard decided to tell them his purpose. But he was still careful, not knowing the current thinking in Philadelphia. He explained that he had been the official negotiator for the peace treaty and that was how he had met Franklin. They both had been frustrated by the lack of progress and Britain was starting to lose patience with apparent dallying here in America.

"So I resigned my commission and decided to come here to try and find out what is going on. I did not strictly deceive. I have large estates in Virginia and did live there many years; very happy years they were, too. "

"We did not consider deceit for one moment, my dear friend," Sally Ann replied. "We just sensed that there was something more to you than first stated. In actual fact, there is to everyone, of course. We would all be strange figures if our characters were all painted on our chests for all to see at first glance. It would ruin the joy of getting to know people and trusting them more and more."

"Thank you, Sally Ann, that is kind of you to say."

"We too do not understand the delays in getting to a treaty. We *were led to believe it to be the arrogance of the British, but it would seem that this is not the case. We want peace quickly and amiably so that everyone can get on with trade, get back to how it was as soon as possible. It is a civil war between two peoples that should be one family."*

"Ma'am, I don't believe it can ever go back to how it was before. The war has seen to that."

"No, dear Richard, that is not what I meant," Sally Ann replied quickly, a little anxious suddenly, glancing at her husband.

He frowned at her and said, "I believe what Sally Ann meant is simply to get back to friendly relations as soon as possible. Everyone over here knows it can't be back to how it was before. When the weather clears I will make enquiries on your behalf discreetly and see if we can establish a way forward."

Ben drained the last bit of his beer and looked at the clock on the wall. It was a quarter to one in the morning and he had to be at work at 8am, leaving the house by seven. He stripped off his clothes, brushed his teeth, and read the closing remarks in bed.

Dearest Ben, that is as far as my research has got. It is dreadfully slow and I seem to be at a dead end. The balance of March has no diary entries by Richard and I know on 15th April he was leaving back for Scotland. I need to find out what happened in that six-week period while he remained in America.

It is lock-down in a moment. I just want to say how much I miss you, Ben, and how much I am longing to see you again on Sunday. All my love from your jailbird, Dakota.

There were six lines of crosses beneath her name, each one longer than the line above, as if she was falling more in love with each passing minute.

So, too, was he.

Two Months to Serve

Val tried to work out how many minutes were in two months of sixty-hour weeks. She had some vague idea of checking them off on a chart when she got home each evening. But mental arithmetic had never been a strong point. When they had done it in school, rapid-fire style, her hand had always been amongst the last to go up. She had a different type of intelligence that did not recognise the relationship between numbers. So, after getting some wildly different answers as she drove to work that first day back, she put the whole 'checking off the chart' idea on the back burner.

It was a shorter drive to work now. That had been her mother's idea. She and Kyle had moved in on the Wednesday evening, intending to go back at the weekend for her other stuff. She had called the landlord, who was not the least bit fussed about the lack of notice.

"As long as it's clean and in good order, I'll be able to rent it out again tomorrow."

But on her first day back she was told that she would have to work this weekend also.

"But I have to clear out my house."

"No, you have to turn up to work when instructed to."

So on Friday her mother and Kyle cleared out the house and scrubbed it clean. She borrowed Verity's boyfriend's labour and truck to move the rest of the furniture into her mother's garage. She put Kyle in the bedroom he had used before and Val into the dining room that was little used.

"Mom, that is so kind. I just did not know how I was going to do it." They were drinking iced tea on the sun deck under the awning. It was hot; no breeze, no movement at all in that part of suburbia. If you listened carefully you could hear a lawnmower several blocks over.

"That'll be a pre-programmed one," her mother said. "They're all the rage now. You can sit on your deck and watch them mow the lawn. How was work today, Val?"

"I saw Dakota today."

"Did you talk to her?"

"Yes, I had a real meaningful conversation. It went something like this: 'Get a move on Jameson, this is not a holiday camp'."

"You know what they say about sarcasm."

"Yeah, but it is such a dreadful place. You have no idea, Mom, it…"

"Actually, I do."

"Meaning?"

"Meaning it ruined your daddy and it ruined our marriage. He worked upwards of seventy hours a week to make a living for us. He spent so long there that it changed him. He became so hard." She stopped, not really wanting to go where her thoughts were taking her. "Come on Kyle, bath time. Your mom is tired and needs to sit and relax. Let's go get wet and play with the boats in the bath."

Val sat musing as a squirrel ran across the lawn. Somebody slammed a car door; someone else called out a greeting. She was feeling sorry for herself again, it was something she kept doing. She told herself she had a good life and was going to make it better. She thought of Dakota who, somehow, was naturally happier than her. I have freedom, income, prospects, a child, a home, a mother, who she was reunited with after five years of distant awkwardness. Dakota has nothing except a loving mother who she could see three times a month on average. She had Ben of course, but so do I have Ben; as a friend, that is. Dakota has nothing material yet she is happier, far happier than me.

Then she thought, it is more than that. Dakota is living in fear. She is not recognised as a human being; more a commodity of little value, or a beast. Yet she is getting on with her life in the best way she can.

"I want to be like Dakota."

"What was that?" her mother asked, bringing Kyle back down in his pyjamas.

"Nothing, I was just mumbling to myself. I'll cook

tonight. I feel like doing something active. After all, you two have killed yourselves today moving all our junk out of the old house."

Val was on duty both days at the weekend, getting Monday off to compensate. She dreaded Saturday because she had heard that Smith was the shift supervisor that day. This was confirmed when she arrived a few minutes before 6am and Smith's sidekick, a weasel of a man, called Carter, was checking off names and allocating duties.

"Bennet to shower duty, then external clear-up."

"Yes, sir." These were the two worst duties. She found keeping order in the communal shower room almost impossible, while clear-up involved slouching around in the fierce heat outside while the inmates made vague attempts to pick up accumulated garbage before visiting hours.

Dakota was not in the showers because of her plaster casts. However, she was required to strip and wash at a basin within sight of Bennet. Bennet had to devote her time to the forty-odd women sharing the showers, crucially preventing fighting and injuries, yet somehow also watch Dakota out of the corner of her eye. Hannah wheeled in Dakota, removed her nightie, and helped Dakota to stand at the washbasin. Then she departed for her shower while Dakota tried to wash herself without wetting the plasters. She struggled and Val wanted to help her. Then she slipped, her right hand caught the wheelchair as she went down, and she yelped in pain as the mending bone jarred with the impact. All this Val saw in slow motion but was fixed to her spot as if tied and bound at the shower entrance. But as Dakota hit the floor, Val rushed to her.

"Are you OK, Dakota? I mean Jameson."

"Get back to your post, Bennet." It was Smith, sweeping in with two cohorts behind her, her backside rubbing against the washbasins on either side so she had to slant slightly, left side of her body forward, to get through.

"Jameson has been hurt, Ma'am."

"I said get back. Carter, pick it up and put it in the

161

wheelchair." Val watched in horror as Carter picked Dakota up casually and slumped her in the seat naked, grinning at the further pain caused. "Take her back to the dorm. Hey you!" Smith hollered at the first inmate exiting the showers, "Get her dressed pronto." Then she turned to Val. "My office, 9am coffee break."

Coffee break came and went with no sign of Val at Smith's office. Smith was planning to keep her waiting the entire break and then send her out to clear up with a flea in her ear. Smith was livid when 9.15 came around and there was still no sign of Bennet.

"Go find her," she almost screamed and three officers scuttled out in search of Val. But they did not find her, nor would they unless they were bold enough to seek her in the warden's office.

"I respect your courage in coming to see me," Mrs Kinderly said, unsure how to handle the strong complaint that had poured out of this young guard at ninety words a minute. "But I don't understand why you are back at work so soon. I was led to understand you had a month of sick leave."

"I was called back under your signature, Mrs Kinderly." She pulled out the letter from her tunic pocket, thanking God that she had not taken it out last night when she had hung her uniform up. Mrs Kinderly looked at it.

"I see; it is my signature, for sure. I don't understand. I was not aware of signing it. It must have been slipped in with some other papers. Well, now you are back so we will live with it. But this is a very serious accusation you are making. Can you corroborate it at all?"

"No, Mrs Kinderly. I am sure that the other guards will back Smith's version of events."

"Well then, there is not much I can do."

"There is everything you can do."

"What did you say, young lady?"

The floodgates were open. Every injustice Val had witnessed in her two years at the prison came out: the senselessness, the injustice, the lack of humanity, the tearing

162

away of dignity. At first Mrs Kinderly tried to counter the points but the tenor and tone built up to a powerful voice for reform and it was convincing, bold and terrible.

"Sit down, Miss Bennet. Now tell me, how do you think this could be fulfilled in practice?"

Valarie Bennet had found her voice.

That voice spoke for prison reform.

And it grew stronger and stronger.

***

Ben noticed it straight away when he arrived with Mrs Jameson the next day. There was a difference in Val. He chatted to her on the way in, thought it may be to do with moving in with her mother or her abusive husband being locked up, but after their habitual discussion at the end of the afternoon he knew it was something else.

"We had an incident yesterday." Val had asked Ben and Mrs Jameson to stay behind after visiting hours were over. She led them into a small room, no windows, to one side of the reception area, and took the main chair behind the desk. "Please sit down. I don't want you to be startled but Dakota was involved in a small accident yesterday." She went on to outline the washroom episode and her subsequent meeting with the warden. "The bad news is that Dakota was slightly hurt and, frankly, treated by Smith no better than cattle. The good news is that I really think this time the warden has taken it on board. She has started an enquiry into Smith's conduct. I suggested that she separates Smith's lackeys and questions them one by one. She did that this morning with Carter. He is also the most loyal of Smith's lieutenants."

She paused, suddenly uncertain, a link with the old Val, before continuing with new determination. "I also called Professor Medici last night and asked her to send in a written report on Smith's behaviour in the hospital when she so obviously wanted to manacle Dakota, regardless of her discomfort or the minimal risk Dakota posed with her limbs in plaster. She said the report would be delivered on Monday morning first thing."

"I'll do a statement as well," Mrs Jameson said. "I was there in the hospital. I saw it all. I was the one who went to get Professor Medici."

"Good, we need every bit of evidence we can if we are to rid ourselves of this scourge and prevent other guards from stepping into her shoes. I have evidence that Smith has been stealing from inmates and I want to get her charged with theft and abuse of her position." Again she paused and looked at her friends before continuing in a more timid vein. "Please remember Dakota was not hurt badly, just a bruise. After I saw the warden I got her to send the doctor to Dakota's bunk but they found her in the library, working away."

"She did not mention it today at all," Ben said. "But that is just like her not to complain."

"I'm changing my role here as well," Val announced, a hint or pride creating a half-smile. "Mrs Kinderly has asked me from Monday to be assistant deputy warden, responsible for inmate welfare. I accepted, although I told her I was thinking seriously about my future so could not commit to the long-term."

"That is fantastic, Val. You will be brilliant in that position. You are just what this place needs."

It was a lot later, getting dark, by the time Ben and Mrs Jameson left the prison for their long journey home. Val had spent almost two hours outlining some of her ideas to involve the inmates more in the running of their lives, so that they had some responsibility and something to work towards.

"She's a new person," Ben said as they drove away, the perimeter fence bending to their right and heading back towards the prison buildings, their car turning left for the way home. It was a long drive and he had to be at work at 6am the next morning.

They made it in record time, Ben abandoning fuel efficiency to gain an extra thirty minutes of precious sleep at the other end. The bank balance would have to take a bit more strain.

***

Val was early for work the next morning. She had to explain to Kyle that, while she had expected to have Monday off, she now had to go in to start her new position.

"Why aren't you wearing your uniform, Mom?"

"Because I don't need to anymore. Do I look OK?" She was wearing one of her mother's smart suits, a blue pinstripe with a light pink shirt the colour of a spring sunrise. She felt new in every way.

"Mom, if you wore your pyjamas you would look great."

"There's my boy!" She ruffled his hair and said, "Flattery will get you everywhere."

"Why aren't you in uniform?" Val had to explain to the duty assistant supervisor about her promotion. She stiffened when Val mentioned 'deputy assistant warden' and asked Val to take a seat in reception while she made a phone call.

"Mrs Kinderly will see you now," she said on returning to reception, her world turned upside down, a junior officer promoted several ranks overnight and in civvies, too.

Mrs Kinderly met her in the hall outside her office with a remark about how smart she looked but queried why wasn't she in uniform.

"None of the other deputy assistant wardens wear uniform," Val replied. "Have I done the wrong thing?"

"No, I suppose not. I hadn't quite meant it, well, no matter. It's just that you are so young. I'll take you to your office." She led Val along the corridors to the back of the prison, finally stopping at a door at the end of a long passageway populated by utility areas and storerooms. "At 8am we have a management meeting in the conference room to decide new responsibilities. I expect that meeting will start to define your job." Mrs Kinderly closed the door to Val's tiny, windowless office and looked for somewhere to sit, selecting to perch on the edge of the metal dust-covered desk. "Bennet, some things have been troubling me for a while. I want you to work towards a better relationship between guards and inmates. Right now, we have a huge overtime bill for guards and if we can cut it by promoting more responsible behaviour amongst inmates then we are going to look real good at annual review." She had to raise her voice to be heard above the laundry below.

Val bit her tongue. So this was the reason for her sudden promotion and the warden's apparent conversion. It was all about saving money.

"I'm sure we can work towards that objective, Warden. I've got some ideas already around job performance and also visiting times. I think they will both boost morale."

"Frankly, I am more interested in cutting the overtime bill. It has mushroomed this year. I want to reverse that as soon as possible."

"Yes but Mrs Kinderly, by boosting morale we increase the inmates' sense of self-worth. This will make them better behaved, hence less supervision will be required. Most of the bad behaviour comes from low self-esteem." As Val replied she thought it did not matter how an opportunity comes about, more that it does come about. She would get the reforms this place needed on the back of the warden's precious efficiency drive. The end justifies the means.

But that night, after Kyle had gone to bed, Val and her mother sewed her Deputy Assistant Warden badges onto her uniforms. She would have to explain to Kyle in the morning but it seemed more appropriate this way.

Daniel Roberts Esquire

Daniel was never called Dan anymore, not since his university tutor had started using the long version and it had stuck.

"It sounds more substantial," he had said. "You need a certain amount of substance and gravitas if you are to get on in this world." He had not added that if you did not have natural presence you needed to cultivate it. Daniel's parents had welcomed the change and 'Dan' was consigned to the scrapbook of grade school pictures, Boy Scouts outings and first tentative girlfriends. They took the tutor's advice to heart; after all, they were paying extra for it.

Daniel had been a good-looking teenager, blond wavy hair to just below his collar, and a habit of tossing it away from his face; blue eyes and perfected teeth. He was an only child, which meant he had all his parents' love and resources ploughed into him. He kept growing through to his early twenties, reaching just over six feet tall by his 21st Birthday party; a weekend with a dozen friends on a rented motor yacht in the Caribbean. He had been allowed to choose half the friends, while his parents carefully selected the other half. They had chosen wisely, as his later career demonstrated.

His drug phase was a distant memory. It had only really lasted for half a semester in 12th grade. Just like smoking in 7th grade, it was cool for the moment. It was forgotten so he could happily fill out forms for employment stating he had never taken illegal drugs. In fact, while he had bought and sold on the fringes of the criminal world, dipping in like someone checking the temperature of the bath, he had never enjoyed consuming the substances and had often pretended to be high for effect.

He was proud of his résumé. Sometimes, he did things just to put them on it. Hence the soup kitchens, the charity runs and the boring church committees. Now at the age of twenty-nine, his résumé was the perfect door-opener and it had led to the steps of Congress. Angela, his gorgeous wife and the mother of his two children, had just told him that her daddy had decided to retire this year. He had a commanding majority and was gifting it to his son-in-law.

Angela was in love with Daniel. He knew because she was always so eager to wave him off in the morning, lining up the two little children before the nanny took over. Early morning was their family time for most evenings he or Angela would be out at functions.

His phone rang as he got into his Mercedes. It was his new PA. He had chosen her two weeks ago when his previous one had suddenly handed in her notice to move to Oregon. She had been a league and a half above the other candidates: sensual with silky dark skin and a perfect résumé. He was looking forward to working with her.

"Mr Roberts, would it be possible to move your 11am appointment to 11.20 so we can fit in the photo shoot at 10.30? I picked up your new suit from the tailors and also took the liberty of selecting a new shirt and tie for the occasion. I went to Tamary's and put it on your account." She had initiative as well as looks. "Good, I'll call the Town Hall right now and put them off to 11.20. Remember this evening you are driving to DC for the first election strategy meeting and Angela is getting driven in later for the dinner."

He eased the Mercedes around the wide suburban roads and onto the freeway. He hit the CD player and Mozart thumped out. He did not like classical music but was trying to get familiar with it. He would play this symphony with Angela on the way home from DC tonight and hum along with it.

The phone rang again. He hit the switch to put it on speakerphone, but left Mozart playing. It sounded impressive in the background.

"Yes."

"Its Tess, sir." His PA's sexy voice came over the speakers. "I have someone trying to get in to see you. He is a British aristocrat." Daniel rushed to turn the music off but hit the wrong button and rap music blared out. He hit the switch in frustration and turned the volume up to full. Finally, he silenced the noise with the correct switch, then had to correct his swerve into the next lane.

"Say that again?" This was not the image he wanted to have with Tess.

"Sir, there is a British aristocrat wanting to make an appointment with you as soon as possible."

"Can you fit him in?" This was impressive.

"I think in a couple of weeks."

"No, sooner than that, as soon as possible."

"Well, Mr Roberts, if I cancel the cancer charity planning meeting this afternoon I could squeeze him in between the review of your speech for dinner tonight and the Zanesville Chamber of Commerce meeting."

"Squeeze away, Tess, squeeze away." He loved hearing her husky voice, especially with the natural deference towards him. "What is this guy's name?"

"Sir John Fitzroy. "

"Is he related to the King?"

"I'll have to ask, sir." It was only after he had terminated the call that he realised that he had not asked what the meeting was to be about.

***

"So, Sir Fitzroy."

"It's Sir John."

"Sure, so Sir John, exactly how are you related to the King?"

"He is my second cousin," Sir John lied; it was actually that they were fourth cousins of a sort, in that Sir John's stepmother was descended from Queen Victoria.

"Wow, so you are real royalty then?"

"Yes, but that is not what I came to talk to you about." They had decided to make a direct approach to Daniel Roberts in the hope that he would say something to incriminate himself. Sir John had a small recording device in his pocket. He switched it on as he sat down.

"I've come about Dakota Jameson."

"Who?"

"An old flame of yours from 12th grade. She went inside on a drug conviction just after leaving high school."

Daniel rocked back on his chair and thought hard. The name was familiar, but there had been so many girls. Probably some he had never known the names of, most others had been long-forgotten.

"I don't recall anyone of that name," he said, with apparent sincerity. "Can you jog my memory?" Momentarily, Sir John thought what if Dakota really was guilty and was leading them all on a dance? But then he pictured her open, honest face and knew it not to be.

"Dakota Jameson, long blonde hair, deep blue eyes, pretty face, very attractive." He showed a photograph from the yearbook.

"Oh, her!" Daniel exclaimed. "I hardly knew her."

"She was put away for carrying drugs just after graduation from high school."

"So? She will have served her time and I hope she has sorted her life out and got on the straight again." He did remember something of her now, but it had been a wild time; memory of each event was vague. Then he had a thought. "Are you collecting for her? Has she started a foundation to help others? I would be glad to donate…" It would look good and he could afford it.

"No Mr Roberts, she is still inside. She got forty-two years."

"No? That is insane!" This conversation was turning a bit uncomfortable. He now had the slightest memory, long buried, of some involvement. But that could not be for he was clean of drugs, always had been.

"It is insane, but it happened. She is due out on 1st November 2059 a few weeks after her sixtieth birthday."

"My God!" was all that Daniel said. Sir John wondered whether he was making progress, dashed at the young man's next words. "But I don't see how this can have any bearing on me. I am not yet in Congress so can't really take up her cause. It would be pointless right now."

"She was caught with drugs on her," Sir John tried again.

"I imagine so. But that is quite a sentence."

"They were your drugs."

"Impossible. I've never taken drugs, never even seen any. I don't believe in that stuff." A scene flashed into his mind of a brown paper package, a cousin when he did not have any.

"You asked her to mail a package to your cousin." The brown paper package, he had dictated an address: 3196 Cleveland Avenue. Or had he? Surely not? How come an address had come to him? But he had never had anything to do with drugs. It had to be wrong.

"Well, that proves it. I don't even have a cousin. Both my parents are only children, like me." Said as if it was both an accomplishment in itself and a conclusion to their conversation: absolute proof. He leaned forward across his desk, the image of a young man going places, his doubts suddenly receded. "It would seem to me that this young lady, who I had the very slightest acquaintance with a decade or so ago, has been reading up on my success and is leading you to believe a pack of lies. She clearly thinks that throwing accusations around will take some of the heat off her and maybe she can achieve a reduced sentence. Now, if you have nothing else, I would like to move on to my next meeting."

***

"So I failed again," Sir John reported back to Ben and Frank at the Little Kitchen, now their established meeting venue. "I don't seem to be able to make any impression on these people when I confront them. Truth is, I would be terrified if someone came up to me with accusations like this, but both Daniel bloody Roberts and Albert bloody Essington just seem to shrug them off."

"Maybe, but I am not so sure. I think you planted some seeds. You mentioned that he seemed flustered," Frank commented thoughtfully. "I've told you about the set-up with Albert 'bloody' Essington. Maybe we need to think outside the box with our up-and-coming congressman as well." His use of Sir John's 'bloody' eased the gloom and caused all three to smile. They talked on with plans, while May served them pizza and another huge salad, shared from a central bowl with chillies and other peppers. Ben was relaxed about payment but had something he very much wanted to raise with Sir John. He grabbed his opportunity as the focus of their discussion moved to Dakota.

"Sir John, I think you should come meet Dakota on Sunday. Mrs Jameson and I are going as usual." He explained that Dakota seemed stuck on her research into Richard Sutherland. "He just seems to travel to Philadelphia on his own initiative and then disappears for six weeks until he travels back."

"I'll come gladly; looking forward to meeting her at last." Truth was, he also looked forward to immersing himself with another expert in the past. Sometimes the present was just too difficult.

May came by with the coffee pot.

"Pie for y'all?" All three confirmed. Then Sir John pulled something out of his jacket pocket.

"I've got something for you," he said to May and unfolded the paper he had pulled out.

"Hear that, Mavis? Shakespeare's got me a prezzie. What you got, Shakey? Did you get something for Mavis, too?"

"It's for both of you." Sir John was absolutely solemn, playing the part perfectly. Mavis came over and they both listened to Sir John's explanation. "It is a recipe for an ancient and traditional British dish." He flattened out the computer print-out as he talked, as if preparing a prize presentation. "I am an historian by profession and I can verify that this dish goes back to the times of the ancient Britons. Think Boadicea. That fearsome queen is known to have had a partiality for this recipe. It is as old as the hills. Julius Caesar is said to have invaded in order to obtain the ingredients. The Gauls tried to barter gold for it. It's a very special pudding called..." he paused a second to check he was getting maximum attention from the other diners, "it's called

Spotted Dick."

That brought the house down. Mavis and May could not stop laughing for ten minutes and everyone in the restaurant was caught up in it.

"You have it with custard," Sir John explained.

"Spotted Dick and custard! Whatever made you bring that up?" Frank asked in the parking lot when they had finally got out.

"Just for fun. I thought they would appreciate it. Look, they are still laughing, you can see them through the window."

"On to more serious stuff," Ben said, although he had been giggling with all of them. "I'll pick you up on Sunday morning at your hotel at 6.45 sharp. I don't want to be late."

After Ben and Sir John left the parking lot, Frank sat a while in his car before driving off. He was going down to Charlottesville for the weekend. He had a lot to think about and it was always easier to think on the back of a horse. Finally, he started the engine, turned up the air conditioning, and slipped his truck into Drive. There were two big circles of problems swirling around, sometimes meeting before going off in different directions. There was the constitutional circle and the incarceration circle. Both had to be solved and it was clear that Sir John was not a problem-solver. Ben would be able to help but the problems were really firmly on his shoulders. He sighed as he slipped onto Interstate 66 and eased into the flow of traffic. Tomorrow he would go for a long ride.

Revelation

On impulse, Frank decided to go to Zanesville on Sunday. Rather than drive from Charlottesville, he made other arrangements. The helicopter picked up Ben and Mrs Jameson at a small airfield in Great Falls, Virginia, and swung down to meet Frank and Sir John, who had driven down for the riding the day before, at Hunt Ridge. They were met at Zanesville airport by a black Suburban with tinted windows. Their driver was out of a movie, with black suit, white shirt, black tie and dark glasses. But there the similarity ended for 'Cars for the Busy' was a one-man show, with the driver and owner being a small, skinny man in his seventies with a big smile and a bigger voice.

"Contrary to popular opinion, Zanesville was not named after the celebrated author of Westerns, although Zane Grey did grow up here. It was named after Ebenezer Zane, who founded the city in 1797. That is even before my time." He gave a running commentary from the driver's seat as he took the car onto the freeway towards the prison on the eastern outskirts. It was another too hot, too still day, with very few people outside.

"A warning," Ben announced. "There is no air conditioning in the prison."

"So we all have to suffer, regardless of whether we were convicted or not," Sir John replied. "I can't take this heat. Where I grew up we were lucky to see thirty days a year when it reached seventy."

It was Sir John's and Frank's first visit to a penal institution. But to seasoned visitors such as Ben and Mrs Jameson, the changes were obvious and stark. At first it seemed like change for the worse. They were much more thoroughly searched on entry.

"We have to make sure there is no contraband whatsoever," the young guard explained. "Contraband is currency in here and currency is fought over." This said by way of explanation in a co-operative way, rather than as an instruction.

On entering the visiting room, Ben and Mrs Jameson were very surprised. There were new small wooden cubicles to waist-height to give a little privacy. The next shock was seeing the prisoners come in to the room.

Dakota entered and she was walking with a stick, left arm completely out of plaster and right in a reduced plaster. She wore a yellow t-shirt under her orange dress and was completely free of any form of restraint. The manacles she had worn on every other visit were not present. Nor, Ben noted, were they on any of the other inmates. Despite the stick, Dakota seemed to walk on air.

"Hi, Mom. Hi, Ben." She kissed them both warmly and then turned to meet the other two visitors. Behind her, a guard strolled down the passageway between the rows of cubicles. Ben noticed that mothers were touching children, lovers touching each other; this was never before permitted other than on arrival and departure.

"This is Val's doing," Dakota said. "You see, there is only one guard wondering around and Val up at the front. Two guards when before they had six or seven in the room. We can touch our visitors provided there is nothing indecent." To make her point, Dakota leaned forward and kissed both Ben and her mother on the cheek, then stretched out to hold their hands.

This was a different visit to the others. Both Frank and Sir John were not prepared to sit back as Ben had done in the early days. Frank asked for a summary of her case from Dakota's own lips. She gave this over twelve minutes of quiet speech, her voice still at inmate level. She recapped on the points of weakness in her lawyer's work and outlined the possibilities for referral to another court.

"I'm not a lawyer," she said as she finished her summary. "But I can see that Essington did not do several things he should have done and was far too keen to earn fees and not so concerned with obtaining justice."

"We thought it was for the best," Mrs Jameson said.

"Of course you did, Mother. You did wonderful. You

have given up so much to help me." Dakota squeezed her mother's hand and then held it lingeringly, reinforcing the point that they were allowed to touch now.

"Well," said Frank, "we have some ideas to get even here. It might take a bit of time but don't give up hope."

"I've never given up hoping, Mr Williams," Dakota replied firmly. "Sometimes it is all you have to hang on to."

Sir John then took over and turned the subject matter to the past. As Dakota described her studies on Richard Sutherland, Ben noticed her coming alive, her animated voice and good left hand fully employed in making her points. She was a joy to watch.

And her smile lit everything up and rolled back the years of incarceration. She was not a conventional beauty, but something shone from deep inside her. Ben could picture her face perfectly when he lay in bed at night, too hot and too involved to sleep. It was like she was lying there with him as the trains trundled heavily down the tracks; car horns and doors slamming adding melody and beat to the rhythm set by the crickets in their thousands. His nocturnal music was altogether more natural, more varied across space, than Dakota's, where the heavy concrete walls shut her in and all external sound out.

After watching and listening for some time, Ben decided to slip away and seek out Val. She had left the visiting room, replaced by another female guard. He found her downstairs in the visitors' reception area.

"Hi, Val."

"Hi, Ben. Who's that dishy guy in with Dakota?"

"The American or the English one?"

"The American."

"Frank Williams. He's a very wealthy businessman."

"It gets better and better!"

"Tell me about all this. The changes, I mean."

So Val relayed everything that had occurred since their last visit two weeks earlier. She had forced the changes through a lot of resistance.

"It was the financial savings that made the argument, not concern for the welfare of the inmates."

"That sounds about right for this place. But Val, you have done wonders in just two weeks."

"Thanks. That means a lot to me."

***

Sir John kept everyone waiting at the end of the visit by disappearing moments before the end. Val sent someone to look for him forty minutes after all the other visitors had left the prison. The young guard came back saying he had been located in the warden's office.

"There was a lot of joking and laughter going on," he said. Ben noticed that Val got much more co-operation from the younger staff members. Those over forty shunned her or obeyed in a wooden, sultry fashion. She was, at twenty-three, quite possibly the youngest assistant deputy warden the prison had ever had.

"I'll go up there," Val said. "Barnes, stay here with the visitors."

They waited another ten minutes for Sir John to come down.

"Sorry to keep you waiting. I was just getting to know Iris Kinderly, the warden. Doubly sorry because after making you wait for me I'm actually going to stay here. She's agreed for me to work with Dakota for a while here in the prison."

"You mean you charmed her into letting you do this," Ben said, feeling he could read Sir John so well now.

"I was rather pleasant, I suppose. And I did exaggerate slightly my connections back in England. It usually works quite well." He winked at Val as he spoke, including her in his little conspiracy.

"Well, I wish you had got her to agree to daily showers." Val replied.

"I'll work on that. But personal practicalities come to the fore. I said I would start tomorrow with Dakota, but I am without toothbrush and clean underwear, moreover I have to find somewhere to lay my head."

"Easy," replied Frank. "Come back to DC with us tonight and then the chopper can take you back in the morning, complete with all your kit."

It was agreed. Sir John and Val filled out some paperwork for the morning and they were off again, back to the airport.

"It's so nice to see you again," Val said as they filed out of reception. "And so nice to meet you, Mr Williams and Sir John." Was there the slightest emphasis in her voice when she mentioned Frank's name?

"Call me Frank."

"My name's Val." She said shyly, but the emphasis was there.

***

"You have to approach it in a different way," Sir John explained to Dakota. They were sitting in the prison library. "Lord, it's hot in here." He wiped the sweat from his forehead and shifted on his hard chair. "My office is bigger than this library."

"Really?"

"No, I was joking."

"Oh, of course." Dakota was finding it hard to understand Sir John's humour. "What do you mean by a different approach?"

"OK, you're not Dakota Jameson and you're not in this lousy bloody festering prison. You're not even a lady. Instead, you are one Richard Sutherland; enormously wealthy trader, but also a man, an old man nearing the end of your life."

"OK."

"Now, get in the mood of it. You're a wealthy old man, lots of material success, lots of contacts all over the globe. But you have conflicts, two in particular. First, you've never had a happy domestic life. You have four children but none of them are legitimate. Your wife is alive but beyond

178

childbearing age and it was a marriage for advantage, not love. Face it, Sutherland, you're not going to have a legitimate child. Your estates and most of your wealth are entailed to your nephew, Alexander Sutherland, the son of your deceased brother. You are fond of Alexander but don't see him as an effective heir who will continue your business efforts. Furthermore, he has a propensity to spend money. As a careful Scot, you disapprove of this. So you are frustrated and there is not much you can do about the true Sutherland legacy living on and thriving. It is out of your hands." Sir John watched Dakota as she sat with eyes closed, away in another place altogether.

"Now to the other conflict and this one you can do something about, at least you can try."

"What is it?" Dakota asked, getting into the role-play. "What can I try to achieve to balance my frustrating personal life?"

"You have divided loyalties." Sir John was a great storyteller and knew when to pause for effect. A full minute passed while he let the divided loyalty idea sink in and work around her brain.

"You mean two countries?" she said as she worked it out.

"Precisely; and well done, others would have taken much longer to get there, if at all. You love Great Britain and you love America. The saddest day of your long life was when the War of Independence broke out. But you are over that. You have moved on." Another pause, while the prison library clock ticked on the seconds; seconds that represented over a thousand lives being wasted within those grey and green painted walls. Every second on the clock was a thousand wasted seconds, one for each inmate. Nothing Sir John had seen in the last ten days had convinced him that prison was anything but bad for all involved: inmates, guards, wardens, visitors, broken families, taxpayers. Surely the mark of civilisation was not to incarcerate as many as possible but as few as could be managed?

"Now, you want peace between the two countries you love, but not any old peace. Remember, you are a man of the world, a businessman. You want a peace that will allow business to prosper and your two countries to be the mainstays of the trading world. You would have preferred how it had been before but recognise that it cannot be that way in the future so you want the next best thing – two friendly and co-operative nations working together."

"Yes, I get that," Dakota said, eyes still closed. Her mind was in Philadelphia, actually in the Hollingsworth household with Sidney and Sally Ann, sitting out the blizzard, waiting for the calm in order to act. "But what now?"

"Well, that's as far as I know," Sir John replied, snapping the mood. "I can't spoon-feed you all the way through your bloody thesis, dear lady! Now, I think it is time for my Spam sandwich." Sir John had been offered meals in the staff canteen but had declined, preferring Dakota to bring two inmate meals to the library, where they ate as they worked.

***

Mrs Kinderly sat back on her swivel chair and looked at Sir John over the rim of her glasses. She was in her own territory, her comfortable and spacious office overlooking the lawns at the front of the prison; lawns kept immaculate by a team of inmates, heads bowed as they raked and weeded, clipped and edged like beings from another world, like the slaves of old. She often thought how the lawns made the first sight for visitors, other than the fences and walls, of course. It was worth every ounce of effort going into those lawns for they announced to the world the efficiency and order within. Efficiency, in the prison world of course, was measured as the neatness of output with no regard to the volume of input. It was another example of the crazy rules that governed the lives of inmates and guards like top-heavy fractions teetering on the brink.

But if she was in her own familiar territory, why was she so on edge? Behind Sir John was a large glass door bookcase with rows of federal prison regulations on top, studies on prison reform on the middle shelf and guides to rehabilitation on the bottom. It gave a solid impression, though she had to get it dusted regularly, as she did the heavy leather chairs and the enormous mahogany desk she now sat behind. This was her inner territory, designed to be equally impressive and imposing, for visitors and inmates both. Very few people entered without an invitation, her fearsome secretary saw to that. Yet Sir John had strolled in here on several occasions without any difficulties at all. It was his easy-going presumptuousness that set her on edge.

She looked again at Sir John. He was a charming man: light-brown, well cut and wavy hair; very dark eyes; a smile that was cheeky, inviting, yet also commanding. It made her think of a World War II general in a movie but she could not remember its name. His every action and his whole appearance spoke of charisma. Moreover, he had an undeniable knack for always being perfectly presentable.

And what of her, the other party to this conversation which she was not quite sure where it was going? Her marriage had been a disaster, there was no doubt about that. Her husband had had affairs, witnessed in a child that was not hers. It had been a hell of a divorce; bitter, deeply hurtful the things he had claimed. And the irony was that she had stayed true while he had played. She had never loved him, more passion and advantage, as he was a politician and as ambitious as she. And passion fades, just as advantage can frustrate. But then, when free to love, she had been hurt by Declan Dacey, her boss. The only thing that he had brought her was promotion. But was it promotion, to this ghastly prison? Could she bear it as a stepping-stone? And then the trio of misery had been completed with little Stacy. She could not say she loved Stacy; it was too short, lasting just one morning, but she had been enormously attracted to her as a lost, timid soul to protect and cherish.

She had sworn never to love again but she could do with a man like Sir John to add some spice to her life. She thought, but was not sure, that the wife of a baronet would have a title of her own. As the storm clouds built their heavy presence outside her air-conditioned, supremely quiet and pristine office, she imagined for a brief minute that she was a baroness or whatever on the arm of this charming, handsome ornament of a man.

But she knew instinctively that it was all surface stuff with this historian from Britain. He would entertain her and charm her as long as it suited him; there was nothing more to be gained from it.

Unless, that is, she could turn his interest to some form of advantage for her career that had become the central purpose of her life, now that tenderness was banished. But how? He was talking about the ongoing provision of books for the library, which she knew was in a pitiful state. The problem had always been financial. Bennet had blown any discretionary funds on the visitor room refurbishment. She had backed Bennet's initiative, for it gave a good impression and had contributed to a solid reduction in manpower, paying for the outlay already. The report was already in to her boss detailing the substantial reduction in overtime and consequential financial impact. He had called her, obviously delighted. But now the coffers were empty. Savings made were never returned to the prison.

Now, she considered, she had to build on this initial success if she had any chance of succeeding her boss on his retirement, but how to do it without the resources to invest?

"Sir John, nothing would give me greater pleasure than being able to buy more books for the library," she lied, hoping she sounded convincing. "But sadly there is no cash. I can't magic up funds I do not have, much as I would love to engender a true spirit of education and self-improvement amongst the inmates." As the platitudes poured out on automatic, the main part of her mind was thinking furiously as to how she could take advantage of this. But Sir John beat her to it.

"I can probably remedy that. Back at Cambridge we have many thousands of books in storage. No doubt I could arrange a loan."

"But the transportation?"

"I could have words with a few people. There are funds

available. It is just a matter of putting it in the right light."

"Well, that would be wonderful."

"But." Sir John used the pause technique again; it was always successful. Outside, the sky was getting darker by the minute, pressure was building, sending shadows darting across the desk like invading creatures in a second-rate sci-fi movie. Thunder rolled, then lightening attacked with jagged blue scimitars aimed at the prison itself. They were under siege in their climate-controlled room. "But it would be enormously helpful if I could demonstrate the commitment to learning in this facility so as to persuade those who control the purse strings." He left it quiet for a moment, then added, "It could be the start of a great new initiative in prison reform: active encouragement of education at every level, pioneered by Jameson with her MA, no doubt to be followed by a doctorate."

"Is she bright enough?" Mrs Kinderly asked. She had been turned down for a doctorate - bitter memories - and had gone into industry instead.

"She is one of the brightest people I have ever come across," Sir John answered. But this could not be the case, Mrs Kinderly considered; after all, she was dumb enough to be caught with drugs. She was an inmate, after all.

Of Nationhood and All that Follows

Dick Turnby was not in a mood to tolerate anyone, let alone pranksters wasting his time. He was a man of business, drafted into government after a solidly successful career making a good-sized fortune. He was now a household name, instantly recognisable; not someone to give time to dreamers on a fool's errand.

"Dick, humour them for me," the Presiden

t had said. So he would, but for no other reason. "Spend twenty minutes with them, no more, and give me a one-page report. We'll go over it together on the way to the United Nations dinner tonight."

"You've got five minutes." His aide ushered in Marcus Hibbert.

"I'll need a little longer," Marcus replied, holding out his hand but ignored.

"I said five minutes. I meant it." Turnby did not get up from his huge desk, which had enough space to lay out a World War II battle plan, ladies in dark green pushing wooden formations here and there with long rakes. His back was to the large floor-to-ceiling window overlooking the White House lawns' a picture of power; gold cords holding back deep red curtains with a sweep like a lady's gown, matching the red pile carpet that was new that year. His aide had set a single low, delicate, upright chair on its own four feet from the desk. Marcus took in the scene in a moment and decided not to co-operate. He had played the same game himself many a time. There were advantages to a sixty-year professional career. He strode over to an armchair in the corner and sat down, placing his large briefcase on the antique low table that bore nothing but a photograph of Turnby shaking hands with the Chinese leader. The aide was about to say something in an attempt to redirect their visitor to the chair in front of the desk but then thought better of it.

He stood, hands hovering and fidgeting, in a position midway between the two protagonists, for that is what they had become.

"You should listen carefully and report straight to the President," Marcus spoke in a quiet voice so that Turnby was struggling to hear.

"Get out of the way," Turnby roared at his aide. The aide jumped back, hit the table and knocked the photograph onto the floor.

"I'm sorry, sir, I'll stand over there." He hastily put the photo back, adjusted it so that the Chinese leader was looking straight at Turnby behind his desk, then retreated to a corner of the room where the heavy bookcases that lined two walls met. Marcus could see the gold letter plating on the spines of the books behind the aide, seemingly perching on his shoulders like the gaudy epaulettes of a shady African dictator. He could not make out the titles from the distance across the room but they looked too neat to have been used regularly if at all.

"Say again," Turnby said to Marcus. So Marcus repeated his instruction, still firm, but quieter than the first time. Finally, Turnby gave in and walked over to where Marcus was sitting, slumping grumpily in the other armchair by the table. In an effort to appear nonchalant he put both feet up on the table, crossed them at the ankles, and stretched back with his arms behind his head, elbows out like some form of exotic insect frozen while doing a love dance.

It was five past two by then; the exact time at which Marcus was supposed to be leaving. He stood up and picked up his briefcase.

"Where the hell are you going?" Turnby questioned.

"You gave me five minutes on the most important constitutional matter since Independence and those five minutes are up. I hope you have enough to report to the President."

"Sit down... please."

So Marcus sat. He talked in the same quiet voice and Turnby listened. They were still there at five past three and the same at five past four. Now Turnby was asking questions, starting with the obvious.

"How do we know this is true?"

"The documents have been validated by four eminent bodies in Britain and now another three in America, there is no doubt."

"What on earth does it mean?"

"It means, Mr Turnby, that legally America has never been a country. It is still a part of the British Empire."

"How can this be?"

"We really don't know and are still trying to determine how it happened."

Finally Turnby asked, "What do we do now?"

The answer: "Constitutionally we need to wait for direction from the British Government."

"Do they know?"

"No, not yet. But one of my clients is a British citizen. He is obliged to inform them."

"Who are your clients?"

"I can't divulge that right now. I don't have their permission."

"What about the election next year?" This was looming and Turnby hoped to add re-election for the President to his impressive résumé.

"Again from a constitutional perspective," Marcus replied, "there can be no elections because there is no body of law - no constitution - governing them."

Marcus did not leave Turnby's office until after 6pm and then only because the aide coughed and reminded Turnby of his pending dinner engagement. Once alone, Turnby pulled out a single piece of expensive paper. He wrote his report in thirty words, read it over again:

'We're screwed, America does not exist, need to silence these lunatics before it gets out. Hibbert refused to say who his clients are. Suggest top level activity to determine identity.'

He sealed it and told his aide on pain of death to carry it straight to the President and place it directly in her hands.

Marcus made one call from his phone when it had been returned to him after he left the White House. He called the office and Tammy answered it.

"Operation Rewrite has commenced," was all he said, then turned off his phone and placed it behind his front tyre before he reversed back out of his parking space and left the car park.

Then he drove to the airport, where the company jet took him to Roanoke in the Blue Ridge Mountains. A nondescript car was waiting at the airport. He jumped in the back and three hours later, after several twists and doubling-backs to ensure he was not being followed, he arrived at the Williams estate outside Charlottesville, where both Franks welcomed him to Hunt Ridge.

***

When the FBI raided the offices of Hibbert Fisher and Welling that evening they found a dozen lawyers and paralegals working diligently at that late hour, Mike Welling amongst them.

They found nothing despite a team poring over the premises for three-and-a-half hours. There was nothing to link the firm to the clients in question: no files, notes or diary entries. As their frustration grew, so they took less care with the paperwork, flinging whole cabinets onto the floor, a spite taking over.

"Who are the clients you are working for, Mr Welling?"

"We work for a lot of clients." So the conversation went on as they worked from office to office.

"Off-site storage locations?"

"We don't rent any off-site storage."

"We'll get there, just a matter of time."

But time was against them that day for at half past twelve there was a phone call and they all left rapidly.

"We'll be back," the senior investigator said, but it was more to save face than anything.

Mike Welling made one short phone call and then left for

187

his home and bed. They would start the clear-up in the morning.

***

A few minutes later, Sir John's alarm clock rang in his London flat. It was an irritating electronic beep that got louder as it was ignored. Sir John was already in the shower but it penetrated the noise of the rushing water until he finally got out of the cubicle and walked across the bedroom to silence it.

It was a big day and he was already in a bad mood.

Kirsten Fisher was still in bed in the spare room. He would leave her for a while, but they would need to catch the cab in little over an hour to be sure of making their 10am appointment in Whitehall.

He looked out of the window over the old Docklands. There was a buzz to this place that he liked, but only for a few days at a time. He only really felt at home in their old farmhouse outside Cambridge, with its rambling outhouses and selection of thrown-together stables. It was the perfect place for the children to grow up in. When he thought about it he was glad the ancestral home, the ancient Scottish castle, had gone two generations back. It liberated him, although occasionally he had visions of playing the laird with magnificent, never-ending hospitality.

Outside and down below in the streets it was well into the working day at 7.55am. Many of the bankers, he knew from various friends, had been at their desks since before six. He was always thankful that the bends in his life had taken him into academia. It suited him and the alternative seemed indescribably tedious. As an historian he could indulge himself while maintaining discipline amongst a crowd of the finest minds. It was a good life.

He called his wife, who was competing today with her pony and trap, the children going along with her, their eldest competing in a gymkhana at the same place.

"I wish I could be with you," he said, and he meant it.

"Bring your American friend up for the weekend."
"I've already asked her."

***

It was Kirsten's first time to London; first time outside the United States, other than a two-week missionary trip to Peru with her church the summer before she started at law school. Sir John planned to spoil her after their meeting with a whirlwind tour of the main sites: Buckingham Palace, Westminster Abbey, the Houses of Parliament and the National Portrait Gallery, then tea at the Dorchester before catching the evening train to Cambridge for a weekend in the country. They would return on Sunday evening to make themselves available for an early Monday morning follow-up meeting then the British Museum, the Tower of London and possibly his favourite, Madame Tussauds, before her flight back on Tuesday morning.

However, he had not planned on the tenacity and ambition of the Foreign Secretary.

After preliminaries with civil servants, reasonably high in rank to reflect Sir John's status, they were ushered into a large meeting room, offered coffee, and asked to wait for thirty minutes while various people were gathered. If Sir John had seen the frantic activity behind the smooth exterior he would have been flattered at the attention they were receiving, although also frustrated that his plans to impress Kirsten would inevitably be postponed. By noon, he had abandoned the National Portrait Gallery. Tea at the Dorchester went at 2pm. More postponements followed as the day became peppered with meeting after meeting.

Sir John and Kirsten saw a drifting-in of senior government officials from a little after noon. By one o'clock most of the forty chairs around the large oval table were filled. Two ladies in smart corporate-style domestic wear brought around a vast selection of sandwiches. Shortly afterwards the Foreign Secretary arrived. Max Heaton was a giant of a man with untidy silver hair and a vocab that had not moved on from the rugby fields of public school, tidied up a bit by his short service commission spent mostly in the battlefields of the Middle East.

"Sir John, begin at the beginning, don't stop until the end." He might as well have issued an instruction not to interrupt, for nobody did.

For once Sir John did not embellish, nor seek to use his techniques to build up suspense. He obeyed the Foreign Secretary to the letter. Most people did.

"Questions, ladies and gentlemen?" Heaton asked at the end. There was a ten-minute period of questions; the discipline was such that everybody thought their question through before asking it, not risking the scathing rebuke they would get from loose thinking.

After ten minutes, Heaton stood up at the head of the table and summarised the situation. "American Independence never happened. At least, therefore, the original thirteen colonies are still colonies of the British Empire. The holder of the bearer document is (a) automatically a British citizen and (b) our Governor for the colonies in question. The holder is, strangely enough, one Benjamin Franklin, security guard at the White House." Then he paused, looking around the table, much as Sir John would have done if he had dared, before adding, "I can just see Turnby's face as he takes this in. What a picture that would make!"

"You are forgetting one thing." Kirsten's Boston accent cut across the room.

"Being?"

"You have the law on your side but you are dealing with a body of proud people. You are going to get the War of Independence all over again, only this time fought with rockets and grenades rather than musket and cannon."

But Heaton was not thrown in the slightest. "My dear," he said, without any condescension at all. "My dear, you don't know what my plans are and you won't know until I have spoken to the PM. At present I don't know which way this is going to fall so let's not assume mayhem from the get-go."

He pushed his chair back, leaving his half-eaten ham and mustard sandwich on brown oatmeal in front of him and left the room with a final call. "Jenkins, you and your lot come with me, the rest stay here and work on the details of what I briefed you on. Come on, Jenks, chop chop, things to do."

There followed a long session in which government lawyers presided, asking Kirsten and Sir John question after question. The afternoon wore on, the trip around Buckingham Palace and Westminster abandoned.

At a little after 5pm they were ushered out to a smaller meeting room several floors below; probably, Kirsten thought, in the basement, where some serious men were waiting in blazers and regimental ties. They were MI5, still fit despite advancing years, dedication to their country's security etched on their purposeful faces. They grilled the pair for over two hours; no refreshments, no breaks, no discourtesy, no raised voices but certainly no humour.

"My God," said Sir John as they were led out along and up the maze of corridors and stairs. "I didn't think I would get through that."

"It was a grilling and a half, something the CIA would be proud of!" Kirsten replied, resorting to humour because she was at the end of her tether; they both were.

They thought maybe now it was over, but far from it. Sir John, on protesting, was allowed to call his wife to say they would be delayed until the morning. Then they were taken by car the short distance to Downing Street. Heaton was back with them now and explained that they would have dinner with the PM.

"Sir John, Ms Fisher, can I do anything for you?" A member of the Downing Street staff asked as soon as they arrived.

"Yes," said Kirsten. "I need a bath and change of clothes."

"Ditto."

Sir John gave his flat key with instructions on the clothes he needed, Kirsten saying to bring one of the two suitcases she had brought with her.

An hour later they were changed, relaxed in the private

dining room of the PM's flat. Other than the PM there was only the Foreign Secretary in attendance.

"Good to see you again, Bunny." The PM shook Sir John's hand warmly. Kirsten looked surprised. She had not been aware that they were acquainted.

"Sir John and I were at school together. I was a bratty older squit who thought I could order the younger ones around. Bunny, I mean Sir John, did not take orders then, or, I suspect, now."

The PM was very different to Max Heaton. Both were forceful characters but the Foreign Secretary was direct and blunt, staying on subject, while the PM wove around the subject in a sea of politeness. He wanted to know all about Kirsten and much of the evening was given over to seemingly idle chat. Yet over coffee and Scotch afterwards he displayed a crisply clear understanding of the situation without giving anything away. This man was intelligent, shrewd, and, she suspected, could be ruthless, but charming to the grave.

A car took them back to the Docklands late that night. Both were exhausted, Kirsten refusing Sir John's offer of a nightcap.

"I don't know if I am any clearer on what is going to happen," Kirsten said.

"The only thing that is clear is that it's a muddle, but that is government for you," Sir John replied then adding as he thought his joke inappropriate, "I expect there will be talks between the governments over the weekend and we will have an answer on Monday." He did not say it but thought, then I can publish my paper. History books here I come!

"You know the worst thing?" Kirsten was clearly in contemplative mood, despite her tiredness. "The feeling that our founding fathers let us down, that they backed away at the last minute and deserted the cause of nationhood and independence. And what persuaded them to do that? I would dearly love to know that." As would I, thought Sir John.

***

"Richard," the PM said in greeting, already ensuring Turnby would be bad-tempered, by elongating his name. "I believe the firm of HFW have briefed you fully on current circumstances."

"Yes. What do you want?" So now the Brits knew. The wheels of his mind churned, throwing out sleep like water sluicing down a mill. "I'm not disturbing the President at this hour without an understanding of what you want to discuss. Send me an email and I'll call you back." He slammed down the phone and laid back on the empty king-size bed. His wife was in California, visiting their grandchildren. It was even earlier there so he could not call, much as he wanted to turn to Fran. But what was he thinking? He could not even tell her anything about it. The president had sworn him to secrecy for obvious reasons.

Sleep eluded him so he rose and did an extra session in his basement gym, pumping weights first then hitting solidly at the punch bag, his favourite exercise. It rankled enormously that Marcus Hibbert had played him so well. He prided himself on playing others but had not seen it coming to him. But that older, wiser part of him that came to the fore as the energy expelled through vigorous exercise, spoke into his brain, whispering at first then speaking quite loudly and clearly. He was a vain man and this was not a time for vanity. He was also a disciplined man and this was a time for discipline. He would win for his country but not if he also sought revenge for petty matters. With a final slug at the punch bag he made his decision, went to shower and dress, and then to call the President.

Standstill or Showdown?

Sir John and Kirsten Fisher caught a mid-morning train to Cambridge and were at the Fitzroy home by lunchtime on Saturday. The truncated weekend was short and sweet, spent with horses and children, walking in the flat lands of the fens, eating wholesome food and working off the energy by indulging in games of chase and hide-and-seek. On Sunday morning they went to the service in an early medieval church built as if for a film set and supplied along with a vicar who greeted the hats and suits by name with small personal questions and updates; a man in his rightful setting.

It was almost possible during that thirty-six-hour interlude to forget that the buttons had been pressed to change the world that they knew. Like August 1939, there was a sense of inexorable change in the air. They could feel it as they walked down the sunken hedge-lined lanes or across the vast fields dotted with combine harvesters and clumps of straw bales. You could see it in the blue sky, absent any clouds, almost as if Sir John expected a Spitfire in practice for things to come to race across the upper world, drowning the gentle hum of the harvesters and people below.

But this was not a national mood: not something authors would use as a setting for sad romances or the launch of daring heroics; not something poets could scratch on paper about.

For only two people sensed this; only two people in the whole of Cambridgeshire, and they did not mention it to each other, preferring their private experience, not wanting to talk about what they had started or why. Perhaps if they had discussed it, it would become apparent that this was not a nation on the brink, gearing up for greatness, but personal ambition in its most naked and honest form. Both Sir John and the firm of HFW were driven by a sense that they were creating greatness by their actions; as Sir John put it, 'writing history as it happens'. When Kirsten examined her conscience as she hid behind a cleft in a haystack, waiting to be found by the Fitzroy children, she realised that her ambition, albeit for the firm rather than personal, was equal to that of Sir John's. She wanted HFW to be at the forefront of these crazy constitutional developments.

But how would it all end?

If she had known the transatlantic and frantic discussions filling that thirty-six-hour interlude she might have come to a depressing conclusion, but she did not and hence the thirty-six-hour interlude progressed.

**

The PM and Heaton had agreed to sleep on it before reconvening at 9am on Saturday morning. Here they had the advantage of the time difference for, by the time the PM picked up the phone at 10am it was only 5am in Washington.

By 7am in Washington the President and Turnby were together in the White House with a knot of aides, sworn like Turnby to absolute secrecy.

Turnby spoke first. "My first thought was to blast them off the face of the earth. But my second thought was to beat them at their own game. We have to find out who HFW's clients are and then work on them."

"Sir, how long do you think before the press gets hold of this?" That was Peter Naseby, a promising aide with large spectacles underlining a remarkably large forehead that, in turn, underlined a rapidly balding head.

"That's your job, Pete, I want it out of the press at all costs." The President answered for Turnby. "We just cannot afford to let a whisper of this get out until at least we have an accommodation with the British, and hopefully never at all."

"Yes, Madam President."

**

So who broke the press ban? Not a politician, nor an aide, not even a lawyer. Yet word got out. Some people would say the word always does get out somehow. Yet everyone was committed to absolute secrecy.

The answer was the instigator of so much of this and it was a careless mistake, nothing intentional. Sir John mentioned it to his wife; a slip of the tongue, an unguarded moment. He quickly swore her to silence and she readily agreed. The leak would have been sealed at that point, except their oldest daughter, fourteen-year-old Annie, heard the substance but not the warnings and she mentioned it at school the next morning to her best friend. From there it spread like fire. The press picked it up at lunchtime; by mid-afternoon it was everywhere.

It did not change a lot, it just made everyone's job that bit harder.

But it changed Trevor Hardcastle's life forever.

Trevor was not a good reporter. He had been fired from two papers, made redundant from a third, yet was still only twenty-five years old. He had a serious problem with the truth and this had got him in trouble frequently. As if to confuse, he had an engaging personality, a big smile set on a handsome face, itself perched on the body of an athlete, although not one that trained at all. He heard it first, working for the *Makenhall Chronicle*, but bypassed them, scrawling a rapid resignation letter and getting on the next train to London.

He had no problem hawking the story around the Docklands, selling different parts as an exclusive to several papers and internet sites. He was his own agent and proved himself a believable, capable salesman, netting almost a quarter of a million in twelve hours.

He was stoking up a multitude of legal battles for the future, selling stories several times over, elaborating blatantly on the truth.

Thus two sentences uttered in error by Sir John to his wife, Lady Fitzroy, went through the mangle, several mangles, and, like Chinese Whispers, came out as a million printed words.

Then when Trevor reached the grand total of one million pounds, all wired to his account, he disappeared completely.

This provoked another million written words, speculating on his vanishing act. The papers and their insurers hired detectives by the bucket load, but nobody ever found him again.

Sir John knew straight away that he was the cause. Annie told him what she had overheard and repeated and it was obvious. He was in London with Kirsten, had just finished what seemed a highly successful meeting with the British government to find a way forward,,was looking forward to an afternoon and evening showing Kirsten the sights. His wife called as he left Whitehall, putting Annie on the phone almost straight away.

"Annie dear, don't cry. This is my mistake, not yours. Don't worry about it anymore. I will sort it out."

"OK, Daddy, you are so kind."

They had to retreat back into Whitehall. The army of the press bore down on them and beat them back. There were hundreds of questions from dozens of voices, all competing with each other and ultimately merging into a cacophony of 'Why, who, where, when, what and how?'

Inside, Max Heaton was summoned, appraised, and instantly took charge. He had a minimal press release drawn up in an attempt to hold the reporters at bay. He set up a committee to deal with all press issues. He gave Kirsten and Sir John the loan of an office. Then he disappeared again in search of the PM.

Sir John immediately called Ben, but got his answerphone as he was at work, the phone ringing in his locker until it clicked over to voicemail. Then he called Mrs Jameson. She seemed confused but promised to get Ben to call the moment he got in from his shift.

Only Ben did not make it through to the end of his shift. He was summoned by radio to Mr Reading's office. Only when he got there Mr Reading was not in, instead two burly overweight CIA operatives in black suits and red ties, white button-down shirts and almost identical shaved heads, almost carried him from the security office into the White House proper. They did not speak. They left him in a small, bare office with just a table and four chairs, and locked the door as they left.

Ben waited there, fretting, until Turnby arrived.

It was a long wait.

He was left to sweat.

***

Meanwhile, Turnby and Heaton were leading their respective charges. Several phone calls were supposed to be private chats 'to resolve the situation' but were far from private, listened into by aides on either side, scribbling notes to their respective negotiators on anything that came to mind.

"I need your commitment to drop the whole thing." Turnby opened the discussion. "It is plainly ridiculous. We know all the participants and they cannot force through a reversal of 250 years of history." He was bluffing because he only knew of HFW, Ben and Sir John. He knew nothing of the two Frank Williams, then arriving by helicopter at the Great Falls airstrip, Marcus Hibbert alongside them. He also did not know who held the two documents that were rapidly changing their world.

"Max, I say again, I need your commitment to drop this ridiculous claim."

Max was without words, caught between two posts, drifting. He had a vague idea but could not frame it. He looked around his spacious office for inspiration, advice, but his aides looked down, no advice on offer.

"We are considering what to do, Dick. Let's talk again tomorrow."

"But the press..." Dick replied, frustrated at the postponement.

"We should issue a combined statement. I'll get my people working on it and get a draft to you within the hour."

"But..."

"No buts, Dick. This is the best I can do right now. We all need time to consider options." Turnby noticed the resolve returning to Max's voice and knew he had missed the opportunity to press his advantage. He would need to regroup and advance from a different point.

"Sure," replied Dick, "and in the meantime our guys will work on a draft resolution and get it over to you."

***

The two Franks - grandfather and grandson - two of the wealthiest people in America, had little trouble gaining access to Turnby. They represented a different scale to Turnby, a league he could never aspire to play in. Turnby had made many tens of millions whereas the Williams were talking tens of billions in net worth. It bought them respect and with that respect came prompt access to the higher levels of government and serious attention.

But Ben knew nothing of these events, waiting in isolation in his White House 'cell', as if separated at Ellis Island, suspected of some terrible contagion. His escorts had excelled in absolute silence. Ben knew instinctively that his detention was connected to the papers he had found, but nothing else.

The door opened at 4.15pm and Turnby entered, flanked by four aides in sober suits, but none of them heavies.

"Good afternoon, Mr Franklin. My name is Dick Turnby."

"Yes, I know who you are, sir." It was the perfect answer. Turnby held out his hand and shook Ben's with vigour. The vanity of instant recognition was something he could not resist.

"Could you come this way, please? We have much to discuss." They went along three passages and then an elevator took them down two floors, across a hallway and into Turnby's private office in the West Wing.

"Hi, Ben." It was Frank. "Grandpa and Marcus are with the President." Frank seemed in control but only just; there was something about him, like a city dweller trying to survive in the mountains, exposed to the elements and using every ounce of intelligence and knowledge available to him.

199

"Where would you like to sit, Mr Franklin?" Turnby asked, wishing his aides could not see his deference.

Ben dearly wanted to see Frank on his own, to get an explanation, some background. They deferred to him with a politeness that seemed inconsistent with the earlier silence. He was out of place. He was a security guard, not even a supervisor. He had a high school diploma, albeit a good grade average. He did not know how to behave or what to say. He felt the perspiration rising, plus all eyes on him. He was a very small fish in a vastly complicated pond, matted with treacherous weeds and predators. He took a deep breath and looked around the office. With his heart pumping, sweat rising, not trusting to speak for fear of squeakiness, he nodded towards the large meeting table and walked to a chair in the middle of one long side, but back against the wall. It seemed better that way.

Within an instant the other attendees dropped into seats, Turnby at the head with a chair with arms, Frank opting for the one next to Ben, the other aides scattered around. Frank put his hand on Ben's arm and smiled. It was the most he could do right now.

Even a billionaire was lost at that time.

Letter Six

That evening, alone in a spacious guest bedroom in the White House, they brought Ben a suitcase of his clothes, quickly packed by Mrs Jameson, who used her passkey to enter his mini-apartment. He opened the suitcase after a long shower, seeking fresh clothes. The first thing he saw was his mail. A letter from the bank, no doubt lamenting the closing of his savings account as the balance was now too small to retain the account. He did not read it, for underneath was a letter from Dakota. Forgetting his promise to be ready in forty-five minutes, he tore open the letter, seeking what had become the familiar and warm communication from her.

My dearest, dearest Ben, I miss you so much when you are not here, it is like an ache, a cancer in my stomach that will not go away. I wish so many things, of course, but they would all be swept aside if I could just have you. I love you so much. Your last letter was so lovely and kind. Knowing that my feelings are reciprocated makes these walls that hold me vanish. I am completely free when I read one of your letters. You have given that to me and I thank you with all my heart.

She doesn't get it, thought Ben. She is the one giving so much when she has so little. His eyes lost focus a minute as he imagined her sitting in the library writing these beautiful words to him. Sir John had described the library to him as a 'dirty little squalid place with ply-board tables, incredibly uncomfortable chairs and a few miserable outdated volumes on various disparate subjects'. It was typical Sir John talk, but it brought to mind the stark contrast, especially with his current accommodation in the White House. Ben was a guest of the President, in a room full of elegant furniture, with a bathroom bigger than his whole studio apartment and a bell to summon service beside the bed; only he knew he was highly unlikely to use it, lacking the courage.

Grab your beer and read on, my love, for I have made some
amazing discoveries with Sir John's help.

Ben had noticed a discreet fridge in the corner and was
delighted to find a selection of beers within it. He chose an
armchair by the window and went back to Philadelphia in
early 1783.

Richard woke up, groaning from aching bones. Rupert eased him
out of bed. Rupert had stoked the bedroom fire half an hour earlier
while his master still slept, a light snore indicating restful peace.
But the air was still frigid and he could only imagine what it was
like for the old man in his care. One of the house servants entered
with hot water for the bath and Richard, with Rupert's assistance,
slipped into the warm and comforting water.

It was a frustrating time and Rupert felt keenly for his master.

The storm had worked its way out of Philadelphia a week
earlier, rolling towards the Atlantic to pick up more moisture from
the sea. It had been a heavy storm, lasting five days and dumping
almost four feet of snow. Immediately afterwards the emphasis had
been on shovelling, fixing, and replenishing supplies. Rupert had
helped the Hollingsworth household with his practical skillset,
repairing shutters, climbing onto the roof to look for a leak and
sweeping out a chimney that smoked badly; also carrying in sacks
of potatoes and sides of beef to replenish the stores. Everyone spoke
of it being the worst winter in living memory.

"What would we have done without you, Rupert?" Mrs Baker
exclaimed one morning when Rupert was clearing a way to the hen
house.

"I am sure you have survived many such storms without my
presence," he replied, showing teeth as white as the snow he was
shovelling.

"Yes, but that was when Mr Baker was alive," she replied.
"This is the first winter without him." He had heard from Betty,
the young maid, that Mrs Baker's husband had died quite suddenly
at the age of thirty-eight, sitting one evening in front of the fire and
not getting up again. They had a daughter, Flo, who was eight, who
helped around the house sometimes but mostly skipped off with a
cake or scone pinched from the kitchen. Her countenance was every

bit as merry as Mrs Baker's and that of Mr Baker too, he had heard from Betty. Mr Baker's premature death gave Rupert a sobering thought for he, too, was thirty-eight years old. But, additionally, he was far away from his family, who faced an uncertain future within the Dubois' fragile household.

"Are you sure you want to do this?" Richard had asked Rupert on the fourth day after the storm. "You understand the risks?" As soon as he said these last words he felt their patronising tone and regretted them. Rupert was much more intelligent than most free men; he just seemed to have a total absence of white man's ambition. "I just mean that you don't need to do it. We will find another way."

"Master, it is my pleasure. I would not have suggested it had I not considered it carefully and wanted to do it." The truth was, he was terrified of what he had volunteered to do, but had not seen any other way that his master could achieve his objectives. He was concerned for both of them. Richard was dying slowly, while Rupert ached to be back with his family in Paris. Whatever the circumstances of their continued slavery, he had to be with them.

Sidney had made a major discovery, but it made the position so much more confusing. There was a late movement to rescind the Declaration of Independence and to return meekly to the skirts of the British Empire, but Sidney's questions had revealed that it had been resoundingly defeated and the main protagonists sent scurrying up to Canada in fear of their lives.

"So why the delay in getting the peace treaty signed?" Richard wanted to know.

"I've been told as much as I am going to be told," Sidney replied. "I was taken to one side and it was suggested that I don't ask any more questions for fear of being seen as a traitor."

That is where Rupert came in. For who would ever suspect a slave?

Sidney's plan was simple.

"They are crying out for workers at Independence Hall. There is a great shortage because of the war. I can offer to lease Rupert out. I'll have to do it, not you, because they know me. With his practical skills he will be jumped on over there! So he listens and reads

everything available and reports back to us each evening."

It was easily arranged, Sidney explaining that his guest was bedbound and they had found a nurse so he had no need for his servant. He haggled for a high price, extolling Rupert's capabilities, and pocketed two weeks' fee before he would agree to provide Rupert the next day.

So it was on 11th March 1783 that Rupert made his way early in the morning to Independence Hall.

The balance of March was a frustrating time for Richard. He could not go out of the house because he was genuinely ill, suffering from terrible headaches and a chronic dampness in his chest that kept him on a leash, just a few feet from a fire, all day. His speech became riddled with bouts of coughing he could not control. Sidney was out much of the day with business so Sally Ann spent long hours sitting by the same fire, wondering how someone could shiver when the room was so warm. She chatted with a determined gaiety, recognising that their new friend's life was running out and that he was a long way from where he would choose to die. The weather went from cold and snowy to moderate, then in a similar cycle every few days. Rupert strode out early each morning to a day of backbreaking work fixing the bell tower, nowhere near the talk inside. He arrived back at the Hollingsworth house each evening and dutifully reported to Richard before his supper in the kitchen.

But there was nothing to report.

Ben drained his beer just as the phone in his bedroom rung, making him jump and bringing him sharply back to the present. He looked up at the clock on the wall. He was late for Dick Turnby and the others.

"Hello."

"Ben, it's Frank. We have a thirty-minute delay. You were running late anyway, it seems. Did you fall asleep? Come down at 8pm."

"OK." That gave him ten more minutes. But when he looked again at the letter he saw it was Dakota writing as herself. There would be no more visits back into the past that night.

Ben, I got such a lot of help from Sir John. He went to Philadelphia and dug up all sorts of records. There is a descendant of Sidney and Sally Ann still living in the city and she had some records, plus the museums as well.

Then the handwriting changed, becoming shakier, less even.

Ben, I miss you so much. You are the light of my life. I think about you all the time and have to force myself to work on my thesis because all I want to do is think about you. I wonder what you are doing. I picture you reading my letters. I know the room that you have in our house very well. It was Walker's, while I had the room upstairs in the attic. I think of you sitting by the window with the view of the railroad behind. Walker and I were real close. We often played music together in his room. When he was sick I spent a lot of time in there. I used to read to him and chat endlessly while he slept or seemed to sleep. Once he was crying, frightened that his life was coming to an end. I tried to comfort him. But that is how I feel now. My life is at an end. But instead of four months like Walker, I have forty years to die slowly. And all because I was besotted with Dan Roberts and agreed to carry his parcel for him. It seems such a terrible price to pay.

Yes, I have friends. I make the best of the situation. I have a degree and am studying for another one. I try to stay positive all the time. But right now I am so low, so lonely, so defeated.

The phone rang again.

"Ben, we're waiting for you. The President is here."

"The President?" Ben folded up the letter and placed it under his pillow. All of a sudden, he had the slightest of ideas, like a tiny touch of a tune in his head, repeated over and over again for fear of being lost.

He would always be there for Dakota.

Panic Stations

Patrick Kennedy swore, but his gentle Irish accent took most of the force out of the words. "By the love of Jesus, Brad, I can't work any more hours. I have the kids to think about."

"I know, Pat, but this is a crisis." Brad had a voice that, quite innocently, followed the lead of the person he was talking with. Thus, when speaking with Pat it took on a sweet tone, almost singing in harmony with the Irishman. "I have to maintain double security for the foreseeable future, plus the crowd control. There are journalists everywhere." He did not add, because he did not need to, that Ben's sudden need for time off, plus his recent disappearance for a full day, added to the pressure. He had tried to find out the reason for the disappearance but Ben seemed sworn to silence. It was frustrating that Mr Reading, the manager, knew, while he was in the dark.

"Well, Brad, you'll have to see it from our point of view."

"What do you mean?"

"I mean the overtime premium. The union wants time-and-three-quarters for all overtime. It's only fair now, Brad, with all the sacrifices we're making."

"I'll talk to Mr Reading but, I have to warn you, Pat, it ain't likely to go down too good."

But, to Brad's amazement, Mr Reading agreed immediately. There was a wartime atmosphere in Mr Reading's office: bunkering down for the duration. Brad noticed the stack of cookies, the extra coffee, and the microwave in the corner.

"Meadows, this is highest alert. Our country is under attack."

"Where from, sir?" Brad was a reservist and did not want to be called up.

"Don't you see, man, our very nationhood is being called into question."

Brad did not see. As far as he could tell it was a lot of hot air. Nothing could shake America. But he did not say so to Mr Reading.

"I've got to go, Meadows. I've got a high-level meeting with the Director of Security. Report back to me at 1400."

"Yes, sir. I'll report back at 1400." Brad almost saluted, turned smartly, left the room.

***

Trevor Hardcastle had promised himself a second fortune. That was why he was standing outside the White House with a growing crowd of journalists. It was not much fun; raining, jam-packed, watched by a cordon of grim security guards in standard grey uniforms mixed with black suits and sunglasses every fifth or sixth person, almost making a chequered pattern as he gazed along the ranks of those charged with containing the journalists.

It was also why he was travelling under a false passport. He was now officially Peter Porky, a name he had chosen and relished when he had purchased the passport, along with a work permit for the United States as a freelance journalist.

He made that second fortune. It dwarfed the first one and he made it much easier than he had imagined.

But first he had made extensive plans to get away, this time for good. His reasoning was like this: a million pounds would last a while but not forever. Buy a villa in a beautiful resort, pay for a new identity, and pay for the convoluted trip to get to your new haven so that none could follow, and over half the money would be gone. Keep a little back for emergencies and there was not enough left to live a modest life, let alone have fun.

So, instead, he would use the first million to make five times more. That would be sufficient. Hence, he was now Peter Porky, living in a nice but reasonably priced hotel and standing with a bolt of other journalists in the rain.

But that was only stage one.

For stage two he had $100,000 in fifties in his backpack,

secured with a heavy padlock.

"God, what a life," said the journalist next to him. Porky turned to see a squat man; no hair, heavy overcoat, large umbrella, accent indistinguishable, possibly Midwest. "Here." He gestured with his umbrella.

"Thanks, old fellow, much appreciated." Porky moved under the umbrella, stooping slightly until the other man raised it higher. They did the standard introductions, Porky lying through his teeth, claiming several stories from the recent past to be his own, heavy upper class accent, almost stereotyped, but it worked. The American journalist was Chuck Bringer.

"I bring good luck to my colleagues," he joked, but it was the perfect opening for Porky.

"Say, old chap, can one buy a little luck around here?"

"It depends on two things," Bringer lowered his voice, on tiptoes to bridge the gap.

"Two things?" said Porky, wondering what, apart from bundles of cash, it could depend on.

"Yes, sir. First, how much good luck do you want to bring yourself?"

"Well, that's an interesting question. If, purely, being speculative of course…"

"Of course," Bringer agreed, but his tone said to spit out a sum.

"If a bod had, say, $25,000…"

"Not enough."

"I was going to say $25,000 to $50,000. What might that bring in terms of good fortune?"

A minute later they almost had agreement on $50,000 'expenses' and a $25,000 success fee: half now, half later, paid to Bringer. But then Porky remembered something.

"Wait a mo. What about the second thing?"

"I want US exclusive distribution rights. You get the rest of the world." Porky was impressed. Bringer was a highly capable operator and every bit as dishonest as he was.

"Fair do, old man, but I have a condition as well. I need this to happen pronto. I want to be somewhere far away by

Friday."

"Agreed." They shook hands. "And, in the interests of my sanity," Bringer added, "cut the phony accent."

Porky bristled, then relaxed, smiled, clapped his new colleague on the back. "Lead on, mate."

***

"How the hell do they know all this?" Dick Turnby screeched, mouth half-full of scrambled eggs, spilling out of the edges. He made to take a draught of coffee then thought again, opened the drawer to his desk and pulled out a bottle of Scotch.

"It appears there was a security breach, sir." Mr Reading wondered whether he would get fired. In the time it took Turnby to pour whisky into his coffee, replace the lid, put the Scotch back in the drawer and raise the mug to his mouth, Mr Reading had contemplated his future, calculated his pay-off, reviewed his 401K retirement plan and come to the conclusion that the future was bleak.

"Explain," Turnby spoke into his mug, looking at his Security Manager standing before his desk, wringing his hands.

"Sir, it seems like two journalists infiltrated the White House." He liked the word 'infiltrated'; it sounded sophisticated, one professional to another. "They gained access to the comms office and listened in to certain conversations."

"How long, and when?"

"Yesterday evening, about 6pm, for about forty minutes"

"Forty minutes? If we weren't in the middle of the biggest crisis since Watergate I would have you clear out your office."

***

Turnby's next meeting was worse, much worse.

It did not help that the British Ambassador was an ass.

209

But not as a stereotypical Englishman, more a snivelling, unctuous creep.

"Well. Dick, we do seem to have a problem here." Everything about the ambassador was stripes. His pinstripe suit gave way to a heavily striped pink and grey shirt, oddly offset with a tie that matched in colour but clashed because the colours were banded horizontally. His hair could be said to be striped also – vertical zones of black and grey were interspersed with bald patches, hair straggled over them.

He smiled as he talked, always smiled. This revealed long white narrow teeth, slightly translucent, slightly too perfect, but again adding to the stripe effect.

Dick Turnby hated meeting with him, avoided it where possible. But this time it was necessary.

"Let me recap, Dick, so we are on the same page. We certainly don't want to be charging around in different directions, do we?"

Stripes and clichés.

The phone rang and Dick grabbed it; normally would have left it for an aide.

"Turnby speaking. Yes, I'm investigating that now. What?" He placed his hand over the receiver, shouted for his secretary to bring in the Washington Recorder. Forgot the presence of the ambassador as he turned back to the phone. "I haven't seen the papers yet. I'll review and get back to you." Slammed the phone down as his secretary brought in the papers, all of them.

"This is precisely what I was rabbiting on about," rabbited the ambassador, annoyed by the lack of attention, but it continued. Dick grabbed the *Washington Recorder* from the pile, letting the other papers drop to the floor. His secretary picked them up, bending from the waist so even the ambassador stopped talking and observed.

But all this was nothing to Dick as he focused on the headline in the *Washington Recorder*:

The Country That Never Was

And underneath it said:

Exclusive Insight into a Non-Nation in Crisis from Inside the White House.

An article below this, at the foot of the page, simply asked:

Can the President survive? More to the point: will she have a country to be President of?

The phone rang again; Dick's secretary answered it with a neat: "Mr Turnby's Office, secretary speaking. Yes, of course, Madam President. He's right here. Sir, it is the President."

"As I was saying," the ambassador was back into full flow, even as Dick was walking out of the room, "we just need to find a satisfactory way forward, jointly as two friendly, co-operative nations. That way we can solve our problems and present a united front to the world at large."

"Sir," Dick's secretary said, "I'm afraid that Mr Turnby has had to leave to visit with the President. He sends his apologies and hopes you will understand given the delicacy of the situation and the friendship between our two nations."

"What? Gone to the President? Yes, of course, I understand." His words spoke of understanding but his body spoke of severe disappointment. "Another time, of course. Perhaps later this morning?"

"Let me just get my diary, sir."

***

Dick hurried along corridors usually mainly deserted but now everyone seemed out of their office on some purpose. He stopped someone he recognised.

"What are you doing, Digby?"

"Removing files, Mr Turnby. Standard emergency procedure." Digby seemed unwilling to stop longer than the briefest explanation.

"Removing what to where?" Dick spoke to the senior

aide's back. "Wait a second, Dig. I asked you a question."

"Sir?" He had not heard.

"What files are you removing and where are you removing them to?"

"Eh… following standard procedures, sir. Removing files, sir."

"On whose authority?"

"Yours, sir, of course." Digby looked flustered, itching to be moving again, to find a rhythm in the mayhem.

"Who told you I wanted files removed?" But Digby had seen a cart laden with folders, pushed by a large black woman muttering repeatedly, "Mind the way. Good Lord, this is not in my job description. Mind the way."

"Careful there, lady. Those files are category 3C, grade four, I can tell from the colour." The folders were bright green, like new grass in strong sunshine, heading for the light with fury.

Only these folders were going round and round without seeing daylight.

"Stop a minute." But Digby and the lady were deep in discussion about whether they were grade three or four.

"Grade three folders are a lighter green. I should know, I've put in twenty years in file admin. I'm a supervisor, you know."

"Lady, I create these files every day of the week, well certainly several each week. I know my files."

"OK," the lady tried to pull rank, "what grade are you?"

"What does that matter? I know my file grades, for sure."

"Come on, Mister Folder, what grade are you?"

"Seven." Said in a much smaller voice.

"Ah, I'm grade eight, so I outrank you. And I say these folders are grade three. Now, standard emergency procedures say grade three files should be…"

Dick moved on, turned the corner, blocking out the triumphant lady telling Digby what she thought of trumped-up university-educated people coming in with their know-it-all attitudes and causing havoc everywhere they went.

Then he saw Mr Reading, rushing frantically along the

corridor, too late to prevent charging straight into Dick.

"Ah, sir. I was just coming to find you. There's been a development. Can you come quickly?"

"No, I have to see the President. Walk with me... no, Reading, I said walk. Calm down and tell me what it is."

But even Mr Reading was gone, rushing around the corner shouting: "Category B, folks, category B."

Dick moved on, anxious to get to the President's office, one corridor and a flight of stairs to go.

"No admittance, sir." Two marines stood to attention, rifles across their bodies.

"I'm Dick Turnby."

"ID, sir." Dick waved the ID hanging around his neck.

"Sir, I'll have to radio ahead." He blurted unintelligibly into his radio, barked a command at his colleague, and both moved smartly aside.

"Up the stairs and to the right, sir."

"I know where the damn President's office is."

"Sir," was the only response.

At the top of the stairs Dick had another surprise. As he made the steps three at a time he pounded straight into a tall man making his way downstairs. He did not recognise him then saw the press badge on his suit jacket. He knew all the usual journalists.

"Who are you?"

"I could ask the same question, old chap."

Damn it, the man was British; that was all he needed.

"I'm Dick Turnby, Secretary..."

"Of course, please forgive my ignorance. I'm new on this station. Peter Porky, Quality Control Director for the International Press Regulation Commission. We're the bods who keep the mob in order." He indicated in the direction of the crowd of journalists outside. "I've just had a chat with the President. If I could just have a word with you at some point it would be most helpful."

"You've seen Jane; I mean... the President?"

"Yes, my chum, we had a highly agreeable tête-a-tête for twenty minutes, just said my cheerios."

Could this man be real? Nothing had seemed real to Dick since he had left his office ten minutes earlier. Was he having some sick dream? Did people still say 'cheerios' to their 'chums'?

"I'll see you in thirty minutes, got to see the President now. My office is…"

"Got the geography worked out, dear boy, I'll trot along there now and have a whisper or two with your striking secretary. I've heard all about her. Single too, I hear. Well, you never know when your luck is in, old man."

Peter Porky's luck was certainly in that day. After all, he had purchased an exceedingly large chunk of it.

***

The mathematics worked like this. The *Washington Recorder* paid $250,000 for exclusive rights. Not a bad sum for Chuck to pocket on top of the $25,000 success fee and his cut on the $50,000 expenses. But not enough for his entrepreneurial spirit. So, following Porky's example in London, he slipped partial information to other US newspapers, thus earning another $300,000. He totalled almost $600,000 from the exercise, all tax-free.

For Peter Porky, however, it was another scale altogether. By the time he met Dick Turnby at the top of the stairs he was already $4,000,000 up. Newspapers across the world had snapped up the exclusive. Porky, however, was careful about selling the story multiple times and kept strictly to country exclusivity.

"Why not go for a killing like me?" Bringer had asked.

"Principle, old man." Porky forgot the accent request, remembered it and said, "Don't worry, mate, I know what I am doing."

And he did. For he had managed twenty minutes with the President, now would have the same with Turnby. He would not burn his main customers by breaking territorial exclusivity when he had a truly major story to sell on the back of the first.

And the real beauty of it was that Bringer had not bought into the next stage, so he could sell his interviews to the *Washington Recorder* as well as the rest of the world.

"I'll net fifteen mil easily." He chuckled to himself as he wandered along the corridors to Turnby's office.

***

Two days later Peter Porky flew to the Bahamas. Only he was not Peter Porky but Matthew Horne, an eccentric British millionaire, seeking solitude, fun and selected company a long way from the regulatory authorities.

He left a country in turmoil. But his bank account was secure, stable and blossoming.

Diplomatic Niceties

Max shoved his chair back and stood, unable to sit any longer, his bulk causing a long shadow down the right-hand side of the table, casting the players on that side in semi-darkness.

"All of you out," he half-shouted, sweeping his arm across the table and in the direction of the door. "We are getting nowhere. Bel, stay behind." The room was cleared inside half a minute, last man out closing the door behind him with relief.

"They're useless, every man jack of them," Max hissed. "Where the hell is the creativity when you need it?"

"Sir, we are as lost as you," Bel replied, no longer frightened of her boss, just plain speaking.

"We are looking like idiots, not able to take a stance on this. While we're dithering around, my opposite number in DC is taking the initiative." Max Heaton walked over to the window and stared down at the busy street below. Eight policemen were attempting to cordon off the reporters but it was a losing battle. "I am not going to accept this and roll over."

There was a long silence in which Max and Bel watched a cameraman and reporter escape the human chain and get to the door. The police sergeant started to chase them then stopped, realising that as soon as he depleted his force, the rest of the reporters would break through. He hesitated, torn between his two options. It was like watching a silent movie from high up in the royal box. No sound reached them but this made the physical actions seem more exaggerated and obvious. Max could read the sergeant's mind; watch his dilemma like a Shakespearean play evolving its plot. Would indignation at the breakaway team of camera and microphone win over the discipline of the cordon? Where did this man's weakness lie?

The act ended quite differently, for a door opened in the facing side of the building and a small figure with black hair tied in a bun, matching what was probably a pinstripe skirt and jacket - only the pinstripe was lost with the distance - walked onto the steps.

"It's Georgie," they both said together.

"What is she doing?" Bel asked. They could only watch the miming below. The herd of reporters turned to face her. Now the breakaway duo was punished for their initiative, for they were at the back of the crowd. Georgie turned back to the door, her arm waving like an excited choreographer working through something new.

"Look, the door's opening again," Bel said.

The same door Georgie had used did open and several janitorial staff in light brown overalls walked out, carrying armfuls of stacked chairs. They passed them down to the reporters. Bel noted how the first reporters claimed chairs and sat on them at the front, shoving the stack backwards with no regard for the reporters behind them. Such was the competition for news. Then she saw the breakaway duo scrambling for a preferred place, barging through. She imagined angry words, but the distance and the glass muted all, while also seeming to slow down the actions like the moment before a car crash.

Georgie had outmanoeuvred them for, once the chairs were distributed, claimed, fought over, and placed for maximum advantage in her direction, she and her team disappeared, the door closing behind her as the last figure slipped through. Now the stage was empty. There was calmness for a moment, then a slow, hesitant restlessness, spreading like gusty wind across the crowd of some sixty reporters. Someone stretched, another stood up, men and women looked around like a city waking from slumber.

"I do believe she is building suspense," Max laughed. It was the first time he had laughed that week.

And it was clear that Georgie was doing exactly that for at just the right moment, the main door opened. It took a while for this action to be acknowledged for the body of reporters was facing the side door Georgie had first used, their backs to the main door. By the time there was general knowledge of this action the same janitorial staff were in amongst the reporters with two large tea urns and boxes of chocolate biscuits. Max and Bel watched as chairs were shuffled around, some occupants hedging their bets by turning their chair halfway to get sight of both doors. They watched as tea was passed out in plastic cups and boxes of biscuits were handed down the ragged lines. They watched as clearly laughter arose and humour abounded. Only they could not hear it from their royal box vantage point.

They also could not hear the short speech Georgie then gave; not from behind a lectern, holding notes, but ranging back and forth across the broad steps that led up to the door. They could see the laughter, see the cameras whirring, see the reporters pressing for more and see the polite but firm reply from Georgie before she retreated with a nod and a wave; the door closed behind her and the show was over. Max crossed to his desk and picked up his phone.

"Get Georgie Bakaj up here now." He replaced the receiver and winked at Bel but, in an extension of the silent drama acted out below, he did not say anything until the knock on the door announced Georgie's arrival.

"Please explain yourself," Max could see that it was not a pinstripe at all. Her suit was black with feint specks of yellow, red and mauve, like flayed material faulty from the mill, but looking splendid all the same.

"Sir, I just thought I would calm things down a bit."

"On whose authority?" Max's stern façade shook Georgie.

"Nobody's, sir, it was just my idea." Her voice petered out into nothing. Silence had played such a role in their morning and it did again now. There was absolute quiet, Georgie biting her lips, feeling the cuff of her jacket with her long fingers, not moving her legs as she stood, like a child against the tide.

"I applaud your actions."

"Sir?" She had been expecting a blasting.

"Miss Bakaj, I applaud your actions and initiative. Thank you. It is refreshing and stimulating, even though we could not hear a word up here!" Then more seriously he added,

"Keep up the good work, Georgie. You are clearly very much the future of the Foreign Office."

***

"Miss President, Jane, we at least know who is behind this fiasco."

"Yes, Dick, and the Williams family just happen to be one of my largest donors. This is a real mess. We have the Brits on one side, not quite deciding what they are going to do, and the Williams family pushing this along at a hell of a rate. The question is, why? Somewhere along the track there's going to be an almighty train wreck."

"Plus the re-election in November."

"Don't, that hurts." She placed her hand lightly on Dick's knee and then said brusquely, the tone of voice balancing the familiarity with her hand, "The thought of being the first-ever female president but not to win re-election is unbearable."

"We won't let that happen." Dick placed his hand on hers, a gesture of reassurance, then jumped up and started pacing around the sitting room, innately knowing when movement and action was appropriate. The President was single. Opponents had spread rumours in 2024 of her lesbian activities. Dick knew they were incorrect and had not stood the test of time, had dissipated. He had acted many times as her companion on official functions; something he and his wife were comfortable with. The President had put other things ahead of marriage and family. It was just how she was. But at fifty-two years old she was still strikingly good-looking and could, he was sure, drum up a date within seconds. He was flattered that instead she chose him to be her companion so often. They were a political double act that had become formidable over the last few years, but it worked through careful restraint.

"Divide and conquer." It suddenly came to him.

"What do you mean?" In her youthful way she kicked off her shoes and sat next to Dick on the sofa, curling her feet

219

underneath her, looking up at him with her body twisted around.

"There are two components to this problem: the Brits and the Williams. We deal with them separately. We keep each sweet while we sort out the other."

"Perfect." She laughed. "Trust you to come up with the idea to save our sorry selves. The question is, which one first?"

"You know the link is Ben Franklin. He seems to have the Williams' protection and is well in with Fitzroy. Incidentally, is Fitzroy a royal?"

"No," the President replied. "I had someone do the research. His line goes back to a bastard son of some ancient king. Fitzroy means 'son of a king'."

"So he is royal?"

"No way, apparently you only stay royal for two generations. I understand he goes back about ten."

"So we can come down hard on him and it won't cause a major diplomatic incident?"

"Correct, although I don't want any kind of incident. I want this forgotten about come election time." She made to get up from the sofa, unfurling her long legs, but Dick waved her back, came around the back of the sofa and rubbed her neck with his huge hands. It always calmed her. But this bit was not known to Dick's wife; they had never discussed it amongst themselves, never mind mentioning it to his wife.

"Franklin is the key to this problem. Somehow, we need to neutralise him." The manipulation of her neck often helped her see things more clearly.

"Leave it with me, Jane. I'll get something in motion."

***

Sir John turned the air conditioning up full and fiddled with the radio, trying to find something to listen to. Half of the two-hour journey from Pittsburgh was behind him, another hour would see him going through security at the prison, maybe another half-hour would have him in the warden's office, bang on time for his 5.30 appointment. He would ask to see Dakota afterwards. It was not often you got to meet someone with as fine a mind as she had. Not that he would ever tell her that, of course.

He had called Frank's office but was told he had just left for a conference in the Caribbean: lucky him, Sir John had joked to Frank's secretary. Then he called Ben and listened for twenty minutes as he rattled through his stay with the President.

"Sir John, I am way out of my depth here," Ben had said.

"You've got Frank and myself on your side." But afterwards, as Sir John drove between the wheat fields in the summer haze, past brightly coloured barns not needing the extra embellishment of wild flowers, and the occasional planted yard, he wondered whether he was on anyone's side except his own. "I want notoriety out of this. I want to be the go-to person for chat shows and historical documentaries. I want to be known." He spoke to himself in the car, his voice drowned by the monotonous country music that could not move beyond love lost and pickup trucks on the road. "At least I am honest with myself." The words came out of the speakers, the chorus louder and clearer than the verse, as if scripted perfectly for Sir John's thoughts.

"Well, Mrs Kinderly, I have excellent news for you with regard to the books." They were sitting in Mrs Kinderly's spacious office, she at her desk with her back to the large window, he opposite, in an upright armchair.

"Well, that is great news. I have been thinking about you and your books." This was an exaggeration: she had been thinking about Sir John, but no time wasted on the books. She liked the look of Sir John Fitzroy, could imagine him in bed, but considered his interest in literacy amongst prisoners as the obsession of someone with his priorities upside-down.

"We have two thousand assorted books on a boat right now, I would say mid-Atlantic." Outside, he could see a detachment of prisoners in matching orange overalls clipping lawn and hedge, moving slowly in the heat. Sir John counted eight prisoners and eight guards. Through the other window Sir John saw a smaller party with similar guard-to-inmate ratio, whitewashing an endless supply of stones that lay around the VIP car park. His own rental was now almost surrounded by neat white stones.

"Do you like it?" Mrs Kinderly had been following his line of sight.

"Very pretty."

"It is my latest idea for efficiency improvements. The stones should be spaced every eight inches. Do you see that they don't lay them all straight, end facing end, but at a slight angle? I was real happy with that twist. I think it gives a pleasing aspect, especially from the offices up here."

"They are very nice," was all Sir John could say truthfully.

"Great. Now, perhaps we can discuss the arrangements to receive the books over dinner. I know of an ace restaurant near my home, about twenty minutes from here. You could follow me."

"Actually, I need to see Dakota. I mean Jameson, because the books will be here late next week and we need to get them housed. I know it's not my decision but I wondered whether Jameson and the new deputy warden - what is her name? - could work on it together."

"You mean Bennet. She's only an assistant deputy warden and I'm not sure about her being involved in this project." The disappointment in the warden's voice rang alarm bells. He had been going too fast. Sometimes you get where you want faster by travelling slower. "I mean, she is very young. I know she did wonders with the visiting room but that was largely under my guidance."

"I knew there had to be an experienced hand on the tiller somewhere. But I have a better idea. Let's go to that restaurant after all, my treat, and discuss the general principles and objectives to get the policy straight. Jameson and Bennet can wait until morning. They can carry out the strategy we give them."

"Deal!" She laughed. Her playful tones mixed with a sharp retort from one of the guards on the lawn. Someone had been daydreaming. It was the weather for it. Sir John watched the delinquent inmate clip at an edge of the lawn a few times then pause again, leaning on the long clippers. It was slow work but Sir John could not deny that the half-acre of lawn in front of the office block was so perfect you could practice putting on it.

Mrs Kinderly's choice of restaurant was sound and expensive. Sir John detoured to the hotel he had stayed in before, then caught a cab so he could have a drink. They met at 8pm in the foyer to the restaurant, Sir John suddenly aware that she was chasing him. She had changed at home and wore a long black dress with no shoulder straps but a red see-through scarf tied tightly around her long neck, the ends sticking out sideways like a short flag frozen in the wind. Below that was a string of pearls ("my inheritance from my grandmother") and above were very delicate pearl earrings ("let's not go into the story of where they came from").

"Call me Iris," she said as she sat down, the waiter expertly assisting with her chair.

"Hello, Iris, you look wonderful."

"Well thank you. What shall I call you? Sir John is like so grand and formal."

"Bunny." In for a penny, in for a pound, he thought.

"What?"

"Bunny, it's what my close friends call me. It's a nickname."

"Why?"

"Because when I was at boarding school I found a baby rabbit and adopted it when it was obvious its mother was dead. I begged the groundsman to make a cage, but most of the time it lived somewhere on my person."

"How delightful. What happened to it?" This man, despite his sexy, suave appearance, was clearly quite loopy.

"The headmaster's wife ran it over. She used to bring the sweets; the candy, that is, in from the wholesalers to re-stock the tuck shop and she reversed to the door and ran Rabbit over."

"Was that its name? Rabbit?"

"Yes, original isn't it? But I was not going to risk my reputation further by giving it some soppy name like Floppy or Big Ears! My reputation was damaged enough as it was by the adoption. But we gave Rabbit a good funeral with a procession across the rugby pitches to the woods beyond."

"Was the headmaster's wife sorry?"

"Yes, but it didn't save her."

"What do you mean?"

"My friend, Stavington - he's now the ambassador to Ecuador – well, he acted as coroner and ruled it unlawful death. Then Stavington got promoted to trial judge and we had a jury of twelve junior brats who gave the unanimous verdict of guilty. I was the prosecuting attorney but I was also the main witness. She was condemned to a life sentence at Borrell House Preparatory School."

"That was the boarding school you were at?"

"Yes, that was the worst punishment we boys could imagine! And the funny thing was, she did stay there the rest of her life. The headmaster and she were still in place when she died of throat cancer twenty-one years later."

"What a sad tale. Let's change the subject." She looked at her menu assiduously for a moment and then said brightly, "Well, Bunny, I assume you will be having the salad?"

Sir John took a long time to work around to his purpose. He flattered Iris Kinderly enormously, giving her the attention she craved but had never got from her husband and certainly not from work where she was a distant figure of authority, behind the firm guard of her secretary, where the air conditioning worked superbly. He described his work, his interests, his travel, but not his personal life. Most of the time he asked her the same things and listened intently to the answers. He chose the wine but only after consulting her. He admired her intellect, what she had done in her life, her authority. He wondered whether it was lonely at the top.

"Yes, it is," she replied. "My ambition doesn't help me."

"Why is that?"

"Well, I don't see potential friends amongst my workmates, I don't even see colleagues; I just see useful people to help achieve my objectives. I am determined to make Zanesville the best penitentiary in the firm."

"That's laudable."

"Yes, last year we were third-lowest cost per inmate. I am determined to get to be the cheapest. It's all about unit efficiency."

"What is a unit?"

"An inmate hour based on a day. We have just over 2,000 inmates so multiply by twenty-four and we have almost 50,000 penal units or 'PUs', as we call them. You take the weekly cost of running the place, including the imputed rent and a head office multiplier, divide by seven, and then divide by your PU. number That gives you the daily cost per inmate hour."

"Wow! That is quite a calculation. What is yours?

She looked across the table at Sir John, her empty fork mid-air, and spoke with a mouthful of steak; something Sir John detested.

"348.43 cents. But Barstown is at 348.21 and I am determined to get there."

"I like that name for a prison town." But Iris was too focused on her objective and missed the joke.

"When will you achieve that?" He asked instead.

"The key cost is staff wages. And within that we need to cut overtime, that's our manageable variable. We got a 6% reduction last month. That's the biggest reduction I've ever experienced month on month."

"That's Bennet's role, isn't it, to get overtime down? Iris, I think I can help you get those twenty-two hundredths of a penny off the bill. Give me tomorrow with Bennet and Jameson and we'll present a plan to you at the end of the day."

"I can't have you in the prison, Bunny. It caused havoc last time. You are a very handsome man!"

"Well, thank you. Not much I can do about that problem!" he replied, his own mind working on overtime.

They ate in silence for a moment, then Sir John laid down his knife and fork and said, "I have the answer. We'll meet in my hotel room. No, better than that, I'll take a meeting room at the hotel. Have Bennet bring Jameson tomorrow morning and I'll come back with them at five o'clock with a plan. Next month you are going to be the lowest cost prison in the world, let alone the firm!"

***

Very early the next morning, Sir John could not sleep. Despite many transatlantic trips, he had never got used to the jetlag. At least it was cool at 4am. He showered, dressed and drove a quarter-mile to an all-night diner. Inside, he had scrambled eggs, toast, bacon, orange juice and coffee. He declined the grits and the sausage and gravy – that was going too far down Heart Attack Alley. He sat at a shiny Formica table on a plastic moulded red chair, joined to the one next to it, the pair bolted to the floor. The waitress tried to be jolly but, on interrogation, she let slip that she was in the last couple of hours, the tail end, of an exhausting all-nighter.

"I'm saving for my daughter's college. She's a tenth-grader."

He asked her the usual questions about what courses, what she wanted to study and where, but forgot the answers as soon as they were given. His mind was on last night. He had found Iris' naked ambition unsettling and had been glad to call the evening to an end, feigning exhaustion.

"I've been up almost twenty-four hours," he had said, as there had been a hint of a nightcap at her place. "Flying from London, it takes it out of you."

But he had woken this morning with a disturbing thought. He had felt it develop as the night's blackness and quietness sorted out the jumbled thoughts of the day, then woken with it as a conviction. His own ambition was no different to the warden's. It was just as great, perhaps greater, and certainly as aggressive and obvious. He had always considered himself one of the good guys, disapproving of the ways of others but safe in his own bubble of self-adulation. This morning, all he could say about himself as he sat in the near-empty diner with the waitress who saved every penny for the college fund, like a million other mothers in a million other diners, was that the song he had heard on the radio yesterday was true. At least he was now being honest with himself. And by helping Iris, he was helping himself.

Fight Back

Dick Turnby led the charge.

It started at ten to four on a stormy Friday in August. It started with a summons.

Two heavy aides delivered it. Identical black suits, white shirts, black ties and sunglasses, hair cropped, smile cropped, humour cropped also. Two aides who were meant to be taken seriously.

"Where's Franklin?" they asked Mr Reading.

Reading pressed his intercom. "Supervisor Meadows to the manager's office."

"Where's Franklin?" he asked Brad when he turned up a few minutes later.

"He's off this afternoon."

"He was on the rota," the more talkative of the two aides said. "I got a copy."

"He asked to leave early. I didn't want to give him the time as he's had so much recently, but he gave me a long story about needing to go and see some lawyer."

Twenty minutes later, the same two aides were outside the offices of HFW, oblivious to the heavy rain that swept its cleansing over the city, both still behind their sunglasses despite the heavy cloud and darkened sun.

"We're looking for a client of the firm, Ben Franklin." Both aides flashed their identity cards.

"I'll call Mr Hibbert," Tammy responded as she had been told to.

Brief explanations followed: Mr Franklin was certainly not under arrest but there were important matters of state that would be best served if Mr Franklin could accompany them to meet with the President. Yes, they understood that they had met extensively last week, but certain decisions had to be made and Mr Franklin was instrumental in making them.

"I'll come with you," Marcus said. "I'll just get my coat.

It's tipping it out there."

Marcus left the foyer and Tammy went in search of an umbrella for Ben. That was their mistake. They both returned minutes later to an empty foyer. Outside, the rain bashed down on empty streets. Tammy thought she saw a car disappearing in the gloom but could not be sure.

***

"Mr Governor, how nice to see you again, sir." The President extended her elegant, slightly bony, hand while Dick Turnby indicated for Ben to sit at the head of the table.

"You have my name wrong. I am Ben Franklin."

"Sir, we know, of course, exactly who you are," Dick replied smoothly. They were both well-rehearsed. "But you are also Governor of the British Colonies of North America. The papers have been fully authenticated. You, sir, are the First Citizen of these satellite settlements."

"I don't understand. Are you just giving in to the British, just like that?"

"Mr Governor, it is not a case of 'giving in', by any means. We are merely reflecting reality. You are the governor and this is your home." The President swung her arms around her to indicate the whole White House mansion.

"We are here effectively on your invitation and will leave when you require us to leave. We are your subjects as the representative of the Crown."

There was a moment of silence as Ben struggled to cope with the enormity of the idea presented to him. Then Dick turned the knife.

"And we await your instructions, sir."

"What do you mean?"

"I mean, Mr Governor, that the government of these colonies has been returned to you. Please forgive the lack of ceremony but there was no time. There are many urgent decisions to make."

"But you are the administration. I'm American and you, Miss President, you are the President and..." Ben's voice tailed away, lacking the confidence so evident in their subservience.

They judged now was the time for the final twist.

"Sir, if you have no objection, we will leave you to acclimatise. There are some urgent papers here for your attention." Dick placed a huge stack of untidy documents onto the table in front of Ben and the two of them made to withdraw from the room.

"Stay, please."

"Sir, we have no official capacity in this government. It would be inappropriate for us to stay and assist."

"But who will help me?"

"You need to appoint your own administration, sir. Have a good day now." The double doors closed behind them, leaving Ben entirely alone.

Ben sat a long time. There were no sounds of human activity. He might as well have been on the moon. Except that nature was beating in at the windows. Several bees busied away in the flower border directly outside, while pigeons discussed matters in the shrubs and trees beyond the lawn. The rain had temporarily halted as they had entered the White House, as if not allowed to soak the seat of government. But now it started raining again, with steady, large drops. There was no force behind them, no anger; just gravity guiding them down. When the drops hit the windowpanes, they landed with the lightest thud, then slipped down a half-inch, becoming elongated, like dangling earrings glistening in the shaky sun. That sun went in and out of the black clouds, causing a constant change in available light; a trick maybe a horror movie director would use to create suspense. Ben stared at a bust of what he supposed was Washington, on a sideboard. He counted the seconds it was in darkness, then the seconds in sudden brilliant sunshine. The longest period of gloom was twenty-four seconds. The longest period of brilliance was twenty-six seconds. Thus, he decided, brilliance won.

What was he supposed to do? He looked at the first paper on the stack. 'Priority level seven. Security Classified.'

Should he read any further? He did not have full security clearance; not for documents like this, anyway.

But by looking away he kept snatching glances back until he had read the full title. 'Suggested Options for New Procedures for the Safe and Productive Disposal of Bulk Powdered Milk beyond Approved Usage.' He flicked to the back page. It was numbered eighty-four. Take out the title page and the contents and the glossary at the back and there were sixty-eight pages of close type to absorb.

He looked at the next document. 'Options on Change: Education and Retraining for Adults: Costings by Option with Budgetary Impact.' This report was 257 pages long plus the following document was an eighty-eight-page annex on the 'Political Consequences of Recommendations Made'.

Ben moved on to the next document and then the following ones. Once he had flicked through a dozen he had no room to lay them out on the table while sitting down. He stood up and, with greater reach, could devise a system to categorise them all. Sorting, categorising, filing: this he could do, and do it well.

After an hour there was a knock on the door. Ben was too absorbed in delineating between farming subsidies and green initiatives to notice. The door opened and a middle-aged woman in smart business clothes entered.

"Sir," she said, then, "Sir." A little louder, then louder still, coming up to where Ben stood along the length of the table.

"Sir, please."

"Yes, sorry. I'm working on a better way to organise these documents. I'm not quite there yet but if whoever brings them in can…"

"That's me, sir. At least it was when we had a President. As Governor, you will want to bring your own team in." She had been briefed well, trusted with Dick's plan, and was a key part of its execution. "Sir, if I could have a moment. Mr Turnby asked me to stay on today in order not to leave you in the lurch, but only for today. Here is your diary. You are running late for dinner at the annual general meeting of the

Civil Liberties Union. Here is your speech, sir. It is black tie, of course."

"Just a minute, I'm almost there on this filing system."

"The car will be outside at a quarter till eight. Goodnight, sir."

But Ben did not hear her. He had just happened on a thin paper near the bottom of the stack that gave him an idea which totally absorbed him.

***

The call came through to Frank later that night.

"Frank, it's Ben."

"Where are you? We've been trying to get hold of you all evening."

Ben explained where he was, the White House, and why, because the administration seemed to have given up. "Frank, two guys virtually kidnapped me and took me back to see the President. Mr Turnby was here, too. Well they've just left me in charge here. They kept calling me 'Mr Governor' and then they just walked out." Frank instantly saw it for what it was: the ultimate bluff. He had done similar in the business world countless times, because it usually worked.

"So they handed over control of the country to you?"

"I think so, that's what I understood it to be," Ben replied, but was excited to talk of something else. "Frank, I got a whole pile of documents to work through, all sorts of stuff. I've been sorting through them and categorising them."

"That sounds like you." Frank was thinking furiously. His instinct was always to call a bluff but he had never played in politics before. He was having to learn speedily.

"But right at the bottom I got to a real interesting paper. I don't think it was meant to be in the pile. Everything else is real tedious stuff about sell-by dates, wind power grants, monument upkeep, like real long papers on nothing important."

"That's the game they are playing. They're hoping to get you to back down," Frank replied, thinking that they obviously saw Ben as the weak link. I would do the same in their position, he considered, but did not mention it.

"Yeah, but I don't even want to play around at governing the country. But listen, Frank, there is a real interesting paper on the effects of prison reform. I've got it right here and it's only six pages long, unlike all the others. It's called 'The Budgetary Consequences of Extreme Prison Reform'. The first two pages are all about their approach but the last four has a thousand figures all about the savings the government would make by only imprisoning those who were violent or kept offending."

"I think it was a mistake to include that report. They are trying to isolate you in the White House and bamboozle you with heavy, long reports on every trivial subject under the sun."

"I know that, that's obvious." Frank was impressed by Ben's perception, but his friend carried on. "But think what it would mean for Dakota."

Another aspect had caught Frank's attention. Think what it could do for the President, for the country.

***

It was hunger that drove Ben out of the office. It was mid-morning and he had been working through the night. He had started an elaborate filing system but that was forgotten now that he had the prison reform paper. The table was littered with scattered documents as he had searched for anything else on the subject. He had found nothing. He started writing notes around 10pm, filling up legal pads he found next door in the outer office. He found a calculator in the secretary's desk and spent hours furthering the calculations in the paper.

"What if, to start with, every prisoner was released and all federal prisons closed down," he muttered to himself. "Well, that would mean one-and-a-half-million people released and a total saving, including civil servants of…" He tapped and scribbled, seeking out other information from budgetary reports to try and assist. This gave him a baseline. "But clearly, not every prisoner can be released. Let's work it out with 10% being held but let's also assume 15% more funding per prisoner." So as the night wore on, the rain and wind picking up, a constant assault on the White House, he worked through the percentages and variables, coming up with conclusion after conclusion.

The breakthrough had come at 3.39am. He had tried the computer various times but could not get through the password controls. He tried once more, putting in the Presidential Inauguration date, the President's full name in various forms, but none worked out. He remembered then that the President had a cat called Scribbles. All lower case got him through the first stage of security, but he was immediately met with another password request. Then he saw a scribbled note on the desk. It just read:

Fight back this evening, Dick T.

Suddenly, he knew what the password was. He scrambled onto the page and typed 'Fight Back'.

'Incorrect Password, three remaining attempts.' It was the same for lower case and all one word. He sat back in the chair, despondently. That left one more attempt before he was blocked. Feeling like a behind-the-lines secret operative in a spy movie, he considered his last chance to get this right. He read the note again. Of course 'Fight Back' was wrong. That presumably was the fight back against the country being stolen by him and these damn documents he had found. She would have set the password a few days ago, before any thoughts of fighting back. That just left... He carefully typed in 'Dick T'.

And he was in.

Many, with access to the President's computer, would look for the sensational or the scandalous; others for something they could use for their advantage. Of course, Dick Turnby could trace his computer journey from the nearby room he occupied, just as he could watch every move

Ben made on CCTV. He was ready to jump in and stop 'the experiment', as it was known to the inner circle, but as he saw the early pattern of website visits he settled back, relaxed, curious, safe in the knowledge that the information made available was a jungle of statistics and reports already in the public domain. Ben could have gone to the library on Thomas B. Eldridge and accessed the exact same information.

So it was hunger that drove Ben out into the corridors. And Dick was ready for him, sending out people just in time.

"Hey, excuse me," Ben called to the first person he saw. "Can you tell me where I can get something to eat?"

"Sure thing, sir," the janitor replied, quickly checking that his overalls covered the suit and tie underneath. "Along here, third right, second left, up the stairs, then third door ahead of you, down one flight to central concourse, then take the right hand bank of elevators to floor 3A, through Records, you'll see the sign on the door, then second left and you'll find the cafeteria right there."

"So, I go second left, then third right…"

"That's right, sir, sounds like you got the hang of it." He stopped talking, hands in pocket, whistling as he strode off. In the control room Dick whistled also as he watched the performance.

"Brent's overdone it."

But he hadn't. Ben took the instructions as gospel and walked off with purpose, prompted by his hunger.

Twenty minutes later, and several sets of directions down the line, Ben opened the cafeteria door only to find it was a communications room full of servers, disk players and wires everywhere. He groaned in exasperation, retraced some steps, and came to an office full of men and women with headphones on, bent over computers.

"Can anyone help me?" No one answered, not even a glance in acknowledgement. He stepped into the room.

"Sir, you can't come in here. This is the Listening Room." He was hustled gently out by a supervisor. The impression he got from his quick look around the room reminded him of a scene in an old movie about iron curtains and fights in trains rattling across the night-time countryside of Eastern Europe. Dick chuckled at the last-minute inventiveness of his staff.

"I'm just looking for the cafeteria."

"Which one? There are seventeen that I know about."

"Any one, I don't care." His stomach rumbled to reinforce his words.

"Best to go to Section A." The supervisor was a good improviser. "Take the next left, along to third right, then…" But Ben was not listening. Maybe he would never eat again.

Then he saw the machine. Or was it a mirage induced by hunger and frustration? No, it was real. He could feel its sharp outline, could see the choices inside. He fumbled in his pockets, grabbing all his change. Each selection was five quarters. He had nine quarters. So it would be one candy bar only. He inserted five quarters, strangely given his hunger, waiting for each quarter to drop before inserting the next one. Five satisfying clunks and thuds as the quarters hit home. He made his selection – C5 – double-checking the digits before pressing the buttons. The plastic arm inside moved in a spiral, pushing the candy towards the cliff edge.

Then it stopped. Ben stared a moment, not believing it. He shook it and banged the side but nothing fell into the tray below.

It had been an ingenious idea to install the machine the prior evening. The technician had been puzzled as to why the set-up had to be altered so it failed to push out the candy.

"Just do it and don't worry why." The janitor who wore a suit under his overalls had said with a grin.

***

By noon, Ben was frantic. A mixture of lack of sleep, lack of food, and lack of human contact - save inane directions that seemed to lead nowhere, delivered with cheerful smiles and punctuated with several 'sirs' - led to a slumped figure back in the President's office. Even the intercom on the desk led to a choice of options read out by a bright and bubbly voice seemingly untouched by the real world.

"It's like Alice in Wonderland," he said to himself. Dick agreed, applauded Ben's comparison, and immediately renamed 'the experiment' to be 'Ben in Wonderland' or 'BIW' for short. That was the term he used when he reported back to the President at a quarter to one.

"Also, Frank Williams has been trying to gain entry. He's asking for you," Dick concluded his report.

"That presents a dilemma." She was sitting again with her shoes off, feet tucked under her long legs, knees slanted over to one side of the armchair, the hem of her red dress cutting across her knee-caps tightly as if she was a Christmas present half-unwrapped. Dick wanted to complete the unwrapping. The President knew this. The thought of Dick's wife stopped him, but only just. Instead, he rose from his armchair and perched on the other arm of hers, placing his left hand on her mane of hair, wondering how she had time to groom herself so perfectly. He traced his fingers through it.

"You know I've always loved you." It seemed the time for truth. "But…"

"I know, Dick. Say no more."

She looked up into his eyes, seeing the honesty that rode in his face alongside the other aspects to his character: the determination; the ambition; the harshness. People were never simple, rather a complicated posse with riders good, bad and indifferent. After a pause, while they looked inside each other, she added, "For what it is worth, it is reciprocated 100%."

Then they both shook off the moment like dogs shaking off water. They had known several moments of intimacy but never one as intense as this, never one requiring such a bright and breezy response from both to relegate it to a manageable place.

"Frank is a good friend and my largest political donor."

"Yes," replied Dick, "it is the weak point of our plan."

"We're going to have to meet with him."

"I agree but Jane, just remember that he is behind this

crazy idea and we desperately need to sort this out to have any chance with the election."

Frank was shown in fifteen minutes later. He listened carefully to what they had to say. He had been taught to listen by his grandfather.

"No preconceptions," the older generation had always said. "Weigh up each situation as it is, not as you would like it to be or imagine it to be."

"Jane, to resolve this you are going to have to do something for me and for Ben."

"What is that?" If it were half-way reasonable they would find a way of managing it. It was three months to Election Day. Her poll ratings were plummeting with this constitutional crisis hanging over her. It had occurred on her watch, which is all that would be remembered. It did not matter that her opponent would not know what to do, either. She was in charge. She was the President.

But at that moment the private phone rang, Dick answered it.

"President's Private Office, Dick Turnby speaking."

"Dick, how nice to speak to you. I trust you are well, and Marjorie also?"

"It's the Brit PM." Dick handed the phone to the President and had sufficient presence of mind to take Frank to another office, where they discussed various matters intensely.

Then, recognising that 'Ben In Wonderland' had no real chance of success, he took Frank to see Ben in his own office, barked down the phone for a double hamburger, fries and salad. Then Frank and he drank coffee and watched Ben refuel.

"Is this all over?" Ben asked as he ate. "If so, I'll get back to work. I'm supposed to be on long shift today. They'll be wondering where I am."

"Yes, it is all over," Frank stated, then whispered, "Make sure you keep that prison reform paper. I'm real interested in that."

That Failing Feeling

They say the polls never lie, which is a lie, but one that the President believed.

"I'm sunk, Dick. Nobody has come back from twenty clear points behind with three months to go." Dick was about to reply when she continued, "Why does everyone hate me? I think we've had a pretty good four years." It was two days after they had tried to scare Ben into acquiescence. It might have worked if Frank had not intervened.

"Jane, it is this damn constitutional issue. You were several points ahead before this raised its ugly head." He was massaging her neck again, had done it increasingly over recent weeks. "We have the campaign strategy meeting this afternoon. We'll go over everything in detail then. Right now you need to relax."

"I can't relax. Every time I go to any campaign event or press meeting I am inundated with questions about this very subject. I don't know what to do or say."

Sometimes Dick felt like saying, 'get a grip, you're supposed to be the leader', but he never would; great fondness for her would prevent that.

There was a knock on the door. Dick moved away from the back of the President's chair, she put her legs down and slipped on her shoes.

"Yes, who is it?" It was an aide, come with more bad news.

"Madam President, Mr Turnby, we thought you ought to see the newspaper leaders ahead of the meeting this afternoon. I'm afraid they are not too good." The young man placed the papers on a table and made to withdraw, wanting to be out of there as quickly as he decently could.

"Wait a minute, Sam," the President called, gathering up her presence from the scatterings of despair. "I don't have time to read them all, give me a quick précis." Then, when he looked shocked and disturbed she added, "Take a minute to collect your thoughts then give me a four-minute summary, don't hold back. I am not the type to shoot the messenger."

The look of relief on Sam's face reminded Dick of why he was so fond of the President, why he was not remotely ready to jump ship. They would find a way out of this mess.

Somehow.

***

Dick had time before the strategy meeting to make a call. At first he was told Max Heaton was not in but when he announced, a little affronted, who he was, he found himself being put straight through.

"What can I do for you, Dick?" Max sounded tired.

"How the hell do we resolve this mess?" But Max did not want to talk about it, was not prepared yet with his own strategy.

"I'm sure it will sort itself out in a jiffy," he replied with the pomposity of an earlier generation. "Now, I really must dash." He was not yet ready to talk with the Americans. He needed clarity first. He needed a plan.

So as Dick replaced the receiver and sighed, unsure of what his special partners across the pond wanted from this, so Max called on his intercom for another meeting, unsure what they should ask for.

***

The campaign strategy meeting was a disaster. Not for the lack of purpose or the quality of the attendees. There was purpose enough and intellect enough. It was just that no one knew what to do.

"We've got to stress that we are the best pair of hands in a crisis," said one member.

"But we don't know what to do," said another.

Thus the meeting went round in circles, like the circles in the President's mind: no way to break the cycle.

"Enough!" she shouted. "We have to convince people that we are the best to deal with this situation. The question is, how do we do that?"

"We need an initiative that you, Madam President, can then talk about." It was Sam, the nervous aide from earlier. He was supposed to be taking notes only, but nobody would discipline him for giving the only contribution.

"Exactly!" Dick said. "We need something to kick-start us in a direction and then we can rely on the President's well-known speaking skills to get us moving. So we've narrowed it down, thanks to Sam." He noticed the look of pride on Sam's face; another reward of the job he loved doing. "Now we are asking ourselves specifically, what initiative can we come up with?"

But no one knew. Nobody spoke. Eventually, after breaking three pencils with his fingers, Dick whispered a request to the President. After getting a nod of assent, he closed the meeting. He left with the others, rather than stay behind with her, suddenly needing fresh air like a diver after oxygen. Dick left the building on foot, walked a half-mile aimlessly, then caught a cab home, changed, and went to his basement gym.

***

Dakota closed the makeshift curtain on her bunk and lay down flat. She knew the bottom of the mattress above off by heart. Once they had done a strip-search of the dorm and pulled half the mattresses onto the floor. Janice had remade the bed afterwards but the mattress was placed on the narrow boards the other way around. She had to make new pictures from the old stains, now inverted. It was strange how a dragon flying out of a cloud, turned through 180 degrees, became a fish being caught in a net.

Closing the curtain was a signal. Either you were doing something illegal, immoral, or taking an inventory of your contraband. Or it meant you craved some peace and quiet. Because prison was, without doubt, the noisiest place on earth. Most inmates would not interfere with this request. It was, Dakota considered, one of the unwritten rules of prison life. There were many such unwritten but understood rules; for instance theft from another inmate was permissible but would be met with extreme violence while theft from a guard or from the institution made you a hero. Another one stated that you never tried to take another's job. There was a complicated system of shop stewards, paying one's dues and biding time to get the choice positions in the prison.

Because everyone had time to spare.

Dakota had worried that getting a library position would be seen as a bad move, breaking the rules, but she had not counted on another facet. Most inmates would not have given her the time of day until she had been beaten up by a guard. And that guard was going inside for a very long time. She had noticed that many inmates now would greet her gruffly, whereas before they had ignored her, pushed past her, expected her to jump out of the way. One or two had even wanted to join her 'non-gang', expanding the circle from four members to six. But most would not go that far. Dakota was raised in the general esteem but to the level of worm, not eagle. She was still close to the bottom of the ladder; would have to do a lot more to warrant further promotion.

But as Dakota's credibility had risen, her faith and her optimism had crumbled. Her shaved head, now just fuzz, like that of a young bird not yet ready to leave the nest, seemed to encapsulate how low she had fallen. She was like Samson: hair gone and strength with it. If she was honest with herself, she saw no point in carrying on. She had not admitted guilt, because she was innocent. That meant early release was out of the question. She had thirty-three years left to serve. That was five more years than her whole life so far. Her mother was fifty-one and not in the best of health, although improving since visiting had begun. She would not live long enough to see her daughter free again.

Dakota's life had become a nightmare revolving around fear, violence and noise. She clung to her visits. She clung to her mother. She clung to Ben. She clung to her few friends inside. She clung to her research. But even with the research, there was a problem.

Her counsellor had told her that afternoon that nobody had ever done a doctorate from Zanesville. Was there an element of glee in those words or was she just trying to be firm, to avoid later disappointment?

"There is no money, Jameson. Consider that you have already had a degree and now another one underway." This was said as if they were absolute gifts showered down on ungrateful and undeserving inmates. Dakota thought of the long hours working alone, no cosy revision or fun study groups. Also, the constant struggle for materials. "We can't have you hogging all the cash. Be content with what you have and try and put it to some use for the prison. Maybe you should be teaching, something to give back." It sounded like a moral lecture; only her whole existence was in a complete moral vacuum.

"I'd be happy to teach and give something back," Dakota replied, meaning it but thinking also how much she wanted to go on to that doctorate.

"Now, onto your rehabilitation plan. I need to discuss your crime with you, Jameson. As soon as you accept your guilt, we can move forward. You are your own worst enemy, Jameson."

Her counsellor had hit upon the crux of it. It would have been easier if she had been guilty. It would have made sense of the sporadic rehabilitation attempts. It would have meant hope, too; hope that she could have a life outside, with her mother, with Ben, doing a doctorate.

Instead, she had a self-imposed cell within the huge prison complex, constructed of mattress and blanket. She was closed off from the world, doing solitary amongst 2,000 inmates, lights burning, voices raised, sounds clashing and echoing amongst the hard surfaces that make a prison.

That was why most people left the blankets alone, understanding that sometimes only solitude would work.

But not Smith.

She delighted in pulling them down, sweeping the blanket aside with a practised arm. If she got the approach right, one stroke could send the blanket skidding across the floor to go under the bunk opposite. Then the inmate would have to be nice to another inmate to get her blanket back, perhaps pay a toll of a few cigarettes.

This is what happened to Dakota, just as she was in the middle of a daydream about Ben.

But instead of Ben there was Smith glowering down at her.

"Get up, Jameson, I've got a special task for you."

Forty minutes later, Jameson was still cleaning the vomit from the floor of the toilet block. Janice and some of the others had tried to help but Carter had delighted in waving them away.

"Solo effort," he grinned.

She was making good progress, hoped to be finished by lock-down. There were two more doorless cubicles to go, someone had clearly been very ill; they were probably now in the infirmary.

Then, in the last cubicle, she saw the foetus.

It was covered in blood.

It was dead. It was slippery, red and lifeless. She thought she could make out its features, but not its sex. She retched, with enough presence of mind to reverse and throw up in the pan of the next cubicle.

***

"The DNA tests are an unnecessary expense. We have to watch our budget." Mrs Kinderly spoke to the meeting of deputy assistant wardens and above, arranged round the table in the main conference room, but her words seemed directed at Val, standing in the corner due to a shortage of chairs. She was the one Mrs Kinderly expected resistance from.

"I agree, Mrs Kinderly," Smith said from her chair, ranging her eyes over the others, daring someone to express any other view.

"I don't," said Val, just as Mrs Kinderly had expected. "It

is vital to know who the mother is. The poor girl might..."

"You mean the inmate?" said Smith. "I thought you said 'girl'. Don't get soft on them, 'girl'." This produced a ripple of laughter.

"She may be an inmate, ma'am, but she is still a girl or woman."

"Not so," said one of Smith's lackeys, bent on gaining favour. "They forfeit their rights to be human when they come through initial processing."

"I don't agree." Val looked around the room for support, but they were all older than her by a long way. She had supporters in the prison but they were mainly junior guards, not promoted and not hardened. They had no authority. "As I was trying to say, ma'am, this 'girl' or 'woman' may be unwell. She may be dying or in agony."

"Let her go to the infirmary, then." That was Smith again, wrapping up the discussion.

But the debate had nowhere to go for Mrs Kinderly had already decided: based on the budget, they just could not afford it.

Caribbean Conference

Albert Essington II was blissfully happy. Over the last six weeks he had billed well in excess of $50,000 a week. And it seemed the gravy train was a lengthy one. At this rate he would bill $3m this year on this case alone. Combine it with other clients and his usual kick-backs and inflated expense claims and he could be bringing in $4m. He had his eye on a villa in the Caribbean, so when he was told to make his way to St Philippe for a conference he thought he would look around in his spare time and see what bargains were available.

"Bring your wife if you like," Marcus Hibbert had said on the phone.

"She can't make it." Essington was thinking quickly. There would be plenty of others down there. "She's heavily involved with her charities," he lied.

"OK, well bring your contract with you. We will want to review it, with the idea of renewing it. Are you OK on the rate?"

"It's a little on the low side."

"Well, now is the time to raise the subject."

So Essington upped his annual estimate of income from $4m to $5m and called a realtor in St Philippe.

The Royal was the best hotel on the island. As he checked in, he estimated that a single room would cost well over $1,000 a night. He had reserved a small suite and checked that his favourite bourbon would be on ice for his arrival.

"Have the Williams checked in yet?"

"Do you mean Frank Williams, sir, the owner?"

"The owner?"

"I thought you knew, Sir. Frank Williams III purchased the Royal four years ago when he acquired the Dainton Investment Company. It was quite shabby before but he has put a lot of money into it, sir." The duty manager was clearly proud of his hotel. "We all have shares in it now, sir, although Mr Williams has 80% ownership."

"Could you tell him I have arrived?"

"He already knows, sir. When in residence he is updated on all suite arrivals as they check in. Dinner is black tie in the Princess Margaret Dining Room; that is our private dining room, sir. Both the Mr Williams, Senior and Junior, will be there at 7.30 for drinks beforehand."

"I don't have a tuxedo."

"Not a problem, sir, I'll send someone up with a selection in your size. Sir, can I introduce Adelia?" Essington turned and saw a gorgeous girl, early twenties, the long black straight hair he loved tied in trestles and kept in place with a net, making Albert instantly want to loosen it so that it tumbled down over her shoulders. He would do that; he knew he would, perhaps later that evening, after dinner. With green eyes, white skin, and a generous bust, she was a vision made for the taking. She was wearing the hotel uniform of deep burgundy skirt, white blouse, and matching burgundy cravat tied loosely, the skirt being just short enough to show her gorgeous legs. "Adelia is our resident Irish hostess and is assigned to you for the duration of your stay."

"My aim, sir, is to make your stay as pleasant and interesting as possible." Her Irish accent did not ring true, but Essington would not have cared had he noticed.

"Thank you, Adelia. That is an interesting name. Is it old Irish?"

"Yes, sir." She lied sweetly, with a generous smile. "It was my great grandmother's name. She was a great granddaughter of King Leonard the Great." The names had been a great selection, pulled at random out of a names book that morning.

"Oh yes, of course, now he ruled about..."

"1742 to 1768." Now she was adlibbing and enjoying it immensely. "He made his horse a duke and invaded England and captured Birmingham; that's Birmingham, England, of course, not Alabama! I would love to tell you all about my family history if you are interested, sir, perhaps over a bourbon and ice?"

"Lead on, fair maiden." He was oblivious as to the awful cliché. He was smitten.

It took Adelia, real name Ruby Smith, only three bourbons to get the information she was tasked with obtaining. Bourbon One was taken up with more incredible feats of King Leonard the Great, "my great, great grandfather". It mattered little whether she had the correct number of greats in the relationship.

Bourbon Two was a sadder tale. It led naturally from a simple question he had asked while draining Bourbon One, talking into the glass and eating caviar on tiny bits of toast at the same time.

"Adelia, you're Irish royalty, so how come you're working in a hotel out here in the Caribbean? Shouldn't you be hobnobbing with the Windsors on the polo field?"

It was easy to give a heartbreaking account of deception on the one hand and nobility in the face of adversity on the other. She had been born at Shamassay Castle, "the most beautiful place in the world, with battlements and a drawbridge, set amidst the Shelley Mountains", born to wealth and great prospects. But her father had been a gambler and had lost everything to an unscrupulous agent. "One day we were the lairds in our castle, overlooking our extensive estates, the next we were packing a suitcase each of personal possessions and had to leave by noon. I was not even allowed to take my horse, my delightful pony. I never saw him again." So the story developed through Bourbon Two.

"What will you do now?" Albert asked while Adelia poured an extra stiff one for number three.

"Well," she replied seductively, "to tell you the God's honest, I am looking for a husband. I need someone who is wealthy, naturally, but also discerning, cultured and fun-loving." Was she moving too fast? She decided to plunge on. "If only you were available, sir!" The sycophancy stood up and danced across the room like a liberated shadow. She hated the deceit but Mr Williams had told her enough of the background to justify her actions to herself.

Albert could not believe what he was hearing; this from a vision of an Irish lass. He coughed violently, a slug of bourbon going down the wrong way.

"I might be available, actually," he managed to get out, spitting a jet of liquid toast and caviar across the sofa and onto Adelia's skirt. She shuddered but hid her reaction.

"Really, sir? Truthfully?"

"My marriage is on the rocks. We are just about to start a trial separation," he lied, and Adelia knew it for her briefing had been thorough. She fought down her revulsion.

"Wonderful, sir!"

"Call me Al."

"I think even if I was lucky enough to be your wife I would still call you sir out of respect, sir!" Lord, she was laying it on thick. She changed the subject. "Tell me how you make your money, sir."

So Albert Essington, quite inebriated and not quite realising it, spoke of his various money-making practices, several of which were highly questionable but ingenious. Adelia interjected with "Gosh, you are so clever" and "My goodness, how smart" at the appropriate times. And in case he came to a halt she added, "Can you tell me more about that, sir? I really admire highly intelligent men, especially good-looking ones." Then she moved in for the kill. "Sir, please explain again to a simple Irish lass how it is you do that clever thing."

"You mean…"

"Yes, sir, the way you bill your clients for defending them and take fees from the other side to ensure they're put away, as you know they're guilty as sin. So you're doing your bit for society, sir. It is so clever!"

So Albert Essington recounted for the benefit of her hidden tape recorder exactly how he did it, who to, and where he kept the 'real records and expenses and cash'.

"So this girl you're working on now with Mr Williams, she was the first?"

"That's right, Dakota Jameson. I was approached and asked to do a bad job of the defence and that made me think if someone wants something real bad like a conviction they usually will pay for it on the quiet."

"Brilliant, sir! And the secret records are all in the lakeside home on the Far Shore?"

"Yes, but not in the house, that would be too obvious. They're in the boat house, sealed in plastic to be waterproof."

"Mrs Essington is very lucky to be married to you, sir!"

"But enough of me," he said eventually. "Let's talk more about you." He put his hand on her bare leg, just above the knee, while slurping at his drink. "Lesh getta know each other mush better." His words were slurred; he knew what he was trying to say, only the words were running together. He shuffled along the sofa towards her. She was already against the arm, the hard stop.

"Gosh, sir, your drink is quite empty. Let me get a refill. It's so nice to spend time with a man who can hold his drink." This gained her a few minutes. At the bar she poured a huge bourbon and added a little ice, then checked her watch. She should be OK.

"Here you are, sir." Albert drank greedily and moved to another level of drunkenness, the bourbon hitting the blood flow within seconds, it seemed. Adelia had to get the balance right and was concerned she had overdone it when he reached across and fumbled with her hair, trying to pull out the multitude of clips contained within the net, but they seemed to move and evade him.

"Put yar hair down," he slurred.

"This is regulation, sir," she replied, glancing again at her watch.

"I thought you're here to entertain me."

"I am, sir." This was getting tricky. The booze had made him incredibly randy. Her brain ran through the dwindling options. She could just leave, but then the cover would be blown. As he got closer she struggled with the revulsion. He smelt of sweat, booze, and nasty aftershave. His dull eyes were glazed and the folds of fat around his face seemed to multiply as if the fat cells from the bourbon were taking up instant residence. She had an idea.

"Sir, I'm a romantic girl. I want to be wooed, that's all. You wouldn't want a girl who just made herself available immediately, would you, sir?"

"Well I'm romantic, too," he said, but the effort to explain was too much and he returned to her hairclips, determined through the haze to get them undone. That was the challenge he had set himself. He stood up to better manage his task. His clumsy fingers succeeded in getting three clips out and suddenly the mass of black hair tumbled, like a house of cards.

"I shaid I would do it." He grinned and swayed, his rumpled body in danger of landing on her.

Then the doorbell rang. "That must be your tuxedo." She jumped up, straightened her clothes, tossed her hair back and sprang to the door. "Sir, can I select your tuxedo for tonight?"

"Shore thing, my gal." She saw his lust and felt it ripping her clothes off.

By arrangement there was one suit at the end of the rack that the bellboy trundled in. It was far heavier and stiffer than the others, hence much more uncomfortable.

"The perfect one for you, sir." He saw only a black suit. "Now I must leave you to get changed and go to your dinner."

"But..."

"No buts, sir. I am not invited to dinner as it will be business, of course, and I would just be in the way. Just ring Room Service and ask for me later if you need me. I very much hope you will, sir." Then she slid the clips back in her hair and screwed up her courage to lean over the sofa and kiss him on the forehead. "You're a naughty man, sir, I'll get into trouble with my hair a mess."

"But I can't do a bowtie. I've never been able to."

"Nor me either, sir. But the bellboy will do that, sir. He will wait here while you get dressed in the bedroom, sir. Goodbye, sir, until later." With each 'sir' she gave him a light kiss on the cheek, until the final "Au revoir, sir" was a blown kiss across the room from the doorway.

Once outside the room she leaned against the hall wall and shuddered, then sighed with relief. She had done it and the cost had not been too high. Then she made her way to the lift and went down eight floors to report to Mr Williams in the Princess Margaret Dining Room.

She had a lot to report.

"My suggestion is that you butter him up tonight and hit him hard tomorrow morning when he has an almighty hangover. My request, Mr Williams, is that you get him too drunk to pursue me tonight."

"Will do, Ruby. Thanks for a great job. I'll call you if I need you but otherwise the plan is 6.30am here tomorrow."

"Mr Williams, I did this for you but next time I would appreciate a challenge that does not involve my body."

"Understood, Ruby, and much appreciated. Pack a small suitcase for tomorrow and bring your passport. You will probably be traveling. Now leave by the back way in case he is wobbling down here right now. See you tomorrow."

***

The phone was the harshest sound he had ever heard. Harsh and persistent, vibrating against the otherwise still morning, and creating waves that beat against his head.

"Good morning, Mr Essington. This is your wake-up call." Did he request a wake-up call? He could not remember.

"What time?"

"5.30am, sir."

"God!"

He cut the call and dropped the phone over the side of the bed, closed his eyes, wanting to sleep but unable to for the panelling in his head. If he could just have half an hour of peace and quiet, he could get to a manageable condition. He knew because he had been there before. Hangovers, even mighty ones, could be managed.

He got half a minute.

The phone rang again. At first he let it ring, not even sure where the receiver was. It stopped after a long time and silence moved back in. Then it started again. He got out of bed, tripped on the bedside light cord and landed on his hands and knees. The phone was under the bed. He lay down and could just reach it.

"What doya want?" His head was like a shipbuilder's yard, welding and banging rivets, his stomach churning.

"Your reminder, Mr Essington. We always call again a few minutes after the initial wake-up call. So many of our guests drift back to sleep otherwise." The voice was so bubbly, insincere jollity flaking off every word.

"Don't bother me again." He was just about to put the phone down when he heard.

"That's just what you said you would say last night, sir: 'Ignore me if I tell you where to go, I need to get up for the meeting.' That's what you said, sir."

"Meeting?"

"Yes, sir. 6.30am in the Princess Margaret Dining Room."

"Send up some aspirin."

"Sir, I need to get the hotel doctor to visit. No medication to guests without the doctor's approval."

"What?"

"I'll just ask him to come, sir."

"Who?"

"The doctor, sir."

"Forget it and don't call me again."

"Of course, sir, have a good day."

Albert rolled over and tried to sleep but the pain was too much. He lay in the dark, trying to work out what had happened last night. He had gone down to the Princess Margaret Dining Room, feeling awkward in an elaborate dinner suit; stiff, uncomfortable, head already swimming. It had just been Frank Williams and his old grandfather. Those two had drunk him, Albert Essington, under the table. They had matched him, old and young, bourbon for bourbon, until the early hours. He had a vague memory of being helped to bed by a porter. Then he cringed when he remembered the fuss he had made about Adelia coming back. There would be broken glass in the sitting room of his suite. But the porter, the crazy man, had just kept saying he did not know of any Adelia on the staff.

"Sir, I think you need to go to bed and sleep it off." It was only afterwards, drifting off to sleep in a sea of alcohol, that he had thought it strange that a Caribbean hotel should employ a white American with a cultured voice as a porter. But then sleep had taken over.

He reached out for his glass of water in the dark but could not put his hand on it. He always took a large glass of water to bed with him. Finally, he felt a glass but it was lying sideways, so when he touched it the glass span a little on its point of contact. He groaned as he thought of no water. He was too ill to get out of bed for more. He would have to live with the headache, the pain, the dryness that invaded his mouth like a desert spreading across a garden; nature in a fanatical hurry to reverse all cultivation.

There was a loud knock on the door.

"Room Service." A large waiter in impeccable bow tie and waistcoat let himself in and pulled a wheeled trolley in behind.

"Good morning, sir! Wakey, wakey, sir. Rise and shine. It's gonna be a scorcher today, sir."

"Go away."

"But sir, you ordered your favourite breakfast, the instructions said to serve it on the dot of fifteen before six because you had to be out of here by 6.15 for your very important meeting."

"Leave it, then."

"I'll run the bath then, sir."

"No, just get out." The waiter did leave, but not for another four minutes. In that time Albert had to get out of bed, wrap a sheet around his body and search for his wallet. He found it on the floor in the bathroom. He only had twenties so he pulled out half a handful and stuffed them in the waiter's hand, dropped the wallet back onto the floor, scrambled back to bed.

"Bring the tray over here," he croaked, the idea suddenly coming to him that perhaps a decent fry-up would make him feel better.

"Get me a bourbon." He gulped down the fiery liquid. "What the hell was that piss water?" he roared but the waiter had gone, insolently leaving the door to the passage ajar. Albert turned his attention to the breakfast tray.

"God Almighty!" he cried when he saw the grapefruit, melon, muesli, yogurt and peppermint tea staring up as if challenging him, the horribly healthy aromas making war on his senses. He tried to find the phone but it was lost again so he stumbled into the sitting room, hitting his knee badly on a table. A lamp fell down and crashed onto the polished hardwood floor, the noise like shards of china entering his eardrums. He limped to the sitting room phone and called reception.

"I want eggs, bacon, sausage, grits, coffee and lots of toast. I want it now."

"No, sir, we can't do that, sir, can we?" The female voice was horribly reasonable, understanding; slightly official, making a wall he could not penetrate.

"What do you mean?"

"Your instructions last night, sir. 'Whatever I demand in the morning do not give me'," she said, clearly reading from written notes. "Sir, you said you would only have our 'Super Heart' breakfast. That is the one we sent up just now. Enjoy, sir. Please remember your meeting starts in twenty minutes."

Half an hour later, Albert Essington II made his way down the corridor to the lift. His stomach churned while a cranky engine worked his way through his brain, digging and dredging into his mind, pounding against the skull, causing shoots of pain in his neck, his ears, his temple, everywhere. Listening to anything hurt, as did any form of bright light. Thus it was a pathetic sight that stumbled into the Princess Margaret Dining Room.

"Where's the coffee?"

There was none. Frank explained that he and Marcus, the other attendee, were trying to give up coffee.

"It would be a great help to us if you could avoid coffee while with us," they lied, both having indulged earlier with their breakfasts. It was in a good cause.

Frank launched straight in, a complete contrast to the conviviality of the previous evening. "There is going to be one other person in this meeting, Essington." The use of his surname jarred, adding to his discomfort. The door opened and Adelia walked in, as stunning as before but now in a smart green business suit and carrying a small matching briefcase under her left arm. Her long black hair hung loose over her shoulders and spilled down her back, contrasting with her green jacket. Albert's initial reaction was that things were starting to return to normal, although he wondered why she was not in her hotel uniform. She greeted Frank and Marcus and sat down directly opposite Albert, her emerald eyes seeming to look right through him.

"Adelia. Where did you get to?"

"Please meet Ruby Smith. Ruby is a private investigator who works for the Williams Group."

"What's going on? I don't understand..." And then he did understand. Even through the throbbing headache, his indiscretion last night was evident; things he had said kept coming back to swamp him. He put his head in his hands and groaned. "It's a set-up."

But things were about to get a lot worse.

The briefcase contained a videotape and a series of papers. With a nod from Marcus, Ruby slotted the tape into a player and Albert was forced to watch his behaviour the evening before. But more excruciating than his lewd actions was his articulate description of how he made his 'extras', as he called his illicit earnings.

"I think we are talking about twenty years," Marcus concluded as the tape ended with grey-and-white fuzz on the screen. "So, let's see now. You have just turned thirty-nine years old. So, allowing a year for indictment and case preparation, we could aim to deliver the sentence for a fortieth birthday present. I am sure you would appreciate that thoughtful touch. Then you would need to skip the next twenty birthday celebrations."

"Birthdays don't happen in prison. Ask Dakota," Frank put in.

"Exactly, so the next birthday will be your sixtieth."

"What will you do when you come out, Essington?" Frank asked. "Will you work in a grocery store? Some fast-food restaurants have programmes to assist released felons. Maybe they will let you clean the deep fat fryers."

"That would be something to look forward to."

Albert hung his head, sobs of self-pity.

"Do I have any choices?" he asked.

"You're a very lucky man," Frank replied, causing Albert to look up suddenly. "You see, I don't believe in prison other than for violent and persistent offenders. You're scum, Essington, but because of my beliefs I am going to give you an option."

"That being?"

"I want three things from you," Frank said, seeing the hope in Essington's eyes, knowing the price could be almost anything, but nothing was gained by vindictiveness. He would pay a high price, but no more. "Firstly, I want you to agree never to practice law again without Mr Hibbert's express permission."

"Agreed."

"His permission is unlikely to be granted."

"I understand." He had enough money to get by and could get involved in some other deals. This was a big demand but he could live with it.

"Secondly, I want complete and unfettered access to all the secret files you have stashed away, particularly those concerning Dakota Jameson."

There was no point in denying the files. He had bragged about them to Adelia last night.

"Will you agree not to use them against me?"

"Provided you keep to the three conditions we are imposing, but the possibility of disclosure to the police will hang over you."

"What will you do with them?"

"We will reverse every corrupt verdict, starting with Dakota's."

"But that will incriminate me." Albert was worried: he knew the content of the files.

"You said it. But, Essington, I am a man of my word. If you stick to your side of this deal, we will strive not to incriminate you. Devising a suitable plan in each case will not prove easy and will be expensive to me, but I will commit to it if you do likewise."

"I agree. And the third condition?"

"That's easy," Frank said, smiling, standing up and walking towards the window and looking out at the beach below. There was a reef in the bay made from old sunken boats. Frank watched two divers swimming in the crystal-clear water, carrying their oxygen, all they needed, on their backs. Man was an animal. If he could breathe and sleep, eat and drink, what else did he need? But man was not an animal, for Frank knew he needed his integrity. It meant more to him than all his wealth. He had that in common with his father living in two rooms in a rundown mining town, working with food banks, second-hand clothing stores, bunk beds in the dry and warm, coping with crippling disease and disaster and corruption.

But maybe integrity was his pride and hence weakness; just as for Essington it was money and seedy deals and easy women. Perhaps they were all animals.

"The third condition is simple." He turned back and saw a beaten man; caught, caged and delivered up for punishment. He felt some sympathy, but put backbone in his voice. Almost done now.

"I want Dakota's fees repaid with interest. I want the same for every person who has suffered at your hands."

"But…"

"This is not negotiable. You have one minute to decide." Frank turned back to the window and started counting in his head to sixty.

At eighteen, Essington tried again. "That will bankrupt me. And if I can't work, I might as well go to prison." It was a poor bluff and everyone knew it.

At thirty-four, Essington tried to get some measure to all this. "How will you determine this?"

"Easy," said Marcus, "actual fees and expenses paid plus interest for each full year at 8%. We don't want to be unreasonable."

At forty-eight, knowing time was running out, Essington tried to bargain. "4% would be more appropriate. I mean, the cost of money has..."

Frank turned around with a savage look on his face. Albert thought he had blown it. In that split second he heard the cell door slamming and the key turning in the lock. Twenty years.

"I'll accept 6%. Your minute is up."

"I agree." Albert pushed the cell door and it swung open. On the other side the sun was shining, the sea beating against the beach and laughter danced on the waves. He would survive.

"Good. Mr Hibbert will finalise the agreement. Now we can move on to more pleasant matters."

Albert's head jerked up, his expression quizzical, a little hope somewhere in his hungover brain.

"Your continued employment. We want you to undo every bit of twisted evil you have done over the last decade. You can start by getting Dakota Jameson out of jail. Mr Hibbert will go over the details with you. Ruby, come with me."

"Why go so easy on him?" Ruby wanted to know as soon as they were outside. "He is scum, he was ready to molest me and think what he has done to all those 'clients' of his."

"One thing I learned from my grandfather – hit your opponents hard but have a little compassion. If you hammer them completely you just gain an enemy. If you give them a little back, you create a relationship that can be useful to you. Also, with the slack you give them they either destroy or redeem themselves."

"I know which it will be in Essington's case."

"Well, let's wait and see," said with an ounce or two of experience behind the words.

Excursion

"Excursion authorisations have to be in triplicate." Smith's nasal voice spoke of pure hatred.

"I have them here, ma'am, signed by Mrs Kinderly." Smith examined them carefully, hoping to find fault. But Val, called by Sir John late the night before, was prepared.

The signatures had been given five minutes earlier by a glowing warden, who wished her success for the day. "The immediate objective is to come up with a plan for how to handle this great influx of books that my friend, Sir John, has organised for me. You and Sir John will be presenting this to me at 5pm, here in my office. Take Jameson with you." This was said almost as an afterthought, then, "Bennet, your job in this is to come up with concrete plans to reduce overtime. Do you understand me?"

"Yes, Mrs Kinderly."

"Well chop, chop, then; remember I want definite ways to cut overtime. We are within spitting distance of Barstown and I want to run straight past them before the year is out."

"Mrs Kinderly, can I ask a question? What is happening with Miss Smith?"

"What do you mean?"

"The enquiry into her practices."

"Oh, that. Well, if we suspend Smith and her cohorts then the overtime bill is going to shoot up again, as others will have to fill in for them. Plus, while they are on suspension, I have to pay them the average of the last six months' pay, and that is the peak of the overtime. So I have decided to put it on hold for now."

"You mean she is being allowed to stay in place? And in charge of a whole shift as deputy warden?"

"Needs must, Bennet. That is something you are going to have to learn. There is a whole gulf between the ideals you espouse and the practical world."

"But the thefts from the inmates? The bullying and the extortion?"

"Criminal acts against criminals? It has a certain ring to it, right?"

"It's wrong. What's more, if you got rid of Smith and her gang I could guarantee you much lower overtime."

"Case closed, Bennet, get on your way."

"I'll collect Jameson now, Mrs Kinderly." Val was far from happy. Were her precious budgets the only thing that interested the warden? The race to spend the least was going to make the warden's career but leave an absolute mess in her wake.

"Smith has taken her already. She'll pick her up as well. Now get going; as it is, I have to cover your time today while you're out with my friend, Sir John."

If Val was prepared, Dakota clearly was not. The first she knew of it was a kick on her bed-frame during the early morning period of bunk time contemplation. The guard told her to get up immediately, get dressed; there was no time to wash, then she was escorted down to Reception by the guard who was tired and resented the routine change.

"What's happening?"

"Silence, Jameson."

"Can't you just tell me?"

"Shut up, scum." To make the point, she kicked Dakota on the back of her thighs, causing her to stumble forward and hit the rough green wall of the corridor, grazing her cheek. The guard was one of Smith's crew who had tried to put the chains on Dakota in the hospital. Rumour among the inmates was that Smith was in trouble yet she still seemed to be working, still in a position of terrible authority and influence.

Seeing the shock on Dakota's face, the guard joyfully grabbed her head and rubbed the same cheek along the wall for several yards, kicking her in the rear with each step. Dakota took the intense pain, did not react to the bullying. She knew better than that. The blood was oozing out of the cracks in her skin, like bubbling water from an underground spring.

Smith was waiting for her in Reception; Carter, too.

"Hold your arms out and stand still." It was chain time. That meant she was leaving the area of general population, perhaps even going out of the prison itself. As Carter bent to fasten the manacles around her ankles, he rammed his hand into her crotch, then ran it down her leg, only just taken out of plaster the day before. She shuddered but remained absolutely still, not responding, ears alert for orders, eyes focusing on the notice board that listed regulations for visitors on the far wall. She heard the usual click of the padlock and could not help a small sigh of resignation.

"What's up, vermin?" Smith hissed. "There's no one here to help you today," she added with an evil grin that told Dakota to expect more.

And more did come.

The second set of chains was much heavier than the standard issue. And it had three padlocks instead of one. Dakota knew it would be hard to move but she did not try, rather staying motionless, as instructed. She would get through whatever they had in store for her.

She was almost thrown into the back of a prison van and driven off at speed. Carter swerved around corners, throwing her from side to side in a tangle of chains. She had been driven by Carter before. She knew the erratic driving today was deliberate.

But the journey was not a long one. It ended at the Zanesville, a period hotel downtown. Nobody had spoken to Dakota and she was not going to ask again. But why a hotel? She was half-dragged into the reception, where early risers inevitably stared at her. She caught sight of herself in the mirror behind the reception desk and understood why. She was heavily manacled, with a shapeless orange prison dress plastered with 'Inmate Zanesville Penitentiary', and orange sandals to match. Otherwise bare legs, no socks, no tights. Her shoulders seemed rounded, oppressed. She tried to straighten them but the chains were too short. To keep her feet on the ground meant slumped shoulders. Then she saw again her head and felt the horror of the razor. It was still mainly bald, just a lining of fuzz where once her lank hair had been. A ring of livid spots had developed like mushrooms around her left ear, with no hair to mask the invasion. Her right cheek was newly grazed, with blood seeping out to add to the massive bruises on her face from the 'incident', as the prison authorities were referring to it. Those bruises had faded a little but were yellowing like old paper. One bruise under her right eye looked like it was going septic.

"Inmate Jameson for the temporary custody of Deputy Assistant Warden Bennet. Arrangements made by Guest Fitzroy." Suddenly the day seemed a lot better. "She should be here by now. She is? Where, then?"

"I'm here, ma'am." Val had been waiting quietly behind a pillar in the foyer, not wanting to draw attention to herself.

Ten minutes later, after Smith had checked every detail of the required paperwork, Val took Dakota upstairs to a private meeting room on the second floor, where Sir John was waiting for her.

"Val, can you take those damn chains off?" Sir John asked after greeting Dakota with a hug and a kiss.

"I shouldn't. Regulations state…"

"Hang the bloody regulations. Now, Dakota, do you give Val and me your word that you won't do anything silly?"

"I do." So she was relieved of the manacles, at least until 4pm when Smith's crew was due to escort her back to the prison.

The day went too quickly for Dakota. She was indulged by her two companions, who, in their different ways, could not do enough for her. Sir John ordered the best of everything for lunch: fillet steak and an endless supply of salad, and rich, tasty vegetables, followed by apple pie and ice cream. To drink, he ordered two bottles of the best red the hotel could offer. There was endless good coffee, a variety of cookies to nibble, and then early afternoon saw the delivery of a large fruit basket.

"The only fruit we get inside is apples," Dakota said while biting into a huge slice of melon.

"It's disgraceful," Val replied. "I'll try and remember some numbers I was working on in my office. It was a report on medical expenditure. Last year the prison spent something like $740,000 on external medical bills alone. There were eighteen heart attacks, while the insulin bill is sky high. Listen, in 2026 there were twenty-five premature deaths, judged against normal life expectancy. I bet half of those could have been avoided. I reckon $3 an inmate each week on fresh fruit would cost $300,000 a year. This would be more than paid for, I'm sure, by a reduction in medical costs. "

They made progress on their objectives, Val reminding them frequently that no measure would get through unless it could show a reduction in payroll.

"It's by far the biggest cost. Last year it was over $7m for overtime alone."

But their progress was suddenly delayed and their objective threatened.

It was Val's fault.

"Give me your room key," she suddenly shouted, jumping up from the chair.

"What?"

"Your room key, Mr Fitzroy, I mean, Mr Sir John."

"Just Sir John," Dakota said.

"Sorry, Sir John, but I need your room key. Dakota is going to have a bath."

"My God!" Dakota cried. "I've not had a bath since…" She did not finish her sentence.

"Please, Sir John." Val was determined.

"Of course." He produced the plastic card and handed it to Val. "I'll work on the notes for the meeting this evening with the warden while you two do the bath routine." Val took the card and handed it straight to Dakota. "Here's the key. I only wish it was the prison key rather than a hotel room. But hey! Let's get moving."

A moment later, in the elevator, Val asked Dakota if she minded Val being in the bathroom while she was in the bath.

"I'm used to it. Not a problem."

"It's not what you think," Val replied. "I just had another idea and need the sink for it."

In fact, there was a sink in the small kitchen area so Dakota had the luxury of a thirty-minute bath without any supervision at all. It was the first time for nine years.

She relished it.

Forty minutes later, Inmate Jameson D. 174632F was sitting back in the meeting room with gleaming clean skin and a freshly washed and beautifully pressed prison dress. It actually had a little shape to it now. Val had stepped into the bathroom towards the end and had gently wiped the abrasions on her friend's cheek and then put cleansing cream on the semi-circle of spots that the sponge and soap had already cleaned. Dakota felt a new person. Even when the manacles had to go back on an hour later, it did not depress her.

To add to her good fortune, it was not Smith's crew that came for her at 4pm. They had gone off-duty. Nobody came at all. Then at 4.15 Val called the prison and a harassed duty deputy warden told her to bring in Jameson on her own.

"They've gone to a damn union meeting at short notice. We've got eight people sick on top of the staff absences," she explained. "I've had to cancel the training day. You were damned lucky I forgot all about your escapade or I would have called you back today, Bennet. Can you bring Jameson in by yourself? I don't think she is a risk."

"She's a lamb," Val replied. "Ma'am, can I ask when Miss Smith is back in?

"Not till Tuesday, I'm carrying the whole shooting match for the next five days. If you get here in the next twenty minutes you'll find me in Reception so you can hand Jameson over to me and get to your meeting with the warden."

"That's great, thanks." After Val put the phone down she did a high-five with Dakota and cried, "No Smith till Tuesday!"

***

The meeting with Mrs Kinderly did not go as planned.

It was Val's fault. She had to turn it into something bigger.

Thank goodness that Sir John Fitzroy was on hand to smooth things over with his endless supply of charm.

"But we got some real progress," Val said as she and Sir John walked down to the car park later on.

"Yes but it's taken everything out of me!" Sir John replied. "Remember also the time difference. It's only 8.15 for you but it is 1.15 in the morning for me."

"I'm real sorry. Listen, let me drive you back to the hotel and then I'll pick you up in the morning so you don't have to drive." Val was growing in confidence as she got used to Sir John's strange ways and twisted sense of humour.

"Would you like a drink?" he asked as she dropped him off.

"I'd love a lemonade."

"I had in mind something a little stronger!" He guided her to the bar and ordered her lemonade and a large single malt with a little ice for himself. "I mean a little ice, not a bloody avalanche," he said with a wink to Val.

Inevitably, they reviewed the long meeting they had just come out of.

"It would have been a lot shorter if you hadn't gone on about respect and rights and every other thing under the sun." Previously, Val would have been offended by such a remark from the aristocratic Briton, but she had learnt fast during the day.

"Hey, dude…" she started.

"What did you call me?"

"Dude. It's a lot easier on the tongue than 'Sir John Fitzroy' plus a whole long line of initials afterwards," Val replied into a moment of absolute silence, as happens sometimes. The whole bar was suddenly quiet also, just the drone of a baseball commentary from the television. But then Sir John threw his tired head back and laughed, drowning out Val's hesitant further explanation. After a while, she too was laughing, others in the bar looked sheepish; some grinning, not understanding the joke but somehow sharing on the fringe. As their laughing eventually died down, Sir John added in a breathless voice, "It should at least be 'Sir Dude'." That set them off again.

The second bout of laughter lasted only a few minutes. Suddenly they were very serious, as if all available mirth had been expended during their outburst.

"The point I was trying to make is that you really wound up Mrs Kinderly tonight. I think if you had made just a few digs about living conditions and respect for inmates, that would have been fine and you would have made your point, but you went too far," Sir John said.

"But I am incensed about the stupidity of it all. Surely she can see it from her precious budgetary aspect? She is incurring thousands extra on unnecessary expenditure. Not just overtime and medical bills, but what about the theft? I mean it, dude; I can save her buckets of money. She's just got to believe in my ideas."

"Well, maybe she is slowly getting the message," Sir John replied, impressed by the vigour of Val's response. "After all, if the same message is repeated endlessly, it is more likely to be accepted eventually."

"Yeah, but when exactly is this 'eventually'?"

"Well, at least we got the library sorted out. Next week they are going to see a ten-fold increase in books, plus a proper lending programme and reading clubs for different genre, plus a special literacy class. It is a wonderful achievement and you and Dakota should be proud of yourselves."

Val was about to say something appreciative back to Sir John but mention of Dakota moved their conversation another few notches into the sombre. Instead, she said, "She will be in lock-down now. Poor girl. She has so much to give and yet she has to struggle all the time."

"You admire her a lot, don't you?"

"Yes, I sure do," Val replied.

"Excuse me." Sir John swung around on his barstool to see a young and very pretty black-haired girl with extraordinary green eyes. She was elegantly dressed in a smart and expensive-looking business suit, with stockings and moderate heels. She had an American accent but it gave nothing away. She could have been east, west, north, south, or somewhere in between. "I don't mean to butt in to your conversation," she was polite as well. "But I couldn't help overhearing you. I have an interest in Zanesville Penitentiary. That is the prison you were talking about?"

"Yes, are you a journalist?" Val asked. She was forbidden to talk to journalists.

"No, I am a private detective and my client has asked me to find out a few things about the place." There was a straightforwardness about her that appealed to both of them.

"Val is the one you want to talk to mainly. As you can see, she works there. She is the youngest deputy assistant warden they have and she is in charge of welfare."

"I can talk to you but I have to be careful of what I say."

"Let me assure you that my client is an American and has a personal interest only. He wants to find out about the conditions, the treatment of prisoners, the internal justice, what rights they have, and things like that. His interest is altruistic and does not have any malevolence behind it." She was clearly well educated, and lucid as well. "If you like, I can get a written statement from him, guaranteeing the privacy of information and underlying his genuine intentions."

"I can talk in general terms," Val was still a bit hesitant.

"That will be fine. I really just want some general information, really whatever you feel able to tell me. The moment you feel uncomfortable about anything I'll change the subject and back off altogether if you prefer. I certainly don't want to compromise you in any way."

"OK, let's give it a try," Val said, then Sir John stood up and spoke.

"Well, much as I love the company of two very beautiful women, I am going to have to hit the sack. It's been a long day for me. What time in the morning, Val?"

"I'm on shift at 6am so is 5.30 too early?"

"That's fine. I'll be up long before that." Then, turning to the new arrival he said, "Goodnight. It was a pleasure meeting you, even if very briefly."

"What a gentleman," the girl said when Sir John had left. "He sounds British."

"He is. His name is Sir John Fitzroy. He is like a minor aristocrat. His family used to have a castle in Scotland but he is a famous historian at Cambridge University. He is an expert on 18th Century British-American relations so he comes over here a lot. Actually, he has been helping set up a proper library in Zanesville Penitentiary and that's why I've been meeting with him. By the way, I don't know your name."

"It's Ruby Smith. I know your first name is Val."

"Val Bennet."

"I'm pleased to meet you, Val. Can you tell me a little about your involvement at Zanesville? When did you start there and how did you get promoted so young?"

***

After a second lemonade they both moved on to black coffee. An hour of conversation later, Ruby suggested they take a break.

"You have an early start and it is almost 10.30 now. Would it be possible to meet again, maybe tomorrow? I hate to press you but I need to report back."

Val would have been happy to carry on. After a slow start, replying to questions with wooden, short answers, no elaboration, she really got into it and enjoyed espousing her views and experiences. She had run through the waste, the inhumanity, the senselessness, but wanted to add much more about the potential for change.

"Sure," replied Val. "Let me just tell you about what we achieved with the Visitors' Room. You see it was the perfect example of giving dignity back to the inmates and everyone benefitting from the changes. We actually got a 6% reduction in total overtime from this change alone. On an annual basis that comes to $60,000. We spent just $4,000 on materials and the inmates did all the work. Because they were motivated, they did a great job, and with minimal supervision. That's just one example of the positive change that can happen. I have a list longer than my arm back in my office."

"You have your own office?"

"Well, it's not much more than a closet," Val said. "No windows."

"But clearly you are quite senior to have your own office and access to all these records and reports. Do you mind me asking a more personal question?" Val shook her head and Ruby continued, "Do you enjoy working in the prison?"

Val did not answer for a moment. She swirled the remains of her coffee around the cup, refused a refill when the bar tender offered it; thinking hard, thinking in particular of the last few weeks, of Smith, her husband, of Dakota, the long shifts, her move back in with her mother, her cheeky son.

"I love it," she finally said. "I used to hate it but now I can't imagine doing anything else. I want to make a difference."

"It sounds like you are; making a difference, I mean."

"Yes, I suppose I am, but I have only just started."

"Well, enough for tonight." Ruby still had to write a daily report and call Mr Williams before 11pm, when he usually retired for the night. "Can we meet tomorrow?"

"Sure. I would like that. I finish at 6pm tomorrow. I know, why don't you come around to my mom's place, where I live? I'll cook something and we can talk after Kyle goes to bed. It's 14140 Bedchester Street, go past the big mall heading west and take the third right onto Grantham Road, then left onto Lincoln Avenue and Bedchester is fourth on the right."

Letter Seven

My darling Ben,

I am lying in my bunk thinking about you. It is 4.45am on Friday morning and I am seeing you, God willing, on Sunday. Your last letter was so sweet, Ben dearest. When you said "I can never get you out of my mind" my heart thumped and my stomach went like all strange! I love you so much, Mr Benjamin Franklin! I asked you in the last letter whether you considered me your girlfriend. I hesitated a long time before writing that and was so anxious to get a reply, fearing the worst. Your reply was wonderful. Thank you! And, yes, I do consider you my boyfriend. Apart from Daniel Roberts, you are the only boyfriend I have ever had.

So much has happened recently. I will tell you more about yesterday when I see you, but I had a real pleasant surprise and spent the day with Sir John Fitzroy and Miss Bennet, who you know is one of the deputy assistant wardens here.

It was strange hearing Dakota explain the people involved as if Ben did not know them. He knew it was for the censors, who read every word that left the prison.

We worked out a plan for the library and Sir John has arranged for a loan of over 2,000 books from his university. He came in and helped me with the cataloguing all day yesterday. We now have a system worked out, although I have a lot to do before the books arrive next Friday.

OK Ben, it is time to grab that beer.

Ben had not bought any beer that month. However, Mrs Jameson had given him a bottle when she invited him to supper the day before yesterday and he had kept half for his next letter. He took it from his refrigerator, surveying his almost empty shelves at the same time, thumbed off the loose cap and settled down in his armchair, reading light on like a spotlight on stage.

Richard Sutherland was definitely seriously ill by the end of March 1783, clearly in the last few months of his life. His left arm was paralysed and speech was harder, although his thoughts were all there and he could still write lucidly, for instance maintaining his diary dutifully. But walking more than a few tens of yards exhausted him. He was like a clapped-out water pump, leaking and inefficient so that maximum effort was required for small exertions. Then there was the pain. He was determined to be stoical about it but wrote freely in his diary. It kept him awake much of the night, when Rupert's concoctions wore off and the house was freezing cold. Rupert often rose and mixed more medicine but Richard hated to disturb him at night when he was working long hours on the town hall roof repairs by day.

But their plan was beginning to pay off.

In the last week of March, the roof repairs were complete and Rupert, demonstrating that he could read and write, was moved into the records department. Where the roof had caved in, the snow and rain had created havoc with the numerous documents. Rupert, always liking a challenge, worked diligently and was soon trusted with copying sensitive reports and filing them.

Thus, on the last day of March, he learned news that he was sure Richard would want to hear. He begged to leave early, claiming he was worried about his master's health, and ran back to the Hollingsworth house. There had been no fresh snow for ten days but it was still bitterly cold. It was as if the sky willed to send down more snow but had none left in reserve. Instead, it sent freezing temperatures and winds that turned the snow on the ground to dangerous ice. Rupert, in his haste, slipped over three times, once banging his knee badly on a fence post at the corner of the road that the Hollingsworths were on. He limped on two blocks to get to their home and went straight to find his master.

"Master, I have news." He was breathless, lungs gasping, doubled over with cramp in his side.

"Rupert, get your breath back. The news will wait two minutes." Rupert's breath slowly returned to normal. In the meantime, Sidney Hollingsworth entered the room, as eager as Richard to hear the news.

"Sir, there are two treaties signed, as you had started to

suspect. There is to be a big meeting at a place in Virginia to decide which treaty to present to the British. One is the treaty you negotiated with Mr Franklin. The other is something wholly different." He paused for breath and to rub his painful leg.

"You're hurt, Rupert. You are bleeding."

"It is nothing, sir, I fell over in my haste to get here with the news. It is just a scratch."

"What is the other treaty, man?" Hollingsworth asked anxiously.

"Sirs, it is a reinstatement of the colonial possessions of the British Empire, with regard to the Americas, specifically those colonies lately in rebellion against the Crown."

"My God." Hollingsworth spoke first, a tight smirk to his face. "They have actually done it." He punched one fist into the other hand.

"Where in Virginia?" Richard asked, slurring his words.

"A place near Charlottesville."

"When do they leave?"

"On Monday, sir." That was five days away.

"Thank you, Rupert, you have done well. Now, go attend your wound."

When the door closed behind Rupert, Richard continued, "I should leave; tomorrow, in fact. But I shall go by ship, as if going back to Canada. Then I will double back to Charlottesville. I have a large estate there. I know the area well. I must make sure the treaty I negotiated is signed. It is the only hope for this great country."

"You are not well, Richard. I would be happy to go in your place. I can report back to you here safely in Philadelphia."

But Richard would not hear of it, adamant that he would go. "I'll have Rupert to help me. I have to make sure that the right treaty is signed."

They went to dress for dinner, Rupert helping Richard considerably now.

"Sir, do you really think it wise to go on this trip? Would it not be better to stay with these kind people until the weather is warmer and then return to Scotland?" Rupert could have said 'return to Scotland to die' but he was too much a gentleman, despite being a slave.

"No, Rupert, I have to do this. If you will support me and bear with me for just a few more weeks, then we can go home knowing that the job we set out to do has been accomplished by our hands."

"Master, I will always support you."

"You are a good friend, Rupert."

Later that night, Rupert pondered that last statement. He believed it was the first time since his captivity over twenty years ago that anyone had called him a friend; certainly the first time a white man had ever done so. He drifted off to sleep in his attic bedroom thinking how angry he had been as a captured child taken in the boat in chains by someone just like Richard Sutherland. Yet twenty years later he had grown excessively fond of a slave-trader. It was a strange world. Good people did wicked things while sometimes the wicked did good deeds. He had learned something of Mr Sutherland's stern religion and wondered how the simplistic division of right and wrong, good and evil, could work in a complex world. But then he thought, 'I am just a simple savage saved by my betters so I might have a chance of entering Heaven and knowing Jesus'. His final cheeky thought before sleep took over was that he was not so simple that he could not partake in a little sarcasm.

***

Richard found dinner that night troublesome and hard to manage. It seemed like his hosts were barraging him with kind intentions. First, they wanted Sidney to go in his stead, Rupert to stay and look after Richard. Then they declared that perhaps Rupert could go with Sidney while Sally Ann cared for Richard.

Next, they sallied forth with a counter-attack. What purpose could be gained by anyone going to Virginia? Surely Richard had done everything he could. The rest was up to fate. It was not in their hands at all anymore.

"I am going to go, dear friends. I have to go, and that is that."

So from course to course they went; new proposals, new ideas, gradually weakening Richard's defence but unable to claim victory until the last move over whisky that night. Sally Ann had retired and they had retreated to a small study on the first floor.

"I will go with you," Sidney said.

"Sorry?" Richard was much weakened.

"The solution is simple. I will come with you. I can aid you and assist physically if there should be any difficulties."

So it was agreed. Richard allowed his new friend to accompany him, actually welcoming the generosity and his tired mind not wondering why this busy man had so much time for him. Perhaps that was what friendship was about.

***

They had agreed that early in the morning Sidney would go the docks to find a ship. They were not interested in a berth on board but in the complete ship. Richard had sufficient cash to hire or, indeed, buy a ship complete with crew.

"It's the best way, so we can easily divert the ship once it is out of sight of land. We tell everyone we are going to New York to trade, then we head south as soon as it is safe, finding an anchorage where we can easily cut across by land to Charlottesville. When the business is done, I will use the ship to return directly to London."

Sidney had one suggestion, that they take a cargo with them.

"I have sufficient goods to fill the hold and it will only take a day to load them from my warehouse. We will attract less suspicion with a laden ship. I have plenty of tobacco. It would be a perfectly reasonable business venture to load it up and sell in Massachusetts so it fits with our story." Then he had a question. "What shall we say of your health? I have been passing the word around that you are too ill to travel back to your estates in Virginia."

"Tell them I am much recovered."

Sidney actually went first to a coffee house close to the town hall. It was before 6am, outside was dark and bitterly cold and a freezing wind channelled its way down the streets, as if seeking mischief of any type, wanting to cause misery as it passed. He met with several people at several tables, had quiet conversations. Then he went with the last person he met to the docks to look over a ship. He haggled, as was his character, twice walking away, twice returning, on request to further the deal. He purchased the ship for Richard for two-thirds of the original asking price. It came with a crew. He then met with his warehouse manager who drew up a bill of sale for the tobacco. This was Richard's venture, so he must own the cargo. But Sidney knew his tobacco prices.

The loading started and Sidney was back at home by 9am, joining Richard for breakfast. "All arranged. I think we might be able to get away tonight on the high tide. I've offered a bonus if the loading is complete by dusk. I will need a bit more cash to cover the bonus if they achieve this. I also withdrew Rupert's services, saying you were much recovered and eager to start trading again."

***

They did leave that night. The ship was aptly named the Swan. She had an elegance about her as she slipped her berth and glided into the Delaware River with a crew of fourteen. She was a small ship, but served their purpose. And she was fast. Richard retired soon after departure, leaving Sidney to explain the change of direction.

"But why do you want to take tobacco to Virginia?" The captain, a stocky man with a jaw that jutted out like a jetty in the water, asked.

"Sir, my colleague, Mr Sutherland, is dying. He wishes very much to see his Virginia home one more time. We decided to go to New York to sell our cargo but he has a hankering to see his home again. We compromised by loading the cargo here and we will be asking you to drop us at Richmond on the James and then go on to deliver the tobacco to my factor in New York. By the time you have done this we will be back at Richmond waiting for you. Mr Sutherland's house is only four days' easy journey from Richmond so allowing a week at his house, our two arrivals back at Richmond should coincide.

The captain agreed, subject to receiving a sum as surety for the crew's wages and a 1% fee on the value of the cargo. Later, Sidney could report to Richard that all was in order for minimal extra expense. Richard had been reasonably careful with money all his life, yet now seemed not to care for the details, focused on the key reason for the trip. He let Rupert handle the money, just as Rupert had acquired the stores for their short journey, packed their belongings, and guided his master on board, later reading to him as the ship made sail and Richard was grabbed by a fierce headache that would not be controlled. Rupert stayed up long into the night, reading and being a presence for his sick master. Finally, as the wind moaned around the rigging, creating a rhythm, it sent Richard off to sleep and Rupert could also get a few hours on his hammock in the passageway outside Richard's cabin.

The next day, Richard was considerably better. The cold weather of Philadelphia had moderated; a fresh breeze from the west was invigorating, as was the sun that broke through the clouds.

"It's the first time this year I've felt the sun with any strength," Richard said as he walked on deck, Rupert holding his arm. "It feels so good, so warming." The Delaware had broadened out overnight so that only to starboard could they see land as a line in the distance. Looking to port, they could be in the middle of an ocean.

"We'll stand out into the Atlantic a little way." The captain came over to converse with Richard. "Then, sir, we turn south for 100 miles, keeping the Delaware peninsula in sight but at a safe distance. When it ends, we turn back to land and find the James River."

"When do you suppose we will arrive?"

"At Richmond? I suspect in the evening of the fourth of the month; the day after tomorrow, that is. You'll want to stay somewhere in Richmond overnight, sir, and make a good start in the morning."

"So in seven days I could be home, God willing." Richard played along with the deception.

"I should think so, sir. We might lose a day on the James."

"I'll accept that, Captain, if it happens, but ask no more of my patience!"

"I'll do my best, sir. Do you see the wind is picking up nicely?"

The wind did pick up. All day, they raced down the Delaware peninsula, making good time. It was as if a divine power was behind the Swan, pushing it along with its own special wind, its own purpose. That same wind also cleared Richard's head, especially when they placed a chair on the deck and Rupert brought up two rugs.

"I feel better than I've felt for a long time, Rupert," Richard said as Rupert tucked in the rugs around his thin frame.

*"I'm pleased to hear it, Master. I'm here if you want anything."
He stood expectantly by his side, but Richard was content to let the
wind blow in his long grey hair and watch the waves in their
jiggery-pokery.*

***

*There was no grand house at Richard's Charlottesville estate of
Hunt Ridge; just a long, jagged rise of land that gave it the name
and led eventually down to a clapboard farmhouse of eight rooms.
They were unannounced and, because it had been over twenty
years since his last visit, it caused some confusion. The tenant
before had been Alfred Brewster.*

*"That is my father, sir. He died twelve years ago come July. I
wrote to you, sir," she said a little defensively, two small children
hiding behind her.*

*"I recall now," Richard said. He had completely forgotten, but
had been saddened when he learned that Alfred had died in a
terrible accident in the water mill.*

*"You wrote back, sir, and gave the lease to my husband, Simon
Williams. I am Amelia Williams now."*

*"But you were Amelia Brewster? Of course, I remember you so
well. You used to hide from me when I came to visit and I would
have to search for you and pretend not to find you. You must have
been six or seven years old then."*

*"I am thirty-three now, sir. But forgive me my rudeness. You
have come a long way and I am leaving you unattended! My
husband is in the fields but will be back shortly. You must come in
and take some refreshment. Will you be staying long?"*

Goodness, it is now 6.30 already and time to get up.

It always took a moment to break from the story Dakota was
telling.

*I have a busy day ahead in the library, getting ready for our big
delivery of books. I will have to go, but will write again very
shortly. I love you so much, Ben. I am so happy to be your
girlfriend.*

There was the usual high volume of crosses to indicate kisses around her name, but Ben could see they were a little more hurried; scribbled, unbalanced. Although she had to hurry, he could sit a long time thinking of Dakota and how much she had come to mean to him. He could not think of one bad thing about her. Even her faults were things of wonder to him.

The Seat of Government

Daniel Roberts loosened his tie and pulled it over his head. He kicked off his Italian slip-on shoes, a tiny part of his mind thankful that there were no laces to undo. Most of his mind, however, was focused on the lady in front of him as she stripped also, but much more slowly than him so that he was in his underwear and socks while she was still undoing her skirt. Each button to her skirt was undone separately, as if each was accompanied by a solemn statement.

But the only statement Tess Ronzio issued was an invitation made with her large, grey eyes, so striking against her light brown skin and jet-black afro hair. She had been deliberately silent but as she stepped out of her skirt and twirled it away behind her she spoke, her voice more husky than usual.

"Do you want me, sir? Well I'm here for you, sir." She lingered on the sirs, stressing the secretary-to-boss relationship that drove Daniel wild.

"Yes," he squeaked, then repeated with greater control of his voice, "Yes, come to me now."

She walked slowly over to his side of the office and sat in his chair, twisting it around with her stockinged feet, this way and that, leaning against one leather-bound arm and holding him in her gaze.

"I'm here for you, sir. Just for you." She still wore her blouse, her stockings and high heels. "Or does sir want me to be the boss today?" She slipped back in the chair to lengthen the reach with her legs and prodded his underpants with her shoes.

"No, I'm the boss." But again his squeaky voice belied the words.

"Then I await your orders, sir." Said so confidently, so alluringly, so sexily. He could not wait, but pulled down his underpants and approached her, forcing himself down on top of her in the chair, not noticing the sudden look of terror on Tess's face, a picture of a rape victim for the camera.

It was at this point that Ruby started the video. The door to Tess's outer office was open just wide enough to hold the phone centred on the office chair.

"Don't, sir. Please don't." But he did not register the panic. He had to have her. He was the boss. Even when she was sobbing he heard just cries of joy, of ecstasy. Only afterwards, when she slumped on the floor, did he first realise something was wrong.

"Hey, Tess, what is it?" Sated now, his voice had descended an octave. He sat in his chair and poked Tess gently with his foot. "Baby, what's up?"

There is a scale in human behaviour and reaction that goes from oblivious to petrified. No clever psychology professor has attached his or her name to it, so it is probably past adoption now. It operates on a scale of zero to one hundred, the lower the number, the higher the oblivion. Daniel had been happily sub-ten when he threw himself on the chair and thus onto Tess. Sub-ten means he may not have noticed a fire starting in the same room, probably not even hearing the raucous alarm. He was in a special place that only had one person, himself, in it.

And of course, in this instance, the body he was raping.

But by the time he prodded her with his toes, he was in the upper teens. At that level, you hear voices but they are not meant for you. Crossing a road, you would be oblivious to the danger and may easily get hit. The screech of tyres and the honking of the horn would raise you quickly to the mid-thirties. That was where Daniel was when Tess did not respond to his questioning. He was still a way off being alarmed but the needle was moving up the scale.

When Ruby stepped through the door with a shout of "What have you done?" he jumped twenty clear points. Now he had fallen off the yacht and the others on board had not noticed. He had a life jacket so was still not in a critical situation, but it was suddenly a lot more alarming.

By the time Ruby had helped Tess to her feet and he could see her torn blouse and the tears smudging her make-up, it had ticked up again.

But the red on the marker starts at eighty and Daniel got there when he saw the phone in Ruby's hand. Something clicked and he knew he had been filmed. Early eighties on the scale is when you see the broken bottle in the bar and watch it swing in a suddenly silent arc towards your body, wondering where it will land but knowing that it will land somewhere.

There was only one more stage on the scale. Daniel reached 100 when Ruby played back the video on her phone.

Thus they had broken a man, sending him off the scale.

And they had done it on the instructions of their employer, Frank Williams III.

Ruby took charge now. Tess retired to the sofa on the other side of the office. She did not get dressed. She did not wipe the tear-stained make-up. She made no effort to sort herself out. Instead, she whimpered and glared alternately. A good actress.

"What do you want?" Daniel asked.

"Listen to him." Ruby laughed but without humour. "His voice has gone squeaky again."

"What the hell do you want?" He reached for his pocket to take out his wallet, but remembered then he did not have any clothes on. "How much?"

"Nothing," Ruby said.

"What?"

"No money, no pay-offs, just justice. That is what we want."

"You're going to turn that tape into the cops? My lawyers will have a field day with you in court." Confidence returning, but he had mistaken the meaning of Ruby's reference to 'justice'.

What Ruby had meant was very different.

"Get dressed," she said. "You too, Tess. Then cancel all appointments for next week."

"What?" Daniel was indignant. "You can't do that."

"I've just done it." Ruby was dismissive. "You're going to

come with us; voluntarily, of course." She turned her back, not wanting to see him get dressed, then continued. "Of course, how long it takes really depends on you."

***

The President was irritated.

She often was these days.

She hankered after the old days. True, take any period in history, as her nieces and nephews pointed out to her, and she would not have been president at all.

Was it enough to be the first female president of the United States? Would that be her chapter in the history books? Or would she go down as the first female but the last president? That was the real question. Would the election even happen? The country was in crisis, if it was still a country.

She slammed the folder on her desk and looked around at her chiefs of staff. They were all looking to her for leadership. Why were the requirements of leadership so totally unpredictable? What should she do?

"Meeting adjourned," she said. "Get me Hibbert and Fitzroy in here now." Aides jumped to her command. This was a crisis. At least they now had something to do.

It was 28th August 2028; hot, sultry, stormy, on edge. And the President had just heard again the convincing reason why her country did not exist, had never existed. The whole of the last quarter-millennium had been a sham. The most powerful country in the world was built on sand, on false foundations. And it came on her watch.

So far, it had been contained. Not the news. That had been plastered over every newspaper and internet site around the world, leaked by the damn Brits. For what purpose? To embarrass them? It did not occur to her that the leak might have been an accident; tempers were hot, confidence was low... everything was part of a sinister plot against her country.

But her country did not exist, had never existed. It was

too much to comprehend; yet she was the leader. It was down to her.

The containment, she realised, had come from the shock value. Everyone was too stunned. It was like the declaration of war hours after a trade agreement was signed. It was more than that, worse than that, but she did not have the words.

Of course, the government was working night and day. Dick had been a trooper. He always was. Not for the first time, she wished she had married. Being Mrs Dick Turnby would have been fine. He was happy to be the string-puller while she danced on stage.

But there was no time for fantasies. Everyone was relying on her. She needed to sort this out.

"What do you think Fitzroy hopes to gain out of this?"

"That's easy, Madam President," Sir John said in his private audience thirty minutes later. "I am an historian. I want to discover the truth and I want it known that I discovered the truth."

"Is that the most important thing in your life?"

"In my professional life, yes," Sir John replied with conviction. They were sitting in a small office in the White House, used for very private meetings. There was only the President, her private secretary, the Attorney General, Dick Turnby, and Sir John. Hibbert was in the waiting room.

"And is the professional life the most important life?" When the Attorney General asked this, the President's thoughts went immediately to bribery. She was not inherently dishonest; had never involved herself with any form of bribery, yet this was a first-class emergency. The end would justify the means. Yet she had campaigned for the Presidency in '24 on precisely the opposite platform – honesty in government had given her a landslide.

"No, but it is right up there near the top. Look, your founding fathers clearly did not want independence. Otherwise, why would they have immediately reacted against the draft Treaty of Paris with an agreement to stay a part of the British Empire?"

"But did they?" Dick asked. "How can we be sure that the sequence of events you present actually happened in that order?"

"I'm certain, so are the experts," Sir John replied with the cool detachment of involvement without impact. It was not his country at risk. "The new treaty specifically says it rescinds all prior treaties with the British."

"Bear with me a moment." The Attorney General spoke up. "It rescinds all prior treaties but what if this new treaty was signed first and then the Treaty of Paris was signed later? It can't rescind a treaty that does not even exist at the point of signature." It was a clever point but Sir John was one step ahead.

"Fine as a theory but for one little point." Again Sir John used his pause tactic. Storm shadows rolled across the room from the floor-to-ceiling windows. Ben, in that room at that time, would have observed the shapes the shadows made, or calculated their average speed, counting their passage from a marker on the left of the room to one on the right. But Ben was not in that room, rather 200 yards away, doing a long shift on overtime, trying to boost his August income so that he could pay for the Zanesville trips planned for September. Those actually in the room were too serious to worry about shadows and shapes and speed. They had the weight of the country on their shoulders.

A biographer might have described the next few minutes as the pinnacle of Sir John's career. Certainly, everything afterwards was not quite the same. But now, pausing, waiting, building suspense, it was vintage Fitzroy.

"That little point being," he said eventually, but with emphasis on each word, knowing that what he was pronouncing was monumental in consequence, "that there were no other treaties before these two." Then in a sudden rush he finished off, "It stands to reason that the treaty that mentions rescinding other treaties has to be referring to the other of these two treaties. There are literally no other treaties to rescind. I ask you, Madam President, ladies, gentlemen, which treaty has an opening clause that rescinds? There you have your answer."

Nobody answered because nobody had an answer.

***

Albert Essington II had never worked so hard, at least not since he had collected debts after hours as a law student, visiting poor homes with a heavy in attendance and claiming to be a fully qualified lawyer to frighten the clients. He had found the heavy to be redundant, people more scared of the paperwork delivered by a young and aggressive lawyer, and made a presentation to the loan company for layoffs. It had been accepted. An added advantage was that the collection bonus had been split amongst fewer of them.

The deal Marcus Hibbert had presented to him had been remarkably generous. He received a salary that was not exciting but would pay the bills. To earn this salary, he had to review each crooked case he had worked on and reverse the process to the best of his ability. In addition, during any downtime, he had a special project to work on. Marcus had made him team leader on the sentencing reform project which Frank had commissioned.

"He is determined to cut out excessive sentencing, like happened to Dakota," Marcus had explained during the initial briefing.

Albert worked temporarily in a small office in the basement of Frank's block in downtown DC. He had been told to expect a move to Hunt Ridge, the centre of Frank's empire, any day. The office he was in was cramped and lacked natural light, but he was man enough to know when he was defeated. He just had to get on, do the work, and get free again.

"I'm like an indentured servant," he told himself, but would never admit to anyone else, especially not his wife. In fact, it would be hard to open up to her because she had taken off the moment he had explained about putting both houses up for sale to afford the repayment of fees as agreed. She informed him, smiling all the time, that she had only been hanging around for the money and had been sleeping with another lawyer. She was gone that day, taking just two suitcases; interested in the future, not the past.

"Bye Albert dear, it was fun for a while." When he did not answer, she knelt down in front of him and said, "No hard feelings, hey? People come and go, you need to go with the flow." She was chewing gum as she spoke. He had never liked that.

There were more points to the agreement that Marcus presented. He had ninety days to repay the $11m Marcus had calculated as owing. This was to be paid into a trust account. Also, if he completed his work successfully over the next two years he would get a modest bonus to help him start again.

"Define 'successful'." Albert had tried to negotiate but Marcus allowed none of it.

"Successful means I think you have done a good job. It is purely subjective but I would be happy if I need to pay it out. This is important work, Essington."

There was only one thing that was thoroughly objectionable about Albert Essington's new role. He had tried to reason and argue but the decision came from the very top.

There was no way it was going to change.

Albert's boss was Ruby Smith.

And he had to see her now to report on his week's work.

Under Attack

Sir John left his sudden appointment with the President and made his way, late, explaining by phone, to meet with Ben, who had now finished work. They had agreed to meet in their usual place, the Little Kitchen. Sir John was looking forward to it, having found time in England to make up a mock cookbook of silly British recipes.

He never made it.

But he did make the six o'clock news that evening.

He heard the car, but did not see it until too late. He had just crossed Farragut Square and turned right on K Street, intending to pick up a cab. The first thing he heard was a panicked cry from another pedestrian. Then he heard an engine massively revving and the squeal of hot rubber on hot tarmac. He turned and the last thing he saw was the vehicle, a bright red Suburban, racing towards him, left wheels on the road, right wheels on the sidewalk. He saw every detail of the car; the licence plate, the stickers, the scratch on the windscreen, the missing side mirror with two wires sticking out like antennae, the broken aerial, and then the great big dent on the door. He saw the driver, grinning madly; baseball cap backwards, red vest, no shirt, short hair, tattoo on his arm, of some unknown monster. He saw the arm come up, noticed the open window, saw the crowds scatter for cover, but still could not work out what was going on.

"Get down," someone shouted. At last, Sir John broke his trance and ducked down, but there was nowhere to hide. He cowered, hands over head, as the rifle pushed out of the window and six bullets were expended in rapid time. He felt four thuds as the Suburban picked up speed and raced away down K Street. He noticed a brake light out as the car swerved into the traffic.

Then he noticed nothing else.

The news report was thorough; instinct dictating that there was a huge story here for the telling. Several of the pedestrians had taken video footage. They were played many times on television, analysed and re-analysed. It was clear that the British professor, Sir John Fitzroy, was the intended victim. The only questions were who had done it, and was Sir John Fitzroy related to the King?

The first question was answered by a voice-disguised recording sent to the major networks around 6.15pm. It stated that the American Society was responsible. They were a new organisation dedicated to all things American and they despised the pathetic attempts of John Fitzroy to take away their country. It ended with a rousing call to arms for all Americans who loved their nation.

The second question was the subject of much debate over several days, until finally the King of England issued a statement that he was not aware of any relationship but was shocked by the act of terrorism and that the whole country's thoughts were with Sir John Fitzroy and his family.

He needed those prayers, for Sir John had been in and out of consciousness since one of the four bullets entered through his stomach and hit his spine, shattering it. The medical response was fantastic. Within six minutes of a passer-by making a frantic 911 call, there was an ambulance on site. The medics had firearms experience. They knew how serious it was immediately. But they also knew how to stop the bleeding and how to move him from sidewalk to gurney and from gurney to hospital bed in A & E. They saved his life.

"But what type of life will it be?" Anne, his wife, wanted to know.

"I'm sorry to have to tell you but it is highly unlikely that your husband will walk again."

"You mean a wheelchair? Forever?"

"It is the most likely outcome. Several vertebrae have been smashed and his nerve chord largely severed. There are some treatments available; there is always hope and this type of medicine is making huge advances every year."

"But at the moment?"

"Lady Fitzroy, at the moment he is likely to be paralysed from the waist down."

It was only much later, as Sir John started to stir, mumbling in his sleep, that Anne thought about his riding. Would he be able to ride again? Would he even be able to sit on a horse again? What it would be for him never to feel the wind in his face, the gait of the horse, the sweep of the land, as he cantered over the fields of the farm next door, jumping the lower hedges and laughing as he again beat her around the home-made course. She tried to imagine what it would be like for her, then doubled it for her husband; doubled the frustration, the bitterness, the anger.

And how would she tell him? How could she break it to him?

But no need, for Sir John had heard her last conversation with the doctor. He had thought at first they were talking about someone else. Then, when they jabbed him again with another dose of morphine, he had gone into a semi-dream, thinking they were discussing Richard Sutherland and his increasingly crippled state as he struggled to make the peace between nations he so badly wanted. He saw Richard, heard his considered voice, wished he were like him. He was a man of his time. Maybe reviled by the modern world as a slave trader and arms dealer, but a man who made things happen in his own time. He had a morality that looked poor through a 21st Century glass, but he was a leader of his day. What more can you do than be a moral force in your time?

A long time must have passed because Sir John was conscious of the morphine wearing off. It was as if he was the prescribing doctor involved with his own medicine, calculating when consciousness would return. But this annoyed him intensely. He wanted to continue his train of thought through to a conclusion. He fought off the present, snuggling down into deeper slumber. But it could not be held off for long. There was also the question of Anne. She had to know he was all right.

"My darling," he said, flicking his eyes open just long enough to see the vision he had married.

"Oh my God, John, you are OK."

"Fighting fit." But where was his train of thought taking

him concerning Richard Sutherland? He was nine-tenths of the way but nine-tenths does not make a journey complete. "I know about my legs," he said to her. He was so torn between the world he had briefly inhabited and the world that contained his wife and family and all the others. That was the painful world where his back hurt and the depression of his crippled state weighed him down.

"I'm so sorry, darling," she said.

"I will walk again. It is just another challenge." He closed his eyes, aware of white coats on the periphery: walking, talking, juggling instruments, dedicated to a purpose. He did not feel the needle, that nerve had gone, but he did feel the flood of relief like Heaven descending into the world.

"Who ever thought Heaven would come to Earth rather than vice versa?" he mumbled as the lights went whiter than white and the flood took over his entire body. Now, where had he been? More to the point, where had Richard been?

"The good news is that his upper body is not paralysed and his brain seems unaffected," one of the white coats said as he made to leave the room. "Lady Fitzroy, I suggest you get some rest. You've been at his bedside for thirty-six hours now."

"I need to be here for him when he wakes."

"He won't wake for six hours. We have a bed for you next door. Please, Lady Fitzroy, you will need to be fresh for when he next wakes."

Lady Fitzroy let a nurse lead her out to the next room and help her ready herself for bed.

***

Jay Harris flicked through the radio stations as he drove, anxious for his moment of glory. He had many in the two hours it took to get from K Street to the cabin he had built with his brother last year. It was only sixty miles but the last hour was endless twists through ever-smaller roads and dirt tracks, then though two fields. He flicked on the four-wheel drive and a few minutes later drove into the wood they owned, had always owned, as far back as anyone could remember. As the Suburban bumped over roots and scrubland, Jay reached across to the glove compartment to pull out his chewing tobacco. He had just remembered it in time. Placing a small amount in his mouth, he grimaced at the taste and chewed rapidly. He would need to spit well when he reported back to the elders. He pulled his phone from his jeans pocket to check the time. It was 8.18, he was slightly late, but it would not be bad to have them waiting on him for a change. As he entered the dense tree growth, the light of dusk barely penetrated and he had to swerve to miss several trunks. His elder brother would tan his hide if he banged the automobile. But then, he thought, who would know if it was done against a tree by accident or swerving to hit the assigned target back in DC? Smiling to himself, he plunged the steering wheel down, hard left, and beautifully grazed an ancient oak with a screech like a wild animal.

"You been drinking?" Eddie Harris demanded. "I said no drinking on the job." Eddie was much bigger than Jay and nine years older. It seemed to Jay that his arm was always raised, ready to strike in a fatherly way. They had never known their fathers so Eddie naturally filled in.

"No, sir." He had tossed out the empty beer bottles as each one was drained so there was no evidence.

"You hit my damn car."

"Yeah, against flesh and bone, Eddie. That was what I was sent to do."

Eddie seemed to accept this and felt the scrape with an almost reverential air, as if touching something connected to the crime would somehow involve him to his credit.

"You done good, Jay, real good."

"Thanks, Eddie." He accepted the handshake and the slap on the back. Now he belonged.

***

"My God, Dakota, Sir John has been attacked. I just heard it on the radio during my break." Val whispered, not wanting to be seen to fraternize with inmates. She had invented an excuse to come to the library when she should have been processing new arrivals. This was one victory she had achieved; giving new inmates a rundown of the facilities available provided they stayed within the rules. You could not easily measure the results of this initiative but they had collectively shaved four hundredths of a cent off the cost per inmate hour last week. With Barstown increasing by half this amount, they had reduced the deficit to fifteen hundredths.

"Mrs Kinderly, I really believe the wholesome nature of these improvements are building trust, reducing tempers, and allowing a slightly lighter supervisory burden. This is why you are seeing staff costs edge down."

"You might be right, Bennet. I see overtime was down by 112 hours last week."

But right now positive change was not at the top of Val's agenda. As soon as she had heard the dreadful news she had to pass it on to Dakota.

"Is he OK?"

"The report said he was alive, thank God, but in a critical state. I've got to get back to help process new inmates. I'll get news to you if I can. Pray for him."

"I will, Val."

"What are you doing here, Bennet?" The aggressive voice made them jump. Val knew before she turned that she had been caught.

And by the worst person possible.

"I'm sorry, ma'am. I... I just remembered that I had to communicate something to Dakota, I mean to Jameson, about the books arriving tomorrow. I was just leaving."

"You could have asked permission," Smith said, both of them knowing that it would have been denied. "Consider yourself on report." That was a blow, would mean a long interview with the warden or her deputy, probably Smith herself, and loss of six months' seniority. It was also not good to put a guard on report in front of inmates, but Val knew that Smith was enjoying the humiliation she was imposing. But worse was to come for Dakota. "Carter, take Jameson down to the rec room. She is back on general duties for the next seven days. The library is strictly out of bounds. That should remind her that her work here in the library is a privilege and should not be abused."

"You can't do that. The books are arriving tomorrow," Val burst out, not thinking.

"Ten days." Then when Val fell silent, Smith added, "Any more pathetic ranting to come? Any increase on ten days? Am I bid fourteen? No, well that is a real shame. Carter, process it for ten days."

"Yes, ma'am."

***

Val was still fuming as she drove home late that night. Her shift had been due to finish at 8pm but Smith had refused to let her go. She had spent three hours racking up the overtime, reviewing the prior records of the new arrivals.

"I want a report on my desk first thing in the morning detailing all trouble-makers. I'm not having disorder in my prison."

Val had completed the report at ten minutes to eleven and taken it to Smith's office in the central administration block, a floor below the warden's. The office was deserted so she left it on Smith's chair. Val had the next day off so was keen to get the report completed that evening.

She played heavy metal loud on her CD player as she drove home, drumming out the beat on her steering wheel and singing along with the words she knew. It was only when she pulled into her mother's drive and switched off the ignition so that the music died mid-riff that she realised her phone had been ringing. There were six missed calls from the same Virginia number.

"Miss Bennet, is that you? This is Frank Williams. Do you remember we met a few weeks ago when I came to visit Dakota Jameson?"

"Yes, of course, Mr Williams, I remember you well." She had liked the look of him; had thought about him quite a few times since then.

"Have you heard about Sir John Fitzroy?"

She confirmed she had and they spoke for a few minutes on this. Frank, with his contacts, informed her that Sir John was conscious some of the time, seemed in good spirits, but the doctors were very worried about damage to his spine. "He might never walk again."

"My God, if you see him, please let him know that we - that is Dakota and I - are praying for him."

"I will, but I had another reason for calling you." She had felt that there was something else. "Are you free anytime soon? I wanted to see you again."

"Actually, I am free tomorrow, then not again for about ten days. The prison is very short-staffed."

"Are you on for an early start?"

"Yes, actually no, not too early." She had just had an idea. And it was a good one.

"OK, shall we say noon tomorrow, then? I'll come to you. I have your new address."

***

Very early the next morning, long before sunrise, Val was driving back to the prison.

"You're not on today," the duty supervisor said after checking the roster.

"Deputy Warden Smith wanted a report on her desk first thing this morning. I only finished it just now." Val waved a stack of pages with neatly-typed nursery rhymes from a project Kyle was heavily into for summer school.

"Leave it here, then."

"No she said to be sure I personally placed it on her desk." She was getting used to lying.

It went with the job.

Inside Smith's still deserted office Val risked the desk lamp and began a systematic search of the whole room. There were three filing cabinets, one with a few books and magazines stacked on top, and then there were four desk drawers including the central one. There were several notice boards on the wall but no pictures, no photos, no ornaments. Other than three chairs, there was nothing else in the room.

She started with the filing cabinet nearest the door. Inside the top drawer were copies of old duty rosters, filed in date order. She flipped through them and saw there was nothing unusual. The next drawer down concerned building and grounds maintenance documents, while the bottom drawer had nothing but a stack of budgets and financial reports that looked like they had never been read.

The second cabinet was locked but she found a key in the central desk drawer, noting at the same time that it contained nothing of interest, just stationery, blank paper and some old half-eaten chocolate. She unlocked the second cabinet. The first two drawers were filled with copies of inmate files. She flicked some open at random. Other than highlighting and underlining in ink, there seemed nothing unusual.

Except why would Smith bother to go through inmate records marking key parts? She was well known for minimal paperwork, maximum brute force. Val looked again and a trend was emerging. The underlined words were all references to inmate weaknesses, for instance alcoholism, drug addiction; one mention of sodomy had a hand-written exclamation mark by it. The highlighted words were notes of relatives and, specifically, what they supplied by way of creature comforts on a regular basis. She looked up Jameson's file and read highlighted details of her mother and Ben, also that she received three packets of Marlborough every week like clockwork.

"I'm getting somewhere," she exclaimed.

But the rest of the filing cabinets produced nothing of interest. The bottom drawer of the second cabinet had nothing but a spare pair of boots. The third cabinet, once unlocked, contained staff reports. Time was passing but she could not help but look at the one for Bennet, V. It was scathing.

It was also completely untrue.

Val was just about to close her personal file when she noticed a hand-written memo. She read it twice with trembling hands.

Smith, we have to play it slow with Bennet. She has a powerful friend in Sir John Fitzroy and I do not want to upset him. Instead, I will promote her out of her capabilities so that she comes crashing down and has to resign. Don't worry about her. She is inept and pathetic. Time will sort her out. I.K.

It had to be Iris Kinderly. Val sat back on her haunches and thought a moment. The whole promotion to deputy assistant warden had been a farce. Moreover, that meant the investigation into Smith's activities clearly was not happening. Val had been lied to in order to keep her quiet while she walked blindfolded into her own downfall.

But, also, if Mrs Kinderly was soothing Smith, there had to be a reason. That meant they were in league together. Yet Mrs Kinderly had a handsome salary, bonus, stock options, car, pension arrangements, five weeks' vacation. Would she really give all that up for her cut of a few dozen packs of cigarettes?

Maybe it was something much bigger.

Remembering that she had a purpose, Val stood up, put the papers carefully back in the cabinet, and crossed the room to the desk. There were three drawers left. She tried the largest one first. It was full of plans of the prison: drains; electric and other cables; the depth of cement; the location of doors and windows. Nothing of interest.

The small top drawer was empty. That left one to try. As she opened the middle drawer, Val saw it was virtually empty also and her hopes sagged. She had achieved something from this high-risk strategy of searching Smith's office but not enough; nothing like enough. She lifted up the one book in the drawer to see if there was anything underneath. There was nothing but two rubber bands, both broken. That was it, then.

Time was getting on. She would have to get moving. She

placed the notebook back in the drawer, then saw its title.

"*Inmate Welfare*," she read out loud. "That will be a short notebook." She closed the drawer and switched off the desk lamp.

Then she realised that the notebook had been heavy, almost bulging, enough to break the rubber bands. She switched the desk lamp back on and opened the drawer again.

"Some welfare!" she murmured to herself. The book was a complete record of twenty years of extortion. Furthermore, it was in the large loopy letters and figures of Smith's own hand. Val had to copy it and she knew exactly where the copy machine was.

Fifteen minutes later, she was back in Reception.

"That took you a long time." The duty supervisor was not that interested.

"I had to find a copy machine." That much at least was not a lie.

"There's one right outside her office, down to the right."

"I turned left," she replied, letting the main door close behind her.

***

Sir John felt like he had finally joined the ranks of royalty. There was a contingent of doctors, one of nurses, and another of well-wishers and family, all competing around his bed for space. Outside, he had heard, was a larger body of journalists and cameramen. He was getting used to publicity, was enjoying it.

If only his damn bloody legs were still working.

"He's coming around," a nurse said while chewing gum. They wouldn't do that with the King, he thought.

"Young lady, be so kind as to step into the bathroom and remove whatever delightful flavour is filling your mouth right now." She retreated in embarrassment, while Anne Fitzroy smiled. Her man was back from the dead.

Letter Eight

Ben had been looking forward all day to the letter he had received from Dakota that morning. The news of Sir John, however, put it completely out of his mind. It was still in his pocket when he arrived at the hospital. He had waited two hours for Sir John at the Little Kitchen, drinking coffee on the house, wanting a beer but not being able to afford it.

"There will always be a coffee for a customer like you," Mavis had said when he explained that he had no money and had been waiting for Sir John. Sir John had said it was his turn to pay. "It's on the house and always will be. You've more than earned it with the odd jobs you do for us." Ben had sorted out their drains just the other day.

"Thank you, Mav." She insisted thereafter on refilling his cup every time it got below the half-way level so Ben had his fill of hot, strong excellent coffee.

It was just as well, for he had a long night ahead of him.

He first heard of the shooting when driving away; angry at the no-show, hungry, his stomach awash with coffee but nothing of substance. There was nothing at home and he had no cash. All anger evaporated as he turned the car off the freeway and made straight for the hospital.

Only they would not let him in.

"I'm a good friend of Sir John's." But his pleading was to no avail.

"Sir, he is surrounded by good friends, he is a mighty popular person. I am instructed not to let any more in until someone leaves: one out, one in. If you give your name, I'll call you on the Tannoy the moment a space frees up."

Ben gave his name and waited.

He went to a reception area that was fairly crowded, with a constant flow of people in and out, reminding Ben of a metropolitan bus station, only no one had any luggage.

"Can I get you a coffee?" an old man said next to him.

"No thanks." Ben could not afford it. The man seemed to take offence, probably had wanted to discuss his wife's illness with someone, anyone. The old man purchased a single cup from the machine and sat one chair over with his back half-turned to Ben.

That was when Ben remembered the letter.

For a moment, he thought he had dropped it somewhere. It was not to be found.

But then he remembered it was in his back pocket.

***

My dearest, adorable Ben,

I am lying on my bunk thinking about you. I am always thinking about you and can't wait until Sunday. I hope against hope that you might be able to come on Saturday and Sunday, staying the night at a motel. I know it is expensive and you are short of money so it is fine if you can't make it but it would be so good to see you two days in a row.

My God, how would he get the money for fuel? And a motel as well?

Time to update you on Richard Sutherland, although there isn't much to report as I am totally stuck in my research. But at least it gives you an excuse for a beer.

But beer was not on the menu that night.

***

Amelia Williams was dreadfully concerned for her elderly landlord; clearly, he would not live much longer. She confided in Rupert while the slave was assisting her in the kitchen.

"We are both desperate to get back home," Rupert replied. "But the master's business is of vital importance and he won't rest properly until it is done."

"Is that why he came here?"

"Yes, with a little fortune we are close to the end of our journey. We hope to conclude matters in the next few days and have a ship

coming back for us in Richmond shortly. That ship will take us directly to Glasgow in Scotland. I have never been there but I am told it is just two days by carriage from the port to his estate."

Neither one of them stated the obvious, that Richard Sutherland did not have many days left should he even make it back to his native Scotland.

"I don't like the other gentleman," she said.

"Mr Hollingsworth? He has been very kind to us. He took us in on the eve of a vicious storm and has been most attentive to my master's well-being."

"There is something about him," she replied, then added, "Perhaps he has been too attentive."

"Perhaps." Rupert suddenly seemed pensive, miles away.

"Rupert!" she cried. "You have poured the soup away in your reveries."

***

This much I have from a letter Amelia Williams wrote to her sister, who married a lawyer in Richmond. I came across it by chance. In the letter she referred to a diary she kept so I wrote to lots of people in Virginia in the hope of finding out if anyone knew of the existence of the diary. I really did not expect an answer but a descendant's wife, called Kirsty Williams, had possession and she kindly sent it to me. It is amazing that, while a lot of people just do not reply to my letters, some people send treasured family records to a convicted criminal who they have never met! And she did not just send one diary, but the whole collection, starting when Amelia was twelve years old. She wrote me the sweetest letter, saying that her husband was a direct descendant of Amelia. So now I know an awful lot about Amelia Williams, 1750 to 1842, but never once does the box full of diaries mention anything to do with Richard's adventures in 1783. It was as if it never happened. If I did not have a copy of the letter she sent her sister, I would not have known about her at all.

But now I'm for sure at a dead end. Richard, Rupert and Sidney Hollingsworth just seem to disappear. The next report I have is of Richard staying at an inn on the road from Glasgow to his home in

1783. I've not been able to find any more records of Rupert. It is like he never existed. I suppose maybe that is normal for a slave. But Hollingsworth is a different matter. For some reason, he turns up in Canada. He is Philadelphia-born and lived there all his life to date, same for his wife, but in 1794 he has a thriving merchant business based in Nova Scotia. He lives to 1809 and is the wealthiest man in Halifax when he dies. His wife lived on there to 1832, yet their two sons returned to Philadelphia after the war. One went into the ironmongery business and made money on gates and railings, the other became a newspaperman. It's almost as if there was a split in the family. I'm trying to get a copy of the Hollingsworth will to see if they left their wealth to their sons or whether it was a family rift that separated them until their graves. But other than that, I don't know where to turn. I wrote Sir John about it and hope he replies soon. He was a great help earlier. He has a sort of instinct for things. He just knows what to do next and where to look.

So, if you can put up with me a mite longer, I'm going to recap where my story is right now. Richard goes to Paris and gets on real well with Benjamin Franklin. They negotiate the draft treaty but it is held up in the States but no reason is given. Richard takes Rupert, a slave he has purchased from his host in Paris, to America, travelling secretly so that his intentions are not known. He gets to Philadelphia and meets Sidney Hollingsworth. Sidney and his wife put them up when Richard is not well. Rupert works at the Town Hall and discovers a shocking fact. There are two draft treaties, one is the version negotiated by Richard and Franklin, the other is a complete recantation of the Declaration of Independence and a statement that the American colonies will remain within the British Empire. Richard is British but he wants the two countries he loves to be independent and friends again. He wants his treaty to be the one that is enacted. He is very ill and old and knows he has not long to live. He also wants to get back to Scotland before he dies and wants to get Rupert, of whom he has become very fond, back to his family. The convention is moving to an estate near Charlottesville to make a final decision. They buy a ship, ostensibly to trade to the north, but actually to travel to Virginia. That is as far as I get. Why are they going to Virginia? Do they hope to break *into the convention and persuade the delegates to opt for independence? What is their plan? Ben, this is tormenting me!*

Enough of all this, my dearest. Soon it will be shut-down and I need to clean my teeth. I am completely out of plaster now and my hair is a little more than fuzz, although still real short. I love you, Ben, I always will.

***

Ben read the letter through again, feeling Dakota's frustration, knowing that he had the means to alleviate some of it. The documents he had sworn to Sir John to tell no one about would surely be able to help Dakota resolve what happened next? It was out as common knowledge that the country's very existence was in question, that the White House; the centre of power and authority, was owned by the British crown. But very few people knew of his involvement. The US government did. He had been interviewed several times, had spent the night as a guest of the President. Hot and cold treatment. Good cop, bad cop. But it was very much in their interest to keep his involvement quiet. If the press learned about him, they would be all over him, teasing the details out, writing more and more speculative articles.

Mrs Jameson knew, as did Sir John and the two Franks, grandson and grandfather. Then there were the lawyers who he had spent long hours with. But all these individuals had been sworn to absolute secrecy and so far as he was aware not one had broken it.

So how could he?

He read the letter again, willing to find a way to help his love, his beautiful Dakota. When he thought of her, he thought of freedom. He thought of the beautiful prairies, sometimes still with heat, sometimes the wind bending the grass in great waves, as if the ground itself was rippling its muscles, flexing and moving. He thought of Indians, free for centuries to hunt and fight, until the white man hemmed them in with ever-smaller circles to roam. Then he thought of his girlfriend; confined, restricted, governed and watched since the age of eighteen. Her name spoke of freedom but her condition was decidedly unfree.

Once, he had looked up the origin of the name Dakota. It meant 'friend' in the local Sioux dialect. That made Ben think of all she had given him, how happy he was now to have her as a friend, his girlfriend. He thought of Val, and the little that Dakota had said of her friends in prison. How come those with the least can give so much?

At first he did not hear his name being called. When it was repeated, he rushed to the ward reception desk and moments later was shown into Sir John's room. He seemed asleep. There was only one other person in the room, sitting quietly in the shadows created by the bedside light shining on the sleeping, injured aristocrat. He could see that it was a man, a young man. Then he saw that it was Frank.

Ben and Frank sat quietly for a long time, barely saying anything to each other. Sir John stirred once, opened his eyes, smiled, mumbled something, then went back to sleep again. At 10pm, a nurse came in to do routine checks.

"Great Scott," her heavy Jamaican accent made both of them look up, breaking their private thoughts, "we still have some visitors. Visiting hours finished an hour ago. You'll have me in great stick if Sister sees you."

"Have you eaten?" Frank asked Ben as they made their way down in the elevator. Ben shook his head. "Let's go to the Little Kitchen, my shout." Ben was not in a position to refuse.

But he did get his beer after all.

***

"You mean you are going to Zanesville tomorrow?" Ben asked after gulping down a third of his beer. "Any chance of a lift?"

"I thought you always went on Sundays."

"She asked if it would be possible to come both days. Actually, it does not matter." Ben suddenly remembered the motel cost. He did not have the money. He fell silent, looking down at his beer, tilting the glass this way and that so the white foam made patterns on the sides.

Frank looked at him a moment, examining him, realising what it was. "I have a suite booked at the Zanesville. I am doing some research into the prison. It would be most helpful to have you and Mrs Jameson to stay the night if that is acceptable to you. You would be my guest, of course, as there are some matters you can advise me on." He would work out what they were later; best to get Ben on board first, get around his pride.

"Are you sure? I mean, will you for sure find it useful to discuss the prison with Mrs Jameson and me?"

"Yes." Don't explain, don't elaborate, don't allow a chink of weakness.

"Well, I accept. And I am sure Mrs Jameson will, too. She will be delighted by the prospect of an extra visit. I'll give her a call right now." The saving on fuel would mean Ben would eat next week.

"Great, I won't be in your way. I have a meeting with Valerie Bennet and one thing I know, it won't be at the prison. She sees enough of that place as it is!"

It was only much later, in bed, reading Dakota's letter once again, that Ben wondered why Frank was meeting with Val. He was too tired to work it out now. He would ask Frank in the morning.

The Date

Travelling with Frank was always fun. And it was efficient, if somewhat extravagant.

The helicopter picked them up at a small airstrip twenty miles west of DC. They were in Zanesville a little after 11am. 'Cars for the Busy' was waiting to take Ben and Mrs Jameson, while Frank had his own limo waiting.

"I don't know when I will be back from seeing Valerie Bennet so I thought two cars better. These guys will take care of you until they drop you at the hotel after visiting hours."

"Why is he going to see Val?" Mrs Jameson had asked.

"He said it was personal. I think he finds her attractive."

"She is a very pretty girl," Mrs Jameson answered, then added, "The belle of Zanesville Penitentiary."

No, Ben thought. Val is undeniably pretty but there is another who stands head and shoulders above the rest. Not conventionally pretty, certainly not with her head fuzz and poor diet affecting her skin, but a beautiful person.

The driver took them, by arrangement with Frank, to a sweet Italian restaurant, where Mrs Jameson had spaghetti bolognaise and Ben could not resist a spicy pizza, washed down with one beer.

"I don't want to be smelling of alcohol when going through Security."

They were the first ones there for Security, standing just outside the double doors that guarded the reception area. They knew the routine well now. At 12.50 the doors would be pushed open by a guard, clipboard in hand. ID would confirm who each visitor was, then male and female visitors would peel off, left and right, for inspections. These had once been no more than an aggressive pat-down, making it fairly easy to bring contraband in. Since Val had been allowed free rein they had become much more thorough, although also more cheerful. The edge had gone from the guards' attitude. Instead, they smiled and joked and knew regular visitors by name.

By being first in line they would almost certainly be first into the room, giving them maximum time with Dakota.

That was what they both wanted.

***

Val was ready a little before noon, watching the driveway from the sitting room window. She wore a yellow sleeveless dress with a white linen belt and white strap sandals. The bruises to her face were mainly gone now, but a little make-up, applied carefully, hid the faint remnants. She wore her long blonde hair loose over her shoulders with a white hair band to keep it from her face.

She looked calm, elegant, beautiful.

But inside she was a jumble of emotions. She had the evidence to get Smith. She just had to decide how to use it.

"My God, you are beautiful." Frank was clearly taken aback. But he was prepared for the day. He spoke to the driver briefly. Twenty minutes later they pulled up at a small stream running through a wood of oaks and beech trees, with a few crooked, squat walnuts growing in the clearings. They sat in one such clearing, near the stream, underneath a walnut tree that looked older than America. The chauffeur carried the hamper while Frank got two rugs from the car and spread them in a space where the roots were less prominent.

"Thank you," Frank said. "Please come back at 3pm." It was a beautiful September day with a gentle breeze getting muddled amongst the trees and drifting this way and that, giving bouts of refreshment from the heat. The high sun was speckled, as it would be under trees, making patterns amongst the roots and dirt and sparse grass that grew in clusters wherever it could find a grip on life. Birds sang with songs of freedom, perhaps playing hide-and-seek amongst the branches and leaves above.

"I'd forgotten," Val said.

"Forgotten what?"

"Life without concrete, fences, paving, barbed wire, rules

on notice boards. Life as it naturally is."

"Well, I hate to bring that all flooding back." He opened a bottle of wine and poured her a glass. She did not normally drink. She accepted it and sipped, her eyes not leaving his handsome face. It was good wine.

"Why not leave it back there for one day?" she said shyly.

"Because I need to ask you a whole bunch of questions about the prison."

"Oh." She straightened up and looked down at a mad network of roots like a city freeway system. She imagined the beetles and other insects living under last year's leaves and the little slabs of slate that seemed to run in veins back from the stream. He realised his mistake immediately.

"It's not that I didn't want to see you. I have thought a lot about you since we met last month." He took her hand in his, raised it to his lips and kissed it. "A huge amount."

"What did you want to know?"

"I'm sorry, Val, I've messed things up. It's just that to me business and personal are sort of merged into one."

"No, it's OK. I just thought... well, never mind. Let's see what you have for lunch. It's been a long day already and I'm starving!" She tried to make light of it.

One reason why Frank had been supremely successful in his decade in business is that he knew not to climb an impossible mountain. Instead, he would work around a problem and tackle it from another angle. So he started talking and when he had finished Val understood much more. He told her about Ruby Smith and the task he had set her. He also talked about the injustices of sentencing and told her about the work he was doing on reform. He had a team working on it, headed by Albert Essington.

"Wasn't he Dakota's attorney?" she asked.

"Yes, but he sees things differently now." That was said with a firmness that hinted at a whole other story. "He's also working with others on Dakota's case. We intend to get an appeal going."

As they ate smoked salmon sandwiches, grapes and

crackers, sipping on the wine until suddenly the bottle was finished, Frank elaborated further.

"But there is something I don't understand," Val said. "Ruby was asking me a lot of questions about how the prison runs. If you are interested in welfare and sentencing, why bother about administration?"

"Simple," replied Frank. "I intend to buy it."

"Wow!" Val thought back to her first serious conversation with Mrs Kinderly; how she had decided that it didn't matter how you got there, just that you achieved prison reform. Here was Frank Williams saying he would buy the whole company in order to bring about reform. "Won't that be rather expensive?" She grinned.

"About $27 billion," he replied. Not as if it was short change, but not an unmanageable amount, either. "Don't get too sleepy, by the way, we have stage two ahead of us."

"What are we doing next?"

"Wait and see," he teased. "I think I estimated your size just right."

Before the limo came back at 3pm, Val had opened up completely to Frank on her ideas for how the prison should be run.

"There is just so much waste," she said. "Yet the irony is, they are trying to save money all the time, yet wasting it in crazy ways."

"Explain."

"Well, here's a for instance. Mrs Kinderly has an army of inmates cutting immaculate lawns around the front of the admin block. A lot of this work they do with hand tools because the inmates are not trusted with power tools. But the bigger point is that this creates a pretty scene but nothing that adds value. It is as if every inmate is written off on reception so even if you get one hour of useful work out of them in a thirty-year sentence that is a positive!"

"It's like modern slavery, then?" Frank asked.

"No, much worse than that," Val replied. "With slavery there is an investment by the slave holder so there is a motivation to get something back for that investment. This is as if the slaves were sold for zero dollars and zero cents. They become nothing of value."

"So the profit is not in what the prisoners do constructively."

"That's right, it is just in making savings on the running costs. Hence the costs have to be driven down relentlessly." Suddenly Val sat up, excited by the prospect. "Frank, this is so exciting! If your deal goes ahead I want so much to be a part of it. I was thinking about leaving the prison service, but this could be everything it needs. I would love to be involved."

"I'm beginning to understand what a mess it is," Frank said, adding, "You have a really good grasp on the situation. I've never heard such a compelling case for any business I've been involved with."

"You're just saying that because you like me," she replied, pretending to bash him with the empty wine bottle. Frank did not reply, but smiled and thought, *Wow! I've got a real cracker here.*

***

Ben was not enjoying his visit anything like he usually did. Smith, the duty deputy warden that day, was throwing her weight around.

"She adds poison everywhere," Mrs Jameson said, hearing Smith's abrasive, caustic remarks directed at a young inmate who could have been Dakota nine years earlier. She had just been denied a visit from her husband because he had raised his voice at the wrong time.

"I've had enough of you, Wright. Carter, take her back to her cell, lost privileges for ten days. You, hubby dear, get out and take that brat with you." Hence she made a stressful situation multiply, ensuring that without privileges the husband and toddler would not be able to visit next weekend, either.

"What's she in for?" Ben asked.

"Do you really want to hear a sad story?" Dakota asked.

Inmate Wright was a lucky girl. Born into a negligent family, other than the abusive father who gave her a lot of attention, she had struggled all her life. Pregnant at fifteen, in and out of care and young offenders' institutions, always on the shady side of life without doing anything seriously wrong. But she had a boyfriend, also on the edge of society, but somehow the relationship had survived six years of pregnancy, babyhood and incarceration. That is why she was a lucky girl.

"What is she in for now?"

"Some meth was found in her trailer. She couldn't explain how it got there but a lot of people come and go in that community."

"So she took the rap? How long did she get?"

"Twenty to life."

Ben did not enjoy the visit, for another reason. He itched to tell Dakota what he knew of Richard Sutherland. They spoke again about her frustration at the cold trail and both Ben and Mrs Jameson were unable to open up with what they knew. Ben had hoped to ask Sir John for permission but he had not been awake during his visit last night.

"Time. Move out now. Inmates to the rear." Smith's commanding voice rang across the room. Ben almost preferred it this way, torn by the secret knowledge he had that could help his girlfriend. "Jameson, I said move." The voice thundered with anger. Dakota released her mother's hands and moved quickly to line up along the back wall. "Face the wall." All thirty-two inmates turned for the frisking. Usually this was done after the visitors left the room, but Smith had other ideas, enjoyed the look of shock on Mrs Jameson's face as Carter frisked her daughter aggressively.

"Don't you dare treat my girl in that way." Mrs Jameson could speak with authority on occasion. Carter stopped, as if obeying an order, looked to Smith for direction. She nodded a curt reassurance and he turned back to his frisking, treating Dakota rougher than before.

"Get out before I ban you from visiting," Smith said, cold and calculating, like steel cutting through a field at harvest time. She might have added not to mess with the blade.

***

"So after the picnic, where did you go?" Ben asked, draining his beer.

"Swimming in the most gorgeous private lake," Val replied, sitting in the hotel lounge, holding hands with Frank. "Frank is a friend of the Burgess family. They are probably the richest family in town. They have a most beautiful lake home and own the whole lake. It is about half an hour south of here, but worth the drive. I got a new swimsuit into the bargain!" She laughed.

"I didn't want to tell her to bring a swimsuit as it would ruin the surprise. By the way, we thought about dinner here at the hotel, the four of us. Val has to eat early to get back for Kyle."

Sitting in the dining room, white tablecloths and black-and-white waiters, large sliding doors opening onto a small rose garden, their conversation naturally went back to Dakota and the day's visit.

"She is real frustrated about her research," Ben said, looking at Frank, who took the hint.

"What's the problem?"

Ben outlined the difficulty Dakota was finding in tracing the movements of Richard Sutherland and Rupert all those years ago. Frank said nothing of note until after he had escorted Val home and returned to the dining room, where they drank coffee and nibbled on the mints placed on the table.

"Do you think the discovery you guys made would help Dakota?" he asked.

"Definitely, but we can't tell. We promised Sir John."

In reply, Frank flicked on his phone, used speed dial for the hospital and asked for Sir John Fitzroy.

"I'm not sure what exactly the relationship is," he said

down the phone to the receptionist. "But I understand he is close to the King."

"Frank, is that you?"

"Yep, Bunny, how are you doing?" Ben was aware of Sir John's nickname, it had come out once when a little worse for wear, but he would never dream of using it. Was it wealth or success that gave you the easy-going confidence Frank had?

"Listen Bun, I think it is time to bring Dakota in on our discovery. She has done great things with her research but is stuck like a cow in a ditch. Can you release Ben and Mrs Jameson from their commitment not to divulge it and let them share it with Dakota? And Val, of course, so she can discuss it with someone if she gets the chance. I've not seen Dakota today but Val tells me she is a bit down. They all send their love and prayers, by the way. I'll pass on the good news. Now, get some rest. I'll stop by sometime on Monday. Sure thing, goodnight. Oh, I almost forgot, I'm pretty well decided on the acquisition. Opening bid is twenty-seven billion, I expect to have to pay thirty-two."

Frank switched off the phone, then said, "Sir John is much better, more like his old self. He grants total release from prior promise in respect of Dakota Jameson and Val Bennet – the language gives you an idea of his recovery, at least of spirit." Frank went on to explain that Val had asked him to lunch at their house tomorrow.

"What's the talk of acquisition?" Ben asked, then wished he had not, it seemed obtrusive of him.

Frank knew he could trust them after they had sought release of their promise rather than just breaking it. So he drew in his chair and explained his plans to buy Pillars of the Community Inc.

It was another world to Mrs Jameson and Ben. They were used to having a few twenties in their pocket and feeling good. Here was someone who dealt in tens of billions as if it were a couple of hundred bucks.

And he was undoubtedly their friend.

False Imprisonment

Nobody saw it coming.

Not even Marcus Hibbert, who had seen many such twists in his half-century in the capital.

Certainly not Ben.

They came, not in the middle of the night like they usually do, but on his way to work. He jumped into his car, slightly late for a Tuesday shift, and eased into the traffic. He thought nothing of the black Suburban following him. DC had many black Suburbans.

But by the half-way mark by miles he thought it a little strange that there was one either side of him, plus the one behind, all shiny black. He could not change lanes, hemmed in as he was, but luckily his route was straight ahead. He felt more threatened when a fourth black beast turned into the road directly in front of him. He was now driving at fifteen miles an hour in a moving black cage with sunlight glinting off fenders, making it hard to concentrate on the way forward.

The rear Suburban made the first move, bumping into Ben's Chevy suddenly, causing him to slide to the left and hit Suburban number two.

The switch happened so fast. Ben wondered afterwards if they had a mock-up section of road somewhere in their training camps and practiced it all day long to gain perfection. One minute he was listening to Johnny Cash on the radio in his car, the next he was bundled, handcuffed, into the back seat of Suburban number three. He saw two men in overalls hitching his car up to a tow truck that must have been waiting just around the corner.

Ben never saw his car again.

Then they were moving away. An agent leant across and fixed a heavy blindfold, black as the Suburbans, no glare.

They drove a long way out into the country. He could tell because they cruised with infrequent braking and no stops. Nobody in the car would talk to him, in fact nobody spoke other than the driver once on the radio to confirm pick-up. This was not like last time. He knew there would be no guest suite and no dinner with the President waiting for him.

When the car stopped he thought they had been travelling about two hours. That would make it about 7.30am. As they grabbed his jacket and hauled him out of the car he could feel the sun with its still modest heat on his lower face, not yet fired up for the day. That confirmed he was facing east. It also confirmed his idea of the time of day. Concentrate on the practical matters, he told himself. Put yourself in the best position you can.

Up steps, through two doors, down a few steps and then some more. A basement, probably. There was a damp feel. Definitely a basement. They shoved him forward, pulled off his blindfold and slammed the door shut, all in the same practised style as before.

He could see nothing. The blindfold removal made no difference. He stepped tentatively forward, feeling with his feet, unable to use his hands. The room seemed empty. It took a long time to feel his way to the wall. It was dirt. So he was in a cellar. He followed the wall around three sides; nothing broke the continuous wall of rock and soil. The fourth wall had the door and nothing else. Dividing the room up into strips, he ventured back into the open but found nothing except a crude wooden bed, a bucket to relieve himself in, and a three-legged stool. He was in a virtually empty cellar measuring about fifteen feet square, as far as he could tell there were no windows, certainly no fresh air.

***

The directions on your phone would have stated 18.6 miles and a time of twenty-six minutes to get from Ben's place of imprisonment to that of Daniel Roberts' internment. If you had put it in your phone, lacking anything better to do, it would have told you on foot it would take four hours and forty-three minutes. But the locals would know that it was much quicker than that. They would know that you could walk to the top of the woods above the building Ben was being kept in, across the valley and over the brook and you would be on Hunt Ridge land within fourteen minutes. From there it was a steep climb for 300 yards and then a gentle slope down to the house. You would spot the stables from the ridge, away to your right or west of your current location, but you would not need to go to the stables, for Roberts was being housed in one of the guest suites at the mansion. It was still a prison for him.

But it was an extremely pleasant one.

"Mr Roberts, I will give you one last chance to come clean on this. You planted those drugs on Dakota Jameson back in 2018," Ruby Smith tried again, never one to give up, but her approach was wearing thin.

"I don't know what you are talking about. I do know that false imprisonment is an indictable offence and I fully intend to follow up and see you in court. They will be looking for me any day now. The eight days will be up soon. When I don't come back they will know something is wrong." He was right and she knew it. Today was their last chance. It was an ingenious excuse for his absence, more so because it would go down so well with Roberts' father-in-law, a deeply religious man. The eight-day retreat before wading into his political career would go down very well with the old man.

"I can't be contacted at all during this period. It is essential to have total silence for eight days," he had been forced to say on the phone to his wife.

"That's a great idea, Danny my love. I'll miss you," she readily agreed. Eight days without him was a bonus and she needed time for her plans. "If you need longer, just get word to me somehow, whatever way you are allowed to communicate. Bye, Darling." Her casualness had stunted his ego, but not for long. Too many people had told him for too long how good, generous and wise he was, how far he had to go.

Ruby turned off the tape recorder and left the room, angry at the lack of breakthrough, stopping herself just in time from slamming the door. It wouldn't help to let him see her frustration.

"I'll be back shortly," she called to the guards. There were always two guards, day and night, paid handsomely and with moderate shift lengths, but expected to ensure the presence and safety of the object.

"Ah Miss Smith, I've been looking for you." Turning around in the passage, she saw Essington hurrying towards her. That was all she needed right now. She could have feigned not hearing his call and slipped into a side room but she was a professional and, more than anything, she wanted to get the job done. Instead she waited for him, noticing that, while still odious, he had lost some of that domineering, leering manner. He seemed brought back down to earth, a very ordinary middle-class middle-manager, starting the approach to middle age.

But she still did not like him.

"What can I do for you, Mr Essington?" She resorted to the formal.

"I just wanted to report on the Jameson case."

"It will have to wait until next week." Ruby had too much on just now.

"But I have a deadline to meet. I need to get the appeal papers filed by Monday." Hibbert had included harsh consequences if various deadlines were not met. "And it still has to get through legal review, scheduled for Thursday."

"OK, I can spare ten minutes now." She led the way back to her office in the administration wing that Frank had built four years earlier, the year she had joined as a dining room assistant, the year she had received the all-clear after the vicious leukaemia that had torn across her young body, the year she had been able to let her hair start to grow. As if conscious suddenly of the last four years, her meteoric rise to senior investigator, she tossed her long, shiny hair; a gesture that brought back painful memories for Albert following in her wake. She was exactly his sort of girl, but then he shook these thoughts from his mind.

"Miss Smith, I've got all the papers ready for an appeal approach based on two aspects. First is that vital evidence was withheld."

She wanted to stop him there and say 'you were responsible for that' but she kept quiet.

"Second, in case that fails, that the resulting sentence was overly harsh and inappropriate in the circumstances."

Albert laid two folders down on her desk. "Shall we start with the withholding?" He pulled papers from the folder.

He was, to Ruby's surprise, thorough and organised. Every question she raised was answered, either through pulling another paper out or with a simple, not overly legal, reply. He was clearly a capable attorney and an intelligent, thoughtful man who could express complex ideas succinctly.

She was slightly disappointed when he closed the second file, informing her that all was complete and, with her approval, would be presented for legal review on Thursday.

"I approve, Mr Essington." Down a degree or two in formality. "Real good work."

But now, with her office door closed behind him, she was brought back to the persistent problem of what to do about Daniel Roberts.

**

The door opened a crack. Ben naturally stepped backwards and the door opened wider to frame one of the silent guards from the Suburban. Behind him were two more. All were armed, all looked tough and competent.

They were taking no chances with him.

They remained silent, but the lead guard beckoned with his fingers, shining a powerful torch onto Ben to illuminate him. Like a prisoner of war caught half-way down the tunnel, the light swept over the walls of his cell before settling on him close to the back wall.

Ben did not move following the summons. Something told him to be contrary, to push them beyond their comfort area.

Because he did not move, one was forced to speak. "Get over here, the boss wants to see you."

"Southwest Virginia, coalfields accent, moderate education, six-foot-three, 280lbs." Ben tried to sound assured through his fear, as if ticking off identification points at a subsequent identity parade. "What's your name?" Maximum effort into making his voice sound calm.

"Shut up and come here."

Ben did not move. He gambled that they had been told not to hurt him.

He was right. They stood in the door for a minute, not knowing what to do. Then one of the other guards pushed to the front and tried to reason with Ben.

"C'mon buddy, we've just got a job to do." No movement. "It'll be worse for you if you don't come."

"Metropolitan Baltimore, 12th grade but no further, five-foot-eleven, 155lbs." This guy was like wire.

The door slammed shut.

But the torch had shown Ben what he wanted to see.

There was a way out.

But doing it with his hands bound was going to be tough. He would need to think it through, but first he had to wait for their return.

They came back about twenty minutes later.

"Mr Franklin, I wonder if you would be able to come with us. I give you my word that you won't be hurt. It is just that a very senior person needs some questions answered. And he needs them quickly."

Ben thought, but did not say: Ivy League accent, Ivy League education, or close to it, five-foot-nine, 175lbs, bright, not like the others.

"I'm not voluntarily going anywhere with my hands bound like a common criminal. I've been a professional security officer for nine years now."

"Release him."

"What?" Mr Five-Foot-Eleven said.

"Take off the damn handcuffs." Two guards jumped to the instruction and Ben, not believing his good luck, followed them up out of the cellar. It looked around noon, judging by the position of the burning sun.

"What time is it?" Ben asked.

But now it was their turn not to speak.

"Where am I going?" The smug look on the face of Mr Six-Foot-Three said 'you played games with us, now the tables are turned'.

But it was only a short walk. They went under a roof of beautiful oaks, one in a hundred leaves changed to red or brown, like undercover agents suddenly exposed. The guards were grouped around him, following a dirt path with small logs marking the edges, grass shoots invading where the wooden defences were weakest. Beyond the trees, Ben saw numerous sheds and parked cars; beyond that, just empty fields. But ahead was an old mansion, immaculately kept, painted green shutters advertising the joys within. This was where he was headed.

Ben was not unfamiliar with boredom; long hours on shift had given him a tolerance for mindless activities, in which his mind had soared. But now he was keyed up for something else, fear mixing with intense excitement, like challenging himself to do ever-crazier dares.

But the reality was a continuation of the tedium he knew so well. He sat for three hours in a small room, wallpaper with an irritating pattern that reminded him of space invaders jigging along the bottom of a screen. There was no cornicing to examine; no other features, just three chairs and a table. The blinds were drawn over the windows. There was nothing to divert him from the relentless, recurring questions. He was in a quandary, torn between his promise of silence, modified recently to include Dakota and Val, and his love of his country. He grew bored of examining his conscience so he turned the larger part of his mind to how Dakota had taken the news about Richard Sutherland.

It pleased him enormously that he had been able to give her such pleasure.

"Where are the documents, Ben? Your country needs to see them."

"I really don't know, sir." That was the truth. Frank had not told him, but he had an inkling that they were at Hunt

Ridge. If Ben had known that Hunt Ridge was twenty-five minutes' walk, door to door, might he have modified his reply?

Dakota had jumped up from the visitors' room table, clapping her hands and crying out.

"Hush Jameson, not so loud." Val came across the room, wondering what had caused her friend to have such an outburst.

"Sorry Miss, it is just that Ben has given me such good news! On my research, I mean."

"I'll tell you later, Miss Bennet, if you have the time," Ben said, unable to hide his grin, a mirror of joy flashing around the prison room, such that Val was also smiling broadly. Thank goodness that Smith was off duty that Sunday.

"Ben, can you outline the contents of this document that Sir John Fitzroy alludes to? It would be of great help to your nation." This was Mr Five-Foot-Nine; all charm, so disarming.

"I don't understand it all," Ben replied weakly. "But it is some sort of legal document that proves America never got its independence." This would not wash, but then Ben had an idea. "You didn't hurt Sir John, did you? I mean, the government wasn't behind…"

"Of course not, Ben. The government doesn't act outside the law." But it did not ring quite true. They had broken the law in snatching him, so why not on other matters? Besides, Mr Five-Foot-Nine had just confirmed that the government was behind his snatching. Could the government of his beloved country really do such a thing? He did not want to think about it anymore.

Ben switched back to his visit with Dakota on Sunday, a blankness crossing his face like ripping off a facemask. Mr Five-Foot-Nine sighed and wrote 'Simpleton' on the notes he had been given on Ben. He shifted tack.

"Ben, you are mixed up, probably involuntarily, in a nasty, unpleasant business. I strongly suspect that you are being used by sinister agents unknown. We really need to understand this better so that we can protect you. It is the duty of any government to protect its citizens. We can't do that if you won't open up with us."

"On whose authority do you hold me?"

"Emergency Powers."

"You mean on the express order of the Pres…"

"Don't even go there, Ben, you have to trust us in order for us to help you. Some things are bigger than individuals." The slick questioner was using every tactic in the manual.

It did not work. Ben went back to the glazed view, Mr Five-Foot-Nine underlined the single word he had written and stood up to indicate an end to this long session.

"It is out of my hands now, Ben. The next interviewer tomorrow will not be as accommodating as me. In fact, I know something of his methods. Suffice it to say they are not the most pleasant. But this is your choice."

No reply from Ben. He had read the single word upside down to him across the table and felt it might be for the best.

Ben was taken back to his cellar. By walking with his head bent sideways he saw on a guard's wristwatch that it was close to half-past-four. There would be three hours of daylight left, then allow an hour for dusk.

When it got truly dark he would make his move. Somehow.

Just as dark descended, the guards made their mistake. They had handcuffed Ben again before closing the cellar door on him. But they had to feed him at some stage and for that he needed his hands.

"You've got twenty minutes, then the cuffs go back on." Mr Six-Foot-Three placed a tray on the stool and made as to leave.

"I can't eat if I can't see."

The guard thought about this a moment and then pulled a pencil torch from his jacket pocket.

"I want it back when you've eaten."

As the door slammed, Ben wasted no time. He turned the torch on, dragged the bed towards the coal chute and tipped it up so that the mattress and blanket folded into a pile on the dirt floor. It was a perfect size, resting against the wall so that the bed spokes made a natural ladder leading up to the chute. He broke the first rung of his ladder, pulling it away so that the nails came out with the baton.

His mind said eighteen minutes to go.

He climbed the ladder and used the baton to lever open the chute door, but it would not move. It was padlocked on the other side. He could edge open the two doors just enough to see the chain the other side.

Sixteen minutes, he estimated.

He flicked the torch over the whole double door, saw the hinges. The wood around the hinges looked rotten. Using the baton as a hammer, he started to beat the wood around the bottom-left hinge. It gave way easily but he had spent a half-minute changing tack and fifteen seconds destroying the hinge.

The upper-left hinge was another problem. The wood higher up was stronger. He hacked at it for thirty precious seconds, then turned to the lower-right. It came away easily.

Fourteen minutes left at best.

He then placed the baton in the gap created by the broken hinges and heaved up, trying to lever maximum pressure on the locked chain and the whole structure of the two doors. He felt it was giving, but more pressure was required. The baton was straining.

Everything gave way at once. The baton broke; several rungs of his makeshift ladder snapped, and both doors gave way with a screech that filled Ben's ears, seeming the loudest noise ever. Ben slipped down through the broken rungs and then fell backwards as the doors gave way. He fell to the floor, winded, lay there for a few seconds while his senses returned. Then he scrambled up and shone the torch up the ladder. Both doors were snapped horizontally, the remaining attached parts locked in place. Six of the ten rungs on his makeshift ladder were gone, lying in pieces on the floor.

There were, he thought, nine minutes left. He could do it.

Smelling the soup that was brought for his meal, he flicked his torch over the tray: plastic cup of water, plastic spoon, plastic bowl, lump of bread, and a smaller one of cheese. He grabbed the bread and cheese, stuffing them into his pockets, drained the water, and climbed back up the bed. He could just fit through. Beyond the door was a three-foot chute and another wooden door.

But it was not locked. A little light pressure and he was through. He had seven minutes left.

He had seen the top of the chute when walking back from his interrogation; stolen a few glances so as not to arouse suspicion. But he knew how to get into the trees and had seen the wood rising gently up the slope. Using the torch in tiny spurts, he headed quickly and quietly in that direction.

Suddenly he froze. He could see the bulk of Mr Six-Foot-Three coming along the path they had trod together earlier that day. He must have miscalculated the time. He thought he had four full minutes still. He stood, wishing himself a tree, just eight feet off the path. Would he be seen?

His heart pumped, sap rising, as the guard stopped and urinated against an oak. It put him directly in the big guard's line of sight should he look up from his business. But he looked down, then turned and went back to the path.

As soon as Mr Six-Foot-Three went through the door to the building, Ben ran, torch on again in tiny flashes, flicking this way and that to help pick out the best way forward.

He got to the wood just as the guard raised the cry. He dared not use his torch now so stumbled on through the roots and brambles. He heard lots of cries, reached the top of the wood, and plunged through up the meadows on the other side into open country, cries growing louder, engines revving.

Then he heard the dogs barking. The summit was 100 yards ahead, now sixty, now thirty. The dogs were getting closer, heading up the hill.

He thought about water; there had to be a brook down in the valley floor. He reached the water just as he saw torches on the ridge behind. He jumped in; it was waist-high, gravel-and-sand bottom. He waded upstream in great strides, fighting the water as it tried to push him downstream. He swore the barking and growling was getting closer, looked back, stumbled and fell into the water. Something made him lie still rather than get up.

"He's not up this way. He would have gone downstream, like instinctive." That was Mr Five-Foot-Eleven. Ben lay half-submerged, absolutely still, while two dark shapes shone heavy-duty flashlights over the water briefly, believing they were wasting their time, the action would all be downstream. They turned and made their heavy way back through the undergrowth. The last thing Ben heard was an oath as one of them obviously stumbled and fell into the water.

Ben rose as quietly as he could and waded another hundred feet up the stream. It was hard going. Suddenly he stopped, wondering why with no dogs going this way he was making life hard for himself. He climbed out the far side, using a fallen tree to help him, then headed diagonally away from the stream, a gradual uphill becoming steeper, small boulders scattered like dice thrown by a giant. He felt safer but did not dare use his torch, not until the other side of the ridge he was now climbing.

He could not believe what he saw at the top of the rise, spotlighted by the moon behind it.

Ten minutes later, he was knocking on Frank's front door, using the heavy ring knocker that gave a dull and satisfying thud, brass on brass. He reached forward to bang again but the door moved away from him as it opened.

***

Ruby was worried. She had tried for several days but could not break Daniel Roberts. He seemed impenetrable, everything glanced off him. He had reluctantly agreed to come here, not wanting the video sent to his family, but time was running out. She had just come out from a long, frustrating session. Nothing seemed to shake him. Was he too stupid or very clever? She suspected the latter, but it did not matter much. She just had to find a way. She owed it to Mr Williams, after all he had done for her. Her mind went back over the long chemo sessions, the top doctors, the blood transfusions, all paid for with a grace she marvelled at. Then his joy at her recovery. He had lifted her from the chair she had been sitting in and held her like a child in the air, all smiles and jokes. Then there was the job offer, helping the cook and serving at the table. After just three months there was quick promotion to be one of his executive assistants as Frank realised how much potential she had.

She had almost left then because she did not like office work. Before her sickness she had been an apprentice welder, but the shipyard had let her go. She thought she would travel a while. She had written out several resignation letters but not handed them in, finding reasons to delay a day.

But Frank had come to her instead. And he knew why she was not happy. He just could tell somehow. He asked her to do a roving job, seeking out investments, investigating people's motives. Albert Essington was the first time he had asked her to use her beautiful body. She had not liked doing it but it was a body he had restored to full health and he had said it would not go too far. It had not.

She was shaken from her thoughts by a knock on the door to her apartment. It was not strictly hers, but used by important guests when visiting the mansion. Sir John's elegant signature was in the guest book on several occasions.

"Come in."

The door opened to reveal Essington standing there.

"What can I do for you, Mr Essington?"

"I heard someone at the door." She could see someone else behind him now. "It was Ben Franklin. He's been held by someone not three miles away, held and interrogated. He escaped from a cellar and came here by chance. He's asking for Frank, I mean for Mr Williams."

"Come in, both of you. My God, Mr Franklin, you look all-in." She had heard a lot about this man from Mr Williams, and from Sir John.

"Please call me Ben."

"Albert, go into the kitchen and get some soup on the go, it's in the refrigerator. I'll get a towel. I believe Sir John has left some clothes here. I'll run a bath, you'll need it!" She quite naturally used Albert's first name.

"I've got some food of my own," Ben remembered and pulled out the supper he had stuffed into his pockets. The bread was soaked through while the cheese was mushy and waterlogged. "Courtesy of my hosts for the day!"

An hour later, Ben was bathed and fed, feeling much better. Ruby opened a bottle of wine and pulled out three glasses, but Albert shook his head.

"Not for me, thanks."

"Are you on the wagon?" But the unspoken question was whether this was because of his experience with her. He answered both the spoken and the unspoken question in the affirmative. So she made coffee.

Ben ran through the events of the day. Inevitably, they speculated on who was behind this. Ben was adamant that the President could not be directly involved.

"She just wouldn't sink so low."

"But somebody would on her behalf," said Albert.

Somehow, they then started talking about Ruby's problem with Daniel Roberts.

"You know Sir John had a meeting with him and he denied everything, swore blind that he had never even touched drugs," Ben said

"So, Miss Smith, you're saying you lack any way to get Roberts to tell the truth?"

"I think he has actually wiped out all memory of it. It's like he and the 12th Grader Daniel Roberts were two completely different people, just happening to have the same names. And we really can't keep him beyond tomorrow. He signed to say he was coming with us voluntarily until tomorrow. Now he thinks he has the upper hand so he is not going to sign for an extension."

Albert got up abruptly and left the room without a word, his half-drunk coffee refill still steaming in the cup.

"Is it something I said? That guy is weird."

"Frank told me all about the way you got Albert Essington to co-operate," Ben replied. "I would have expected him to be much more sullen. He seems almost cheerful, like accepting."

Ruby had called Frank, who was frantically busy in DC, but said he would be there in the morning. She put Ben up in the spare bedroom to the apartment and called Security, asking them to double the guards. Then they drank another glass of wine, the discussion ranging over Dakota, Sir John, Frank, Roberts, and the people behind Ben's kidnapping.

"You know Frank is buying Pillars of the Community Inc.," Ruby said.

"Yes, he told me at the weekend."

"That is why he is so busy right now. Yet he found time to come down here tomorrow to see you."

"You really admire him, don't you?"

"Don't you?"

"I like him a whole lot," Ben replied. "But I'm real torn about his business practices. I want to believe they are good, because it fits his personality, but I am not always sure."

"Well time for bed. I expect Albert Essington has tucked himself up already!"

In fact, Albert was in his little temporary office, poring through old notes, trying to find a document that was logged somewhere in the back of his mind.

The document would undoubtedly help Miss Smith with her problem.

It was after 3am that he discovered it, deliberately misfiled in a bunch of obscure estate documents. He read it again, for the first time for nine years, then sat back on his narrow chair and thought about Dakota Jameson. He had not seen a kid in trouble with the law, another life to be squandered at the altar of the justice profession. He had not seen what all these others around him now saw; the injustice, the waste, the cruelty, the suffering, nor the spirit, the courage, the fear conquered. What had he seen then?

With a deep sigh he realised all he had seen was a quick dollar coming his way.

"My God, what have I done?" He wept.

But then he started scribbling notes on a legal pad, going

through the document time and time again, writing a succinct summary, working out what to do.

He was still there when Ruby came to find him at 7.40am.

Be Prepared

Frank made it to Hunt Ridge for early afternoon, arriving by helicopter. At first, Ben thought the whirring blades were his captors come for him again. But when he watched the growing speck in the sky it was evident that it was too tiny for sinister intent. Still, he was glad when he saw Frank Williams as the only passenger descending, hair and tie blown by the blades so he looked like he was struggling to make it to the mansion.

He wasted no time, clearly in business mode.

"Listen guys," he said to those who had assembled to meet him, "I can't stay long. I am in the middle of a big deal."

"Can you spare ten minutes for a briefing?" Ruby asked. "It's just that we've found something that is real interesting."

"Of course, but first I have to see Ben." His eyes wandered over the small entourage, smiling when he saw Ben Franklin. "Eric, be so good as to call the stables. I want to ride Dignity; have a suitable horse saddled for Mr Franklin. Maybe Liberty, if she is over her bad leg."

"Yes, sir."

They drove down in an old jeep without doors and most instruments not working. "My favourite vehicle," was all Frank said. It was only when they were mounted and riding up the ridge that Frank spoke again. "Ben, I want you to try and show me the house from the top of the ridge. There are three estates that join our land and I would like to be sure as to which owner held you captive. You can see the roof tops of all my neighbours from the ridge."

Ben looked around, expecting to hear the dogs again. As ever, Frank read his mind. "Don't worry, I have six men in the woods with high-powered rifles. No one is going to snatch you again."

It all looked very different in the daylight. Ben had to measure out mentally the time and steps he had taken. "It must have been right there that I came out of the brook."

They rode a little further down towards the water. "Yes, that was the tree I used to climb out. So go back 300 yards; no, more like 400. You see that little sandy area ahead?" They were riding downstream now, retracing, but backwards and with the advantage of height from the ridge. "I remember the sand on the way in. Look, you can see a whole lot of boot prints, even from here. That is where they all were last night. So I came down straight through two fields, that must be those two. So that means I came out of the woods right around there." He pointed down across the valley to the second ridge, a lot lower than Hunt Ridge. There, you see the three chimneys? That was the house where I was interrogated."

"What I thought. Now, let's get back and I'll tell you about my morning."

Frank had called the President first thing that morning. She had sworn ignorance about the whole thing but promised to investigate and come back to him.

"A man's life is at stake. That man is a good friend of mine," Frank had said.

"I understand, Frankie, I'll get back to you within the hour."

Seventy-five minutes later Frank was sitting in the White House in the private office of Dick Turnby. Just as he sat down, the door opened and the President entered. Dick and Frank stood up.

"Sit down, both of you. Now, Dick, tell me what in hell's name has been going on."

"I've no idea, Madam President," Dick lied easily. Hence the need for Frank to confirm which of his neighbours Ben had escaped from. Dick Turnby had purchased the Blue Brook Estate several years ago. It was not generally known what went on there; certainly farming was a front for something. Now Frank thought he had a better idea.

"Mr Franklin is now free from his kidnappers. Do you want me to get the FBI involved?" she asked.

"No," replied Frank, looking directly at Dick, "just your

absolute assurance that he will not be apprehended or prevented from conducting his lawful business in any way."

"Agreed, but we have tailed him and…"

"I know, and I would not expect any less, but I don't want any more than that."

"That is what I was going on to say."

"OK, Jane, I am happy with this assurance. Now, I have something else to discuss. I am bidding for Pillars of the Community Inc. It is general knowledge as of forty minutes ago so I am not breaking any confidences. You are probably aware that they are a massive service company with a multitude of federal contracts, including being the largest private prison operator in the country. Our due diligence shows a number of security and other issues with these contracts. I wanted to reassure you and Dick that with a change of control these contracts will be much better managed in future. You know from my ownership of FMP Services that we took over a number of troublesome federal contracts and have turned them around to everybody's benefit."

"We have been impressed with how you have turned around FMP," the President said. "Go on."

"Well, this is the first time we have got involved with running prisons and it has become a real passion for me. We intend to change the management and operation of the federal prisons drastically. We want to change the ethos from pointless, mind-numbing punishment to positive rehabilitation. There is a young girl, for instance, incarcerated for forty-two years at the age of eighteen for a relatively minor drug offence. Putting aside the question of guilt for a moment, it is crazy that a whole life is taken away for a moment's stupidity." Frank paused a moment, reading the thoughts on Jane's and Dick's faces. How does this affect me? Did the girl not deserve a lengthy sentence? Then he struck with his true intention. "Jane, I want you to consider a very serious proposal from me. I think it will make all the difference to your re-election prospects."

Afterwards, when Frank had left, rushing off to catch the latest on his bid situation, Jane and Dick sat in Dick's office, both breathless with the audacious proposal Frank had made.

"Do you think he really meant it?" Jane asked.

"That level of cash is small change for someone like him."

"But do you think it would make a difference?" Jane turned it over and over in her head. The more she considered it, the more she liked the various aspects of his idea. "Let's go through it one part at a time."

They discussed the incredible donation to the re-election campaign. But could they accept the conditions?

"Frank will be the Campaign Strategy Director, essentially running the campaign from now on," Dick said.

"I think it might be just the thing to have someone who is not a politician in charge. I'm sorry, Dick, because it means you moving aside, but this is appealing."

"Jane, I just want you to succeed and to play some part in that success." Again a lie, they both knew it, but were so fond of each other that the deceit did not matter. "But the real issue here is the central theme of the campaign going forward. He wants it to be all about prison reform. Do you think that will connect with the average voter?"

"Yes, I think it will, for sure. It has such a sweet ring to it; wasted lives, wasted money, wasted opportunity."

"It sounds like you are on the hustings!"

The President smiled at the joke, but looked deep into Dick's eyes. The look said what the words did not, that she knew he had been behind the kidnapping, despite his denials. His return gaze told her that he knew she knew. It went further, accepting that Frank's appointment was a direct result of his action, now seen as foolish.

But he had done it for love for her. And that made it different. Now he stretched out his hand and took hold of hers. She responded by twitching her fingers ever so slightly. It was the most tentative of advances, one that could be withdrawn, pretended to be nothing at all, should circumstances require.

But they both knew what it was. So, with eyes searching deep inside each other, seeking out the souls that lay within, they stood, moved together like dancers doing a waltz, but slow-motion, silence for music yet keeping the time.

They kissed first and for both it was entering paradise. The physical contact that for decades had been confined to holding hands, occasional massages and brushing past each other, now opened to a new garden that brought with it a new intensity of joy. It was new to the spinster and new to the married man.

They could have made love on the floor behind Dick's oak desk.

But they did not. Instead, they lay on the floor together, still searching with twin eyes locked, their combined moral structure tottering, guilt against pleasure, loyalty against love.

But it held and then normality returned. They rose and Jane smoothed down her skirt while Dick took off his tie and retied it. Their thoughts were now on the normal, the practical. And so they spoke of normal things to break the silence of their passion.

"Dick, you don't mind, do you? About Frank, I mean. If you do, I won't..."

"Jane, I don't mind, I really don't."

And this time he was telling the truth.

***

On the ride back to the house, Ben, loving being back on a horse again, decided to ask his friend for a favour.

"Frank, I'd like to stay here a few days."

"That's fine, you're always welcome."

"Can I ride each morning? I'd love that."

"I'll tell Eric to have Liberty ready. What will you do the rest of the time?"

"I met Ruby last night. She told me about the Records Room you have here."

"That's where I got the trunk from to give you."

"Well, if you're OK with it, I'd like to see if there is anything else that can help Dakota with her research."

That was fine with Frank, who then asked Ben to sit in on the briefing he was going to with Ruby.

"Then I have to be off, back to DC via Chicago. This deal is at a real critical stage."

***

"Do you mind if Albert attends?" Ruby asked. Frank assented. They sat in the Orangery, where Ben had eaten lunch the first time he visited. They had coffee and sandwiches - Frank having skipped lunch - served by a young girl, again without hair. She seemed hesitant and tripped when carrying the coffee pot for refills. Ruby was up in an instant.

"Don't worry, Bethany. The rug needed cleaning anyway." She helped Bethany to her feet and sat her by the window. "Take a second to get your breath back. Look, there's enough coffee left in the pot for Mr Williams to have a second cup. The rest of us are awash with coffee anyway." Ben saw the tears in Bethany's eyes, rubbed quickly to oblivion with a bony, freckled hand.

"So Ruby, what's up?" Frank answered.

"Well, sir, as you know from my daily briefing, we are making little to no progress with Daniel Roberts and he really should be released today." She stopped talking a moment, looked behind her at Bethany and called, "Beth, go and have a lie down in your room. You look all-in. No, it's important to rest. I'll talk to Mrs Murray to get you covered." The girl stood and mouthed 'thank you', then fled. Ruby watched her go and then turned back to the trio waiting for her briefing.

"She's not well, Mr Williams. I'm worried about her."

"Get Mrs Murray to call the doctor in. Send me a text when you know more."

"Yes, sir."

"Now, what about Daniel Roberts?"

"Well, Albert came up with something from the past. He found the receipt for a payment to his firm from one Mr Roberts."

"You mean...?"

"Exactly, Daniel's father. He paid Albert $50,000 for 'legal advice' back in July 2018." Naturally, all eyes went to Albert who studied the pattern on the floor tiles.

"Albert, do you not recall receiving payment from Daniel's father during Dakota's case?"

"No, sir." Then he looked up directly at Frank and said, "The extent of my wrongdoing is becoming more and more obvious every day. If you want to take me to court, I will not contest it. I will plead guilty." He was looking at Frank but it was Ruby who answered.

"Don't be stupid, Albert. We need you if we are to succeed in this."

"Lord, I have to go." Frank broke the momentary spell, jumping up. "Eric, where are you? Great, get the chopper pilot back on board. I'm going to be late for the Chicago meeting. Ruby, walk out with me so we can strategize a bit. Bye, the rest of you."

Ben went straight to the Records Room, seeking out Mr Urquart, who kept the room in order and made documents available to visitors by appointment. The room was a large alcove to the stately library, Mr Urquart filling the position of records custodian and librarian.

"I'm looking for records from the early 1780s, particularly anything of a political or diplomatic nature. Also, anything to do with land transactions around that time."

Mr Urquart was ancient, with wire bifocals and clips on his shirtsleeves; accoutrements from a different age. He was delighted to help and was able to set Ben up with several boxes at a leather topped desk that sat by a long leaded light window looking onto the ridge above them. Ben felt quite the scholar as he settled down to a long afternoon with yellow notebook and Mr Urquart's fountain pen.

But the afternoon brought nothing by way of discovery. Two boxes in, stomach rumbling, he leaned back on his chair and stretched, then noticed Albert sitting at a desk in the adjoining library. He stretched again and then went over to him. "You know you ruined Dakota's life."

"I know." But infuriatingly he remained deep in his legal book, answering by machine.

"Nine years, most of them in maximum security. Another thirty-three to go."

"Mr Franklin," now Albert looked up, "I'm trying like crazy to make up for it." Then he corrected himself with evident humility. "I can't ever make up for it. I should be in there instead of her but Mr Williams has given me a chance to try and do some good, to repair a little of the damage I've done. And, sure as hell, I'm trying."

"See that you do," was all that Ben could reply, then he thought better of it. "What are you trying to do?"

"Take a seat." Albert got a clean page of his notebook and drew several circles. As the shapes cleared, Ben could see that they were Venn diagrams. "This is the total population." He wrote '44' in the largest circle that encompassed all the others.

"What is the population?"

"The people I screwed and ended up in jail. Now here is the population still inside." He pencilled in '27'. "That leaves seventeen that have been released over the last nine years. And yes, before you ask, Miss Jameson was the first one. I was three years out of law school and had just set up on my own."

Albert added a further circle breaking across the '27' and '17' circles. "These are the ones that Marcus Hibbert and I agree were genuinely guilty. I know it's not right for us to play judge and jury but, as Mr Williams said, you have to start somewhere. So that reduces the twenty-seven to eighteen and the seventeen to nine."

"So you're concentrating on the eighteen deemed innocent and still rotting in jail?"

"That was the priority that Mr Williams set. Second priority is the nine innocent now released from prison. Then I am to go over the 'guilties' and check each one thoroughly."

"So how are you doing?"

"It's tough; a lot of work for each one. I need to get a cast-iron case together each time, knowing I am risking prison myself as the details of each case will become known to the authorities. But," now he looked directly at Ben, "I put myself in this position and I have to live with the consequences."

They fell into silence, Albert bent over his research, Ben watching him. Then Albert looked up again.

"Part of the problem is that I deliberately kept very scanty records, for obvious reasons."

"I can appreciate that. I'm trying to find records a lot older than yours and I get the feeling that they also didn't want to leave much of a trace." Ben went on, with Albert's gentle enquiries, to explain what he was trying to do.

"Mr Franklin, can I see the documents you found?"

There was no 'Call me Ben'; he was not ready for that yet. "Why?"

"I just would like to read the words, see if it prompts any ideas."

"I'll ask Marcus to email you a copy. I don't have one."

Ben stood awkwardly a moment longer, not sure what to say, if anything. Then the door opened and Ruby walked in.

"Ah, there you two are. The kitchen is preparing dinner for us at seven o'clock." She looked automatically at her wristwatch. "That's thirty minutes. I said we'd eat in the Orangery again as it's so pleasant in there."

"How's Bethany?" Albert asked. Ben had quite forgotten about the young girl.

"She's not doing too good," Ruby replied. "They've taken her back to the cancer centre at UVA in Charlottesville. Frank asked me to organise flowers and chocolates. She is a chocoholic! Getting her in and arranging all that has taken up a chunk of my afternoon, so we'll have to see our friend Daniel after we've eaten."

The meal was pot roast, beans and fried potatoes, served by two recovering cancer patients who seemed to be well on their way, cheerful and dropping in casually to their conversations, as if themselves on the guest list. It reminded Ben of the Little Kitchen.

"Frank told me pot roast was your favourite," Ruby said to Ben, who nodded in confirmation, his mouth full of the excellent food. Frank Williams seemed to spread thoughtfulness everywhere he went; yet he was clearly an effective businessman with all that entailed. "We've got to be pretty quick as I want to get Roberts sorted out tonight," she continued.

***

Daniel Roberts had quite enjoyed his 'enforced' stay, or retreat as he had told his family. The rooms he had in the mansion were luxurious in every way: beautiful furniture, aspects and service. He had been able to indulge in flicking through the television channels; saunas; drinks at the ring of a bell; fine food. The only thing he lacked was company. He missed female company or 'a bit of skirt' as he called it after hearing it in a movie years ago. He also missed male company, a crowd to strut amongst.

He had contemplated calling home to say he was extending the retreat for a few more days. He was on a great spiritual journey, a preparation for the great political career that stretched out in front of him. But something held him back from doing this. Would they start to wonder about him? Would they call the retreat house and discover the pretence?

Had he called, he would have multiplied his discomfort many times over. His wife was not there. He would have got the nanny or the housekeeper, both of whom could lie with expertise. But it would have left a sense of deceit that he would not have been able to shake off.

It was just as well, all things considered, that he was going home in the morning.

There was a knock on his sitting room door.

"Enter." Nobody usually disturbed him in here, unless it was those imbecilic maids without any hair or just fuzz, so unattractive on girls. "Oh God, what do you want?" It was

Ruby, followed by two people he did not know.

Only one looked very familiar.

Something, somewhere. In the past.

"I'm about to eat," he said, slugging on his bourbon and ice, lots of ice.

"I put the kitchen on hold," Ruby said. That angered Daniel, who rose from his bed, shuffled into his shoes and uttered various expletives. But Ruby was completely unfazed. "I am sure you remember Mr Albert Essington. The other gentleman is Mr Ben Franklin."

"I thought you died over 200 years ago." It was a silly joke, but his mind was working on the other man. Essington. He knew that name. He looked like a lawyer, although in jeans rather than a suit.

"Very droll, Mr Roberts."

The next twenty minutes were the worst of Daniel's life. After a minute of introduction, he spent the next four in violent denial of his involvement.

"Denial is pointless," Albert said. "The evidence is here in black and white." He was being creative with the truth, for the evidence only proved that Mr Roberts Senior had paid money to him nine years ago, not what that money represented in terms of services.

But for Daniel, it was turmoil. He had convinced himself, almost born again to an honest past, all suggestion of dishonesty banished, but now flooding back to drown him.

The sixth to eleventh minutes of this interview were spent not in denial but in fighting back.

"If you take me to court you will go to jail yourself." This was the first effort, quickly dismissed.

"Mr Roberts, I fully expect to go to jail. That prospect holds no fear for me now." It was another lie, but in a good cause.

"My father is senile. His word means nothing anymore. He is a jabbering idiot." Second attack, but again Essington was prepared.

"It does not matter. He was perfectly *compos mentis* nine

years ago."

"My wife is very wealthy. She and her father will fight you every inch of the way, starting with false imprisonment."

The counter to this was easy – Mr Williams was the third most wealthy person in America, the ninth richest in the world. He had at least a thousand bucks for every one Daniel could lay hands on. Plus, they had the video.

"How supportive would your lovely wife be when she sees it?" Albert asked.

"She loves me. She'll forgive a little indiscretion."

It was then that Ruby played the second video. The one that featured his wife.

And her lover.

And when he saw her lover, the beautiful Tess Ronzio, smiling in all her sensual beauty, naked other than her heels, he hung his head in his hands and wept.

The remaining nine minutes took the form of a briefing. He was asked if he had any questions, had none, was sure he understood it, then had to repeat it back to be sure. "I am to sign a confession drawn up by Essington. This will be kept by Williams and not released to anyone unless I break the terms of our agreement. I am to continue outwardly with my marriage, giving the impression of a happy family to all observers. There will be no more children. I may visit whores provided discreet but no affairs. I will certainly be elected come next November. I am to make a particular cause of prison and sentencing reform throughout my congressional career. I am to push it inexorably. At all times the confession will hang over me and will be sent to the authorities if I break one single condition of the agreement."

"Just a minute," Ben broke in, "what about Dakota? Her innocence? Her appeal?" It had suddenly come to him that she was being sold out. If Roberts avoided prison then, by implication Dakota, the perceived guilty party, would remain behind bars.

"Ben," it was the first time Albert had used his first name, "not now. Trust us, we have her interests at heart."

"Like nine years ago?" Ben stormed out, slamming the door behind him.

***

It was several hours later that Ruby found Ben, sitting alone in the Orangery, lost in his own thoughts. She crouched down to be at chair level and took his hand in hers.

"It's a complicated situation..." she started but he interrupted her.

"It's just not complicated at all," he said, pulling his hand away. "Dakota has been nine years in prison in the most awful conditions. Everything you take for granted, she doesn't have. She lives with aggression, anger, hatred and violence. She should not be there. That Roberts is the one who should be behind bars, not Dakota. And then there's Essington, who sold young people like Dakota into penal servitude for cash. You're supporting these people and denying Dakota her chance, her one chance of liberty. It disgusts me. Do you have any idea what it is like?"

"I do, actually."

"What?"

"Well, not of prison, but I had a real rough start to life." She told him then of the first twenty-five years of her existence. She told of the drunkard mother and the abusive father. She did not know to this day whether he was her father. She told of the filthy trailer, the party every time the adults chanced on a few dollars, kids sent out to roam the trailer park while they put the radio volume right up, ignoring neighbours, management, just hell-bent on trivial enjoyment. She was close to prison, seeing two of her half-brothers inside, one in and out for petty crime, the other life-without-parole for a gruesome vehicular homicide when high. He had been seventeen, was now dead, killed with the leg of a plastic chair fashioned into a knife. She had been arrested several times for car theft, shop-lifting, drunkenness and street-fighting, somehow managing to stay one pace away from prison each time.

"I was raped when I was fourteen. The local police said it was natural justice for a slut like me. Plus, what did I expect, looking so hot?"

Then she told of her time in care; more abuse, more cruelty, more hatred, marginally less hunger and filth. "They received money from the state for taking me in. I was a cash cow. But at least I got some schooling."

Then came the cancer.

"That was more vicious than anything I had experienced so far. I started losing weight and feeling ill, vomiting, and such headaches. I was twenty-three and working off and on in a hamburger place. They let me go pretty well straight away. I went to a Medicaid doctor who told me my diet was bad. Ben, I ate anything I could just to have something. It got worse and worse; more sickness, weakness. I started getting real dizzy, too. The fourth time I went to the doctor he referred me to a cancer charity in Salt City for screening. They paid for the tests. They came back positive. I had leukaemia."

"How did you get involved with Frank?" At some point in the story Ruby had taken Ben's hand again, rubbing it slowly, as if the words as well as being spoken were travelling from limb to limb into Ben's very soul.

"Through his father. He lives in Salt City. He raised money for the charity, actually about a dozen charities. Five years ago, when I was twenty-four, he drove a busload of us cancer patients up here and we camped on the front lawn. Well, that was the idea, but Frank, his son, would have none of it. He put us up in his best rooms, gave a whole pile of money to the charity, set up a branch locally and has been involved ever since. He paid bucketloads of money for me and the others to get the best treatment here at the cancer centre. To cut a long story short, I got into remission and came to work here, just like Bethany. If it wasn't for both Mr Williamses, father and son, I would be moulding away in the ground right now."

When Ruby had finished talking, there was little else to say. They stayed where they were for a while until Ruby started getting cramp in the back of her legs. She stood up and said, "Ben, please believe me, Frank is the best sort. He will not let Dakota down." But Ben was thinking not of this, but how Ruby's life had changed so much, so suddenly. There was always hope.

"But now I think we need to get some sleep," Ruby said, flexing the back of her legs and stamping on the paved floor. "Oh, by the way, Frank gave me this for you. I forgot earlier with everything that's been going on. Frank went to Mrs Jameson's this morning and picked up some of your clothes and this."

It was a letter from Dakota.

Letter Nine

My Darling, I am so excited!! The information you told me is jump-starting my research. I can't wait to tell you what our friends from the past have been up to! But first of all, I want to thank you for this and for everything you have done for me since we met seven months ago, indeed for what you've done for my mother for almost four years now. You are a dear, kind man, and I love you to pieces. My whole life has been waiting for you to come along so keep telling me you love me and you're not allowed to change your mind!!

V. (if you know who I mean) tells me that Sir J. is quite a lot better. She gets her updates from Frank. But apparently he is going to be in a wheelchair. That is so sad. There are plenty of people in here who've developed quite a crush on him. But not me, I've only got eyes for you!!! Talking about crushes and eyes for people, V. is wondering around starry-eyed, forgetting half her tasks.

As well as the revelations you gave me on Sunday, I have also received a partial diary from Richard Sutherland himself, sent from the National Records Office of Scotland. But I also received more letters from Kirsty Williams who, you will never believe this, is the mother of V.'s Frank, the one who you brought in to meet me with Sir John. She explains all this in her letter. She married Frank's father, also Frank, although he has nothing to do with the family business.

Ben stopped reading a moment and thought. He was, this very day, staying at the Hunt Ridge Estate that Richard Sutherland had owned and had visited in his desperate attempt to prevent the wrong treaty and the wrong type of peace. The Frank Williams he knew was, obviously, a direct descendant of the tenants of the estate when Richard Sutherland was alive.

But Ben, it is time to grab that beer and listen to what I've been able to piece together.

In the kitchen to Ruby's apartment there were several beers to choose from and she had said to help himself. He selected an earthy-looking local craft beer, with a picture of a man being chased by a bear. He opened two and took them back to his room. It was called 'Bear Beer' and the neatness of the two words appealed to him.

It had a delicious, malty taste. Ben read on.

When Richard got sick again, staying in Amelia's clapboard farmhouse, even he did not expect to live long. It seemed like his chest was hollowed out with coughing and spluttering, phlegm coming up constantly. His right arm was now paralysed and the right side of his face hurt all the time. He was exhausted, dizzy and frail, only an inner core seemed still alive. Being a Christian, he imagined this was his soul preparing to leave his worn-out body and, he hoped, soar with the angels. Maybe others would call it the spirit or essence, those that do not believe.

Then he started coughing blood.

And his vision and concentration were next on the list to revolt against his will, battering down that will. Perhaps it was a parallel rebellion to the one he was trying to end between the two great nations he loved. Both rebellions had an inevitability about them, both would happen regardless of who or what tried to stand in the way.

So why then did some people stand so obdurately against the peace he had negotiated with Franklin? Was it like expecting immortality, a never-ending constancy that kept all things in their place, Great Britain to rule its empire forever? But Richard knew, on reflection over his long and varied life, that nothing was constant. Even faith came and went.

He corrected himself then. There were constants: love and fidelity and truth, for instance. In later days, at the height of Hollywood, they would make movies around these constants, simple movies with simple values standing up to the evil forces stacking up against them. But Richard thought of them differently, was not aware of future moralistic positions. He was touched, as all educated men were at that time, by the Enlightenment. He could step outside his body, his life, his trade and occupation and sense what had been right sixty years ago, at the start of his long career, was not right now.

So he changed his will and freed all his slaves.

***

Sidney Hollingsworth watched the deterioration in his new friend with interest, but also with frustration. He was tired of playing the part and wanted to move quickly to a conclusion satisfactory to him.

So, he made his move. And he timed it perfectly.

"Richard, my dear fellow, I am so sorry to see you in this way. I hope we can conclude matters speedily and get you home to your beloved Scotland."

"Thank you, Sidney, you have been very kind to me over the last few months."

"That is what friends are for, Richard." Did this dying man really think they had met by coincidence on that cold evening before the storm? "My only thought is speeding you to comfort and ease and I have an idea that may help in this regard."

He went on to explain that there was a general concept in law that may assist them. If they did an exchange of land that was unequal they could write in a covenant that would bring it to equality.

"What do you mean?" Richard's head was throbbing as he and Sidney sat alone in Amelia's parlour. The fire burnt strongly, Richard was less than a yard from the flames, but felt cold as he ever had been in Philadelphia, colder with each day that passed.

"I mean that I have a little land near the Potomac River, just a few acres. It has no significant value. You have a very large estate here, some several thousand acres. That would be an exchange of different value clearly."

"Clearly it would."

"But if we placed a covenant on the Potomac land, stating that it would always be a part of England forever, then the value to you is increased considerably."

"I don't understand why it would. I see the argument on the land exchange but fail to see why it would increase with the covenant and my ownership."

"Because, my dear friend," Sidney was prepared for the next part of his persuasion, had rehearsed it many times, wanted a successful Virginia estate so badly, "that gives you a piece of England over here to secrete the other treaty on, the treaty you aspire to keep from the public. Nobody will be able to gain access to take it from you. That way you can forever keep it secure and out of the public eye. Nobody need ever know or suspect of its existence. Trust me," he lied, "I have had it checked by my attorneys. It all stacks up neatly."

"But it depends on gaining possession of the treaty that prescribes the Americas to remain in the British Empire. That is where your idea seems to fall down."

This was exactly where Sidney had hoped the conversation would lead, because by convincing Richard of this subsidiary point he hoped to take pressure off the main point; the exchange of land. He also had another trick up his sleeve, but hardly dared think of that at present.

"Easy, my friend. We steal it. Or rather, Rupert steals it on our behalf."

The deal was done the next day. Richard, his senses failing, clasped enough about him to argue that the Hunt Ridge portion, some 1,000 acres of beautiful countryside, stay out of the deal. It left almost 7,000 acres, and a fine site for a mansion, to pass over to Sidney Hollingsworth.

The same lawyers did another unequal transaction, charged to Richard's account. A grant of Hunt Ridge, all 1,500 acres, was made to Amelia Williams, the covenant being that it was never sold, would revert to Richard or his heirs if no Williams were to inherit and inhabit.

Richard had signed both documents and now retired to bed, exhausted. Rupert helped him up the stairs. His master seemed to be talking nonsense, rambling in his mind about land deals and covenants. He needed to rest. Rupert put him to bed with a dish of hot chocolate to wind down the mind that seemed so intent on these peculiarities. When Richard finally dozed off and stopped muttering, Rupert sat on the end of the bed and wondered whether he would ever see his family in Paris again.

Sidney lost no time, in fact had prepared for this outcome. He spent the next day with a firm of architects from Richmond, deliberating on the mansion they would build for him. He was annoyed about the Hunt Ridge land, for it had the most commanding positions, but realised that obtaining nine-tenths of his objective was better than nothing at all.

And he still had his trick up his sleeve. That, as the architects rattled off in their carriage with hours of work ahead of them, was what Sidney now turned his mind to.

He was entering the gentry with his acquisition of an estate. But he wanted something more. Above all, he desired a title.

And he knew how to go about it.

***

Picture the lawns around a new-built mansion in a slave state. Those lawns will be perfect. There is the desire to match the fresh woodwork and paint, neat greenness offsetting the pristine white. And there is the workforce to carry out the painstaking care: clipping, edging, mowing, watering and weeding to perfection.

This was the lawn, not so large but boasting consistency of rich colour, forming a border around the lavish town house. This was the house that contained the document, the house they needed to penetrate in order to gain the treaty.

Or rather, that Rupert needed to penetrate.

But right now those lawns were just a memory from the five times they had driven past over the last two days, for it was pitch black, ten o'clock in the evening and no moon; even starlight masked by banks of sultry clouds. The conditions were perfect for burglary.

"Rupert, you do understand the arrangements, don't you? Let's run through them one more time."

"Yes, Master. I am dressed as similar as we can manage to the servant dress of this household. There is a big gathering today so they will have drafted in more slaves to help with the festivities. I am to be as one of them. I am to scout out the place and locate the treaty you wish me to procure. If I can, I will then obtain it. If it is too awkward so to do, I will return empty-handed and we shall

discuss what to do next. I am to take no risks and to abandon the project should I fear detection or a level of suspicion that merits retreat." He had learned the instructions to the word. Richard asked a few questions, although his mind was weak and the effort to discuss matters was hard. Then he sent his slave on his way with best wishes and a private prayer.

Rupert was gone from the carriage at ten minutes after ten, back at twenty minutes past eleven. He had no documents with him. Sidney rapped on the roof and the carriage moved off, silently on muffled hooves.

"How did you find matters?" Richard asked, shivering with the cold boring into him, not noticing the look of shock on Rupert's face.

"I think I have located its position within the house but there was no opportunity to take it tonight, sir. It needs a quieter time." He was not very forthcoming and Richard, after asking a few more questions, decided not to pursue it any further at the moment. He was tired and needed warmth and rest if there was to be any life in him the next day.

There was a knock on Ben's door. Ruby wanted to talk with him. He would have to read the rest later. He carried his beer out to the sitting room. Ruby had one already.

"Ben, I've been on the phone to Frank. He is confident that the deal will go ahead, although it will take a few more weeks to be finalised. He suggested that we all go up on Saturday and Sunday to Zanesville, to the prison. That means leaving in the morning. It will be you, Frank, Albert and me. I need you to let me know how to get on the visitors' list. Albert will be fine for entry as her lawyer."

"Hold on a second. Do you think Dakota is going to want Albert as her lawyer? After what he did to her? He's a son of a bitch. I don't even want to be in the same room as him."

"Ben, look, he's actually not a bad person. He's trying real hard to make amends and he is the best person to do her appeal. He knows what he did wrong and can right it this time around. He's expecting to go to prison for a long time. You've got to give him a chance. He is Dakota's best hope, believe me."

"He's filth."

"Can't we let Dakota decide? You and I can visit first, put our prospective cases to her and then let her choose whether to see Albert or not."

"OK."

"Listen, Ben. This particular 'son of a bitch' has been working night and day on Dakota's appeal. He's covered every aspect of it. It went through legal review today with HFW. They praised it, said it was one of the most impressive case preparation they had ever seen. I thought the same as you a few weeks ago but this guy is really something special and I'm convinced he is genuine in his remorse. Nobody could work harder. This morning, when we found him in his office, he wasn't just in early, he had been there all night working the angles to get Dakota out of jail."

"You know, I don't want to think about it right now. To get in as a visitor you need to fill out an online form. And then fax your driving licence or passport. You can go to the federal website but I found the Pillars one much easier. There is a form there for legal representatives as well."

"Thank you, Ben. Goodnight." She seemed pleased that Ben had added the form for lawyers to visit. But Ben did not register this, just thinking to finish Dakota's letter.

Ten minutes later he was in bed, a borrowed bed, wearing borrowed pyjamas and having used a borrowed toothbrush. He opened the letter to continue reading, but found that the story ended right there, reverting to the present with Dakota back centre-stage.

Ben, my dearest, that is as far as I can go right now. I know that Richard left on April 15th from Richmond for Scotland. I know he arrived in Scotland months later. He travelled immediately to his half-built house and died there on New Year's Day 1784. But I need to do a lot more research to find out what went on in the first half of April 1783. It is time to get up now. I have been disciplined for talking to a guard instead of working and was put on general duties for ten days, mainly washing floors and cutting the edges of lawns, but am back in the library today, I hope. All the books have arrived but they have been sitting in crates for eight days.

I love you so much, always yours, D.

***

Ben read the last words again and again, then laid back and thought of her. He had often seen inmates tending the lawns in front of the admin block, like orange ants swarming across the lush green; black-and-white clothed guards in almost equal numbers. It annoyed him to think of Dakota's fine mind diverted onto clipping, sweeping up the cuttings to make the lawns perfect. It was just like the lawns she had described in colonial times, cultivated to perfection by a never-ending army of slaves.

He was annoyed by so much right now.

Then he folded up the letter, set the alarm for 5am, switched off the light and fell asleep instantly, the events of the last two days causing sleep to sweep over him.

The State Versus Jameson

Ben woke with his alarm. Still exhausted, he rose, washed and dressed, made his way back to the records room. He expected to see it deserted with the lights off, but there was one powerful desk lamp on and bent underneath it was Albert Essington. He did not hear Ben enter or cross the library floor to the records room.

Ben had no intention of talking to him and soon lost himself in his search for clues as to the events surrounding the last days of Richard Sutherland in America.

Around 7am, having just opened an interesting box full of letters from the war period, he was jolted out of his research by a cough.

"I was getting myself some coffee, thought you might like some."

"Thank you." Ben did not look up, but did want the coffee.

"What are you researching?"

"Something to help Dakota with her thesis."

"I didn't get the email from Mr Hibbert."

It took Ben a moment to work that one out. In that time, he broke his own hastily imposed rule and looked up at Albert. It came back to him. He had said he would get Marcus to email a copy of the documents they found in the chest.

"I forgot, sorry. I'll do it this morning." It might have ended there. Ben had a choice. He could have looked back down at his work, could have pulled a letter from the box, signalling that the conversation was over. But he did not.

Instead, he sipped the coffee, now looking over the rim of the mug directly at Albert, like a boss might regard a subordinate.

"What brings you here so early?" But as soon as Ben asked the question he knew that Albert was not here early. He was here late. He had not slept again last night, confirmed by stubble and dark rings below his eyes, plus clothes unchanged since yesterday.

"Final preparations for the appeal. I am visiting Miss Jameson with you today and then plan to file it on Monday, first thing."

"Do you think it will work?"

"I think it is 50:50. But Mr Williams told Miss Smith that he has some plans to hatch so I think he is trying to pull some levers at a high level."

"Why are you doing this?"

"Because I was a real bastard. I just want to do what I can to make up for some of the damage I caused."

"You've taken the best years of her life, may have taken most of her life." The anger was rising. "She was eighteen when her parents came to you, put their faith in you to represent her. Instead, you sold her like a slave. You took every penny they had and also took money from Daniel Roberts to get him off the hook and all blame passed to Dakota. Mrs Jameson is still paying on two mortgages."

"I know, I think about it every waking moment now." Saying nothing more, Albert returned to his desk and picked up a folder to review. Ben watched him for a few minutes as he worked, hating his very existence, wanting some comeback so that he could retaliate. He wanted to fight him, to give him a little bit of the pain he had inflicted on others.

***

Ben clutched the letter he had found as the large helicopter burned its way through the sky; woods, fields, more woods, and small towns with tall churches made up the view below, cars buzzing along the ribbon-like roads, climbing and descending the undulating land. Soon, they crossed the truck-laden interstate, huge cargoes north and south. Then the trees got heavier.

"National Forest," shouted Frank, seeing the direction of Ben's eyes. Then he looked at Mrs Jameson, brought to Hunt Ridge first thing this morning in Frank's 'get-about chopper', the little three-seater. She had a shine to her eyes, an expression on her face, of someone out of her league but enjoying the day, regardless. She was, after all, going to see her baby. Twice in the next two days. They had booked in for both Saturday and Sunday. They were staying at the Zanesville again, Frank had insisted.

It was pretty well trees all the way from then on, making Ben think he really was transported back to Richard Sutherland's time, when the country could still boast of being brand-new.

Or had the country never come into being at all? Ben doubted this was the case, but maybe Sir John was right. Maybe the treaty he had found was the genuine one.

He hoped not.

Although it would be a great outcome for Sir John.

"Frank, have you heard how Sir John's doing?" Ben had to shout above the engine noise.

"As well as can be expected. They think he will be paralysed, at least from the waist down. I spoke to him last night and he was pretty chirpy."

Ben noticed that Albert still had his head buried in papers. He was not going to ask him what they were about, would not volunteer a conversation. He would try and have a word with Frank about not selling Dakota down the river for some bigger cause. He didn't like 50:50, even if he believed Albert. Failure now would mean another ten years until a new appeal could be heard, provided that someone came up with the arguments.

Well, he mused, at least Albert had made some arguments. Ruby and the lawyers thought his approach was real good. Time will tell, but these people will no longer be my friends if they even hint at Dakota being sold out.

Ben could not avoid Albert, however, for the lawyer approached him immediately on getting out of the helicopter.

"Mr Franklin, I've read the documents Mr Hibbert sent through. They're real interesting. I need to understand the background a bit more. Can we discuss it for a few?

"There's no time. We're late for Security so we'll be

cutting into visiting time if we're not careful."

"What are you two talking about?" Frank asked, calling across the tarmac, walking towards them.

"Nothing," Ben said.

"Mr Williams, I was asking Mr Franklin to brief me a bit about Miss Jameson's historical research. He just said we were running late and would risk cutting into visiting time."

"Easy, we have to take two cars to the prison anyway. You two go in the first car and the rest of us will bring up the rear. Also, I think it is time you started using first names. We're all in this together now. Does anyone have any objections?"

Ben wanted to say he did have objections, but it looked small, mean-minded. Instead he just grunted and walked towards the first car.

***

"Wow! Party time," laughed Dakota on seeing the five of them lined up along three sides of the table. "Or is it the inquisition?" Then she recognised Albert and her tone changed. She just said. "You?"

Frank asked everyone to leave for five minutes. "I need to talk to Dakota privately a moment." Ben stomped out first, the others followed.

"What's up, Ben?" Ruby asked. But she knew, of course, and just wanted the opportunity to work on him quietly. "Are we allowed outside, ma'am?"

"Just on the lawn directly through the door," the guard replied.

Ruby led Ben out, pairing with him so that Albert and Mrs Jameson were left alone together in the reception area.

Thus all three of them, by design, had their roles to play, working on their selected partners. Albert had possibly the easiest task, although it was hardly easy, squaring things away with Mrs Jameson, the loving mother of his first victim.

"You cheated us of all that money?"

"Yes."

"You're guilty of theft?"

"Yes. I expect to be prosecuted and go to jail."

"Good, you're an evil man, Mr Essington, thoroughly evil. They should throw away the key when they lock you up. Just think of the lives you've destroyed by your greed." He hung his head in shame, could not defend himself. "Wait a minute, that means you cheated Dakota of her freedom?"

"Yes, I did."

"So when can she get out?"

"It's not that easy, Mrs Jameson. This is the plan that Mr Williams has come up with. We need you all to agree to it."

By contrast, Ruby had it harder. On the one hand she had worked on Ben already, but certainly he was no less angry for it.

"This is the damn lawyer, more like crook, who ensured Dakota was put away in the first place." They were walking around the small patch of immaculate lawn immediately outside the reception area entrance, a guard watching over them. Beyond their patch were the several acres of equally pristine lawn, stretching like a lake into the distance, harboured by the wire fences that were visible everywhere.

"Yes, but people change and Frank and I are convinced that this change is genuine. I despised him at first, just like you. But if you saw the countless hours he's put into turning this around…"

"You can't turn around the theft of time."

"True, but you can work your butt off to try and do something about it."

"He's just trying to save his own butt."

"Ben, come on, he's actively putting himself in harm's way. He's not holding back for his own safety." Ben could not disagree with that. Albert seemed to have reconciled himself to a long prison sentence and did not seem to be out for himself any more. So he moved on.

"But this approach is all wrong. You are expecting to challenge the conviction on the grounds that Dakota was an accessory and not the main culprit. But, at the same time, you're offering a great deal to the culprit. The result is,

Dakota remains guilty."

"But guilty of being second fiddle. Remember, we don't have to prove there was a main culprit, just prove beyond reasonable doubt that Dakota was not that person. Then we argue that a forty-two-year sentence is totally disproportionate for the crime she is actually guilty of. We get the sentence reduced and Dakota gets out."

"She will never plead guilty to anything. You don't know her like I do."

"Well, why don't we ask her?" Ben could not argue with that. He grunted and made back for the door.

But he had to wait with the others because Frank and Dakota were still talking. The five minutes extended to fifteen, then twenty before they were summoned back by one of the guards.

So what conversation took place during those twenty minutes? Between two people who only really knew each other through reports from others?

That conversation started as many do, skirting around like fencers, probing, getting to know the other party.

"Your hair is really starting to grow," Frank began.

"It was a shock and a half having the barber in," Dakota replied. "I doubt it will grow back like it was before."

"It will," Frank said.

"How do you know?" She looked at his classic casual clothes; his tailored hair; fine, closely shaven face. What could he know of brutally shaved heads and prison life?

"I shaved my head last year, for cancer." He went on to explain his involvement in the Last Chance Cancer Home, the charity his father had set up and he had expanded.

"And then you employ them in your household and offices to give them a new start? That is fantastic, Mr Williams."

"Please call me Frank."

"Have any of the people you've helped gone on to anything else? I don't mean to be disrespectful, Frank, but being a house-help may not be everyone's idea of a long term career."

"Well look at Ruby…"

"She was one?" Dakota was amazed.

"Sure thing, she came to work in our kitchens just over four years ago. Now she is my head of research."

"But her hair? I mean it is fantastic, such lovely healthy black hair. And so long!"

"She was bald during the chemo, also down to seventy pounds."

"My God, the recovery is incredible."

The first stage had worked a treat. So now Frank closed it. "Prison, as it is now, is like a cancer in society."

"Too right!" Dakota replied.

"I aim to cut it out." So then he explained about the bid for Pillars of the Community Inc. and about his efforts in sentencing reform. Dakota was mesmerised, taking in every word, a born-again Christian listening to the Bible.

"But there is a price for all this." Frank ended his description to shining eyes, eyes that had been dead for nine long years, which now saw hope where hope had not been ten minutes before.

"Surely worth paying?" she replied, then thought, *My God, Val has a cracker here for a boyfriend.*

"I think so, but it is not me paying the price. Well, I'm funding the campaign and buying the biggest prison operator in the country, but it is not me paying the real price."

"Who is? What is it?" Dakota was hooked.

"It's you, Dakota. I need to have a young and upcoming congressman on my side and there is none better suited than…"

"Dan Roberts," she interrupted. "So you want me to be guilty still? Any appeal is provisional on Roberts not getting convicted for anything?"

My God, thought Frank, *Ben has got a bright one here.*

***

That evening, Frank and Val went out together so the others

walked down to a hamburger place near the hotel. The sky, as they walked, was thick with cloud, as if pregnant, expecting, monitoring changes to come. Ben walked behind the others, letting Albert chaperone Mrs Jameson. He could not talk to them, none of them. When they turned into the restaurant recommended by the hotel staff, he just kept walking.

"Leave him," said Ruby.

So they were down to three for dinner.

Ben would not have eaten anyway. Instead, he walked. When he tired of walking, he drank a beer. Then he walked again. He repeated the process many times, still walking and drinking long after the others had left the restaurant and Ruby had said again, "Leave him." But this time with a little more explanation, "He needs to work some things out, best alone."

If he had got into a vehicle at midnight and switched on the engine, the cops in the car across the street from the bar would have been justified in stopping him and then taking him in for a sample. Instead, they tailed a group of four guys who lounged around the street corners, lighting cigarettes then putting them out on the cobbled sidewalk. But they knew better than to drive and walked to their friend's apartment so no arrests were made that Saturday night.

Ben was, by beer six, drunk but sober. He would have failed the blood test, likewise with urine, but he was still walking in a straight line. He was full up with beer but, like the clouds in the sky, there was a dead weight that hung about him and kept all elation, frivolity, light-heartedness, humour, well away.

He just could not believe what Dakota had said to him that afternoon. "Ben, my love, you can't know what it is like in here. I'll agree to anything if it meant a chance to get out."

"But the truth...."

"There is only one truth in here, Ben. If you're an inmate you deserve shit and you get it, whole bucketfuls at a time. There are no innocent people in here." Then later, sensing that her explanation was not getting through, she added,

"Ben, I don't want to spend the rest of my life in here. I see the older inmates. I don't want my life gone just like that, shuffling to the showers, watching my back, making friends who then get ripped away, seeing people coming in younger than you until finally someone says 'Hey grandma, what's up?' and then you know it is all over."

At 1.20am, it started to rain. For three minutes it was just an announcement of what was to come. But at 1.23am those dark clouds responded to a crack of thunder and shattered themselves on Zanesville. There was nobody on the streets then, nobody but Ben. He walked on in the rain; angry, upset, hurt, arguing with Dakota in his mind, arguing with himself, with Frank, with Albert, with Ruby, with anyone who dared cross him, although nobody did.

The cop car cruised past at 1.56am. It did not stop because neither of the cops wanted to get out in the rain. But at 2.44am, running around the circuit again, the driver felt obligated. He wound down the window a crack.

"Hey feller, you OK?"

"Yes, sir." Ben was dragged from his thoughts, wanted to get back to them.

"Where do you live?"

"Staying at the Zanesville."

"I suggest hitting the sack then, buddy." But Ben did not answer and the rain was slanting into the police car, causing the officer's shirt to get soaked. "Son of a bitch," he said to his partner, winding out the rain and driving off.

They did not return. They finished work at 3am. The next shift was a skeleton one and would not venture out in the rain unless called. And if they had ventured out, all they would have found was driving rain washing empty streets, for Ben had eventually returned to the hotel.

Where he found Mrs Jameson and Ruby waiting for him in the foyer.

"There you are. I was about to call the police. I was worried," Mrs Jameson said.

"I'm sorry, Mrs J. I just needed time to think. You shouldn't have stayed up."

"We sent Albert to bed. He couldn't keep his eyes open. I couldn't sleep and Ruby said she would sit up with me. Sit down a moment, Ben." He did as told, small puddles of water marking his route across the foyer, steam rising from his body, giving the appearance of a mythical creature come out of the sea seeking vengeance. "Ben, you've got to see it from Dakota's point of view." Her mother could see it clearly. "The most important thing is to get out of prison, nothing else matters. She has a life to lead; she has so much to catch up on. I would love it if her innocence could be proved, but most of all I just want her home. It is enough for me that I know she is innocent. I don't care what other people think."

"And," Ruby added, with a killer blow, "you've got to be careful that your pride doesn't get in the way."

"I'm going to bed." He was too angry, now with a new anger that hurt and dug at him. He left for the elevator and pressed his floor before they could rise from their chairs and follow him.

But he lay a long time awake, as the electronic clock marked the minutes in bright orange, his anger slowly being replaced with a kernel of a thought that perhaps they had a point.

***

First thing on Monday morning, Albert Essington lodged the appeal in Washington DC.

That same morning, Frank Williams swung into action with the first part of his plan.

The press conference was well attended.

"Ladies and gentlemen, there are two announcements to be made today." Frank stood on the makeshift stage in the main conference room of the Coliseum Hotel, just down the street from his DC offices. "First, I would like to report that the acquisition of Pillars of the Community Inc. has been agreed at a cost of $27.9billion, payable in full on completion. This represents a price of $42.45 a share or a premium of 32%

over the pre-bid price. There will follow a short period of due diligence and we expect to close around Monday, October 2nd. The entire board of Pillars of the Community is resigning on completion and there will be a number of senior management changes. We will start to announce these over the next two weeks, leading up to the change of control." He paused a moment; a tactic learned from Sir John? "Ladies and gentlemen, there are going to be substantial changes to the operation and ethos of federal penitentiary operations conducted by Pillars of the Community. This takes me onto the second announcement today. But this announcement is not being made by me."

This created a buzz in the room, plus the noise of the metal chairs shifting to look around for the next speaker. Afterwards, one journalist claimed to have deduced the next speaker from the number of black-suited men with dark glasses and radios. But he said nothing at the time so history can debate the validity of his claim. But not right then, for the curtain pulled back and the President strode out.

She had made her name in politics on two counts. The first was her undoubted integrity. The second was her undoubted oratory.

She held the room spellbound. They all knew this was a definitive moment in the campaign of 2028. It was a moment of change, the bottom of the curve of fortune for the President, the moment in which the fight back started. With a rush and slowness of words, she weaved a future for herself and her administration, blowing away the doubts like dandelion seed in a spring wind.

But they could not guess the subject she dwelled on.

"Americans, we have rights, guaranteed by our constitution. These give a special obligation on all of us to protect the rights of all, especially those who are less able. It is why a past president encouraged us to ask what we could do for our country. This, ladies and gentlemen, is our country and, if we are called to fight for it now, just as we were called to fight for it over a quarter of a millennium ago, we will fight and fight. The news has been full of the apparent indecision of some of our Founding Fathers, hedging their bets and even signing a second treaty that some say has jurisdiction rather than the Treaty of Paris of 1783. I say to you and to all Americans that this may be the case."

The room went silent. Was the President admitting the situation, giving in?

"It may be the case," she repeated. "But we will never know for sure. The fight back starts today. All we know for definite is that we are Americans and that makes the difference. We claim our country, just as our forefathers claimed it. We are our forefathers, melded into one nation. We are the American people."

Frank gave her the thumbs-up from the edge of the stage. She had their total attention.

"Ladies and gentlemen, we can all of us, every man jack of us, be founding fathers of our great nation. Perhaps that is the nature of re-invention. Perhaps the first founding fathers meant us to re-address this in some distant future time not known to them. That time is come now." She looked around the room, saw several hundred journalists, almost the same again of on-lookers, diplomats, officials, even a couple of waiters skiving off their duties to see history unfurling. "Remember, Americans, this is our country and we shape our country as we see fit. Perhaps our founding fathers decided to throw in uncertainty to make us address these serious issues again, as we must do now." Her voice rose like a swallow, but with the strength of lions. Dick watched her with such pride; this was the President, his President.

"And, Americans, I am today launching a great new campaign. 155 years ago, another President made an address to the nation. It was during a time of great turmoil for our country, racked by civil war; far greater turmoil than we face today. President Lincoln made all slaves free. He did this to unite our great country. Remember, the pursuit of unity often causes division along the way. But if the end is right, the motivation is true, then the unity far outweighs the dissension." She looked for support: Dick was smiling,

smiling broadly. That was his sign to her.

"I am but a pale shadow of that great man, not fit to wash his feet. But I have learned some lessons of statehood and leadership, particularly over the last few months when turmoil has revisited us. I look around and remember our commitment to life, liberty and the pursuit of happiness, set for us by the first Americans. I look around our prisons and see modern slavery in action. I see the same cruelty, the same disregard for fellow humans, but mostly I see the terrible waste of human lives through incarceration on an industrial scale. I don't say open the prison gates and let all out. I say let us work to rehabilitate, to give chances, to hold back on punishment when we can. I say let us as Americans give light to the world, to show the world our commitment to life, liberty and the pursuit of happiness."

She was spent, a few questions answered with spirit and she backed away, Dick taking over. The following question-and-answer session lasted over ninety minutes. Frank stepped up on the stage alongside Dick and showed his own particular mastery in front of an audience.

But Dick was a natural.

And the President had found her way.

Back in Charlottesville

Ben had no desire to go back to DC, preferring Charlottesville where he could ride in the morning and spend the rest of the day trying to find any information to help Dakota with her research. Convinced the appeal would fail, he badly wanted something to soften the blow for Dakota. He had told her on Sunday how much he had enjoyed riding across the countryside. For a few minutes Dakota had allowed herself the fantasy of a horse farm with Ben, she also learning to ride, and cantering in the early morning then coming out of the trees at a mad gallop, laughter blown on the wind. Her life was an awful lot of monotony punctuated by moments of intense fear and humiliation; sometimes a dream or two and a happy thought to mix in was no bad idea.

When Ben got back into the records room on Monday afternoon he found that Mr Urquart had been busy.

"I came in over the weekend because it seemed such a huge lot to wade through." The kind old gentleman had gone through several dozen boxes, condensing relevant papers into four stacks on the table, but all referenced so they could be put back in their proper location. "The first stack contains the ones I thought were particularly interesting, but you will be a better judge than me." He moved off to greet some students from the University of Virginia who had access, by arrangement, to the Williams archives.

Ben settled down, coffee and a bar of chocolate to sustain him, powerful overhead lights and an open window to give freshness to the air.

It was a long day, as were the next three. Mr Urquart had mistaken Ben's objectives and most of the papers, all those in the priority stack, were of little interest; account books, hunting records, a visitors' book, architects' plans for a mansion. He realised they were the plans for the house he was in right then, built in the early nineteenth century by one of the descendants of Amelia as the family started to make serious money.

But he found no reference or insight to Richard Sutherland. The visitors' book mentioned his arrival, but no date was given for departure and no comments from Richard were included. Had he left in a hurry? Quite possibly; most other entries included a departure date.

The days formed into a natural routine. Ben rose early, had breakfast, indeed all meals, with Ruby and whoever else was staying, then went riding on Liberty, a fine stallion with one white sock and a mane that changed colour in light and shade almost magically. After the first day he asked to learn how to saddle him and then always did so, taking joy in the simple physical task. After each ride, he removed bridle and saddle, rubbing Liberty down and turning him out in a pretty meadow of late summer flowers that ran down to a tiny stream at the front of the house. He would lean on the fence, under the shade of a huge forked oak, and watch the young horse charge around the field, quite free. Finally, hunger would drive Ben indoors for lunch.

Then the afternoons and evenings were dedicated to research. Mr Urquart was often available for interpretation and advice and gradually understood better what Ben was seeking.

"I think you need the personal papers, Mr Franklin," he said on Thursday afternoon. "I need Mr Williams Senior's permission for these as some of them are quite fragile. Leave it with me and I'll see what I can do."

The next day, Friday, the day before he was due to see Dakota again, Ben saw a new stack on the table when he came in after his early lunch with Ruby and Albert, who was now back to brief Ruby before going to visit Dakota on Saturday. The other four piles had been removed to the far end of the library, where Mr Urquart was busy re-filing them. Ben settled down to what he hoped was a more productive session.

The seventh paper Ben picked up blew his mind. He found the style of writing hard to get to grips with and the antiquated language did not help. But he knew as he made out the title 'An Account of my Adventures with Mr Sutherland' that this was going to be an incredible find.

"Mr Urquart, look what I have found!" he called across the library to the bent back of the old librarian.

By nine o'clock that evening, they had a very rough paraphrase of Amelia Williams' account, although whole passages were unintelligible, so to Ben it did not make much sense.

"I'm sure Dakota is more used to the styles and the language and will make much better sense of it," Mr Urquart said soothingly.

"What do you mean?" Ben asked. "She couldn't get release for her father's funeral so they are not going to let her out to study an old journal."

"If she can't come to the book, we may just have to take the book to her," Mr Urquart replied with the dimpled cheeks that accompanied his smile. Then he explained. "Mr Williams Senior said that if you found anything of interest you were welcome to take it to Miss Jameson."

"That's fantastic!"

"There is a proviso," Mr Urquart added, with the same dimples.

"What is that?"

"That I accompany the document as its guardian! I just did not realise it would be the very next day."

Mr Urquart was thrilled to have confirmation from his boss that he was definitely needed as custodian. After a quick phone call home, to get ultimate authority for his jaunt, he delighted in telling Ben, Ruby and Albert at a late supper that night.

"I told Mrs Urquart that I was going to prison tomorrow. She almost fainted with shock." When Ben heard this he thought, *So too would I faint, for there is not one unkind or dishonest bone in your body, Mr Urquart.*

Frank was already in Zanesville but sent the little chopper for Mrs Jameson and the big one for the others so they converged at the airport. 'Cars for the Busy' was waiting, a refreshing wind blowing the cap off the old chauffeur's head as he tried to hold the door open for his customers. He chased after it, the wind teasing him mercilessly, until finally it was lodged against a concrete bollard set there to stop people wandering onto the runway. On his way back he could not find his keys, until Mrs Jameson suggested he look in the ignition. Tension should have evaporated with these escapades, yet Ben deeply resented sitting next to Albert in the back row of the seven-seater.

"Ben, I am really interested in the documents Mr Hibbert sent over." But Ben would not respond, would not acknowledge the lawyer, would not admit that maybe there was some sense in their approach. They risked selling Dakota down the river. Even Mrs Jameson was in on it, although he could not bring himself to ignore his landlady.

The fifteen minutes from the airport to the prison seemed to take forever, as did waiting for Security, then Security itself. Val was back on duty, in charge of the visitors' room. Ben barely responded to her; she was associated with Frank, who had persuaded Dakota to accept guilt. Ben thought back to the first time he had met the billionaire on his day trip to Charlottesville when he had first ridden, fallen off, remounted and then picked up the fateful trunk. He clearly remembered the strong disquiet he had felt that day and in the days afterwards. Frank's obvious kindness to him and the cancer patients he nurtured sat oddly with the casual way in which he destroyed lives.

Like Ben's own mother's.

Could people be good and bad? That did not fit with the world he knew. Certainly, it would make Hollywood a lie. He tried to think of movie stars who had played ambiguous characters; either good people who did bad things or bad people who did good deeds. But that made him think of Dakota. She was a good person who did a single stupid thing. And was paying the price. Also, because they had subordinated her appeal to boost their cause, she likely would be paying a lot more over the coming years.

He wished he had never met Frank.

But then he thought that without Frank he would not

have been in a position to help Dakota with her research.

And she would not be lodging an appeal right now, however 50:50 or worse it might be. At least it was an appeal.

"What's up, Mr Franklin? You look real sorrowful today." Val always used formal names when on duty. It helped avoid accusations of favouritism. He looked up and saw her radiant face, returned to its pre-assault beauty.

"I don't know, I'm just confused about a lot of things right now." Dakota's face, in contrast, still had some way to go to repair itself. Her beating had been more damaging than Val's as her arms were chained to the bars. She had not been able to protect herself from the blows.

"You still have fifteen minutes until visiting starts. Will you walk with me outside?" Val asked. "The situation is under control in here." She paused, a vein of the old uncertainty, as if she was not good enough for the situation, but a beautiful happiness was escaping from every part of her and could not be suppressed, even for work.

"Sure."

***

He had always liked Val, would have asked her out if he had met her before Dakota. He bristled when she first mentioned the appeal and its prospects as they walked anti-clockwise around the oblong lawn, September sun in their faces for one shorter side before they turned left to run the full length to the gravel parking area beyond.

It was the same lawn he had walked with Ruby the previous weekend. But now he had a guide who knew every aspect.

"I did some research," Val began. "This one area of lawn is almost exactly half an acre. So far this year, do you know how many inmate hours have gone into tending it?"

"Tell me."

"8,422 hours, Ben. The bigger lawn the other side of the senior staff parking area has had over 15,000. So on this little lawn there has been over four man-years of work and we are not done with September yet. I should say woman-years, of course, as inmates did it all. But here is the second scary thing. The guard hours dedicated to overseeing this work are running not much less at 6,012 hours year to date."

"My God, so the best part of $100,000 to keep a lawn pretty."

"Plus the wasted inmate time. You know, Mrs Kinderly does a monthly inspection of both lawns. She sees it as a standard-setter for her prison."

They walked another circuit in silence, Val working out how to get to the subject she needed to discuss. Finally, as they turned from sun behind them to sun on the left flank, she decided just to say it.

"Ben, we need you on board here. It's great that you are putting Dakota first. She has become my best friend and I would never do anything that risked her safety…."

"What about her liberty?"

"I was just about to say 'and liberty'. Ben, it's real important that you see the bigger picture here. Frank has set up a massive campaign involving the President and her re-election. There is so much at stake here. Think of all the other inmates in desperate need of help."

"Hey, Val, who was it who first thought of prison reform? Who was it that got Frank involved and got him excited about it? Who was it put the idea of buying the business into his head? Exactly." He responded to her gesture, indicating him. "So, don't give me the 'bigger picture' story. It was me that first thought the bigger picture."

"So right, Ben, but you've got to keep seeing it. You remember when we were in the cafeteria at the hospital? You convinced me then that I had hope on my side. You did good but did I follow it up? I was still thinking small country roads while you were on the interstate, cruising west. It took me a week to summon up the courage to go see Dakota. And when I did, well, things have been leaping forward ever since."

They made another circuit and a half in silence; Ben simmering, Val struggling for the right language.

"Even Dakota sees the benefit of this approach." It was close to visiting time, there was time for maybe one circuit left to convince him.

"She's clutching at straws with Essington."

"It's you that's fooling yourself, Ben, my friend. Things have changed. Albert Essington is turning out all right. Dakota is content to be a part of a much bigger thing. You've got to let her give the way she knows how to give. She wants to be part of a bigger thing. I understand Dakota now much better. She is all about giving and sometimes that involves some risk, but you can't keep her from that. It's who she is, why she is, what she is."

Their time was up; in fact, they were ten minutes late. When they entered the visiting room, Mrs Jameson, Frank, Albert and Mr Urquart were already there, bent over the document Mr Urquart had brought along with him in a worn leather briefcase with 'J.U.' in faded gold letters on the flap that closed it.

They were bent over the document until they became aware of the presence of Val and Ben. Then Dakota jumped out of her chair and flung her arms around Ben.

"Thank you, Ben, my dearest. This is the best birthday present I could ever ask for. It is fantastic." He had forgotten that Dakota had turned twenty-nine during this last week.

"It was really Mr Urquart," Ben said, to which they all burst out laughing. "What did I say?"

"Albert said you would say that! You are a lovely man, Ben. If I ever get out of here I am going to marry you and then keep you as my prisoner for the rest of our lives."

She was crying with pure joy, she who had so little. It was more joy than was allowed for an inmate, of course, far more than allowed.

And Smith was on duty that weekend.

But this time Val was ready for her.

***

"Jameson to control room." Carter's ominous voice rang

across the prison.

"Good luck," said Janice as Dakota sprung to her feet, not wanting to be late. "I'll keep working at my letters as promised. Probably be able to read fluently when you get back."

"Stand there and wait," Carter said. "Don't fidget, in fact don't move a damn muscle." Smith was in no hurry. At that moment she was enjoying overseeing a cleaning detail, toothbrushes to scrub the cracks between the tiles in one of the bathrooms.

"Ma'am?" said one of the inmates as her toothbrush handle snapped and the head scuttled across the floor and down the open drain beneath the metal sinks.

"Shut up, keep scrubbing." So the inmate, one year into a twelve-year sentence for stealing a car when high on meth, carried on scrubbing the floor with the broken handle of her toothbrush.

Smith's radio went and she answered it. "Good," she said. "I'll be along directly." Then she looked around for another guard. "Bennet? Over here now!"

"Ma'am, I'm just in the middle of something."

"Correction. You *were* just in the middle of something but that something just ended right now." Smith could not help leering as she spat out her orders. "Get over here and take over. I want this floor so I can eat my dinner off of it. No slacking, you sluts, I'll be back before you know it."

"Get back to work." Val's imitation of Smith was like well-watered bourbon to the real thing. But as soon as Smith left, her tone changed again. "Guys, stop working and listen to me. The floor is fine. Stand up, all of you. I don't have much time." She pulled out a large notebook from inside her tunic jacket. "Now, I want to check a few details from our earlier conversation. Dickson, you said Miss Smith has been stealing your supplies for how long?"

"Jameson, you're in big trouble." Smith licked her lips, one hand pounding into the other.

"What have I done, ma'am?"

"First thing you did wrong was get a fancy education. Slum bitches like you should keep right away from books and ideas. Best thing for you is cleaning detail. It's the sort of work you fit right into. Ain't that right, Carter?"

"Yes, ma'am. Scum like Jameson should be licking your boots, ma'am."

"Good idea, Carter." Smith turned back to Jameson. "Get on your knees and lick my boots. I want them sparkling."

"No, ma'am." Said very politely.

But politeness only incensed Smith. She grabbed Dakota by the back of her neck and forced her down to the floor. Her anger blanked out the scene around her, just concentrating on Jameson and the need for her boots to be spotlessly clean.

Thus she did not see Val standing there, nor Mrs Kinderly and a cohort of other guards.

Nor the police officers.

***

Mrs Kinderly accepted the cup of coffee Val poured her. Her hands were shaking, eyes wide with panic at the police presence in her office.

Would she be arrested along with Smith and Carter?

"Sir," began Val, "the warden is obviously very shaken by the evident corruption and gratuitous violence going on behind her back. She takes great pride in the smooth running of her prison."

"I commend your loyalty to the warden, Mrs Bennet."

"Ms Bennet, if you don't mind."

"Of course." Everyone in the local police knew of Val's husband and what he had done to her and to inmate Jameson. "But I do have some questions for her. I can come back later if that is easier for her."

"I understand, Detective. Best to handle it now." Mrs Kinderly was wondering how long it would take them to find the memo she had sent Smith. Why on earth had she done that; in her own handwriting, too?

The questions that followed were all centred on

determining whether the warden knew anything of the corruption going on. Mrs Kinderly answered them all, explaining that she had her suspicions but nothing definite to go by until Bennet had come up with the proof earlier that day.

"Ms Bennet has shown a great deal of initiative. You should be proud of her."

"I am."

Mrs Kinderly was a great deal prouder and a lot less nervous after the police had gone, because that is when Val told her about the memo she had found.

"Yes, I wrote it," Mrs Kinderly could see little point in denying it. "You must understand the pressure I was under." So then it all came out. How Smith had found her, in a moment of weakness, having sex with a particularly attractive inmate; little Stacy, poor little Stacy.

"It was three years ago, just after my boyfriend broke up with me. It was when I was new here, in my first month. I was so lonely and dejected. I'm not that way normally, at all. She got me to write a confession and then I had to turn a blind eye to what she was doing. She had control of me."

"I know, Mrs Kinderly."

"You know? How come?" So Val told her boss about her discoveries in Smith's office.

"My God, so the documents are in there? The police will find them."

"No, and no." When pressed to explain, Val simply said, "I removed all the incriminating evidence, including the confession. It is quite safe now. Frank Williams has them."

Letter Ten

A letter from Dakota was hand-delivered to Ben on the last day of September. He had spent the previous two weeks searching the records for anything else that shone light on Richard Sutherland, but nothing came up. But it gave him a chance to ride and to think in a way that only the countryside can encourage. Practical matters came first; grooming Liberty, then calling the vet when it seemed the lameness might return, rubbing on a poultice twice a day, walking Liberty gently in his meadow, the flowers now a little tired of life and the constant beat of the sun. Then after three days of medical attention he was given the go-ahead to ride Liberty again. For two days he just walked him, but Ben could feel the horse ready to go and on the third day he galloped and galloped, over the ridge, into the fields beyond and up over the back way to the mansion that he now knew was completed in 1829.

He had written to Dakota every day, telling her of the problems with Liberty, but also how much he loved riding. He wrote about coming up on Hunt Ridge from different directions, seeing the land below from different perspectives, different angles.

And all the time the different angles were working on Ben, sorting the jumble of conflicts in his mind, settling his turmoil, a little more each day.

But strangely, although he wrote each day, he received no letters back. Once he phoned Val, getting her after several attempts.

"I'm sorry, Ben, it has just been so busy here," she explained, almost breathless.

"What's happening?"

"I can't talk about a lot of it because of the pending acquisition. But you remember Smith? No, not Ruby, but the assistant warden here, the real nasty one. Well, she has been arrested along with her sidekick, Carter. The police have been all over the place. They've pretty well finished now."

"I haven't heard from Dakota for a while. I'm concerned about her."

"Don't be. She is fine. She is in the library all day every day, trying to finish her thesis. She is so excited about the document you found. She's literally working every moment of every day to get it done. We've had to drag her out at lockdown!"

The next afternoon, as Ben was settling in the library after a long ride, Mr Urquart rushed in from his little side office.

"Phone call, Mr Franklin," he gasped. "It's from Zanesville."

It was Dakota, apologising for not writing. The words did not matter to Ben, it was the tone of her voice that made him sit and stare afterwards, research unattended for the rest of the day.

There was a richness about her voice he had never heard in the muted prison environment. Also, a volume never before present. She was alive again. He could imagine how she had been as an eighteen-year-old, before her incarceration.

"My God, I love that girl."

"I'm sorry, Mr Franklin, did you say something?" Mr Urquart was passing Ben's desk.

"Just muttering to myself," Ben replied.

"You know what they say about talking to yourself." Maybe Ben was going mad, but madmen can have brilliant ideas. And Ben had just had one.

***

The letter was hand-delivered by Frank four days later. He had flown in early on the morning of Saturday 30th September. Hunt Ridge had been frantic all the day before. Marcus Hibbert headed a large team of lawyers, arriving in several cars and including his two partners, Kirsten Fisher and Mike Welling. Mike and Albert had been closeted together for hours, missing meals, sending down to the kitchen for coffee and snacks.

"They're working on the appeal," Ruby had explained to Ben. "They've got a date for the hearing. It's November 8th, the day after the election!"

"That's fantastic! Mike Welling is a top attorney, right?"

"Ben, he's the best human rights lawyer in the country. He won that case…" But Ben was not listening. He was thinking of Dakota. And hoping.

Frank was in a rush but was determined to fit in a ride with Ben. It was a short one. As they mounted, Frank started talking, aware that his time was limited. Ben led them out the back of the stables, across the barrelled bridge and down to the main gate. From there they went across a lightly wooded area, past the observatory Frank's great grandfather had built, and then up the drive to the house.

"I've got a letter for you from Dakota. I've just come from there this morning. I'll get it for you when we get back to the house. I wanted to talk to you about Dakota's appeal but don't have much time. This Pillars of the Community deal is keeping me very busy."

"I can imagine. Go on; about Dakota, I mean."

"The appeal date is set for November 8th. Ben, I daren't sound too hopeful but Mike Welling - he's the partner of Marcus who specialises in human rights - well he thinks Albert has done a first rate job on the appeal."

"I know he's worked real hard."

"That is an understatement if ever there was one!" Frank joked. "He's created a chance for Dakota. Mike thinks he's created a real chance."

"He put her there in the first place. No, I take that back. That was mean-spirited of me. I hated the man so much but even I can see how hard he's working."

"There's something else he's been working on as well. He went to see Sir John the other day," Frank said then, spurring his horse, he shouted, "Race you to the house."

"You're on!"

Ben won easily.

***

Ben had a beer in mind, two bottles placed by him at the back of the fridge. It was called 'Wild Stallion' and was a dark porter. When he opened the first bottle he knew instantly that the Kentucky brewery had hit home. The beer had a beautiful balance of malt, fruit and spices, giving the impression of a beer crafted with love and care. Also, the horse in the picture on the front of the bottle looked just like Liberty, only it had two white socks rather than one.

My darling Ben, the paper you dug out of the archives is a goldmine. I am so happy that you did this for me. I'm working like crazy to finish my thesis. I've done the work, just adding notes, and then I have the bibliography to do. I've sent a copy to Sir John. I hope you don't mind him seeing it first, but I wanted to get his opinion and then write to you a special letter to give the ending of the story about Richard Sutherland.

Sir John sent a cross note back saying he might get round to reading it if the hospital runs out of old magazines on cooking and knitting. But Lady Fitzroy put a note in with his saying he had not put it down and will not talk to anyone while he is reading it!

Beer time, Ben, so I can start.

Richard Sutherland grew weaker by the day, relying on Rupert and Amelia for care and Sidney for direction as to how to pursue his objective. The land deal had been done; Sidney now owned a vast estate outside Charlottesville, Amelia and her husband owned the Hunt Ridge estate, still in the ownership of the Williams family today, as you well know.

"Will we be going back to try again, sir?" Rupert asked as he bed-bathed Richard, who now shook with fever and slurred every word, such was the effort to talk. Sidney answered for him.

"We must go tonight. They will be breaking up their meeting in a few days, from what I hear. You must go in there in the dead of night and purloin the document. We will wait for you as before."

Same scene as the last attempt, same carriage and same dark street. Only the time was different, now it was almost 3am and all the candles were out save one in the hallway, giving a yellow glow to the window through which it shone. Rupert slipped out of the carriage, his soft slippers silent on the cobblestones. He was forty yards from the front door. But that could not be his entrance, as it would be well secured. Instead, they had devised a plan for Rupert to enter by a basement window that they knew entered into a pantry off the kitchen. The door from pantry to kitchen had not been locked when Rupert had acted as a servant during the previous visit, but there was a key in the lock. The whole plan depended on it being left unlocked at night.

To get to the window he had to go around the house, directly across the glow from the single candle and to the back, descend the steps that led to the kitchen door, but then scramble up the stone side to lever open the window.

All without making a sound.

He moved very slowly through into the front garden, placing each slippered foot down carefully, feeling for anything that might raise alarm. Then, taking a deep, even breath, he darted across the block of light that could not be avoided, moved on six more paces to the corner of the house and stopped and listened.

He was a cat at night. Nobody had heard him. Richard and Sidney had seen the sudden shadow flash through the light, but had not been able to make it out as human.

Rupert rounded the next corner of the house with slow, quiet steps and went on to the stairs. He imagined there were eight steps until he could reach up for the window, open it and haul himself in. But the steps were steeper and deeper and it was only six until he was in the right position.

Richard sat up suddenly, straightening his slumped posture.

"What was that noise?" he whispered.

"I think it was the window, creaking as Rupert opened it," replied Sidney, wondering to himself exactly how glory would come, how it would play out.

There was a second, louder noise from the back of the house as Rupert lowered himself from the window and landed on a crate of wine, cutting his ankle so that he gave an accompanying cry of pain.

He waited ten minutes, straining against the light wind and the crispy leaves to hear for any pursuit; stock-still, not even daring to take out his handkerchief to try and stop the bleeding. There was no

381

disturbance above him, so eventually he moved forward. And found that the pantry door was unlocked.

The next stage was easy. He had seen the head servant place the huge bunch of keys in the cupboard at the entrance to the kitchen, where the stairs rose up to the ground floor, his destination. He lowered the bunch, making sure not to clash any two keys together, and made his way up the stairs, across the hall, picking up the candle to give him light, then into the dining room where the safe was, hidden inside a cabinet against the far wall.

Ten minutes later he had the draft treaty in his hand. He placed the other documents back in the safe, locked it and retraced his steps back downstairs. The exit was the exact reverse of the entrance, like a story read backwards. He even managed to cut himself again, this time the sole of his foot on the broken glass that lay beneath the window of the pantry. But he made it outside, with slightly less care now; slightly more hurried, keen to get away. A dog barked, just as Rupert turned the corner of the house and ran along the side, a candle lit in an upstairs room as he turned the second corner to the front of the house. The window opened as he darted back across the glow of light that seemed to flood the front garden.

"Who's there?" came an angry voice. Rupert froze. He had rushed too much, risked all in his desire to be away.

There were cries now from inside the house, feet clattering on the stairs. Rupert ran the last thirty yards to the carriage, arriving just as a shotgun blasted out into the night, followed by several more, firing wildly. Torches were lit and lanterns held high as they looked out into the night.

"He's getting into that carriage," came the cry.

But there was no coachman. The coachman was taking a leak, so Rupert, without thinking, jumped up, released the brake, and urged the horses on. No need for silence now; they were discovered and would be pursued.

Unless they could slip away immediately and disappear into the night. There was another cry to the left. Could they have made that much ground already? No, it was the coachman, scrambling back onto the moving vehicle, grabbing the reins, understanding that rapid departure was the best hope for their safety.

They drove like fury in the black night, with no lights, risking potholes, ruts, fallen trees. They went in a straight line for Hunt Ridge, thinking speed a better ally than deception. They were right. There was no sound of any pursuit. It was as if the night was closed, opening up to accept them in their hurry, then closing around them again, enveloping them in blackness and silence.

"Are you alright, Master?" Rupert had climbed from the driving seat into the carriage compartment, swinging out wildly as they took a sharp bend at speed, then falling into the compartment as it righted itself from the corner. He banged his damaged foot as he landed.

Richard was white-faced and in pain. As Rupert sat down he first realised the pain he was suffering as well. He placed his hand on his right ankle and it was very bloody. Richard had murmured a reply.

"Good, sir, I am glad you are alright. I have the document." He handed it to Richard and closed his eyes to concentrate on the pain.

Sidney took over then. On arrival back at Amelia's house on Hunt Ridge, he lost no time in seeking fresh horses to go straight to the Potomac.

"We must deposit the treaty where it can never be found by an American," he said. "And what better place than on what is now permanent British soil? The irony is most appealing. We hide the treaty giving the colonies back to Britain on British soil. I have had the attorneys prepare an extra copy of the deed of exchange so we can deposit it with the draft treaty. I also have had someone make up this trunk to contain them. But we will not simply put them in the main body of the trunk. For that I have taken the liberty of securing some of your old letters and copies of letters I discovered you had left in Philadelphia."

"I left behind some letters at your home?" Richard looked puzzled, then looked to Rupert.

"Sir, I was not aware of us deliberately leaving behind such correspondence but, if you recall, I did inform you of a disappearance of certain papers shortly after the big storm."

"You did, Rupert. I remember it well." Richard was reassuring. But his expression spoke of something else. "No matter," he added, perhaps a little too breezily, "they clearly are serving a good purpose elsewhere."

"See what I have done?" said Sidney, keen to get back on subject. "I have had a carpenter create a secret chamber in the lid of the trunk. That way they will always be secure."

"You've thought this out well, sir. We are indebted to you," Richard replied. Again a calmer man, on hearing this, might have thought he was a little too stiff in his response.

Richard insisted that before they go Amelia take care of Rupert, binding his cuts. Richard carefully handed the document to Sidney, who then observed him placing it in the secret chamber of the trunk, before closing it and locking it.

"There, that is done. Now, as soon as Rupert is repaired we are to leave."

"I must just see Amelia about some pressing business first."

"Can it not wait?"

"No Sidney, I don't think we can count on someone my age and condition returning on a future visit. I must see her and her husband alone for a little while before we depart. No, I will see them alone. It is private business, as I mentioned." The firmness quite exhausted Richard and he had to sit down a while, the others leaving to give them the privacy Richard desired. Amelia's only maid brought him tea and some fried mushrooms with garlic; a dish he had always enjoyed. It was strange sitting in this small farmhouse that he had often visited as a young man, knowing that he would never sit there again. Doubly strange that so much intrigue was going on when it had always been a quiet place of work and business before.

They were away at last, the new sun poking into the horse's eyes, making them skittish. Rupert hobbled with a stick, his foot wrapped in bandages, their luggage packed by Amelia's maid who admitted with a grin that all she had done was scooped up piles of belongings and placed them in the cases they had.

"We'll sort it all out on board, sir," said Rupert, worried that his master may be concerned.

But Richard had bigger worries right now. Which is why he had insisted on seeing Amelia and her husband alone.

Ben paused, as there was a knock on his bedroom door.

"I'm sorry to disturb you, Mr Franklin." It was Albert, head and upper body wrapped around the door. "I just thought you might want to see this." He placed a small collection of papers on the end of the bed and made to leave.

"Just a sec, Albert", Ben stressed the use of the first name, "can you tell me what it's about?"

"It's an acceptance by the prosecution that the original sentence was harsh. It means that any judge reviewing the case would be likely to make a reduction in the sentence."

"Would it be the original judge again?"

"No, she died last year. Anyway, it would be an appeal judge. We've got Judge Julie Jefferies, a second-generation Kenyan immigrant. She was married to a Harvard law professor who wrote his doctorate on sentencing reform. Now, I've done some research and of the 112 sentence appeals she has ruled on over the last eight years, seventy-nine of them have been sentence reductions. The average reduction was eight years or 28% of the original sentence. But, here is the significant bit…"

"Sit down, Albert, and call me Ben if you like."

"Thanks, Ben," said with a sudden element of shyness. "That's good of you. Now, as I was saying…"

Albert gave fact after fact about averages, rates, age and gender differences. Every conceivable element of Jefferies' sentence appeal work had been analysed in detail.

"So to summarise it," Ben said, the facts and figures appealing to him, "Judge Jefferies appears to have a slight bias towards female prisoners in terms of reducing sentences on appeal, plus a more marked bias towards younger prisoners. These two should help Dakota."

"Also, she does seem to have a tendency to reduce sentences generally, even for middle-aged men there is a 55:45 split."

"So Dakota's odds are increased a little?" Ben suggested.

"We pulled strings to get Jefferies. Our research said she was the second most favourable for this particular situation. The best option has just gone on long-term sick leave."

"That's great work, Albert, thank you."

Albert stood up to leave then turned back and said, "I know what it took to say thank you to me. I don't for one minute think you've forgiven me, but I am trying to get her free, to undo a little of what I've done. No, don't say anything else, Ben, let me get back to work. Sometimes words don't help."

Ben sat for a moment, half-lying on the bed, three pillows supporting his back. He rearranged them as he sank back further. That made him think of a joke Dakota had made about prison pillows being so rock-hard you could take them surfing. He chuckled, then remembered the letter. He opened his second beer and continued to read.

The three of them plus a driver made good progress. By noon they had covered twenty miles of difficult roads, changing the horses at an inn mid-morning, Richard paying for the very best on offer.

"This is crazy," Sidney said. "It will take us three days to get to my land on the Potomac, I mean your land, then another three days to get back to Richmond to meet with the ship. Six days on the road is going to be hard on you, Richard."

"Considerably hard," Richard replied. "And I am tiring rapidly. Do you have any ideas?"

"No, but I will think on it."

A neat five minutes later, Sidney spoke again. "I have it. We split up. I take the trunk to your land and deposit it securely there, while you take a separate coach to Richmond to board ship."

"But..." spoke Rupert, voice trailing away after seeing his master's reaction.

"Excellent idea, my dear friend," Richard said, would have continued but for a bout of strong coughing. Rupert forgot his misgivings, forgot Amelia's warning words, dedicated instead to tending his master.

So Sidney made the plans, while Richard coughed and spluttered. They would split up at the next inn. Sidney would hire a light phaeton and take the trunk to the Potomac at speed. The sooner it was secure, the better. Richard, with Rupert caring for him, would turn for Richmond and be there in two days.

"I won't see you again," said Sidney as the plan was finalised.

"I will visit my cousin in Baltimore, then make my way back home."

They spent that night together, Sidney in good form with joking and laughing but a little falsely so, as if the dearness of his new friend was dying with his friend and Sidney was moving on to better things. Rupert thought him excited, exaggerating his attention to Richard but in a somewhat triumphant way. To Rupert, Sidney Hollingsworth's faults seemed large upon his face that night. Amelia's words kept coming back to him. 'I do not like nor trust that man and think only bad can come of his association with Mr Sutherland.'

In the morning, Rupert spent an extra hour caring for Richard, who seemed slower and sicker than ever. By the time they were ready to depart, the innkeeper told them that their companion was long-gone.

"No matter, we were due to split today," said Richard, suddenly seeming a lot better. "Now, we must get away. Rupert, is everything ready to depart?"

"Yes, Master. I'll just check the horses are hitched."

Richard then turned to the innkeeper and asked for a fast rider to take a message back to Hunt Ridge. A man left a few minutes later, his charge just a single piece of paper.

"But speed is of the essence."

"I understand, sir." Before cantering off.

Three days later, they arrived at Richmond.

There they found the Swan waiting for them.

But Richard was in no hurry to board.

"I will rest tonight in this fine inn," he decided. "I will have enough of the swaying motion of the ship when we set out to sea. Rupert, be so kind as to take this letter to the master of the Swan. It gives direction to head not for Philadelphia but across the Atlantic to Glasgow. Please also give him this money as the letter requires him to provision for a longer journey immediately. Help him if necessary and because you know my likes."

"Yes, sir. Will he be willing to go on such a journey, sir?"

"I think so, for his reward is the ship. I make a gift of the Swan to him when we are safely back in Glasgow. To step from ship's captain on a salary to owner clear of all liens is a significant *improvement in wealth and status and I don't know any that would turn it down."*

Rupert was away some considerable time, going with the ship's boat directly to the warehouses and chandlery. Thus he did not see Amelia and Simon Williams arrive by horseback, mounts with frothing mouths and heaving sides.

"Mr Sutherland, it is so good to see you. Are you bearing up?"

"Yes, Amelia. I am better for seeing the end of my mission. We are close now. Let us go to my room, for I have the paper to give you."

At that moment Rupert returned, tired from several trips in the boat and from helping load stores for much of the day.

"Mr and Mrs Williams, I did not expect to see you here. Can I get you anything?"

"No, Rupert dear. We are not staying long at all and have already had refreshments." Then she turned to Richard with enquiry on her face.

"Yes, by all means. Rupert should know everything, especially as tomorrow morning we will be away. You please tell him."

So Amelia and Simon took turns to recount the quickly planned events of the last few days.

"Mr Sutherland asked us to build a trunk just like the one Mr Hollingsworth has taken now to the Potomac land. The real document is to be kept in the trunk at Hunt Ridge."

"I don't understand. Mr Hollingsworth has the document." Rupert broke into the explanation.

"Correction," said Richard, enjoying the suspense he was creating, "Mr Hollingsworth has a document but not the document."

"But I saw you hand it to him, Master."

"You saw me hand a document to him, but it was not the document in question. That one is safely upstairs. You see, Amelia alerted you to her distrust of Hollingsworth, but she also, out of dear friendship, spoke to me. Now, we don't have much time to waste. I want Mr and Mrs Williams away from here long before we sail." Turning back to the Williams couple, he continued. "You are sure about riding tonight? I hate to see you going out into the dark without rest, but it is important if I am to rest easy on the voyage

that I am certain as I can be of your earliest return to Hunt Ridge."

"Yes, we have rested a short while and can leave as soon as we have the paper."

This was handed over in the bedroom and they quickly left on fresh horses after hugs all around, fellow conspirators drawn even closer together than from natural ties.

"Sir," Rupert asked in the silence following their departure, "might I ask what the document you gave to Mr Hollingsworth would be? As I deal with your correspondence, I feel obliged to say I am not aware of any document not in its proper place."

"Oh, it was just any old piece of paper, nothing of any importance." Richard did not want to mention that it was the only thing he could pull from his pocket at the time was the manumission papers for Rupert and his family.

I can always replace them, thought Richard.

But thoughts are not always the same thing as action.

***

During the night, the weather broke. They woke early to low clouds, mist and a ruinous damp in the air, condensation forming wherever it could find a hold. Rupert looked out of the window of his tiny attic cubicle and saw great puddles in the road with new drops being added in spreading circles all the time. As he stood there dressing he noticed two large puddles break their boundaries and merge together. Like a marriage he thought, two people becoming one, to be further expanded if God blessed the match with children. He wondered if it was raining now in Paris where his family was waiting for him. He wondered if Monsieur Dubois had recovered from his financial difficulties and if things, therefore, would all return to normal. He was so homesick.

But he was going home.

Looking back afterwards, it all seemed so normal for Richard. He was woken early by Rupert, as requested. He was helped through washing, shaving and dressing. Then he had breakfast in a small parlour next to the main room where others, including Rupert, shared a communal breakfast.

There were no early signs, no warnings, no omens. It all seemed so ordinary. He remembered feeling sadness at leaving America for, almost certainly, the last time in his life. He remembered expressing that sadness to Rupert who, being over forty years younger, had no sense of end, of finality. So Rupert's reply was all looking into the future and hopeful, about reunions, family, new visits another time.

Richard remembered vividly boarding the Swan, the master unable to hide his smile and gratitude for the sudden change in circumstances. He remembered the master fussing over him, showing him to his cabin, even though he knew it well enough from last time. He would never forget settling down, looking forward to pleasant days reading Shakespeare out loud with Rupert. But first they would go back on deck.

"I want to savour my last view of America," Richard had said.

So they arrived back on deck just as the commotion broke out. It was the far end of the quay, so may have been nothing to do with them; some dispute between traders or a criminal trying to escape capture. But Richard looked at the source as it moved closer and, with sinking heart, he recognised the bulk of Sidney Hollingsworth.

It happened very quickly. Sidney shouted, "You villain, Sutherland, I checked the paper. It's some damn manumission document, no statement of allegiance at all." Richard looked at Rupert then, who suddenly knew to whom it referred.

"Thank you, Master," he said. He knew, although it meant little to him, it was the greatest gift the old man could give.

It was the last words he uttered. The pistol shot had been aimed for Richard but hit Rupert in the heart. It had been a good shot, going straight for its target, but Rupert threw himself at Richard and pushed him away against the railing, taking the bullet himself. He died instantly; a look of shock spreading across his face to replace the gratitude demonstrated a second earlier. He slumped, Richard tried to catch him, but he was too heavy for the old man. He hit the deck just as the mooring lines were cast off and the Swan slid away from the quay, bare-footed sailors running across the rigging in a silent dance, only the creaks and groans of mast, rope and block marking out the time.

The end of time for a man who had spent all his adult life a slave, but died a free man.

Richard wrote just two letters on that journey home, a journey extended by countless storms blowing them off course. Thus they did not sight Ireland until late June and then were thrust back into the Atlantic by another storm, a purgatory for Richard from start to eventual finish. The crew kept away from him, as much as was possible in a small ship. But they need not have concerned themselves to avoid him because Richard was in a trance most of the time. He stared out to sea from dawn to way past dusk, as if the succession of waves were a measure of time and, maybe, the currents and the tide and wind could somehow push them to a different end. But time, though lengthened by the contrary weather, kept the same beat, the same count and no reprieve for Richard Sutherland; trader, slaver, politician, diplomat and friend.

The hardest letter he wrote first; typical of the man to do so. He wrote with the stern windows open, sea spitting in his face, trying to wash away what he had witnessed, or water down the pain. He wrote to Rupert's widow, a long letter full of his sorrow and what a good man her husband had been. He wrote a sentence, then sat a long time looking at the sea, seeing what might have been and what should have been.

They had buried the body at sea. Each time Richard closed his eyes he saw the off-white sail patch used as a shroud and the makeshift board that pivoted on the railings so that Rupert's body slipped inch by inch, gradually gathering momentum, until it crashed into the sea and was gone in an instant. He once heard a sailor telling his colleagues that he had seen Rupert's arm swing up in a final salute as the body entered the turbulent water, seeking peace in the still depths far below the choppy surface. But Richard had watched every second of Rupert's slide into the sea and had not seen anything that could be construed as movement. He put it down to gossip, from which folklore grows.

The second letter was easier, more factual, more a relaying of terrible events. He wrote to Amelia, filling four pages with the happenings of the twelve hours immediately after she and her husband had departed.

When Amelia eventually received this letter it was mid-October; a time for apples, nuts and berries, a time to cut firewood and mend roofs. She cried bitterly, then wrote back to him. She then wrote the 'Account of my Adventures with Mr Richard Sutherland', attaching the letter she had received to the inside back cover of her notebook.

Ben, that is the end. I don't know whether Richard ever received the letter from Amelia, telling him the documents were secured in the hidden chamber of the lid of the trunk the local carpenter had built, identical to the first one he had constructed a few days earlier. He had a habit of scribbling notes between the lines. So I would have to go to Scotland to see if the letter still exists and whether he did make notes on it, meaning he had read it.

Richard was very ill and had a difficult winter. He did not finally arrive at his home until October, having to see several physicians in Glasgow and one in Edinburgh. Perhaps the October day when Amelia read of the death of Rupert was the same day Richard arrived at home for the last time. Such coincidences make a neatness about history when they sometimes happen, but they rarely do. I like to think it is God's way of marking something of significance, but that is just a fanciful idea I have developed.

Some of his old colleagues from London planned to go and see him in the new year, but Richard died alone; - his wife was planted securely in London and would not move - on January 1st 1784.

Everything makes sense now regarding Sidney Hollingsworth. He was a member of the Empire Association and had been tipped off about Richard's visit to America. My contention is that he deliberately found Richard and Rupert in the streets of Philadelphia and ingratiated himself with Richard in order to learn his plans. He was a fanatical, for sure, but not what we normally think of in using that word, for he was firmly on the other side; not of rebellion and independence but of empire and order. After the war he had little choice but to flee the country. He went to Canada, along with many other loyalists and started a new and very successful life there. As far as I can tell he was estranged from his two children, both of whom had fought for independence in the war. It seems he never saw them again and never went back to the United States.

So that, my dearest Ben, is the story behind my thesis, and my

MA work is almost over. I expect to tweak it when Sir John gets back to me and then I shall submit it. It would not have been possible without your great find and I would have floundered months ago without your constant encouragement and enthusiasm for my project. I thank you and want you to know how much I love you.

Ben lay back on his pillows. So that was the end of her story. And it was the start of Ben's story for the papers Amelia had hidden in the lid of the trunk were the same papers he had discovered. For almost 250 years they had lain at Hunt Ridge under the guardianship of the Williams family. They had first found a spot in the farmhouse then, when the mansion was built, had been placed in the library. It was probably much later that they were moved to the records alcove. Mr Urquart had said he set it up as a young post-graduate in 1980 and moved all the old records from the rest of the house in there at that time.

It struck Ben that there was a far greater coincidence than whether the letter arrived on the same day of October 1783 that Richard arrived home in Scotland. The greater coincidence was certainly marked out by God for its significance; he agreed with Dakota on that.

The end of Richard's story was the start of his, thus history took us from the distant past through a chain to the present. And because it was the start of the new story, it promised to take them on into the future also.

Trade Off

It was not Max Heaton's idea but he wished it were.
    It was obvious. It was simple. It was ingenious.

Georgie got past the secretary by slipping in when she went for coffee. She knocked on the heavy panelled door and entered without an invitation.

"I'm sorry, Mr Heaton. I just popped out for a second." His secretary, coming up from the rear, tried to shoo Georgie out again.

Max hated unscheduled interruptions. He was about to blast both secretary and intruder but stopped, mouth open and framing the first word, when he saw it was Georgie.

"It's polite to make an appointment," he said instead.

"I'm sorry, Mr Heaton, but you really need to hear this." Georgie ploughed straight in. "You know you tasked me with finding a solution to the United Nations permanent seat crisis. Well, I think I have it."

"You certainly seem excited about whatever your idea is." Then he added, a touch gentler still, "Come along then, let's be hearing this wonderful idea." There was no sarcasm, Max neither recognised nor utilised it. "Sit down for a moment, Georgie, you are making me dizzy with that prancing about."

Georgie sat on the edge of an upright chair, fingers under her thighs to stop her fidgeting.

"Sir, I have a possible answer to the problem."

"No, Georgie."

"What do you mean?"

"Your language, my dear. Answers are for questions, not problems. Problems hopefully lead to solutions."

"Ah, of course. So, I have a solution to the problem."

"I'll make out my bill for language tuition later on."

"Don't you want to hear my answer; I mean my solution, sir?"

"Of course I do. Fire away!"

***

A first-world country can do pretty well anything it wants.

At least in diplomatic terms.

Thus, His Majesty's Government turned an idea on Tuesday morning into a delegation, flying First Class, on Wednesday. Twenty-four hours to organise the team, the itinerary and security. It meant headaches for quite a few people, mostly the corporals and sergeants of the diplomatic world, but it happened.

The top team selection was easy.

"Who do you want?" the PM had asked Max.

"We should both go."

"Agreed. Who in support?"

"It should be the Foreign Office in support, not Number 10," Max replied. The PM thought about this a moment. It would mean responsibility and glory would go to the Foreign Office, hence to Max. Could he afford to boost a rival? Yes, it was too serious a matter. He sipped his coffee and tried to calculate the chances. Was it high risk? Did the Americans have any choice in the matter?

No, that was the wrong question. The President and Dick Turnby were good sorts: they would do the right thing. The question really was could the Americans pull it off? Did they have the authority? That was where the real risk lay.

"Of course, Max. I took that for granted. I meant who will you have on your delegation?" The unspoken part of this conversation, stated in glances across coffee cups and in the tone of innocent words, said 'pull this off and you will succeed me'.

So they had agreement.

"I want Bel and young Georgie. Other than secretarial support, I don't need anyone else. And for you, Peter?"

That meant the PM could only have one senior diplomat. It would have to be the Cabinet Secretary. It would be a grave insult not to take him.

With a brace of parliamentary under-secretaries, both bright, hard and going places, and the right level of back-up and security, the delegation was kept to two-dozen people. The press would be invited, of course, but only four elder statesmen journalists would be invited on their aeroplane, the rest would travel independently.

It was the first time Georgie had travelled First Class.

***

Three thousand miles across the Atlantic, similar preparations were being made.

But with a key difference.

"Jane, this is a fantastic opportunity," Dick said over an early breakfast. "A successful summit could wipe away the whole constitutional issue at a stroke. We're rising in the opinion polls."

This hurt because since Frank had taken over from Dick in leading the campaign, the polls had moved significantly in the President's favour.

"What are they saying right now?"

"Averages overnight are twelve points deficit. Two weeks ago we were twenty-plus down. We've got four weeks to go. We might just make it."

The unspoken conversation was different, too. Dick would never take over from the President. They both knew that. Their glances over their coffee cups spoke a different story. *Do this for me*, the President said, *and I will love you forever. It's too late for us to be together, you won't break your marriage and I don't want you to do so, but somehow we will find a way to be intimate. We will deal in what could have been.*

"What do you think they are going to propose?" the President asked.

"I have no clue," Dick replied. "I've been so wrapped up in (a) our election campaign and (b) trying to sort out the main protagonists in the constitutional issue. I just haven't had the time to concentrate on it."

The President looked at the love of her life another short moment. His reference to (b) confirmed her suspicions that he had kidnapped that security guard, despite denying it.

And she knew that he had done it for her.

And, as he met her gorgeous gaze, he knew that she knew. He had to look away.

***

"Good evening, Prime Minister. I hope you are well."

"Good afternoon, Madam President. I am fine thank you, and you?"

"Good, thank you."

That was the preliminaries out of the way. They kissed while Max and Dick shook hands, Dick also placing a hand on Max's upper arm, as was his way.

Dick and the President knew nothing would be revealed that evening. Nothing until the formal negotiations started in the morning. This was just the four of them in the White House for a pre-summit supper.

Likewise, the journalists, outside in their hundreds, knew that no statement would be made that evening; nothing until the next day. But they could speculate and fill the airwaves, building suspense like Sir John would tell a story.

While four enjoyed elegant dining, the best the White House kitchens could offer, hundreds camped outside, munching hotdogs and wasting calories on trying to appear busier than their rivals. Some scribbled, some dictated, while others placed themselves in front of large cameras that moved like aliens across the lawns and sidewalks. It was each one to their own, whatever made them feel important.

But one man, not far away, closeted in a hotel room, could not care what the newspaper and television people did. He was immersed; saturated, even, in something far better. He worked at his computers, flicking endlessly between screens, referring left and right to leather-bound volumes that never got read normally.

Except by him.

For what had started as just a whim, the vaguest of ideas, had turned into something so important to him.

A chance to make a difference. A difference to Dakota

and, through Dakota, to Ben and Ruby and Frank.

Everyone he cared about.

***

Fast-forward to Thursday morning, early. The British contingent arrived fresh from the Embassy where they were staying, fuelled in the normal manner by bacon, eggs, tomatoes, mushrooms and buckets of hot tea. Dick and the President had eaten porridge and *pains au chocolat* with all the coffee they could drink, over a hastily convened strategy meeting.

Dick observed the British team as they filed in, shook hands, took seats. The PM and Foreign Secretary were clearly heavy-hitters, for whom he had great respect. Bel, he knew less well, had on several occasions got the impression of a harassed but intelligent aide; someone who in the business world he would promote to divisional leadership but not main board. The ambassador was jostling for position, over-courteous to his bosses, obsequious as ever; the least said, the better. He was not someone to worry about. Georgie caught his eye: neat, clearly not indigenous British, obviously intelligent but inexperienced. He decided that, if she worked for him, he would promote her early and often. Perhaps that is what Max had done.

He looked at his own team: smaller than the relatively small British team. That was because of the election. Normally, they would outnumber any visiting team by two to one with a knot of fresh-faced aides, ready to jump at any instruction, copious note-taking on brand new legal pads. But today it was strictly the essentials. The President, himself and the Attorney General each had an aide they could trust with their political lives, plus two taking notes, heads down and pens out. And then there was Frank Williams, of course; here alone, no aides, very smart business suit, slender briefcase from which he pulled just three pages. He liked Frank, everybody did. But he would not have had him in the conference. He was on the fringe of politics, a sideline to the administration. But Jane had insisted. Dick was conflicted, even he could see that. Frank was Jane's saviour in electoral terms. Dick dearly wanted to be her saviour, but was so glad she had one, even if it could not be him.

He considered the wider scene as the British settled, stirring their white coffee cups and placing their silver spoons on matching white saucers, pulling out A4 pads and buff folders which were actually surprisingly slim given the importance of the subject matter. He looked at the folders of his aides. They bulged as if they contained muscles, flexing and rippling, anxious to get to work. Surely that was the way to start? What negotiating strength could be brought to the table with folders less than a quarter-inch thick?

Outside, he had seen the ever present babble of journalists on his way in, could hear them if he opened the window, but didn't. The journalists had split into two camps, Reading had told him, with his neat analytical approach. There were the 'die-hards' who had been there all night, a few cheats amongst them getting their interns to sit out the long darkness shift, but most committed to the cause. Then the other party had drifted away after midnight, but now appeared refreshed and invigorated, ready for the day, although a handful had drunk the night away and were the sorriest of the entire collection, lacking the slightest principle behind their red eyes and messy clothes. The 'die-hards' had survived on coffee, hotdogs and hamburgers from a mobile café that made a killing every time a newsworthy item broke. The 'drift off' party brought back neat white polystyrene containers with lukewarm scrambled eggs and soggy toast weighed down with butter.

The other cast member was Albert Essington. But neither the British contingent nor the Americans knew of his existence, had ever heard his name. He had done virtually another all-nighter, crashing for an hour or so around three in the morning, waking again to order fresh coffee. He was on a roll, more than most could boast of that second Thursday in October.

The day the weather turned and Fall moved in to

establish its cooling tendrils across the land.

But typical of the change of season, it started by pretending no change at all. The weather forecast spoke of stillness, heat and humidity, like every day had been since late May.

What actually happened as the British contingent unloaded from their borrowed black vehicles and strode to the entrance, flanked by a guard of black suits and shaven heads, was a rising wind that lifted Georgia's skirt and made her wish she had worn trousers like her boss.

The wind continued to rise as they gathered for the summit, the words of the journalists whipped away from them before they reached the microphones so that viewers relied on the images to determine what was happening, while listeners on the radio were lost.

"We both have problems." The Prime Minister stated the obvious, causing Dick to bristle. But he remained silent, aware of the greater cause, determined to remove this problem from the election campaign. "You have a problem with the, shall we say, historical position on the question of Independence, while we have a unique concern we would like to put to rest." In Dick's opinion it was a typical British statement. It said everything but nothing, made an argument but allowed for compromise.

It provoked a side discussion on whether the Americans had a problem and, if agreed to be a problem, it had any significance today. But this was led by the subordinates, determined to make a mark. It was silenced by the President.

"Ladies and gentlemen, I would like to hear the Prime Minister's concern. Pray hush while we attend to his point."

As the President brought quiet to the room, one young American's voice was still heard; part of the heated discussion now silenced but her final words rang out to the quietened room.

"Even if it was an historical problem, it has no relevance today. All we have to do is declare independence again and you won't be able to stop us." There were shades of Kirsten's defiance in her voice, remembered well. This, Max thought, is what it might come down to. A new Declaration of Independence would be made and, if Britain wanted to contest it we could, but good luck to us against the might of America.

But it was the perfect opening for the PM.

"Young lady, you're forgetting one thing."

"What is that?" Dick took over from the civil servant.

"The United Nations."

"What about them?"

"Permanent seats, my friend, permanent seats."

"Explain." The President leaned across the table, seeming to pin herself onto the PM.

"Influence, Jane. If you make a new claim of independence we will not stand in your way, far from it." The multiplier to military strength was tenfold, possibly more in terms of industry. "But to make a claim for independence, you are de facto agreeing that you are not currently a country. If you are not a country, you can't be a member of the UN. The only way to be a member of the UN is to apply; meanwhile, some other country will snap up your permanent seat. There's quite a waiting list, I hear, and we know all about these things, of course."

Suddenly, the President was bored of the games, bored of the careful manoeuvring, bored of diplomacy.

"Peter, you didn't come over here to tell me endless problems, nor to revel in our issues. Why don't we cut the crap and go straight to the point?"

"Where's the fun in that?"

"This is not fun, Pete, this is real tedious and, right now, I'm dog-tired of tedium."

It worked, a slightly chastened Prime Minister rolled out the deal that Georgie had told Max and Max had relayed to him.

"It's simple, Jane. You would like this independence problem to go away. We are in a position to either pursue it or not. Nobody else can because either America is American or it remains a British colony. We only want one thing in return and that is merely a reflection of the status quo."

"Which is?" Dick Turnby could not help but ask.

"The little issue about our permanent seat at the United Nations."

The deal was done within minutes; in fact, there was little more to discuss when the way was set by the two leaders. Max would put together a draft statement expressing complete British backing for an independent United States of America, independent since the Treaty of Paris in 1783. In return, the USA would support the United Kingdom wholeheartedly and effectively in the matter of the permanent seat.

"One other thing." Max Heaton now spoke up. "There should be no recriminations against anybody. I don't want to find Sir John Fitzroy suddenly arrested, nor anyone else, for that matter. Let's agree to leave everyone alone, regardless of whether they are British or American citizens."

Dick was less than keen to accept this element of the resolution. He had lashed out at his punch-bag that morning, pretending it was Sir John Fitzroy, wheelchair or no wheelchair. He could understand the amnesty for the Williams family; they were important donors and carried much influence. But on reflection that left only Sir John Fitzroy and Ben Franklin, and Franklin was a nobody. In fact, if anything, the White House security guard had impressed the administration with his honesty and patriotism. He could understand Ben's dilemma very well, likening it to his torn loyalties to a wife who was always in California and the President he loved beyond anything. That left Fitzroy as the obvious target, but now ruled out as a candidate by Max's insistence.

"Agreed, but reluctantly." He sighed. "I don't know why you guys can't understand that sometimes someone needs to pay the price." He meant that Sir John Fitzroy Bt., third cousin to the King through his stepmother, principal architect of this preposterous situation, should be the one to pay the price.

"An eye for an eye doesn't get rolled out too often on our patch," Max replied. "At the end of the day, we are all just struggling to get along. Saints sin and scoundrels do good turns."

But there was someone who would pay the price for his ineptitude, Dick considered, however small his role was. That morning he had signed the order that, milled through the multiple layers of human resources, would result in the dismissal of Reading from his post. But even this had a slight sting he found unsatisfactory. Reading was not being turned out on the street, but offered a different position. He was being loaned to the Veterans' Administration for three years, after which he would be offered early retirement on reasonably generous terms; terms he would be a fool to reject.

"Saints sin and scoundrels do good turns," he muttered to himself.

"What was that, Dick?"

"Nothing, Jane, just a reflection."

And at that precise moment, Albert Essington, bent back and tired eyes, was a scoundrel heavily engaged in a good turn.

Prison Reform

The balance of October was a blur. Days merged together, creating grounds for argument as to which event happened first; much contention for future political biographies. But not one person was thinking biography; events were too fast and too immediate.

Opinion polls were moving. Jane, Dick and Frank had pulled off a coup, it would seem. Suddenly, just as the skies darkened, nights growing in length and strength, dampness settling in like rheumatism, hopes soared, like spring come again, out of season, out of time.

Ben received a letter from Mr Reading. His position was terminated for non-attendance. It was understandable. He had not been at work for over a month and was two months' behind on his car payment, for a car that he had not seen since he had been snatched by those working for Dick Turnby. The letter included no final cheque. But the next day he received one from Brad Meadows, newly appointed to replace Mr Reading. It contained a cheque, explaining that the period of non-attendance had been reassessed as sick leave, his statutory right, plus a severance payment of two weeks for each year worked. It was sufficient to pay off the remaining car loan and pay rent to Mrs Jameson for October, November and December, plus his mother's rent for the same period. He was OK for a short while.

It also contained the good news, written in Brad's handwriting at the foot of the letter, that Patrick had been made up to Supervisor.

"You should go to university," Mr Urquart had said. "I'm sure Mr Williams would consider funding you. I could raise it with him, if you like?" But Ben swore Mr Urquart to silence. He would not take charity, even although he dispensed it freely with what little he had.

Ben and Albert and Ruby watched the election progress with interest. Ruby put up a chart on the wall in her apartment, tracking the opinion polls. Beneath the chart, she worked a computer programme that predicted the likely outcome.

"There's no doubt that Frank has got it right," Ruby said most days. "The idea of prison reform has hit a chord with the public."

"It's such a neat connection between the constitutional pursuit of happiness, the need for budgetary savings to spend on other things and matching the idea of entrepreneurialism with rehabilitation. It is a major game-changer in American politics." Albert was sitting on the sofa next to Ruby, a rare moment off for the workaholic.

But it was not their main interest. Not even their secondary interest. Topmost priority was Dakota's appeal and here progress had been dramatic.

"We abandoned the appeal against conviction," Albert said one day, again sitting next to Ruby on the sofa; this time Ben noticed her hand lightly on Albert's leg, tracing patterns, as if dancing with the possibilities.

"Why the hell...?" Ben wanted to know.

"Because she agreed to admit her guilt. Ben, let's not go there again, please accept that everybody is working in Dakota's interest."

"Now, maybe." That was unkind of Ben and he knew it as the words came out. Albert ignored it but Ruby stiffened a little, her fingers now drumming on Albert's leg.

"Yes, but it has given us a rock-strong case on the sentence," Albert continued. "And in that regard, we have some great news we would like you to pass on to Dakota when we visit on Saturday."

***

Frank had a heavy document still to read before he could get to bed. It had been a long day in a long week. And the long week had been part of a hectic month. But progress was evident on all three fronts: politics, business and personal.

He paused a minute, poured two Scotches, and invited his companion to sit. It was 1.45am; both had to be up early.

"Let's review where we are politically," he said, sipping the twelve-year Malt. "We are two weeks away and the polls range from negative-five to plus-four. We've decreased the gap steadily."

"Thanks to you. I have a lot to be thankful for," the President replied, leaning forward and chinking her glass against his. At times like this the twenty-year gap seemed nothing at all. He saw an attractive lady, shoes off, legs tucked under her on the armchair, hair loose, golden and springy. She could be a student working through an all-night revision session. "And I don't think the full impact of the settlement with Great Britain has yet worked its way into the opinion polls. Did you see the Bert Wise show last night?"

"No, I was finalising my plans for Pillars of the Community."

So she flicked open her phone and found it online. They watched the best bits, the venerable political journalist predicting a landslide for the President. "Only half a handful of times in the history of our great country has a president risen to the occasion as this one has done."

"It sounds like a political speech," Jane joked. Frank smiled, but said nothing. He had primed Bert Wise yesterday afternoon, given him 'script ideas' rather than daring to present a speech. It had worked perfectly.

"By the way, how is the deal going? I shouldn't really be asking, of course, but you know I won't do anything to influence it one way or another," the President said.

"We got the corporation for $27.9billion, less than we expected. Their defences fell away after they rejected the first bid – that's to be expected – and we held firm. We ended up paying a 3% premium on the first offer. With acquisition costs and reorganisation expenses we are looking at an all-in price of around $31billion."

"That's a lot of money, Frank."

"It was a steal. I shouldn't talk any more about it but you will see what I mean shortly enough. Now, finish off your Scotch, it's high time I left and we both got some sleep!"

"Good night, Frank, and thanks."

"Oh, there is one thing, Jane. Could you take a look at this file and pass it on to the appropriate authority?" Frank passed over a slim folder. "I don't want to influence your recommendation but suffice it to say that if you saw fit to grant this it would be a huge personal satisfaction to me, no business gain, purely personal."

***

Frank was right about the opinion polls. Come Saturday 28th October all the papers and internet sites were showing a lead for the President. Frank reviewed the papers in the helicopter going to Zanesville, together with Ben, Ruby, Albert and Mrs Jameson. There was one article of particular note; Ruby read it over his shoulder.

"Wow, a landslide predicted for the President. That is awesome news."

"Let's not celebrate just yet, Ruby. There are ten days still to go. Anything could happen."

"But it is such a turnaround."

"And you have all helped make it happen," Frank said, looking at all his guests, then explaining, "The mainstay of our electoral comeback has been prison and sentencing reform. You've all helped in that regard."

"And the way the President sorted out that disaster with Great Britain," Albert said. "That was a remarkable bit of negotiating."

"She was remarkable," Frank replied. "I'll tell you about it someday." Frank could not avoid reminding his friends that he had been present for the negotiations.

To Ben, it was a great unloading, like being caked in mud and grime and then swimming naked in the sea, or learning that your child's leukaemia scare was just that – a scare and nothing more. He felt like summer break, school out, just days messing about in the lake as he had done in those long, hot summers in Still City.

Except there was a shadow over his world and that shadow was Dakota. If only the appeal against her sentence was successful, maybe she could be out in five or ten years. Then summer would stretch forever.

"Penny for your thoughts." Ben was snatched back to the present by Frank's words, only to realise that he was not offering Ben a penny, but Albert.

"I was just thinking," he said, "about what Ben showed me of Dakota's research. Something does not add up."

"What do you mean?" Ben tried to stand up, but the harness held him tightly.

"Oh, don't get the wrong meaning from my words. I was thinking about the constitutional and legal aspects."

He would be drawn no more, stating that he had some facts to check first with Dakota. The truth was he knew no more, at least not clearly. Something was bothering him at the back of his mind. There was an inconsistency somewhere, but he could not place it.

"But there are more important things to concern ourselves with now. We have to update Dakota on the progress of the appeal," he continued.

It was then, as Mrs Jameson leaned forward and took Albert's left hand in both of hers that Frank, logically, looked for his right hand. It was locked with Ruby's left as they sat side-by-side in the bench seat of the helicopter, now making ready to land at Zanesville airport.

Like last time, Frank did not go with them to see Dakota. Instead, he had meetings with the prison management. He had already been to three of the prisons they had acquired the contracts for and made substantial changes at all of them. But this one was going to be different. It was going to take every inch of leadership he could muster.

He admitted it to himself. He was nervous, incredibly nervous.

***

Dakota greeted her four visitors as she usually did, now that the restrictions on physical contact were relaxed. Her mother got a long hug and several kisses, Albert and Ruby polite but

408

warm handshakes. For Ben, however, time seemed to slow down as she raised her arms and looped them over his neck, bringing him into a long embrace.

"Ben, my Ben," was all she said.

Ruby and Albert waited while the greetings went ahead, waited while they caught up with news, waited while Dakota soaked up Ben and Ben soaked up Dakota, Mrs Jameson watching and approving quietly.

But Ruby and Albert had something to say, something they badly wanted to bring up. It was Mrs Jameson who made it possible.

"I think these two have something they're itching to tell," she said, loudly to be above the good-humoured chatter that filled the room. Suddenly, all was quiet, as if she had announced the start of the main performance.

Ruby spoke first. "Dakota, we want to ask you a favour."

"Sure thing." But what could she do for them, stuck inside the prison?

"We want you to be our bridesmaid."

"What?"

"At our wedding. Albert asked me to marry him."

"And you said yes?" Ben spoke up, still miles behind the plot. "To Albert?"

"Yes," she smiled in reply, her eyes dancing, hands clasped together again, this time on top of the table in full view, "I admit I hated him at first but I have come to love him deeply."

"Congratulations, my dear, and you too." Mrs Jameson looked at the man who had effectively imprisoned her daughter, saw evil, but faded; saw honesty too, shining like a child that cannot lie. It was new honesty, like a new person. "Well, I never." She spoke to herself, then smiled. Despite her daughter's imprisonment this felt right, felt whole. She could condone this, somehow, not that they needed her blessing.

"You haven't answered our question, Dakota," Ruby said.

"I can't, unless you want to be married in here." She glanced around the room, a look of amusement on her face;

smiles resulted.

"Ben, give her an update," Ruby said. "Then we'll update the update."

Ben gave a matter-of-fact account of recent happenings, relayed from his discussion with Ruby and Albert during the week.

"The appeal is underway, set for November 8th. It is an appeal against the overly harsh sentence, not the guilty verdict. You had agreed to that last time when Frank and Albert came," Ben finished up.

"That's right. No bones about that decision. I'm happy with that now."

"OK," Ruby was itching to take over, "now for the latest. First, we have news on the appeal hearing. The judge hearing the case is going to be Judge Julie Jefferies." She paused; no response, no one knew who she was. "Dakota, she was our first selection. She is known for her views on excessive sentencing."

"We couldn't have asked for a better judge," Albert interjected. "A few months back she quashed an eighteen-year sentence and replaced it with a four-year one. The guy walked free the next day."

"Wow." Dakota looked suddenly embarrassed.

"Also," Albert spoke up again, "Judge Jefferies made a point of demanding a pre-appeal hearing on bail conditions."

It took a few moments for this to sink in. Dakota tried to grapple with the biggest change in almost a decade, but not definite, just possible. She took Ben's hand, then took her mother's also, for reinforcement, to try and understand. A Hispanic toddler threw a plastic ball across the room. It landed on their table, knocking over the paper water cup. The cup swirled around in an arc on its bottom rim, spilling its contents in two directions, two puddles on the table-top, one going east, the other propelled west. The west contained more water and had the smallest distance to travel. It spilled over the table edge and onto Mrs Jameson's lap. She jumped back, knocking against the low wooden cubicle wall Val had had constructed. The thin ply-board shattered, sending shards across the gangway behind them, while Mrs Jameson landed on the floor and lay there, facing up at the strip lights.

"Here, let me help you." Ben was first to her side. "Are you hurt?" She was not, in fact was laughing as she struggled to get up, leaning heavily on Ben's arm.

"What does all this mean?" Dakota asked, after checking her mother was OK.

"It means there is a chance, just a chance, nothing definite, that you will be allowed out on Wednesday week."

"For how long?" It was impossible to take this in. For Ben also. He had known of the sentencing appeal but not the bail application.

"I can't say," Albert replied. "It will be at least the duration of the sentencing hearing but, if that goes well, it could just be forever.

"But I need a job, somewhere to stay, all sorts of things."

"That's in hand, Dakota. Frank Williams will have a job for you and it is a live-in position. Mrs Jameson, I hope you will be able to stay with Mr Williams, at least until we know Dakota's future."

"It is the same position I started in," Ruby added. "Frank is extending his programme to include released prisoners as well as cancer survivors."

"Free? Me? Next week?"

"Yes, quite possibly. Now, we will leave you to talk with your mother and Ben. Albert will be back on Monday morning to talk about the hearing." They shook hands again, Dakota's smile steadily stretching across a face, magic back in her eyes. For Ben it was like a horror movie played backwards: unhappy start flipping to become happy ending. Had someone put the tape in backwards?

Full Week

The first full week of November was when everything seemed to come together.

It started, innocently enough, with a speech on Sunday 5th, in which the President announced the United States of America's full backing for the United Kingdom retaining its permanent seat at the United Nations. Her tenor and content were eloquent, her delivery masterful. She spoke warmly, generously, with wit and perspective. It was her side of the deal that Max Heaton had bargained for.

And it worked. Not just for the United Kingdom, but for the President.

Frank Williams had decided to spend election night at Hunt Ridge, but did not arrive until long after dark, the helicopter lights showing up the crisp leaves that lay on the lawn, picking out colours like nature making a patchwork quilt. He found his guests in the Orangery with a large television screen masking the two lemon trees in the corner, the chairs arranged in a semi-circle around.

"Where's Albert?" he asked, after the greetings.

"He's gone to bed early. Big day tomorrow," Ruby answered.

"So nice to see you here, Mrs Jameson. I hope everything is comfortable."

"Yes, real comfortable. Thank you for inviting me to your gracious home. Now, I too need to get to bed. It is a big day for me tomorrow, too." Ben followed soon after, desperate for sleep to tick off some of the remaining minutes until Dakota might be freed, unable to stand the waiting any longer.

That left Ruby and Frank to watch the results coming in. They drank good Scotch and ate the chocolates Mrs Jameson had brought with her.

"Will you give us your blessing, Frank?" Ruby asked, as Kentucky and Indiana raced to be the first to declare results.

"Are you sure about Albert?"

"Yes." No more words needing saying, Frank knew his protégé well.

"Then I bless it wholeheartedly."

They missed the first two states as they hugged, then Frank led Ruby in a little dance around the Orangery. "I'm so happy for you." As they made it back to the screen they saw two wins notched up for the President.

"Where will you live?" Frank asked as they waited for Virginia to declare.

"We're going to buy a house in Charlottesville. Albert hopes, after jail, to get a job assisting those on low incomes with legal advice."

"There won't be any jail," Frank responded as Virginia declared for the President.

"What do you mean?"

"I made a request to the President, for immunity. She reviewed the case personally, sought the advice of the Attorney General, and agreed to it. I just heard this afternoon. There will be no prosecution of Albert Essington II."

"My God!" Ruby jumped up. "Thank you, Frank, my darling." She jumped on him, splashing kisses all over him. "Let me go tell Albert."

"No, I would prefer you to wait until after Dakota's hearing. Can you do that for me?"

She agreed; what else could she do?

"You're going to have to be careful Frank Williams III; if Albert proves unsuitable I might just make eyes for you!"

"Too late." Frank replied. "I have my sights set on someone else, but to me you would be a damn good second choice."

And then they sat, Ruby snuggling up to the man she loved second to Albert, pinching the last chocolate with a deft finger movement, laughing, crying, and laughing again. They were there when Florida declared and when Ohio did so shortly afterwards. But they did not wait up for the West Coast.

"Barring a miracle, it is all over," Frank said as they kissed goodnight.

***

Analysis of the numbers filled pages and hours over the next few weeks and into the future. Suffice it to dwell on just a few facts. It was the biggest swing from pre-election opinion polls since polls started. It ranked as the third-largest margin of victory ever in a presidential race, pushing Franklin Roosevelt into fourth place. It was the largest comeback in living memory.

It was a landslide.

***

The Bell 505 Jet Ranger X, red-and-white striped like a soccer shirt, had blades whirring as Albert put on his jacket, straightened his tie and grabbed his coat. It was 5.15am. The hearing was set for 2pm, but he did not want to be rushed. It was a three-and-a-half-hour flight, four hours door to door to the Potter Stewart Courthouse in Cincinnati. He knew he was ridiculously early but he still wanted to run through things one final time with Dakota.

No breakfast, just half a cup of coffee, nervous. The others would come on later, but he had to be there early. It seemed right.

He checked his briefcase and made for the chopper, saw the pilot in place, presumably doing final checks. He clambered in and closed the door.

"I thought you were never coming," Ruby said.

"What are you doing here?"

"Do you really think I would let you go alone, my darling?" She held out her long, graceful arms, shook her deepest black hair, and hugged him. The pilot, glancing back to ensure all aboard, thought, *Some guys have all the luck.*

She had brought a small hamper with her.

"One of the kitchen assistants made it up this morning," she said. "Plenty of protein to give you a good start." There were sausages, bacon and egg in a bun, plus a yoghurt drink and a flask of coffee. Albert felt his nerves settled as he munched, but considered that the most wonderful thing was Ruby Smith, her coming with him.

"You must have had no sleep at all?" Albert said.

"An hour and a half," she replied, tossing her thick hair in the way he loved, looking like she had slept for ten.

For Dakota, the journey was a little different. The distance was much less, but the mode of travel much slower. At half past two the previous day, election day but she could not vote, the manacles had been slapped on. She was wearing a freshly-laundered orange prison dress, faded like they all were now, but preferring the dress to the overalls ever since she had first worn one with her broken bones. White socks and orange sandals, plus the regulation manacles on hands and feet, necessitating a shuffling walk from prison admin to prison bus and from prison bus to destination.

She at least had Val as her escort. Val was strictly too senior for escort duties, another promotion under her belt, but insisted on accompanying her friend.

"So what's it like to be an assistant warden?" Dakota asked, as soon as the bus left the Zanesville outer fence. "You must be the youngest ever!"

"Yeah, but it doesn't come with all the responsibilities. I am assistant warden responsible for inmate welfare and staff-inmate relations. I don't have staff reporting to me. It's like a dotted line thing." She was clearly shy about her elevation. "Besides," she added, with a grin, "it helps when you're dating the CEO!"

They laughed, then grew more serious as fences faded in the rear-view mirrors and daylight moved down a notch or two.

"You deserve it, every bit of it, Val. Or should I say 'Ma'am'?"

"I hate that," Val replied. "Every time someone says that I think they must be talking to someone else." They laughed again. "Keep it for when we have company," she added, closing the screen between them and the driver.

"What's happening with Mrs Kinderly?" Dakota asked. "Nobody has seen her for days."

"She's been moved; promoted, actually. She's gone back to Head Office in Chicago. She's got responsibility for every prison budget we have. It's right up her street, that type of work."

"Frank again?"

"Yep, I told him about Smith and the blackmail. He took pity on her but also got others involved. He wouldn't put her into a job she was unsuitable for so she went for some interviews with his staff and they determined this was the best route for her. Mr Chambers is taking over temporarily until we hire a new warden." Dakota could not help but notice the use of the first person plural. Val was involved now, more deeply involved each day. She doubted that her friend had sent any job applications recently, doubted she ever would again.

"And Smith?"

"Charged with blackmail and abuse of federal office. I heard she has told prosecutors about all her accomplices to try and reduce her sentence. Frank thinks she will get about eight years but will be in isolation because of her background."

"That's less time than I've spent behind bars," Dakota said.

"But hopefully you will be free long before her, hopefully real soon." That thought sobered the two friends. They sat in silence a while, the heavy bus lumbering at fifty miles an hour, slowing for each curve in the road, no hurry ever in the prison world.

"That's Columbus," Val said eventually, as a modern city rose before them. "You know, I've lived all my life in Zanesville but never been to Columbus."

"Same with me up to the age of eighteen; apart from being born in Dakota, I never left the DC area."

"What happened then?" Val was not thinking at all, rather thinking of other things, of Frank and of tomorrow for her friend, of what she would do in her job with her new role.

"Well, the government sent me on a tour of the United States of America, all expenses paid," Dakota replied, causing laughter, when it registered, that repeated itself half-way to Cincinnati.

They had to split when they got to Cincinnati. Val was bound for a cheap motel, but first Dakota had to be delivered into the custody of the city police. She spent election night in a common cell with people coming and going all night, up to twenty-six girls at the maximum around 2am. Many were prostitutes, some drunks and druggies, two car thieves, a burglar and three fighters, one taken quickly to hospital with a livid knife wound to her thigh. Most were not strangers to police cells but few had been inside for any serious length of time.

"If you add it all up," one older prostitute with a torn red top and matching torn skirt, somehow rigged as a fashion statement, said, "it comes to a lot of time but nothing like you've done, babe." She evidently held Dakota in some awe. "What's it like? I mean doing serious time?"

"Keep away," Dakota replied, swirling the muck they served for the evening meal, then raising her voice. "Seriously, you guys, whatever you do, keep on the outside. Nothing is worth the humiliation. It doesn't make you a hero or hard, it just sucks, day in and day out. I was a real idiot to end up in there. Just stay away."

A little later, she was touched on the arm by a young girl, maybe just turned eighteen; the age Dakota had been when she went in.

"Hi," she said, then, "My sister is in Zanesville."

"What's her name?"

"Julie Wright."

"I know her," Dakota replied. "She's got a kid. I've seen him and the father." Memories of Smith denying a visit came back to her, breaking up the family for her own sick enjoyment. Wright had got twenty-to-life for drug possession, had served maybe eighteen months now. Was the younger sister going in the same direction?

"That's right. They live here in Cincinnati. They have a trailer and I stay there sometimes when…"

"I know, you don't need to say it. Your father."

"Yes." She looked about fourteen years old, could almost be put in pigtails.

"What's your name?"

"Sammy."

"Sammy, that's a nice name. Listen, do something for me, will you? Stay away from trouble. I'm twenty-nine now and I've spent almost ten years as a convicted criminal. Those are years I'll never get back."

"Sure, Dakota. I'll do that." But would she?

It was a long night, with little sleep; there was no spare mattress, although Sammy offered her one, but Dakota declined.

It was like being inside in one respect. As dawn settled in, the place fell still, exhaustion taking over. She leant against the cell wall and closed her eyes. Then she heard Val's voice.

"I've come for Federal Inmate Jameson. Here are the papers. No, I went straight to bed last night, didn't see the joys of Cincinnati. Maybe next time."

The police officer redid the manacles in the foyer right outside the common cell, handing the key to Val. It gave Dakota a chance to seek Sammy through the bars.

"Sammy, tell your sister to get hold of Albert Essington. He will try and get her sentence reduced." Sammy looked blank so Dakota tried again. "This is Assistant Warden Bennet, tell Julie to go to her, she'll help. Remember the name Bennet."

"Sure I will, thanks Dakota. I really like you."

"That girl is high as a space ship," Val said as they walked through the police office and down to the street to the waiting bus. "Who were you talking about?"

"Julie Wright. I don't know her number."

"With the sweet kid? I'll go see her. So that is her little sister? She's heading the same way if you ask me."

"God forbid."

"Calm down, Al." It was the first time Ruby had shortened his name. He liked it. He loved it.

"I'm nervous as hell," he whispered back, stroking the back of her hand with his.

"You'll be fine," she said, flipping his hand over and clasping it. "You've rehearsed it about a hundred times."

"It's just that it's..." He hesitated.

"I understand, Al, it's real important to you. We're all cheering for you." She indicated the small crowd behind the attorney's bench: Ben, Mrs Jameson, Frank, Mr Urquart, and two more from Hunt Ridge. A full helicopter load.

Dakota was ready in the dock, her orange dress creased from an overnight stay, her manacles hidden from view below the wooden structure that surrounded the dock. Behind her sat Val, resplendent in her best uniform, flanked by a pair of court security guards. Val's eyes flicked between her charge, Dakota, and her boyfriend, Frank. But she was strong, disciplined, she kept her attention mostly on Dakota. This was her time.

The door shut at the back of the courtroom with a satisfying thud, stating that this was a serious business, with solid matters to discuss. Albert risked a look around. The court was full to bursting. As well as the usual interested observers, season ticket holders, there was a large clutch of journalists, not an inch to spare.

But then the door opened again. Everyone turned to see who had the audacity to turn up late and expect a place.

There was only one person Ben could think of who fitted that category. But he was in a hospital room in DC, paralysed from the waist down.

"Make way, make way." The clear, upper class British accent cut into the room. "Push me over there." He pointed to the aisle next to Ruby, herself next to Albert. "Then make yourself scarce, no room at the inn, dear fellow. I'll holler when I need you again." The attendant pushed Sir John exactly where he was instructed to and left immediately, closing the door behind him.

"I'm sorry, sir, but you can't sit there."

"Well I most certainly can't sit anywhere else, can I, man?"

"He's with us," Albert said. "We need extra space for our representation. If you haven't got room for him you're going to have to deny someone else."

"Essington? I never thought to see you here. I must say it is jolly decent of you to offer me the internship, especially at such short notice. Luckily I was just passing when the offer came my way. Now, what do I do to help out? Shall I run errands? This go-cart can move pretty damn fast. It's all in the technique. Shall I show you?"

"That won't be necessary, sir." The court official did not want this British man causing chaos in his courtroom. "Under the circumstances, given your recent employment offer, I think we can allow you to stay right here. Have a good day, sir."

***

The bail hearing lasted seven minutes and fourteen seconds. Ben timed it on his watch. Judge Jefferies dominated throughout that time.

The prosecution had two minutes to make their case. It consisted largely of 'Dakota Jameson is a convicted criminal serving a long sentence. She is highly likely to run if allowed out as the alternative is another thirty years of incarceration'.

The defence also got two minutes. Albert sat back down after eighty-eight seconds. Ruby memorised his speech.

"Your Honour, we are not here to decide whether or not Dakota is a criminal. A court has already decided that she is. We are here to consider that, at the tender age of eighteen, Dakota was taken from high school and charged, imprisoned for forty-two years, for a simple mistake. It was a grossly disproportionate sentence by a judge whose own child had suffered as a drug addict. The prison service took responsibility of her and abused that responsibility in an horrific manner. One of the senior guards, charged with watching over her, with rehabilitating her, raped her and broke no less than six bones. The facial bruising was awful. At long last, we have a chance to redress this sentence, this abuse, this horrible punishment. I appeal to Your Honour's sense of what is right, not necessarily what is strictly legal. Precedence, in both this court and others, suggests she has served enough time. She is no danger to the public, has never been so. She is no flight risk. She has a job and a place to live lined up. Her mother is alive and will vouch for her. She has friends who will stand by her. I ask that she be granted immediate bail."

Albert sat down and Judge Jefferies asked about the job, the place to live. She asked if anyone was prepared to stand surety.

"Yes, Your Honour. Mr Frank Williams will stand surety," Albert responded. Ben looked at Frank, sitting next to him, focusing on Val, eyes flicking between her and Dakota.

The judge then asked for a verbal summary of Dakota's prison record. Val stood up.

"Your honour, Dakota Jameson has been an exemplary inmate. She has worked hard at whatever tasks were given to her, caused no trouble, and has been a help to other inmates. She has also earned a degree in history and has, a few weeks ago, submitted a thesis for her Masters." She sat back down, blushing heavily.

Now it was time for the decision.

"This court is prepared to offer bail under the following conditions. Surety is set at $5m. She will reside at the residence offered to her and, as it is also her place of work, she will not leave except for a medical or other emergency or for the purposes of attending federal court proceedings regarding her case. She will be subject to police checks and will wear a tag at all times. Is surety at this level offered?" She looked around the courtroom, knowing full well who Frank Williams was and where he was in the room, also that

$5m would be small change.

"Yes, your honour. I will transfer this amount immediately on leaving the courtroom," Frank said, hastily standing up.

"Dakota Jameson, you will be released on bail from Zanesville Federal Penitentiary at noon on Friday November 10th. You will travel directly to Hunt Ridge, 5884 Old Hollow Road, Charlottesville, Virginia, and remain there until you are summoned back to this court. Do you understand?"

"Yes, Your Honour. Thank you."

"Out in time for the weekend," shouted Sir John.

"Quiet, please," the usher said.

"Now," continued the judge, "as to timing for the sentence hearing. I do not have any availability until early February. Would the first full week of that month suit you both?" This was a question for the attorneys, both of whom confirmed. "Good, then this case is adjourned until then. Now, as to the rules I like to follow in my court, let me just remind you…"

***

"I've got to see Dakota." Albert rushed past the others coming to congratulate him. He need not have worried, for Val was in charge of Dakota again and she would not deny her a chance to talk with her attorney.

"Dakota, I must ask you, your thesis, did…"

"My thesis?" Why was that important?

"Yes, Ben talked to me about it. Something has just come to me. Did you determine during your research that the deed never made it to the land Sidney Hollingsworth exchanged for Sutherland's Charlottesville estate?"

"That's correct, Richard Sutherland placed the manumission document for Rupert in the trunk. The land deed never left Hunt Ridge. But why is this important? And why now?"

"It just came to me, while the judge was talking. It has been niggling away at me the last few weeks, ever since Ben told me."

"But why now, Albert?" Frank asked, coming up behind the lawyer.

"Don't you see?" Albert was almost shouting. Several journalists, who had been hurrying to write up their stories, now stopped, turned, sensing something big in the air. "I read the deed a hundred times. It got me every time. I couldn't see the simple truth."

"Out with it, old chap." Sir John, in his wheelchair, had run over two feet and some folders in his rush to get to the front. Had he missed something? He, also, had been over that deed multiple times. Good Lord, had not the experts pored over it from dawn to dusk?

"Well, if the deed never left Hunt Ridge, how can it have any effect?" Albert said, as if playing a game of chess verbally.

"What do you mean?" Frank asked, but Sir John suddenly got it and answered for Albert.

"My God, man, you're on to something. The deed only has effect when physically placed on the eighteen acres. We have all assumed it sat happily there for hundreds of years, therefore had legal force. But Dakota has demonstrated that it never got there. It never came of age, as it were."

"So the whole thing was a myth?" Ben asked, reliving his agonies of division and soul-searching. "It never had any legal basis at all?"

"Exactly, young fellow," Sir John replied. "Now, I see another myth I hope very much will become a reality. It's the myth that Cincinnati is home to some half-reasonable beer. Let's see Dakota off and then check it out." Said in a hurry before Frank could say anything; before he could even frame a response, in fact.

Frank went through the motions over the next two hours, arguing with Sir John about who would pay the bill, yielding at the very last minute to give Sir John satisfaction; both in fact were playing a game. Frank's body was there; certainly it paid attention to the others reliving the highlights of the bail hearing, but his mind was on the President and Dick Turnby.

Had Frank jumped to conclusions too early? Had he assumed the validity of the documents too blithely, thus contributing to the mayhem his country, his United States of America, had gone through?

More to the point, had he started a chain of reactions that put his close friend in a wheelchair?

"Everyone thought the same, even that army of bloody specialists I hired." Sir John had wheeled over next to him, did not need to ask Frank his thoughts.

"But it hollows out my contribution to the President getting re-elected," Frank replied, allowing a selfish reflection.

"Too bloody right," Sir John said. "But at the end of the day the best candidate won and that's all that matters. The method is bugger-all. It is the end that counts. You got her elected despite ballsing up a few things."

"Hey Bunny, I'll thank you to remember that you made about a hundred critical mistakes and have cost me a pretty penny in legal fees, all to chase dark shapes and bumps in the night."

"Precisely," Sir John replied with his humour undiminished. "That's what friends are for... buddy!"

***

The bus looked the same, her manacles were the same, her prison dress perhaps even more crumpled by a second night in the police cells in central Cincinnati. For the bus driver, a civilian worker, had quoted the rules and refused to drive that night back to Zanesville.

"It's more than my job's worth," he whined when Val pleaded. "No journey to last beyond 6pm. It's almost 4pm now and we have four hours plus ahead of us."

So Val had no choice but to take her friend back to the police station, see her chains come off and cast into the same cage, then leave to find another cheap motel for the night. She was determined that the bus driver would not enjoy the best Cincinnati could offer, so she went with a quick meal at the local diner, followed by an early night. If the bus driver wanted to sample the nightlife, it would be on his own dime.

Dakota got no more sleep than the night before; less, in fact, because the men's cell in the other corridor was the scene of a riot, or at least much disturbance. Every time Dakota's eyelids dropped down it seemed the yelling increased, as if propping up her eyes with the yelling. She looked around for Sammy Wright but did not see her at any time that night. Maybe that was the one and only time the youngster would see the inside of a cell. Dakota certainly hoped so. She wanted to ask a police officer, but she barely saw one with the trouble next door.

No evening meal, no breakfast; all too busy or exhausted for that, but chains again at 9am, as soon as Dakota came in.

"I'm going to have to leave these on," Val whispered to Dakota as they crossed the police reception office. "The driver has been giving me a hard time about rules already this morning."

"Don't worry, Val. I don't feel chained inside, that's what really counts."

They ate lunch at a coffee house called The Express. The driver took a separate table at first, but then slid in beside Val with a grin.

"No point being lonesome."

"Be our guest," Val said. The driver took it literally and made no attempt to pay his bill.

They arrived back at 2.45 that evening, gone over forty-eight hours for a seven minute and fourteen seconds hearing. Val removed the chains.

"Go say goodbye to your friends, Jameson. You're getting out tomorrow."

"Yes, ma'am. Thank you, ma'am."

She meant it.

Epilogue

Albert's divorce came through on the middle Monday in April 2029. Ruby and he were married that Saturday at Hunt Ridge, Dakota their only bridesmaid. They had no honeymoon because it was right in the middle of Dakota's lingering sentencing hearing. Besides, Albert had a list of other cases requiring urgent attention, including young Julie Wright's. However, on the Sunday everyone helped them move into a rented apartment above a garage in a long tree-lined road in Charlottesville. The owners lived in the house next door but went away to Florida each winter. They liked someone permanently there on the property. It had four rooms, with a rickety external staircase covered in wisteria. It did not take long to move in because they had no furniture and few belongings. Frank's wedding present of $5,000 was spent in the junk shops and used-furniture stores of Charlottesville. They also visited every yard sale that spring and purchased a beautiful mixture of the practical, the beautiful, the useless and the downright ugly.

They were in love, not just with themselves, but with their causes also. Ruby worked part-time for Frank and part-time for the cancer charity. Albert worked for his own legal practice, given permission by Marcus Hibbert to recommence law in his own name. He kept strictly to helping those who could not help themselves and made a very low income as a result.

Frank surprised everyone in May 2029 with the announcement of the sale of Pillars of the Community. However, the details, when understood, showed his true genius. He sold everything except the prison management business for $38 billion; a profit of over $6 billion on six months of ownership. The prisons business earned $14 million in that six-month period: profits promised to be way higher on the radical new approach. Mrs Kinderly renegotiated contracts, under Frank's guidance, to include a fixed fee as the contract progressed and the remainder based on rehabilitation, judged over time by re-offending convictions.

"It means that, provided we get it right and cut down on re-offenders, we will make a lot more money in the long run," Mrs Kinderly explained at a board meeting. "The real mark of success is not cost management, screwing down every penny, but how we keep these people from coming back to us. We really don't want to see them again when they leave!" She had repeated that joke several times: it always got a laugh.

They trebled the education resources, doubled work release. Plus, every inmate had a progress review at monthly intervals. "And the best thing of all," Iris added, looking over her spectacles at her audience around the board table, "is that we have added four major new prison contracts this year already."

Frank spent a lot of time in Zanesville. The Bell 505 Jet Ranger was traded in for a new one, such was its use beetling in a triangle, the three corners being DC, Hunt Ridge and Zanesville. Val got more time off as incidents in the prison fell steadily. In March, the board asked her to roll out her programmes to other prisons in the group. This gave the helicopter more airtime than ever, but also gave Val long weekends with her friends at Hunt Ridge.

Mrs Jameson, her loans repaid from Albert's assets, moved temporarily and then permanently to Hunt Ridge. At first it was just important to be with Dakota, but she fell in love with the estate and rented a ranch house a half-mile behind the stables, looking up to the ridge and down to the river. She started a garden and soon was supplying both vegetables and flowers to the main house, piling them into the back of an ancient pick-up truck three times a week, inevitably then staying for lunch at the mansion.

Sir John was paralysed from the waist down. It did nothing to diminish his personality or his energy, nor the volume of his voice. He still flew regularly to the States from his Cambridgeshire base. He often came to Charlottesville, where he was a major part of a new initiative involving Dakota, at the University of Virginia. Dakota was offered a research grant for a doctorate in history at the university, provided she was not sent back to jail.

There was sad news in late May. Frank brought it to Hunt Ridge. Dick Turnby, fitter than most in their mid-sixties, had suffered a massive heart attack in his basement gym.

"He was dead when the paramedics arrived," Frank told them all, gathered in the Orangery. "The President is distraught. There was always something close about those two." Close, yes. Out of control, no. They had come to the edge, both of them, and turned back because of love and respect.

They joined hands in the Orangery and Frank led them in a prayer.

Then Frank gave them an update on prison and sentencing reform.

"Daniel Roberts seems to have taken it to heart," he announced.

"I wouldn't trust that man an inch," Ruby replied, then looked at her husband, remembering similar comments about him. He squeezed her hand and smiled. He understood.

"What's he been doing?" Albert asked.

"More like what's he not been doing? He's on every committee on the subject, giving speeches more days than not. He even started a penal reform pressure group and the membership has rocketed. They're talking about him as a potential president."

"God forbid!" said several people at once.

For Ben it was a strange interlude. He was with Dakota but she was not free. He had been liberated of the burden of his country's future and very existence, the terrible secrets, the awful responsibility. Yet nothing seemed quite right. He found himself looking at Sir John during his visits, wondering whether he had taken everyone for a ride. There was no doubt that Sir John had received enormous fame from the whole escapade. But life in a wheelchair was a high price for the notoriety; not a price he would choose to pay.

Then he considered Frank. Another friend he sometimes thought he did not know. Yet at other times he could predict his reactions perfectly. In the end he decided not to think too deeply; better to let the wind blow away the worries as he cantered with Dakota.

Ben had proposed to Dakota three times at Hunt Ridge, all three times out riding. Each time the answer was "Yes, my dearest, just as soon as I am free." That was combined with the warmest of embraces.

Dakota, like Ben, had taken to riding, although it was much harder for her to learn. She seemed all fingers and thumbs but she developed a deep love of it, even persuading her mother to try. But that was a disaster and no one thought to suggest it again. However, Mrs Jameson did insist that she be allowed to pay for Ben's education.

"You above all have given me by girl back," she said. "I know others did great things but at the end of the day it comes back to you. You were always there for her. I want to do something for you now." He was enrolled in the University of Virginia to start his undergraduate studies in August, selecting history as his major.

Frank had one last surprise, but not for Dakota, nor for Ben. He called everyone together one hot, sultry July day when Sir John was visiting and staying at Hunt Ridge. They met at the stables. Frank disappeared into a stall and led out a beautiful palomino stallion with a white mane that it shook in the deep sunlight.

"Meet your new horse, Bunny."

"But I can't ride." His eyes were fixed on this wonderful horse.

"Bloody nonsense! You bloody can if you just bloody try." Frank tried to imitate Sir John's British accent. It sounded more Australian but got a long laugh.

Frank had devised a mechanical mounting block that raised Sir John out of the wheelchair and then swung him onto the special saddle with raised sides for support.

"But my legs? They won't work."

But Frank had thought of this too.

"The horse has been specially trained. You don't need to use your legs. Just use your voice and a gentle prod to the neck. I've seen others ride him in this way."

It worked perfectly. Sir John was hoisted up and half an hour later was trotting. Before the day was out, he was cantering.

"What's this beauty called?" Sir John asked as he took his first tentative steps.

"Oh, that was easy." Frank replied. "His name is 'Bloody Independence'."

***

If freedom was the trigger for Ben and Dakota to get married, it was also their frustration, for, despite Albert's hard work, Dakota's final release remained tantalisingly out of reach. There was a shock in June, when the sentence was reduced from forty-two years to sixteen. On the face of it this was good news. However, it left a balance to serve. Even with a decade of exemplary behaviour at the new rates introduced by the President earlier in the year, it left two years to serve. Dakota was returned to Zanesville, issued a new bunk in a new dormitory, only to be released four days later on renewed bail. Albert had found a loophole in the law, in fact had not slept for those four days, scouring every possibility.

It was only in early August 2029 that Dakota received the news they all hoped for. The sentence was further reduced to fourteen years. With time off for behaviour, Ben calculated she was a free woman. She had one return trip to Zanesville, in order to leave correctly. Ben went with her, as did Mrs Jameson. They waited in Val's office until Dakota was led in, her last time in the faded orange dress.

Ben saw, for a second, the girl he had first seen in the visiting room. Dakota was much changed: hair grown out, skin much fresher; more colour, more confidence in her stride. If Mrs Jameson had thought to judge her health in the same way Dakota had judged hers on the visits in the early days at Zanesville, she would have marked her an eighty-five score. Not 100, not in the nineties, because prison took a long, long time to fade, but well on the way.

But Ben saw, not the post-graduate, but the inmate for one last time. He did not see his girlfriend, the academic, about to start a doctorate at the University of Virginia; he saw a fragile being, strangely attractive, compelling, dressed in prison orange, doing what she was told.

But that was only for a moment.

As soon as Dakota tossed her auburn hair and looked first at him, then at her mother, eye to eye, he knew that was the past.

He took her then in his arms, did not need to ask again for she just said one word.

"Yes."

THE END

Also by Chris Oswald:
2024: A History of the Future

SOMETHING HAD TO CHANGE. SOMEONE HAD TO LEAD THAT CHANGE. BUT WAS HE UP TO THE TASK?

George was an intellectual, a journalist, a writer: more theory than practice. Could he lead the country to a new beginning?

Someone had to stand up to the tyranny, the controlling force that had crept up to overtake their lives. Someone who could espouse the principles they all believed in. But George had always been on the sidelines, involved but not committed. A product of the establishment but not a driving force. Until now.

Until he made the ultimate decision. A decision that would dramatically alter the fate of their country. Britain was a sorry state; controlled, whittled down, oppressed and depressed. Until now.

2024: A History of the Future is an engaging tale of the struggle to make change to a nation and to all those involved. Both historical novel and political thriller, it will take you into the future and back into the past, tying the two together in one story. One drama to fashion our future. Through the Past.

Printed in Great Britain
by Amazon